Murder
in
St Paul's

Richard Dale, an Emeritus Professor at Southampton University, has a degree in economics, a Ph. D in Law and Economics and a professional qualification in law. Having published widely in the field of finance he has focused his writing more recently on history and is an elected Fellow of the Royal Historical Socety. *Murder in St Paul's* is his first work of historical fiction.

Murder
in
St Paul's

Richard Dale

Matador
9 Priory Business Park,
Wistow Road, Kibworth Beauchamp,
Leicestershire. LE8 0RX
Tel: 0116 279 2299
Email: books@troubador.co.uk
Web: www.troubador.co.uk/matador
Twitter: @matadorbooks

ISBN 978 1838590 451

British Library Cataloguing in Publication Data.
A catalogue record for this book is available from the British Library.

Printed and bound in Great Britain by 4edge Limited
Typeset in 11pt Adobe Casion Pro by Troubador Publishing Ltd, Leicester, UK

Matador is an imprint of Troubador Publishing Ltd

Dedicated to Notre Dame, sister cathedral of Old St Paul's.

Like martyrs, they burned.

"Whoever sheds man's blood, by man his blood shall be shed, for in the image of God has God made man."

Genesis Book 9, Verse 6

———————

"God has purchased from the faithful their lives and worldly goods and in return has promised them Paradise. They will fight for the cause of God, slay and be slain."

9th Surah, Verse 111, The Koran

INTRODUCTORY NOTE

THE STORY OF RICHARD HUNNE'S CONFLICT WITH THE Church, his death in Lollards' Tower and his post-mortem trial in St Paul's is recounted in Foxe's Book of Martyrs. Some details of his legal challenge to the Church have been preserved as has the original coroner's report on the corpse found hanging in the Bishop of London's prison. Many of the events and characters presented here are well documented though history tells us little about Hunne's family other than that he had a wife, Anne, and a daughter, Margaret. Women in early sixteenth century England had no voice, least of all the outcast widows of convicted heretics, but I have recreated the bereaved Anne as a forceful figure in her own right and this is her story.

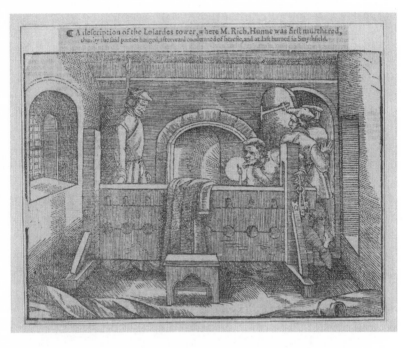

Woodcut depicting the murder of Richard Hunne, Merchant Taylor, in Lollards' Tower. John Foxe, Acts and Monuments. London. 1583.

AMERSHAM 1506

A MAN WITH HIS DAUGHTER LOOKED ON AS THE sheriff's men prepared the fire. Alternate layers of straw and wood were being laid around the stake, care being taken to leave a narrow passage through which the prisoner could be led.

The archdeacon, in his purple cassock, stood out from the crowd. He was speaking to the man beside him who wore a doublet and tabard.

"Sheriff, it has been agreed with the bishop that those who abjured must lay the last faggots. Also the prisoner's daughter, Joan Clark, will be obliged to set the straw alight when everything is in place. This is her penance."

"All has been arranged," the sheriff replied. "I understand, too, that the chief culprits will be branded. A blacksmith from Aylesbury will be arriving in the morning to stamp the cheeks of the miscreants with a hot iron. No local man can be persuaded to undertake this task."

"No doubt they are Lollard sympathisers," the archdeacon retorted. "This whole town is infested with heretics. But let us hope that we set an example to them this day. The priest has checked off each person present. All parishioners are now here as required by the bishop. We can begin whenever you are ready."

Bound with ropes, the prisoner was brought out and led into the centre of the pyre. He looked dazed as he murmured prayers and repeatedly called out "Lord save my soul!". Once he had been chained to the stake the narrow passageway through which he had entered was filled up with wood and straw.

The man held his daughter in front of him and looked around at the fearful faces of his fellow parishioners – among them yeomen, labourers, weavers and basket-makers, all wearing their workaday homespun. They were gathered on a hill above the town, a position of sufficient prominence to send a message to neighbouring villages.

The man tightened his hold on the girl and covered her eyes with his hands. He watched as the sheriff motioned to one of his deputies and a group of men and women, their heads bowed, were led towards the stake. A symbol representing faggots had been sewn onto their clothing and they carried faggots on their backs which they heaped up around the prisoner. The sheriff's deputy, holding a flaming torch, pulled a young woman away from her husband towards the stake. She was resisting and tearful and averted her eyes from the prisoner. The torch was thrust into her hand and forcefully put to the straw.

Driven by the wind, the straw flared up and the timber was soon alight, billowing smoke over the onlookers. The prisoner's legs were quickly engulfed in flames but the wind blew the fire away from his face and torso. The crackling of the fire and the screams of the sufferer mingled with the cries of the onlookers. The burning body was visible only dimly through the haze of smoke and the acrid smell of scorched flesh hung in the air.

After some minutes the upper part of the prisoner's body tilted forwards slowly before falling into the fire, the legs having been burned away. The gaping mouth still moved but its swollen tongue stifled any sound.

When at last there was no sign of life from the blackened corpse, the stunned crowd began to disperse. But others, some sobbing, watched for a time over the smouldering remains. The man with the daughter turned to his neighbour and muttered "Just like an infernal scene from hell."

"That is what they intend", replied the other bitterly.

The man led his silent but shaking daughter away. When they reached home he held her close and said: "Anne, my dearest child, we must be packed up by this evening. For people of our way of thinking this town is no longer safe. We shall be off at first light to stay with our kinsmen in London." But Anne was in no state to make any response.

Shortly before nightfall, Anne's father returned to the scene of the burning. A labourer was scraping up the ash and whatever else was left over and depositing it on a handcart for disposal in the river. When the labourer had gone, he picked up a small fragment of charred bone that had been missed. He would keep it in remembrance of his good friend, William Tylesworth.

PART I

❧ *1514* ❧

OLD ST PAUL'S

❧ *April* ☙

SHORTLY AFTER MIDNIGHT ON THE TUESDAY FOLLOWING Easter, Benjamin Slather, chaplain and secretary to the Bishop of London, entered St Paul's. The cathedral doors were locked at night but the bishop's palace, where the episcopal staff resided, had its own private access to the building through a door in the north wall. Slather, though limping awkwardly, moved stealthily from the north aisle into the nave, a large leather pouch in one hand and a lanthorn in the other. The flickering light from his candle cast tremulous shadows against the cold walls while tapers burning in the side chapels and chantries created small circles of light along the whole length of the cavernous interior.

Slather stopped beneath a candlelit statue of the Virgin Mary that had been affixed to one of the four central pillars supporting the cathedral tower. He placed the pouch and lanthorn carefully on the stone-flagged floor, detached two keys hanging from his belt and inserted one of the keys into the strongbox that sat immediately below the holy icon. He then inserted the second key into the double lock and opened the box.

The shrine's takings had been swelled by Easter offerings from the faithful and Slather now began to sort through the horde of coins of varying denominations. The clinking of metal broke the eerie silence as he set aside some of the higher value coins – shillings, sixpences, groats and an occasional gold angel – and left the pennies, half-pennies and farthings untouched. He dropped the selected coins into a purse that he produced from his cassock and relocked the box.

Slather stood in the heart of the cathedral looking up at the vaulting beneath the tower. Amid the stillness, silence and shadowy expanse of the great basilica he paused for reflection. It was now four years since the bishop and the cathedral chapter had disputed the right to receive the oblations of the Virgin's shrine. The warring parties had eventually agreed to divide the spoils equally, and to ensure that this was put into practice the bishop's chaplain and the chapter's sacristan had each been given a key to the offering box, which they opened jointly once a fortnight in the presence of two brethren. But, as Slather had explained to the sacristan when asking to borrow his key, it was only just after all that, in return for their special responsibility, the two key-holders should receive some personal benefit from the shrine.

As he contemplated his good fortune, Slather set about the rest of his night's work. Picking up a large sheepskin pouch he crossed to the south aisle and hobbled between the chantry altars where candles were burning. He snuffed each taper and, with a small penknife, removed the unburned stem, put it in his pouch and replaced it with one of the wax stubs he was carrying. He would return in the morning before the cathedral doors were unlocked and light the candle ends which, to all appearances, had been burning all night.

Making his way back towards the bishop's door he congratulated himself on the cache of beeswax he had gathered which he would sell to one of the less reputable chandlers who plied their trade in the streets neighbouring St Paul's. He reassured himself that the souls of the departed had no need of beeswax, a scarce commodity best used in the service of those here on earth.

He opened the side door in the north wall and looked back. The cathedral was now in total darkness except for the glow from a single burning taper that threw a wavering halo of light around the Virgin's image.

❧ *July* ☙

John Colet, a graceful, cerebral and somewhat austere man, sat in the library of the deanery, gazing across the close at the sunlit cathedral and the bishop's palace beyond. He looked forward to his long-planned pilgrimage to Canterbury with his close friend, Erasmus, who he had no doubt would entertain him with his witty and scholarly conversation.

Many years had passed since the Dutchman, after taking monastic orders, had become passionately involved with a fellow monk; and a long time, too, since he had been unceremoniously dismissed as tutor to a young man in Paris. All these things were behind him and now he was acknowledged as one of the foremost scholars in Christendom. After studying in Paris, Turin and Venice he had been appointed Professor of Divinity at Queen's College, Cambridge where he complained about his discomforts and the bone-chilling cold. Colet felt comfortable in the company of a man who, like himself, did not hesitate to criticise the Church's excesses but was loyal to his calling and restrained in his reforming zeal.

Just then Erasmus – gaunt, sharp-nosed and hollow-cheeked – appeared at the library door. Colet looked up.

"We have to leave for Canterbury soon. Are you ready?"

"Yes," replied Erasmus, "My baggage is in the passage. But since we have a little time I wonder whether you would show me your great cathedral."

The dean was only too willing to oblige. "I would be delighted – especially as we can temper our admiration of everything we see with a little scepticism. Let us go now – at such an early hour there will be few visitors."

The two men walked across the close, past the canopied open air pulpit known as Paul's Cross and approached the cathedral through the north door. Here, a great rood stood beside the entrance and the dean began his guided tour:

"This cross, a piece of which they say was borne by Joseph of Arimathea, is an object of great devotion." Erasmus looked up at the revered artefact and gave a wry smile: "I have seen a few of those in my time," he said.

"I can tell you in confidence that the offerings amount to as much as £1000 per annum. Most of this – but by no means all – goes towards maintaining the fabric of the Church."

Colet was full of pride as he directed his friend's attention to the soaring columns around them. "The building of St Paul's began in the 11th century on the site of an earlier church but the original Romanesque basilica has been transformed over many generations into the English style that you see before you."

Erasmus peered down the length of the central aisle towards the choir. "This is the longest nave I have ever seen in all my travels through Europe. The proportions here match the scale of your great city."

"Yes, indeed. And if you were to come here in the afternoon you would see merchants and people of fashion walking up and down, discussing business or sharing gossip. The church then becomes the people's meeting place."

"Like the Roman forum." Erasmus had begun to examine the tombs set out along the north wall: "I see you have two ancient sepulchres inscribed here as those of Sabba, 7th century king of the East Saxons, and Ethelred, King of the West Saxons. These must have been removed from the old church."

"Just so. And here, among the Bishops of London laid out in their tombs throughout the church, we have William Norman. He was present at the submission of the English after the Conquest."

They advanced slowly along the twelve bays of the nave which terminated in four mighty pillars supporting the tower. There were numerous chantries and side chapels set within the bays. They paused opposite one of the chantries where a priest was praying aloud for the soul of some departed benefactor before a candlelit altar.

"I could fault his Latin", whispered Erasmus, "but what patronage there must be to support all this piety."

Colet was doubtful about the value of what they were witnessing: "The result of prosperous times, my friend. There are some fifty chantry priests serving in the cathedral, all paid for by the bequests of the departed. But I cannot say that I approve of this kind of redemption."

"I am glad to hear it", replied Erasmus with a sardonic smile.

Colet then pointed out a statue of the Virgin Mary, affixed to one of the columns beneath the tower. "A taper has burned every night for 150 years before this cherished icon. The oblations at the shrine are so large that, some time ago, the bishop decided to claim the revenues which should rightly belong to the dean and chapter. Sadly, such disputes are not uncommon in these troubled times."

Erasmus held his friend's arm for a moment: "My dear Colet, it is the same throughout Christendom. The wealth of the Church is the cause of covetousness among its own spiritual leaders. I dare say we will see such jealousies when we visit St Thomas's shrine in Canterbury."

As they approached the choir, Colet pointed at the entrance to the crypt. "Our crypt is curious because part of it has been set aside for the use of the parish of St Faith. So there is worship here above and worship down below. And I am afraid to say that the parishioners are more attentive to divine service than our own canons – who are inclined to self-indulgence and their worldly needs. Shamefully, they are often absent."

The tour continued past the choir to the altar, which stood beneath the cathedral's celebrated rose window with its elaborate tracery and polychrome glass. Colet called his friend's attention to the richly bejewelled shrine that stood behind the altar against the eastern façade.

"This is the reliquary shrine of St Erkenwald, a revered seventh century bishop who has a reputation for miraculous healing – especially for those with failing eyesight. Pilgrims come from far and wide to be cured and here, of course, there are again rich takings for the Church."

"Mere superstition," Erasmus said. "How credulous the faithful can be."

Before Colet could reply a wild looking figure suddenly sprung forwards from the shadows of the apse. Erasmus shrank back. The dishevelled man, for a man it was, was gesticulating – pointing first to the shrine and then to his eyes. He began to speak but Colet held up his hand and dismissed him gently. "Alaric, there is no need to disturb our friend here who is well aware of the healing powers of our great saint's relics." The man fell back into the shadows and Colet turned to Erasmus. "I am sorry if our faithful servant caused you alarm. Alaric is employed by the chapter to testify to the miraculous properties of St. Erkenwald's shrine – he being now sighted after he was made blind. Such testimony from one who has been cured gives encouragement to those who may wish to make offerings to the shrine."

Erasmus ran his finger along the rail protecting the glittering reliquary. "And what benefit does Alaric receive for loosening the purse strings of the faithful?" Colet was embarrassed. "The chapter has given him the right to sell wax tapers to those who wish to burn a candle for a loved one. Let me add that I personally do not favour any of this. However, the chapter is insistent that the presence of a *miraculee* is beneficial to shrine receipts. You know how awkward our brothers can be. I cannot thwart them in everything – least of all in matters touching the Church's revenues."

Colet looked up at the cathedral clock. "I could show you other prized relics, such as a stone of the Holy Sepulchre and a rock taken from the very spot of the Ascension. But I'm afraid our time is up and we must make ready for our journey to Canterbury."

Erasmus nodded. "It is just as well your cathedral is blessed with so many profitable images and relics, considering the cost of maintaining such an imposing building – not to mention all those employed in its service."

"Well, you have a point", replied Colet. "We have many mouths to feed. Four archdeacons, a precentor, a chancellor, a college of twelve minor canons, thirty greater canons with their vicars and deputies and a multitude of subordinates – sacrists, vergers and servants of all kinds."

As they walked slowly back to the deanery, Erasmus asked about the three-storey tower standing at the south west corner of the cathedral. Colet felt ill at ease as he explained the purpose of the building. "This is known as Lollards' Tower. It is the Bishop of London's prison where he can, at his discretion, detain those suspected of heresy. As dean I have no jurisdiction or authority over what may pass within its walls."

Erasmus looked up at the latticed windows. "And does the bishop confine many so-called heretics within this gaol?"

Colet paused before speaking very deliberately in a low tone. "As you are my trusted friend, I will tell you what I would impart to no one else. Church leaders, and especially my own

Lord Bishop have declared war against the reformists. Some are detained, maltreated and forced to abjure. Those who are unflinching they burn. If they continue on this path the people will be provoked into revolt."

Erasmus took Colet by the arm, all traces of wry amusement gone from his expression. "It is the same throughout Europe. Christendom is ready to erupt. But, my friend, we are scholars not warriors and cannot be expected to lead the charge." His thoughts were interrupted momentarily by kites squabbling noisily over the carcass of a dog. As they flapped off he continued. "Perhaps a great figure will emerge to rouse the people against the Church's decadence and wealth."

"Ah yes", Colet responded. "I, too, believe that an upheaval is coming. But will it be at the hands of a prince or a religious zealot? And what will be left of the Church as we know it when all is done? Great changes bring turmoil and disorder." He paused and gazed up at the kites now soaring above them. "Sometimes I despair at the present and fear for the future."

As the two men entered the deanery Erasmus tried to lift their spirits: "Do not let these gloomy thoughts weigh on us. Let us enjoy our pilgrimage. With humility, of course, but also light-heartedness and some mistrust."

❧ *Monday 4ᵗʰ December* ❧

Shortly after 7 o'clock Peter Turner, an assistant gaolor serving the bishop's chancellor, made his way in the half-light towards St Paul's. Although the sun was not yet risen the streets surrounding the cathedral – Paternoster Row, Ave Maria Lane, Creed Street, and Amen Corner – began to stir. The stationers, printers, parchment-makers, text-writers and sellers of religious books and rosaries who dwelt in the neighbourhood were just beginning to organise themselves for the day's business.

This morning Peter had to attend to the one prisoner held in Lollards' Tower. He entered Paternoster Row where the familiar figure of Thomas Symondes, stationer, was preparing his stall with the help of his wife.

"Good morrow Peter." Thomas gestured towards the walled cathedral precinct. "We saw Charles Joseph just now coming out of the close. He seemed in a hurry and barely acknowledged us. Then he disappeared into the murk. What business does the bishop's summoner have in the cathedral at this early hour?"

Peter was unwilling to offer any opinion and merely shrugged. "I have to see to the needs of the bishop's prisoner."

"Well you can tell your Richard Hunne that we tradespeople, along with most others in this city, wish him a quick deliverance from his ordeal. What is more …" But his words tailed off as he responded to a powerful nudge from his wife.

Peter carried on and entered the close through the north gate, his slowing steps betraying the anxiety he felt. There had been rumours of late about the fate awaiting Richard Hunne and the reported sighting of Charles Joseph only served to increase his unease. Once inside the cathedral he looked for his fellow gaolor, John Spalding, to obtain the only set of keys to the prison cell. Being unable to find Spalding he had to wait until the end of morning mass to track down the keys which, as it turned out, had been given to another gaolor named William Sampson.

Why were the keys being passed around? And who had held them overnight? Peter, now convinced that something was amiss, and fearful that he might be blamed for whatever had occurred, sought out two church officers to accompany him to Lollards' Tower. He led the way up the winding stone staircase and paused before unlocking the cell door.

Entering the poorly lit chamber the three men found the prisoner hanging by his own belt with his face to the wall. Shaken by what they saw they hurriedly retraced their steps and reported their discovery to the Bishop of London's chancellor, Dr William Horsey, who was in the cathedral. Peter and Dr Horsey, accompanied by the sub-dean, the Master of the Rolls and various other Church dignitaries, together with their servants, climbed the stairs to the prison cell to view the body.

As the clergymen entered the room, a draught wafted through the open door ruffling their white cassocks. The movement of air also caused the corpse to rotate slowly so that it now confronted the onlookers. The ashen face, with eyes closed, appeared spectral and recriminating to those staring up at the suspended figure. Someone closed the cell door and the body swung round again to face the wall.

Those present were at first silent but after some minutes they began muttering anxiously among themselves. The sub-dean voiced their concerns. "Brethren, this is a pitiful sight but it is also a tragedy that endangers the Church. We know that Richard Hunne was a London citizen, highly respected within his community and among his fellow tradesmen. News of his death while in our custody will further inflame the people against their spiritual leaders."

Dr Horsey, the bishop's deputy, took charge. "If this should get out in the wrong way the consequences would be incalculable. The bishop must be informed and a suspicious world must be told straight away that Hunne has destroyed himself. A placard to this effect should be affixed to the north door. It must be made as obvious to others, as it is to ourselves, that the Church's hands are clean."

"But will they believe us?" asked the Master of the Rolls nervously.

"That I cannot say," replied the chancellor, "but whatever their thoughts, they will not dare to challenge our verdict."

Turning to the sub-dean Dr Horsey added: "Have one of our priests make a pronouncement from Paul's Cross. Let it be known that Hunne, by taking his own life, exhibited his guilt; and that as a self-murderer and heretic he is beyond God's redemption, his estate forfeit and his family made destitute. This will put fear into those who might count themselves his supporters."

The chancellor spoke softly but Peter sensed the menace in his voice as he continued to give instructions.

"Send messengers out to inform the bishop at Fulham Palace. Also the sheriff's office in the Guildhall, as well as the Lord Mayor. A notice should be pinned to the cathedral's north door stating that a suspect heretic, one Richard Hunne, has died by his own hand in the bishop's prison, thereby committing the grave sin of *felo de se* and offending the dignity of God and the Church."

Peter noted that no one thought to inform the dead man's widow in nearby New Fish Street who would no doubt learn of her husband's fate soon enough.

The Lord Mayor, George Monoux, was going through routine administrative documents at his office in the Guildhall when a messenger brought news of the death in Lollards' Tower. The Church said it was suicide. But the Mayor knew that London's citizenry would share his own deep suspicions. After all, given what Richard Hunne had done, there had to be powerful figures with every reason to be rid of him. As Mayor, he would immediately instruct the coroner, Thomas Barnwell, to conduct an inquest into the cause of death. And, given the urgency and sensitivity of the case, he would need to talk to Barnwell himself. The truth had to be ascertained – regardless of where the investigation might lead.

2

Bishop's Move

The Bishop of London, Richard Fitzjames, had been staying in his country residence at Fulham Palace when a messenger had brought news of Hunne's death. His chancellor had arrived later by boat on the following morning in a shocked and dishevelled state to explain the circumstances of the grim discovery in Lollards' Tower. They had been in private conference together most of that day and now, twenty-four hours later, the bishop was alone in his study planning his next move.

When duty called him to London, Fitzjames resided at the bishop's palace adjacent to St Paul's but he much preferred the quiet life of a country squire at Fulham where he could enjoy the spacious gardens, entertain his friends and indulge his passion for building. He had erected a fine quadrangle with a gateway bearing his coat of arms, and within the main house he had constructed a splendid panelled hall as an inscription over the chimney piece testified. Here, too, in this tranquil setting he could refer to his unique collection of theological works: volumes by Jerome, Ambrose, Augustine, Isidor and Bonaventure, many of which he had studied during his Oxford days.

He recalled that it was only five days before, on Saturday December 2nd, that Hunne had been brought down from St Paul's to Fulham Palace to be examined by the bishop in his chapel. Hunne had been required to answer to a number of charges, including his reported objection to the payment of tithes and his support for the views of a neighbour, Joan Baker, who had been found guilty of heresy some time before and made to do public penance. At the end of his examination, Hunne had not formally recanted by signing a declaration nor had he admitted, in precise terms, the charges against him. He had, however, acknowledged in his own writing that he had spoken inadvisedly and submitted himself to his lord's charitable and favourable correction. After this inconclusive hearing, Hunne had been taken back to Lollards' Tower.

The bishop sat in his study tapping the arm of his great oak desk chair. For some time he had felt that everything that he and his fellow prelates stood for was under threat. Now the danger was close at hand. He had to act quickly to stifle an outburst of anti-clericalism among the citizens of London who, already openly critical of the established Church order, would now be incensed by the death in custody of one of their own.

An austere, gaunt and slightly hunched figure in his late seventies, the bishop was a battle-hardened champion of the Church establishment. An able administrator, he had served as bursar and then warden of his old college, Merton, and for fourteen years as Treasurer of St Paul's before appointment to his first episcopal see at Rochester. He understood that the Christian path was a narrow one and, in carrying out his diocesan duties, his main aims were to ensure regularity in Church administration and to keep his flock from straying from the course that God had ordained. In recent years he had been deeply troubled by self-styled reformists and new thinkers who sought to challenge the traditional ways of the Church. Among such he counted his own dean, John Colet, who had, in the bishop's view, disgraced his office by criticising from the pulpit the supposed shortcomings of the priesthood he served.

The bishop's face hardened as he adjusted the shawl around his shoulders. John Colet. The very name was an anathema. Here was a man who, no longer content to accept the Church's time-honoured teaching, had joined with others and especially that perfidious Dutchman, Erasmus, in disseminating new and dangerous interpretations of the Gospel that undermined the authority of the Church hierarchy and confused the faithful. He was himself convinced that Colet's offence amounted to heresy but so long as the King – and therefore the Archbishop – gave him protection there was nothing he could do about this fox lurking in his own backyard.

Richard Fitzjames had given his life to the service of God and the support of an institution that he believed was under threat. He knew that the Church's special status within the realm was safeguarded by its great landed wealth, its courts, its own canon law and its law-making body, Convocation. None of these mainstays could, of course, be swept aside. Nevertheless he was acutely aware that some of the Church's privileges, which previous generations had taken for granted, were now being challenged. Worse still, the teaching of the Church and its doctrinal underpinnings were being questioned by reformers and Lollards. If they had their way, they would destroy the priestly order by denying the miracle of the sacrament of the altar, abandoning confessionals, destroying images and allowing ordinary worshippers, however humble, to read the Bible in English and interpret it without priestly guidance.

The bishop had already acted decisively against some of the more flagrant heretics. A score of Lollard suspects had been investigated, forced to recant and do penance under pain of death while two lapsed penitents had been burned at Smithfield. But these cases were surely only the visible tip: those who were caught were simple souls but he did not doubt that there were many more subtle apostates in prosperous households who knew how to avoid detection.

Hunne's death had now brought matters to a head. If this man were to become a martyr in the eyes of London's rebellious inhabitants, the entire Church order would be put at risk. The bishop narrowed his gaze: attack was the best form of defence and he knew what he had to do. He rang for his servant and asked to see his two senior legal advisers, Dr William Horsey, chancellor, and Dr Thomas Head, commissary, who were waiting in the anteroom.

William Horsey was a pale faced man of scholarly appearance aged about forty years. He had a slight nervous twitch that affected the left side of his face and when he spoke he did so in a hushed voice, though with the deliberation and precision of a man used to addressing his own court. He had a doctorate in canon law from Oxford and had been the bishop's loyal friend and right hand man for many years. As chancellor and vicar general he presided over the consistory court at St Paul's and had a special role advising on all matters connected with proceedings against heretics. He shared his bishop's religious conservatism as well as his passion for regularity, good order and procedural correctness in all Church affairs. He had a clutch of preferments to augment his income: Canon of Wells and Prebendary of Wedmore; Canon of Lincoln and Prebendary of Scamlesby; Canon and Precentor of St Paul's and Prebendary of Finsbury. He spent his income on his library of manuscripts and books, a private collection of holy relics and his principal indulgence: a taste for finery in gowns and cassocks. His prize possession was a fingernail from the hand of St James which he had managed to obtain (for a fee) from Reading Abbey. He had set this relic within a ring, which he rubbed nervously when under stress.

Thomas Head, commissary, a smooth faced man with an ingratiating manner, was Horsey's junior. As the judge who presided over the bishops' commissary court he spent long hours enquiring into the sexual conduct of those brought before him. But he was also a competent administrator and he would be happy to step into Horsey's shoes if that should prove necessary.

Both men looked strained, but the bishop's chancellor – drawn, unshaven, apparently unslept and still wearing his travelling cloak – was very much more the worse for wear.

The bishop addressed his first remarks to Dr Horsey. "William, we all know that the London rabble are falsely convinced of your guilt and that they're after your blood. I trust to your good sense to ignore such false accusations, but it would probably be better for your own peace of mind to stay sometime with the Archbishop under his protection. What do you say?"

The chancellor was quick to agree. "My Lord I think it is for the better. I dare not appear in any public place and if I could ride out the storm in a secure house perhaps the people's anger will subside and I can again resume my duties."

The bishop was relieved that this little matter had been resolved. He had already sent a letter to Lambeth Palace and they would make whatever arrangements were necessary. But before his trusted deputy departed, he needed his advice on the next crucial steps. Horsey was an acknowledged expert in canon law and everything had to be done in accordance with its ordinances.

The bishop leaned forwards and looked his chancellor in the eye. "William, we are all aware that there is a great deal at stake here. We must ensure above all that Hunne does not by his death deliver us a fatal blow. What I intend is that the charges of heresy against him should be heard in St Paul's. The bodily remains can then be condemned and entrusted to the sheriff for burning. All this to be proclaimed publicly with the full authority of the Church so that others may take note and be warned. In your knowledge is this procedure sound in law?"

The chancellor had to give this some thought and began deliberating aloud. "The great statute *De Heretico Comburendo* enacted in the time of Henry IV does, of course, authorise diocesan authorities to try a man for heresy and hand him over to the sheriff for burning. But this is on condition that the convicted heretic either refuses to recant or that he does so but later repeats his offence. The statute states clearly that in such cases the sheriff should, before the people and in a high place, cause them to be burned that such punishment might strike fear into the minds of others who could be tempted to stray."

The bishop drummed his fingers on the arm of his chair. He was impatient to reach a conclusion but he knew he had to hear his chancellor out.

Horsey caressed his ring. "The problem is that Hunne, at his preliminary examination, showed a degree of penitence. Can he be burned if he has not been given a proper opportunity to recant? Furthermore, can a corpse be tried for heresy? We must weigh these considerations as well as the fact that suicide is itself a grave sin which compounds the original offence." After further pondering he finally gave his opinion.

"I believe that what your lordship has in mind can be justified in law. There is, after all, a powerful precedent. John Wycliffe, beloved of Lollards and source of all our troubles, was condemned as a heretic by the Council of the Church in 1415 some thirty years after his natural death. When the Holy Father later commanded that the body of Wycliffe be destroyed, his bones were exhumed and, in the presence of the sheriff, his remains were damned to an eternity in hell by the Bishop of Lincoln and the canons of his diocese. The body was then burned and the ashes scattered in the river. This case can be the justification for our own actions and it is therefore in order to proceed as you suggest."

The bishop nodded in approval and then turned to his commissary. "Thomas we must lose no time. First ensure that you secure every piece of evidence against Hunne that we can lay hold of. I know his house was searched earlier but I now want the place ransacked for hidden religious works. Interview his manservant who may now be more willing to talk – especially if the threat of wider heresy proceedings is put before him. Having gathered whatever evidence you can, draw up charges for the hearing which will of course be in St Paul's. Also draw up the conviction and sentence in solemn form since the conclusion is not in doubt. This will be an audience court with myself presiding but other bishops will be in London to attend Convocation and some of them will also be present. We must be very particular about the trial proceedings because the whole world will be watching us. I shall ask Benjamin Slather to take care of all the administrative arrangements – invitations, seating, positioning of the open coffin, incense and so on."

Dr Head told the bishop that a wherry was ready waiting for him and that he would return immediately to London to carry out his instructions with as much despatch as possible. But before leaving he raised one final point. "My Lord, by the time of the trial, the body of Hunne will be perhaps two weeks in decay. Should he then be laid out before the court and assembled company in the Lady Chapel or would it be more seemly to bury him and try him in absentia?"

Fitzjames was in no doubt. "The body must be there and the evil air will serve as a reminder of the stink of heresy that we find in our midst. If he has already been buried he must be dug up for the hearing."

The three men said their farewells and the bishop was left alone to contemplate the fight that lay ahead. He was aware that the coroner had already empanelled a jury to investigate the cause of Hunne's death and that this very day they would probably be viewing the corpse in Lollards' Tower. He had to preempt their deliberations. Hopefully a properly constituted heresy trial held in public, with irrefutable evidence brought before it, followed by destruction of the body at Smithfield, would put an end to further speculation. The book could then be closed on Richard Hunne.

Or could it? For there was one further matter that still troubled him. Hunne, through his great proceeding, had sought to attack the Church within its own stronghold. He must have had confederates and powerful backers. No man could have done what he had without such assistance. Once the trial was out of the way he would have to discover the identity of those who stood behind Richard Hunne.

3

A Widow's Vow

ANNE HUNNE TRUDGED SLOWLY TOWARDS ST PAUL'S, her tall figure bent against a blustery wind and her heart heavy with the news that would transform her life. Since learning of her husband's fate she had been in emotional turmoil. She and Richard had been joined in love, companionship, work and worship, and now that he had been taken from her she felt alone and abandoned. But she also felt guilt. The world knew that Richard had been held captive not because of his supposed heresy but in savage reprisal for his great action against the Church. Had she not encouraged him in a course of conduct that exposed him to extreme danger? Should she have restrained him? Surely, she was at least partly to blame.

There was fear, too. Fear for her own future and that of her child, now that she had no means of support.

But it was increasingly anger that she felt burning inside her. The Church thought it could do what it wanted with impunity to those it opposed because its clergy were not answerable under the ordinary law of the land. That, to her, was an abominable injustice.

At times of crisis in her life Anne had always prayed with meekness in her heart. But this was a turning point. The life she had known was no more and she would have to find a new purpose – one inspired by the sense of outrage that was consuming her soul. She would no longer seek in her prayers the divine path to forgiveness and reconciliation. Instead, she would call for vengeance on those she held responsible for her loss. Did not Leviticus say that whosoever injures a person so it shall be done to him? *Fracture for fracture, eye for eye, tooth for tooth?*

Anne paused outside her own parish Church of St. Margaret's but could not bring herself to go in. Too much had passed and too many memories crowded in on her. She continued with heavy steps along Watling Street and when she approached All Hallows, Broad Street, she caught the sound of morrow-mass being conducted within for the benefit of those who had to go to work.

She entered the church and stood at the back while the priest delivered his incantations in Latin. His richly brocaded chasuble and silken stole contrasted with the dull woollen workaday clothes of the congregation. After tinkling bells had been sounded to signal the sacrament of the altar, all eyes were fixed on the priest as he raised the Host aloft. This was the moment of the awesome miracle that those ordained by the Church were empowered to perform each day: the transformation of ordinary bread and wine into the very flesh and blood of Christ. After reciting further Latin prayers, the priest concluded the service by reading out the bead rolls – a roll call of the departed who had bequeathed money to the church so they might be remembered in the prayers of the faithful.

Anne stepped outside the church and, in the half-light of early morning, watched as the metropolis began to awaken. Porters, carters and servants were already going about their business: a woman carried a large pitcher towards Cheapside to collect water from the public conduit and a shopkeeper was preparing to open up, the upper shutters being hooked up to provide shelter and the lower folded down to form a counter.

As she continued slowly through the eastern gateway to the cathedral close, Anne recalled what had been said in their Bible reading group only a few months before. Someone had recited the account of the last supper given in St Mark's Gospel. After the reading Richard had commented that there was nothing in this or any other scripture that could justify the supposed miracle of the Eucharist. In his opinion, the bread and wine, being only a symbol of Christ's sacrifice, remained unaltered. As he put it, "The object of the Church in claiming the real presence of Christ is to overawe the congregation. This trick, together with the priest's incomprehensible mumblings in Latin and the obscurity of a Bible that cannot be read in a man's own tongue, is intended to blind the people and raise the priesthood above the flock it is supposed to serve."

"In the same way priests' teaching of purgatory, which cannot be found anywhere in the Bible, is used to instil terror into the people," one of their friends had added bitterly. "It is because of this fear that the faithful go to confessionals, give donations to shrines, purchase indulgences and make bequests to the Church."

The assembled company had murmured their assent and Richard, who was looked upon as their leader, had spoken for them all in concluding the discussion. "Take away these superstitions and the priests are shorn, because every man and woman can then be their own priest. Take away the superstitions, too, and the Church's coffers will be emptied. Therefore the bishops will pursue with every weapon at their command those who deny such false teachings."

With this reminder of the dangers they all faced, the group had dispersed. As for Anne and Richard, they had long been convinced of these truths but they continued their daily devotions at their parish church partly because they believed in the simple message of the Gospels but also because regular worshippers were less likely to fall under suspicion of heresy. But now that Richard was dead, Anne felt strangely liberated. She would not trouble herself anymore with outward appearances. Rather, she would pray directly to God and eschew altogether the false ways of priests.

Preoccupied with these thoughts she crossed the cathedral close, entered St Paul's through the north door and deliberately averted her eyes from the great rood that stood at the entrance.

At this hour, the cavernous interior was hushed and she was conscious of her own footfall. Tapers burned in several of the side chapels where chantry priests were already intoning their prayers for the departed faithful. A cold draught wafted through the great nave carrying the faint aroma of honey from beeswax as well as the lingering scent of incense. She made her way down towards the choir at the east end and there she descended the steps that took her into the crypt. When the cathedral had been extended to the east it had enclosed the parish Church of St Faith and part of the crypt had been given to the local community as their parish church. It was in the privacy of this makeshift house of God, situated directly beneath the cathedral choir, that Anne chose to offer her most solemn prayers without any human witness.

Kneeling in front of the altar she waited some minutes in order to collect herself for the task she had come to perform. She then spoke firmly and without hesitation. "Dear God of Heaven and Earth I beseech you from the very bowels of your great Church, console me in my grief and take pity on the soul of my departed husband. He wished no man ill, gave to the poor and upheld the teachings of the Bible. He died in pursuit of a true Christian cause which is the right of all men and women to read the Gospels for themselves in their own tongue, to worship without idolatry and to be served by a priesthood unblemished by corrupt practices, avarice and false doctrine. God give me strength to bear my loss and, as a mere woman, to carry on the noble work of my dear departed so that his death may not be in vain." Here Anne was forced to pause as the memories flooded in and the tears welled up.

After some moments, she recovered herself and quoted from the prologue to Wycliffe's English Bible with which she was so familiar. "*God grant to us all grace to know well and to keep well Holy Writ and to suffer joyfully some pain for it at the last. For the common people cry out for the scripture to know it and obey it with great cost and peril to their lives.*"

Then her voice grew stronger and less submissive as she invoked the God of the Old Testament and vowed to take her revenge on those who were responsible for her husband's death. She prayed that God should make her the instrument of his retribution and she recited the *Song of Moses* from the Book of Deuteronomy which she had learned from the English Bible. "*See now that I, even I, am He, and there is no God beside me; I kill and I make alive; I wound and I heal; and there is none that can be delivered out of my hand. For I lift up my hand to Heaven and swear, as I live forever, if I sharpen my glittering sword, and my hand takes hold in judgement, I will take vengeance on my adversaries, and will requite those who hate me.*"

Anne then raised herself, climbed up the stairs to the nave and retraced her steps from St Paul's back towards Carter Lane where she would pick up her little daughter, Margaret. Her grieving was done for now and her prayers had been heard. Iron had entered her soul. She would champion her husband's just cause at whatever cost to herself and she would fulfil her vow to pursue those pitiless evildoers who had brought about the destruction of Richard Hunne.

PART II

ॐ *1511–1515* ॐ

4

A SON IS BORN

RICHARD HUNNE ALWAYS LOOKED FORWARD TO THE great annual banquet held at the Merchant Taylors Hall on June 25th. It was, of course, a celebration of their patron saint, St John the Baptist, but it also united the hundred or so liverymen of the guild together with ambassadors, knights and other distinguished guests in an atmosphere of conviviality and splendour. At one end of the Hall was the gilded statue of St John, standing in his golden tabernacle and framed by flaming torches. The walls were hung with embroidered tapestries portraying the life and death of the saint; ewers, basins, cups and other plate embossed with images and symbols of St John were laid out on long tables and the whole scene was illuminated by scores of scented wax tapers.

For Richard, this feast day was a double celebration. His wife had given birth to a daughter two and a half years before and today she had announced that she was with child again. He dared not tempt fate by voicing his hopes but he could not help wondering whether he might not this time be blessed with a son and heir.

"Well, Richard, may God bless your wife and your child to be. If it is a son, may he live to pursue his father's trade and fill the ranks of our fraternity." The speaker was a liveryman of long standing whom Hunne could count among his close friends. "And there is another cause for congratulation, Richard. You have since last year moved above the salt to a position of eminence." And he pointed to the master salt placed carefully in the middle of the table.

"True," replied Richard, "but sadly my elevation is due to the passing of several of our fellows, most recently our venerated beadle. I would much rather stay below the salt than witness the departure of such men."

The conversation moved on to business matters as butlers moved between the tables bringing successive platters of food: a meat course of beef, mutton, sheep's tongue and deer's tongue; a fish course of salmon, pike, lobster and carp; and poultry consisting of swan, pheasant, capons, duckling, cuckoos and owl. All this was washed down with Rhenish and Gascony wines.

The celebration ended with solemn prayers and a special commendation of their late sovereign, Henry VII, from whom the guild had received its charter.

It was a balmy summer's evening. As Richard strolled back from Cornhill he was reminded by all the pageantry that it was almost exactly two years before, on June 24 1509, that Henry's son had been crowned King. On the preceding day, Richard had watched the coronation procession in Gracechurch Street as it wound its way from the Tower to Westminster. The young King, mounted on a white stallion, was accompanied by four barons of the realm holding a canopy of gold over him. Henry VIII himself was resplendent in a cloth of gold coat with a collar of rubies and Catherine, his queen, reclining in a canopied litter, wore a gold, pearl and silk circlet on her head. Richard had been one of the liveried guildsmen lining the street which was hung with tapestries and cloth of gold, while Anne had viewed the pageant from a window above. And on the coronation day itself, when the royal couple had processed on foot from the Palace of Westminster to the Abbey behind twenty-eight bishops, Richard and Anne had both joined the jubilant crowd marching through the City. They linked hands with the throng and passed doors decorated with greenery and flowers, all to the accompaniment of drums, lutes, horns and the soft piping of recorders.

Two years on and the King was still a youth. No one yet knew how he would fulfil his sovereign duties as a man. But for one thing Richard was thankful: the Tudor monarchy had brought prosperity to England and especially to those like him in the cloth trade.

Nearing his house in New Fish Street, just north of London Bridge, he contemplated the cloudless sky above and counted himself a fortunate man: his business had brought him considerable wealth; he was blessed with a fine and loving wife; and he would soon have another child, perhaps a boy. All this, and the comradeship of his fraternity, made him well content with his lot. He was determined to acknowledge the bounty that had been bestowed on him by undertaking charitable works and serving God in his own way.

———————

At home early in the new year, Anne and Richard celebrated the safe delivery of their son Stephen. They were proud of their little daughter, Margaret, but now there would be an heir to carry on the family name and the business. The gathering of friends and relations was in joyous mood as they feasted in honour of the newborn baby. Richard turned to his maidservant, a neat young girl with auburn hair, who had been busy carrying platters of vegetables and meat dishes to the festive table. "Martha, bring from the pantry the flagon of Burgundy wine that I have set aside for today's celebration. We have some wassailing to do."

When the wine had been poured into everyone's goblets, Richard's father-in-law stood up. Thomas Vincent was tall and dark like his daughter. He had his own draper's shop nearby and now that he had reached fifty was hoping to bring a nephew into the business and take things more easily. Holding his goblet aloft he addressed those present. "Friends, we all welcome the arrival of Stephen and thank God for blessing the family of Richard Hunne. Let us drink to the health, happiness and prosperity of Richard, Anne, Stephen and Margaret and may they all serve God faithfully."

There was a chorus of approval round the table as Richard rose to reply. "Thank you for your benediction, Thomas. To my dear kinsfolk and friends I wish to say that this is the happiest day of my life. I thank God for my good fortune and for the honour he has bestowed on my family. Let us now drink to baby Stephen."

After the maidservant had cleared the debris from the table, Anne turned to her cousin Rebecca. "Thank you for recommending Agnes Snowe as nurse to little Stephen. She is a good, caring woman. And although Whitechapel is some walk from here, I can manage it quite comfortably, even in my weakened state. Richard and I visited yesterday and I could swear that baby Stephen already has the look of his father."

Richard was not so sure. "But I don't care much who he takes after so long as he doesn't have the appearance of our parish priest. Then I would be truly suspicious."

They all laughed. It was widely suspected that several women in the neighbourhood had born the children of clerks in holy orders and John Cawood, priest at their own parish Church of St Margaret, New Fish Street, was thought to be not entirely blameless.

"No", said Anne good humouredly, "it is only poor maids, simple wives and lone widows who fall prey to such men. I am none of these and so intend to remain."

When the manservant had closed the door after bringing more fuel for the fire, Anne's father, Thomas Vincent, adopted a more serious tone. "The folly of women can take a different form," he said in a lowered voice. "I heard only yesterday from Gervis Baker that his wife, Joan, has got herself into serious trouble by declaiming loudly against images, pilgrimages and the avarice of priests. She did so in front of her own parson at St Margaret's, who then reported her. She is cited to appear before the commissary court in a few weeks time. She will be made to do penance, that is certain. And her imprudence may place suspicion on us all."

There was a pause in the conversation as the maidservant came in to brush the table. When she had gone into the kitchen Richard turned towards his father-in-law. "It is true that Joan was unwise to speak so forcefully and in church, but none of us present here today would doubt that what she said is correct. The time has surely come for people of our way of thinking to be more openly critical of the failings of the Church and the need for reform. The views we hold are, after all, shared by many around us, as well as by some eminent churchmen, among whom I count the Dean of St Paul's. I believe we should no longer hide ourselves away in secret conference but in a reasoned way declare our opposition to those Church practices that cannot be justified by scripture. Above all else, we should press for the freedom of ordinary worshipers to read the Bible in their own tongue."

Thomas placed his hand on Richard's shoulder. "Richard, there is a time for boldness and a time for caution. Pray be careful. You have a family. It is only a few years back that I had to witness the pitiless burning of my friend William Tylesworth. I have seen with my own eyes what the Church can do. And at times such as these the guiding principle for us must be caution."

Richard accepted this gentle rebuke with good grace and embraced his father-in-law.

The party broke up in good spirits but the news about Joan Baker had cast a shadow over their celebrations. It was said that the Bishop of London had taken up arms against supposed heretics and many must have wondered whether the bishop's summoner might not soon come knocking on their door.

5

AN INFANT'S ROBE

TWO WEEKS AFTER THE JOYFUL FAMILY GATHERING, came news that baby Stephen had fallen gravely ill. Agnes Snowe, who was nursing the infant in Whitechapel, reported that he suffered looseness and fever. After a physician had administered wormwood, mint and balsam there was a brief respite and hopes were raised. But the disorder returned. Stephen's small frame shook with fever and he could take no milk. The physician said there was no more to be done and the distraught parents could only look on helplessly as the life drained slowly out of their beloved son.

Richard prepared for the worst. One evening after Margaret had been put to bed he said to Anne, "Sweetheart, we must have Stephen baptised straight away. We cannot allow him to leave this world without the sacramental graces granted by holy water. The parson at St Mary Matfellon in Whitechapel, Thomas Dryfield, has agreed to perform the baptism on the morrow. We can then rest assured that his soul will be at peace. Look – I made this christening gown to wrap around his poor wasted body." And here Richard brought from his workshop a richly embroidered vestment cut from finest silk. Anne caressed the fabric. "Yes", she sighed, "it is fitting."

The next morning they walked together along Fenchurch Street, through London's eastern gateway at Aldgate and down Whitechapel Road to the Church of St Mary Matfellon. There they were met by Agnes Snowe, a large motherly figure, carrying baby Stephen. The baptismal service was performed and Stephen and his parents parted for the last time because he passed into a better world the very next day.

Anne was too upset to attend the burial service and so Richard made the by now familiar journey to St Mary's on his own. After the infant's corpse had been interred, Parson Dryfield, a sly looking man with a pinched face, sharp little eyes and unkempt grey hair, took Richard aside. "I wish to extend my deepest sympathy to you and your wife in your grievous loss. May God relieve your sorrow and fortify your spirits." He then lowered his voice: "Regarding other matters … you are, I am sure, aware of the mortuary fee now due. As is the custom, I will be obliged if you would deliver to me, as payment in kind for my services, the baby's christening robe, this being the one article of value possessed by Stephen at the time of his death."

Already distraught by his bereavement, Richard flatly refused: "I have lost my son and now you want to take from me the one remembrance I have of him." He raised a reproving finger. "You should know that, in law, a deceased infant cannot own anything. The robe is therefore mine not his, and I say you cannot have it."

The priest's manner changed abruptly. "You had best think again. No one – least of all a rich merchant – refuses to pay a burial fee. To do so is certain to provoke the wrath of the Church. If you persist in this attitude, you will live to regret it."

Richard turned on his heels and returned home determined not to yield to the parson's demand. Back at New Fish Street, Anne expressed her support for her husband's decision – even though they were both aware that there would be trouble ahead. As she put it: "Demanding a deceased infant's christening robe for burial services is like claiming the wedding ring in payment for a marriage. It is an abuse of the sacrament."

Life gradually returned to normal. As the weeks went by, the pain of Stephen's death abated slightly and his parents were able to console themselves with the thought that they might in due course be blessed with another son. That summer, on the feast days of St Peter and St Paul, there were traditional festivities in New Fish Street. Oil lamps were hung outside front doors to burn all night, garlands of white lilies were displayed and neighbourhood bonfires were lit both to celebrate the season and to purify the air. The wealthier residents, such as Anne and Richard, set out tables of sweet bread and drink in front of their houses and invited both neighbours and passers-by to partake.

These happier times were short-lived. One day in early October, Richard and Anne were working in the yard at the back of their house sorting through a new delivery of cloth when they heard a sudden commotion in the parlour. It was Anne's cousin, Rebecca, who had appeared unannounced in a very distressed state. The news could hardly have been worse. "My darling Anne" she said, breathlessly, "a most dreadful thing has happened. The bishop's summoner came to your father's door early this morning and cited him to appear before the bishop's court in St Paul's on a charge of heresy".

Anne was lost for words as Richard asked, "And where is he now?"

"He was taken away. He is to be held in the bishop's prison and brought to trial with other named persons next month on All Souls day. He is allowed no visitors. I have heard all this from a neighbour."

"On what grounds was this charge laid?" Richard queried.

Rebecca shrugged her shoulders. "I do not know precisely but I understand that two unnamed neighbours were witnesses against him."

The three of them stood there helplessly. Richard knew there was nothing to be done since no witnesses could be called in defence of Thomas Vincent, no lawyer could be appointed to defend him and none of those present knew of any persons in high places who might have influence with the bishop or his officers.

———

In the weeks that followed, Anne was in anguish not knowing how her father fared or what the future held for him. She prayed, as was her habit, but her prayers now had a sharper edge and a more unforgiving tone.

On the first Sunday in November, Anne awoke to the pealing of bells from the Jesus Bell Tower at St Paul's. This was a summons to Paul's Cross and Anne guessed that the important announcement that was to be made concerned the fate of her father and those who had been tried with him. At breakfast she asked Richard who was receiving customers that day, to keep an eye on Margaret. It was only a few minutes' walk to the cathedral and, full of trepidation, she joined the throng of curious onlookers gathered around the canopied pulpit. A priest climbed up to the raised platform and read from a scroll. Against each of the half-dozen listed names, he read the charges, the verdict of the court and the sentence imposed. Anne's chest tightened as the name of Thomas Vincent, Draper, of St Margaret's parish, was proclaimed.

"Thomas Vincent, will abjure and renounce his false and heretical beliefs before the people at Paul's Cross. He will be whipped three times before a solemn procession around the cathedral. This will take place on three separate Sundays and he will also submit to six whippings around his own parish church. His priest will follow immediately behind him on each occasion in order to certify that the whipping has taken place."

But that was not all. The priest's voice was now shrill and piercing:

"And Thomas Vincent will be obliged to wear an embroidered faggot on his outer garment at all times as a reminder of the fate that awaits him if he should repeat his offence. The faggot is to be worn for the whole remainder of his life and removal of the same will incur the penalty of relapse, which is an immediate sentence of death."

The priest paused and looked slowly around the assembled company. "And let the fate of those who have been justly sentenced be a warning to any who might be enticed into religious error or wicked opinions."

The convicted prisoners with faggots tied to their backs and signed recantations pinned to their shirt fronts, were released to their families. Anne tried to comfort her father as she helped him back to their house in New Fish Street. There they were met by an anxious looking Richard.

That evening, sitting in the parlour over steaming potage, Thomas, white faced and broken, gave vent to his feelings.

"I can bear the pain of the whipping but the mark of heresy will be branded on me for the rest of my days. My neighbours will shun me, my customers will desert me, thereby destroying my living as a draper. And I will never again be able to join in Bible readings or make known my religious views – all for fear of burning. Even as things stand, my life as I have known it has been consigned to the flames."

Later that night while Thomas slept, Anne and Richard tried to console each other. But there was little comfort to be had. "The Bishop of London is now in full cry in his crusade against heretics." Richard said. "As a further warning of what lies in store for straying members of his flock, he has committed two men to the stake at Smithfield in a fortnight's time. After their earlier conviction for heresy they had recanted but now they are judged to have offended again – for which there is no mercy."

Anne, further incensed by this news, gripped her husband's arm. "We shall not be cowed as our enemies want us to be. The humiliation of my father and the burning of those who share our beliefs show that we must prepare ourselves for the battle that is to come. We shall not submit to our ravening bishop and his henchmen."

As Anne contemplated the dangers ahead an image floated before her. A girl stood in front of her father amid a crowd of weeping onlookers. She felt the heat of the fire on her face, smelled the wood smoke and something more and heard the prisoner's cries turn to moans amid the crackle of flames. And between her father's trembling fingers she caught a fleeting glimpse of a scene that would be forever seared into her consciousness.

Anne understood the Church's use of terror, but recent events had pushed her past the point where she could be intimidated.

6

THE COURT OF AUDIENCE

ON A WET AND BLUSTERY MORNING JUST AFTER EASTER Richard put the finishing touches to a fine tunic for a valued customer. He lay down his cutters and looked at his apprentice, John Birtwistle: "John, I shall not be working on the morrow because there is jousting at Smithfield. I will be attending with some fellow guildsmen. In my absence you will be looking after things here."

John seemed happy to oblige. "Yes master. I saw this week that they were preparing the tilt yard and setting up scaffolds for spectators. I hope you will enjoy the tourney."

Richard was about to give further instructions to his assistant when there was a loud knock on the front door. His manservant, Thomas, seemed agitated as he introduced the caller. "Sir, John Huxtable here says he is an emissary from Lambeth Palace sent to deliver a court document to yourself."

Richard motioned to the surprise visitor to come in. He noticed that the official wore the insignia of the Archbishop on his black gown: three shells surmounted by a goat.

"Mr Huxtable, what cause has His Grace to concern himself with a humble merchant such as myself?" The reply was offhand and brutally curt:

"Richard Hunne, you are cited to appear before the Archbishop's Court of Audience in the Long Chapel of St

Paul's on the morning of the 24th day of this month. You will answer to a charge of wilfully refusing to pay a mortuary fee owing to one Thomas Dryfield. Failure to appear at the appointed time will be a grave contempt of court, warranting immediate imprisonment. Full particulars are contained in this summons."

The emissary delivered a scroll into Richard's hands, bowed and let himself out. Richard was stunned. He had expected to be called to appear before an ecclesiastical court but his alleged transgression was surely a diocesan matter to be dealt with by his own bishop. Now the Archbishop had assumed jurisdiction over the case, which was to be heard not by the consistory or commissary court but by the highest ecclesiastical tribunal in the land. Clearly the Church authorities believed that the challenge to their priests' customary dues had to be dealt with at the most elevated level.

Over supper Richard explained the situation to Anne. "The court I must appear before will be presided over by the Archbishop's legal representative, Cuthbert Tunstall. He is a renowned scholar and, they say, a rising man. I must seek good advice and have one of the leading proctors present my case before the court."

Anne looked downcast. "This will surely mean great expense in court charges and extortionate payments to those avaricious Church lawyers. But I suppose we must defend our cause as best we can."

"Certainly we must", said Richard. "I have decided to absent myself from the tourney and have sent word to Merchant Taylors Hall so they may grant my place to another. I must go straight away to Doctors Commons in Paternoster Row. They have many lawyers there who deal with Church disputes. Rest assured, I shall present the Archbishop's Court with the best case I can."

Next day Richard left his tailor's shop in the hands of his apprentice. He walked up Gracechurch Street, along Lombard Street and on to Cheapside. The rain had stopped but there were pools of water lying in the muddy roads and while skirting round a particularly large puddle he was distracted by the sound of horses galloping towards him from the direction of the Tower. As the cavalcade splashed by, spattering mud over his cloak, he marvelled at the spectacle of jousters in their full regalia riding towards Smithfield. Coloured plumes streamed from their helmets, banners fluttered from the tips of their upright lances and their horses were caparisoned in brightly coloured cloth emblazoned with heraldic motifs.

A large woman in an outsized bonnet commiserated. "I have heard there is a tourney in honour of some foreign visitor. God's wounds, it's all very well but these knights give no consideration to foot travellers like us."

Richard gave an ironic laugh. "They look very fine now. But I wager some of the proudest will return bruised, broken-lanced and bloodied before the day is over."

He turned left into Lombard Street and when he reached Paternoster Row he stopped opposite a large timber framed building that had clearly seen better days. This was Doctors Commons where a body of ecclesiastical lawyers had recently set themselves up as a separate college dealing with canon law disputes.

Brushing the worst of the mud off his clothes he entered through an open door and found himself in a spacious hall full of disorder and commotion. Along the side wall there was shelving stacked high with papers, at the far end scribes were sitting at desks scratching away at legal documents and set within another wall there were alcoves lined with law books and manuscripts. Proctors and advocates in their flowing black gowns were intermingling with each other and their clients and amid the hubbub some were advertising their services with shouts of "Wills!" "Tithes!" and "Marriage!"

Richard pushed his way through the melee and sought the assistance of a bearded clerk in a flat hat with a wide brim who stood apart from the crowd.

"Good sir, I wish to be represented in a case in the Archbishop's Court of Audience in a matter concerning a mortuary fee."

"Squibb's your man," said the clerk. "Graduate of Oxford. Good canon lawyer. Does tithes and burials. Mind, he does not come cheap, especially in a hearing before the Archbishop's Court. He is over here – I will take you to him."

Richard was introduced to a small grizzled man with a beaky nose who spoke in a high voice:

"Herbert Squibb at your service. Tell me your case, Master Hunne."

When Richard had recounted his dispute with the Church, Squibb looked grave, stroked his chin and made a tutting sound, before responding. "Master Hunne, I cannot hold out any great prospect of success in resisting your parson's claim. We could argue that papal decrees have prohibited the payment of fees for burials or we could assert that such cases fall within the jurisdiction of the royal courts. I can, of course, make these points on your behalf. However, it will be no easy matter – and I might add that proctors' fees must be paid ahead of proceedings."

Richard was undeterred. "I am happy to entrust the case to you. My purpose is not only to keep possession of Stephen's christening gown but to establish that in law there is no requirement to pay mortuary fees."

The proctor's manner suggested that he was doing his new client a great favour:

"Sir, I have been persuaded to undertake this task for you, though I will be obliged to spend many hours studying the writings of jurists and canon law scholars. Very careful preparations will be necessary for a hearing before Cuthbert Tunstall who, as you may know, is himself a learned theologian."

Richard was sceptical about how much work Master Squibb would be required to do but terms were agreed and he paid his fee. As he was leaving Doctors Commons he looked back and noticed that money was passing between Squibb and the bearded clerk in the wide hat.

———————

On the morning of April 24 Richard, wrapped in his over mantle, battled through driving rain along Watling Street towards St Paul's, sheltering as much as he could under the eaves of the overhanging houses.

Entering the cathedral he joined the throng of Paul's Walkers pacing the nave and made for the east aisle of the north transept which enclosed the Long Chapel. Away from the shuffling feet and murmuring of tongues the chapel, long used as an ecclesiastical court, provided the solemn setting for the Archbishop's Court of Audience.

Cuthbert Tunstall, slight, pale faced and wearing a white cope with a black stole and cap, was sitting with a small group of advisers and canon law scholars on a raised platform.

Herbert Squibb, appeared diminutive as he prepared to address the court from below while Richard stood to one side.

"Your Worship," the proctor began in his high pitched voice, "I wish to bring to the court's attention a passage from the proceedings of the Third Lateran Council held in the year of our Lord, one thousand one hundred and seventy nine." He held a faded text close to his failing eyes. *"It is a scandal that in certain churches a charge is made for burying the dead. No payment should be made for this or any other sacrament."*

Squibb cited other papal pronouncements with a similar theme and referred also to the work of jurists. He concluded with a look of self satisfaction. "Learned gentlemen, the verdict of the papal see as well as scholars of divinity is that burial services are as much part of a priest's duties as the Eucharist itself."

Squibb then moved on to his second line of argument. "Your Worship, disregarding for the moment whether my submission on the papal prohibition against mortuary fees is good in English law, I wish, on behalf of my client, to make a further contention. My client wishes to point out that the present charge laid against him arises not out of any spiritual matter but rather concerns rights to property. Such rights, he submits, more properly fall within the jurisdiction of the secular courts, as several eminent legal scholars have declared."

Here again Squibb referred those on the bench to various legal texts before arriving at his conclusion. "My client therefore wishes to express his objection to being called before this court in a suit which he avers fall outside its province."

As the proctor sat down, there was murmuring of disapproval from the bench above. Richard then waited expectantly while Tunstall and his advisers conferred among themselves. The angel shaped hand of the nearby cathedral clock pointed towards twelve and the chime rang out the hour, reverberating throughout the vaulted roof space.

At last, Tunstall rose to give his verdict. "It is determined that, notwithstanding earlier papal decrees, the payment of mortuary fees is established in England by long custom. Furthermore, this court has full jurisdiction over all matters affecting the rights of priests and the ancient liberties of the Church. We hold that in this suit, the said priest, Thomas Dryfield, is justified in claiming the deceased's only possession. The said Richard Hunne is required either to surrender his dead son's gown or else to pay its estimated value of one gold angel or six shillings and eight pence."

With the court cleared and the case now decided against his client, Squibb nevertheless displayed a surprising air of triumph as he took Richard aside. "Sir, I hope you agree that this is the best outcome we could have hoped for. You may keep the gown which you so cherish and the payment in lieu will be a small matter for someone of your standing. It is plain that our arguments pushed them so hard that they were obliged to yield this concession."

Richard was unimpressed. "My good man, I have fought this case on a point of principle. But that point has not been conceded. Indeed, I am being asked to purchase my own property for the benefit of an avaricious priest."

It was clear to Richard that the Church courts were there not to administer justice but to uphold clerical privileges, to exact money from lay persons and guard jealously the jurisdiction of the spiritual power. He turned his back in disgust and left the cathedral by the north door.

The sun had come out, and instead of walking back home Richard wandered thoughtfully around the cathedral precinct. After exploring the makeshift book stalls that crowded between the buttresses he went out through the perimeter gate into Paternoster Row. Here he joined the throng of curious people examining the volumes on display in the bookshops that lined the street. There were works of devotion, copies of the Latin Vulgate Bible, almanacs, law books, books on matrimony and anthologies of medicinal herbs. After some hesitation he picked up and paid for an illustrated volume of Aesop's Fables.

Richard felt the need to settle his mind, so rather than return directly to New Fish Street he walked slowly down to the river in an attempt to focus his thoughts on what his next move should be. He could, of course, pay the fairly modest sum of six shillings and eight pence to his parson and close the matter but this would be a humiliation for him and false enrichment for the priest. Another possibility occurred to him – and here he stopped and glanced back through the river mist at the immense and shadowy outline of the cathedral – he could surely challenge the ecclesiastical tribunal by taking his case to the royal courts. If he went down this route he would need to hire a very good attorney, heavy expenditure would be incurred and there might be other dangers ahead to him and his family.

He turned off Thames Street to Queen Hythe where wooden cranes were unloading sacks of grain from shallow draughted barges and lighters. The corn was being transhipped from larger vessels that were docked in the deeper water beyond London Bridge. He looked out at the great expanse of the City's waterway on which floated a scattering of wherries and canopied tilt boats, plying their trade between the countless stairs and quays that punctuated both sides of the river between the Tower to the east and Westminster Abbey to the west.

Richard retraced his steps to Thames Street, and by the time he reached his front door he had made up his mind. Margaret and the maidservant could be heard upstairs and Anne was alone in his shop painstakingly writing figures in a business ledger. She stood up and looked anxiously at Richard. "My dear love, how went the hearing?"

Richard embraced her. "It was to be expected. They said we could keep the robe but must pay the money. I believe, however, that we should take the matter further."

He began to outline to her his plan to challenge the Church in the royal courts while Anne put away her quill and ink, closed the ledger and listened attentively. After explaining the simmering tensions between secular and canon law and the growing rivalry between the spiritual and royal courts, Richard looked his wife steadily in the eye and asked for her support. "If we issue this writ the Church will be hard hit. It is a battering ram that can break open the bishopric's citadel. Of course, there will be considerable expense, but I should be able to raise the funds. Should we proceed we must expect a counterblow from our enemies. Combat will be truly joined. What do you say?"

Anne did not have to be persuaded. She would support any move against the Church that might help to avenge her dear father and protect the dignity of her lost baby. The battle lines were drawn.

That evening Richard felt the need for relaxation after reaching such a momentous decision. He went upstairs, picked up his daughter and held her in his arms. "Come now little one, it is time for bed. Before you go to sleep I shall read you a story about a fox and a stork from a book of fables that I bought today."

7

HEAVY WEAPONRY

RICHARD WASTED NO TIME IN SEEKING OUT RICHARD
Hawkes, a leading barrister of the Middle Temple who had been
recommended by a fellow merchant taylor. Richard had been
told that when not attending court hearings at Westminster
Hall Hawkes could generally be found after midday in the
Temple Church. On that fateful spring afternoon, Richard said
farewell to Anne and set out on the thirty minute walk from
London Bridge to the Inns of Court situated between Fleet
Street and the Thames.

Turning off Fleet Street to the Temple precinct, Richard
found himself entering a vast building site: banging and shouting,
the erection of scaffolding, horses hauling brick waggons, great
timbers being set into position and a pall of dust overhanging
the whole scene. He picked his way through rubble, building
materials and labourers to the comparative calm of the Temple
Church. On entering he found himself in a round nave ringed by
elegant clusters of marble pillars. He was surprised to see so many
lawyers, many of whom were in conference with their clients in
the bays around the nave. He asked a young man, whom he took
to be a legal student, where he could find Richard Hawkes.

The young man pointed to the bay opposite. "Master
Hawkes is over there in his customary place with a suitor. He

is much in demand these days and no doubt very busy but you may be in luck since he appears to be concluding his present meeting."

Richard walked round the arcaded columns of the circular nave to a pillar where Richard Hawkes was now standing alone. He was a big man with bushy eyebrows and strong features framed by thick black hair. Richard introduced himself, explaining that he was looking for an attorney to represent him in a difficult case. Hawkes's reply was delivered in a sonorous voice that had been deliberately honed to harangue the Westminster courts.

"Good Master Hunne, welcome to the Temple. I'm afraid that we are all inconvenienced at present by the building of yet more chambers to meet the demands of an ever growing body of lawyers and students. I fear that before long they will be encroaching on our cherished gardens and orchards. Now tell me about your dispute and I will see if I can help."

Richard explained the reason for his refusal to pay a mortuary fee to his parson and recounted the proceedings of the Archbishop's Court which had found against him. He now wanted to challenge that decision in the royal courts of justice. Hawkes looked grave. "There is only one way forward if you really wish to pursue the Church in this case. And make no mistake, if you do choose the path I am about to suggest there will certainly be great cost, probably much delay and conceivably some danger of a counter move. Now let me advise … You are correct in saying that the secular courts have jurisdiction over matters affecting ownership of property. But the canon lawyers would no doubt argue that a dispute over burial fees touches on the Church's ancient rights and is therefore a matter properly to be judged by the spiritual courts. The question therefore is finely balanced." Hawkes took Richard aside and lowered his voice. "I believe we should find greater seclusion in the chapel of St Anne if you would be so kind as to follow me."

He took Richard through a door in the nave wall that led into a small chapel adjoining the church. Here they were alone.

"These are sensitive issues," Hawkes said. "Certainly, we may claim that the Archbishop's Court acted beyond its province in hearing and purporting to decide your dispute. To do this we would issue a writ of praemunire which is a legal instrument feared more by the Church authorities than any other cause of action.

"The Great Act of Praemunire, as it is known, was put on the statute book in the reign of Richard II. The original purpose behind the enactment was to restrict the pope's jurisdiction in England. However, in recent years it has been invoked chiefly to challenge the right of ecclesiastical courts to hear cases that should be heard by the temporal or royal courts. The boundary between the spiritual and secular spheres therefore lies at the heart of praemunire suits. By issuing this writ you will be striking at the very pith and marrow of the ecclesiastical body."

Richard, undeterred by the enormity of what he was undertaking, asked Hawkes to act on his behalf and to prepare a writ of praemunire.

His newly appointed attorney explained the procedure. "I propose that we issue the writ against Parson Thomas Dryfield and the bishop's summoner, Charles Joseph. Of course, if the suit is successful it is the Archbishop's legal representative, Cuthbert Tunstall, who will be found to be at fault. But it is more politic to cast our net over the smaller fish in order to catch the larger."

When all was agreed the two men left the chapel by another door and walked down towards the river and away from the noise of the building works through the Temple gardens. The apple trees had begun to blossom, the air was scented and there was the sound of birdsong. Richard reflected that the air of rustic tranquillity was far removed from the world of Church politics and adversarial legal suits.

———————

Richard's case against the Church was set down to be heard in the Court of King's Bench a month later. On the appointed day, wearing his best fur-trimmed mantle, he took a wherry up river to York Stairs. From there he made his way to Westminster Hall where, outside the entrance, he was jostled by hawkers and beggars. As he passed through the open doorway a hunched and dishevelled man grabbed his mantle. "Good sir, I can be a witness for you for a mere shilling," he pleaded. "Any testimony you wish I can provide."

Richard brushed the man aside and joined the throng of people inside the Hall. Beneath the great hammer-beam roof, small shops and booths were set up along the walls selling books, millinery, stationery, jellies, sweetmeats and much else. Within the body of the Hall there were loose boxes formed by wooden partitions and it was to one of these enclosures that Richard was directed by an usher.

Within the Court of Kings Bench, the Lord Chief Justice, flanked by two other judges, sat on a raised bench. All three were wearing scarlet robes lined with ermine and the Lord Chief Justice wore a gold collar embossed with the Tudor Rose. In the well of the court, beneath the bench, there was a table covered with green baize at which clerks sat with their parchment rolls, quills and inkwells. The court officials were separated from the litigant and his counsel by an oak bar.

Richard was led by the usher to the bar where Hawkes was already standing with a sheaf of parchment under his arm. After some minutes of murmuring among the seated officials the marshal of the court rang a bell for silence and announced the commencement of formal proceedings.

Hawkes recounted the events leading up to his client's refusal to hand over his baby son's christening robe. He then challenged the right of the Archbishop's Court of Audience to hear the suit against his client. In a resounding voice he concluded his argument:

"Since the dispute over the deceased child's robe is a dispute about ownership and property it is a temporal matter that falls outside the jurisdiction of the spiritual courts. Accordingly all those appearing in the action against Richard Hunne have transgressed the royal prerogative. Under the provisions of the Great Statute not only they but all prosecutors, maintainers, abetters, supporters and counsellors of such traitors should be placed outside the Lord King's protection and should forfeit their lands and tenements, goods and chattels and should be arrested in person."

The Lord Chief Justice then deliberated with his fellow judges one of whom lent forwards. "Master Hawkes, I wish to know why your client is unwilling to pay the value of the christening gown, now that the Archbishop's Court has determined that he may keep the article?"

The attorney's reply was unhesitant. "My client wishes to establish two legal points. First, that the christening gown at issue is his own and no one else's property. And, second, that any challenge to his right of ownership of the same should be brought before His Highness's courts and not an ecclesiastical tribunal which has no standing in the matter."

The judge sat back expressionless and the Lord Chief Justice concluded the proceedings. "Master Hawkes, your submissions on behalf of Richard Hunne have been heard and you and he may now stand down. There are, however, weighty issues to be considered and you must not expect an immediate decision."

After conferring briefly with his attorney, Richard returned home.

While waiting anxiously for news of the court hearing, Anne had busied herself in baking bread and instructing the maidservant, Martha. Though she maintained an outward appearance of normality and calm she had begun to have misgivings about the full consequences of their legal challenge. There was, of course, the cost, which was worrying enough. But suppose the praemunire suit looked like succeeding. Would the bishops and their acolytes simply stand aside and watch while their powers were whittled away or might they intervene in some unexpected way that would harm her family? Certainly, she must back Richard now that they had come this far, but she worried that their little household might not be secure against the wrath of a mighty Church.

Anne was preoccupied with these thoughts when Richard appeared. While they were alone at supper he described the inconclusive court proceedings. He held her hand as he explained how he saw the situation. "Sweetheart, I believe the judges are facing a great difficulty. If, as loyal servants of the King, they uphold my claim they will be delivering a great blow to the Church. For they will be denying its right to try cases in the spiritual court. But if, as faithful adherents to the Church, they maintain the powers of the spiritual court, they will affront the Crown. They will be saying that it is lawful to appeal to a higher authority than that of His Highness."

Anne was puzzled: "So how will these learned men come to a decision?"

"My attorney tells me that this adjournment may be followed by further delays and postponements. That way the judges may hope to empty my purse, force me to withdraw my suit and thereby enable them to escape a judgement that could cause grave upset."

Anne was now concerned. "But how can we pay for all this legal expense? Surely the court will be the cause of our ruin."

"You need have no such fear. I will continue to provide for my family. I have funds set aside to see me through this impasse – and in due course the court must reach a decision."

Anne was not altogether reassured and also amazed that judges who were appointed to declare the law could be so fearful as to evade the obligations of their office. She conjectured that the outcome of this case must be momentous indeed.

But she was unaware that Richard had been approached in utmost secrecy by a prominent figure who could give powerful support to their cause.

8

LOLLARDS' TOWER

As Anne later recalled only too well, it was on the Feast Day of St Bruno, October 6th 1514 that the Church took matters in hand. She was upstairs at their home in New Fish Street teaching Margaret to read when she heard loud voices in the hallway. As she reached the landing she caught a glimpse of a tall figure at the front door who was talking in a commanding voice to Richard. Then two burly men burst past him and took her husband forcibly into the street. Anne rushed downstairs intending to follow them but a fourth man, wearing a hooded cloak, blocked the doorway. By now she was crying out for Richard but she could not escape the grasp of the stranger in her doorway.

"Mistress Anne," he said roughly, "Your husband has been detained by the Bishop of London's summoner. Our instructions are to take him to the bishop's prison at once without farewells or pleadings. You should be thankful that you yourself are still at liberty. Your manservant may bring necessaries to the prisoner but he is allowed no visitors."

The nameless official kept guard outside the house for the next hour before disappearing. During this time it dawned on Anne that the confinement that her father had endured was now to be suffered by her husband. But she and Richard had discussed the possibility of such a vengeful step by the Church and she knew that she had to be strong. She called the apprentice boy to the parlour: "John, Master Hunne may not return for some time. We must together ensure that the business carries on. I can deal with customers and ledgers and we are well stocked with cloth. Can you, working on your own, ensure that all the orders we have are met?"

John, whom she had come to think of as shy and rather lacking in confidence, surprised her. "I believe I can do what is needed Mistress Anne, so long as we take no new orders." Reassured, Anne next sorted out articles to be taken to Richard including linen, warm garments, a Latin Bible, rosary beads and sweetmeats. She turned to her manservant. "Thomas, please take these items to the bishop's prison in St Paul's and ask whether my dear husband is in need of anything else."

When the manservant returned later that morning he had bleak tidings. "The gaoler says that I may bring necessaries but no food is permitted, nor any materials for writing. I myself am unable to speak with Master Hunne who is kept alone in his cell."

Anne's anxiety at the turn of events deepened but she knew that she must not let her feelings overwhelm her. Margaret would soon be missing her father and she needed to maintain an outward appearance of calm in order to comfort the little girl.

In the afternoon Anne left Margaret with the maidservant and walked over to Carter Lane to see her kinswoman and confidante, Rebecca. She was married to Samuel, a well to do haberdasher who had a shop and warehouse in Wood Street. He sold ribbons, beads, purses, gloves and ladies' hats and he encouraged his petite and coquettish wife to try out these items in the company of her friends who often met together in his shop. She would pass on to him their comments on his merchandise and in this way he was able to keep in touch with the changing fashions of the times.

Rebecca was in a great state of excitement when Anne arrived. "Anne, what is your opinion of my newly borrowed French hood? Samuel says I may keep it if others approve its style because then he will sell more!" But Anne's demeanour prompted an abrupt change of tone: "My dearest Anne. I am so sorry to see you downcast. What has happened to make you look so wretched?"

The two women embraced in silence and when they had drawn apart Anne recounted the events of that morning. "First my father and now my dear husband. Both caught by the vengeful reach of the Church. Richard and I understood that such a thing could happen but now that it has I blame myself for encouraging his intransigeance."

Rebecca took her cousin's hand. "No, Anne, Richard chose this path knowing full well the dangers. He is a strong and resourceful man and will survive his incarceration. But we must find a way to communicate with him. If he is not allowed pen and ink and no visitor may speak with him we must devise something."

"He has forbidden books," said Anne. "Although these are held securely in a secret place I fear that someone might inform against him. Also he has spoken openly against tithes which some churchmen say is a mark of heresy." She gave a deep sigh. "But, of course, it is because of his praemunire writ that they have seized him. I am full of dread for the fate of my dear husband."

A month passed while Anne waited anxiously for news about Richard. Each week Thomas took fresh linen to Lollards' Tower and collected the old but he was unable to exchange words with the prisoner. As he returned from St Paul's one Sunday with a bundle of washing, he confided his thoughts. "Mistress Anne, the gaolers are very particular about items I take into Master Hunne's cell. But they do not trouble themselves much with what I bear away. Maybe there is an opportunity here."

Anne gave a good deal of thought to Thomas's observation. The days were drawing in, there was a late autumn chill in the air and she pictured Richard confined in a dank, dark and unheated chamber with no one to share his miseries. Not being able to communicate was becoming unbearable but then she hit on a simple idea. Taking a linen shirt into Richard's workshop at the back of the house she found the lead stylus that he used to trace out the shape and design of apparel for his customers. She tested it on a piece of parchment and, satisfied with the results, sewed it carefully into the seam of the shirt. She guessed that anyone wearing such clothing close to the body would soon feel the sharpness and discover the cause.

She set aside the shirt and, from their small collection of devotional works, took a prayer book. This contained opposite each prayer a blank page on which the devout reader could inscribe his or her own supplication. On the first blank page Anne wrote in her own hand *Scribere ad me*. Pleased with her handiwork, she called her manservant.

"Thomas, please take these fresh clothes and this prayer book to Master Hunne. I believe he may contrive to write a letter which he can conceal in his old linen. Be aware of this when you next collect raiment from him, and let us hope the gaoler does not carry out a thorough search."

Anne was not to be disappointed. When Thomas returned from Lollards' Tower the following week she found in the bundle of washing he brought back a page torn from the prayer book. She read the short message written on it again and again:

"Sweetheart, they are questioning me about my supposed confederates and fellow believers but I have said nothing. They hold me in the stocks several hours each day. Sometimes they put a heavy metal weight on my shoulders as if I were a

beast of burden. They, meaning chiefly the bishop's chancellor, are trying to break me. However, I have received kindness from the gaolers who are simple men with no hatred towards myself. This place is damp and very cold and I fear the ague has come upon me. I long to be reunited with you and the little one.

Richard"

Anne was mortified to hear of her husband's mistreatment. When she later told Rebecca, her devoted cousin wondered aloud whether enforced silence would not have been a greater comfort than these images of suffering. The following week Anne received another letter which served only to increase her apprehension. Richard said that the bishop's chancellor had interrogated him fiercely and warned him that grave charges against him would soon be drawn up. But worse news still was to come as the winter advanced. On the afternoon of Sunday 3rd December Thomas returned from his customary errand to St Paul's. Anne eagerly unwrapped the bundle of linen he had collected and found some sheets tucked into the hem of Richard's smock. She read the shaky pencil script on these torn scraps of parchment:

"Sweetheart, my fate is now in God's hands but I am fearful. Last morning I was taken by barge and brought before the bishop and his chancellor at Fulham for an examination. I was asked many questions and had answers to most but I was made to write and yet not to sign a letter of contrition for speaking inadvisedly. I was taken back to St Paul's and this very morning the penitentiary was sent up to me to make holy water and holy bread. Later the chancellor knelt down before me and prayed forgiveness for all he must do to me. From all this I judge that my life may be endangered.

If this be so, keep faith with God, take care as I know you
will, of our little daughter, and keep remembrance of your
husband who always loved you and does so still.
   Richard"

Reading these scribbled lines with some difficulty Anne was too overcome to weep. But the last piece of parchment, which had not been written upon, conveyed the most baleful message of all. The page bore the imprint in blood of Richard's hand – that familiar hand, with its tailor's scar, which many a time she had kissed and many a time had caressed her body. He must have cut himself with a nail or other implement, pressed his palm to a bloody slab and left his brand on the page as a final leave-taking.

That night Anne prayed for Richard's soul and in her troubled dreams had visions of the apocalypse. The next morning, after attending mass with Margaret in her parish church, she left her daughter with her cousin in Carter Lane and walked over to St Paul's. Entering the precinct she saw that people had gathered round the north door where a placard had been pinned up. Before she could discover what news was arousing such interest a priest mounted the steps to the canopied platform of Paul's Cross. A crowd formed quickly as the priest made an announcement about the prisoner in Lollards' Tower:

Richard Hunne, who had already caused great offence to God on
account of his wicked beliefs, last night died by his own hand in the
bishop's prison where he was held under suspicion of heresy. The act of
self-murder is itself a criminal deed which testifies to the guilty mind
and heretical opinions of the said Hunne. He has, we understand, a
family and these unfortunates will now be made destitute since the
estate of any person who commits felo de se is, by long established law,
forfeit. Hunne has therefore betrayed his God, his Church, his King
and his family. He has also dishonoured the company of merchant
taylors of which he was a member. I speak on behalf of the bishop

when I say that Hunne's fate and that of his wife and child, should be a warning to all those who are minded to support the mischievous views of Lollards, Wycliffites or other heretical sects.

As the priest stepped down it was apparent to those around her that Anne had fainted. Concerned neighbours and acquaintances tried to revive her and, having failed in their efforts, carried her back to New Fish Street, where she was tended with strong smelling herbs and barley with honey in hot water.

9

The Coroner's Inquest

George Monoux, Lord Mayor of London, was a man of substance. A former sheriff, he was one of the most successful merchants in the City and had just served the first of what were to be seven terms as Master of the Drapers Company. He had extensive property interests, a brewhouse in Southwark and an impressive moated mansion in Walthamstow, known as "Moones", which was surrounded by several enclosures of land and many large meadows. He was irascible and overbearing but he also knew his duty and took his responsibilities as Mayor very seriously.

Monoux was a traditional Christian worshipper and was later to obtain a special licence to have the sacraments administered in his oratory at Moones. However, like many merchants of his time, he resented the financial impositions of the clergy. He found it outrageous that the Church, with its extensive monastic land holdings, accounted for around one third of the total rental value of all London property. He was also opposed to the burden of tithes. In London tithes in kind had been commuted for cash payments, the faithful being required to make an offering of one tenth of their income to their priest. For house owners tithes were also payable on the rental value of their house and for tenants the tithe was fixed at three shillings and five pence for every pound paid. He reflected that it was all very well for a man of his great wealth but for many London citizens the tithe was a heavy burden – often paid only on death from the sale of the deceased's property.

Monoux also strongly disapproved of the Bishop of London's fanatical drive against supposed heretics which was striking terror into many of his fellow tradesmen and citizens. When he heard of Hunne's arrest he had been shocked. Hunne was well liked and respected as an honest merchant, and if he were taken who might be next? He knew that this was a spiritual matter outside his control, but he had nevertheless approached the Dean of St Paul's, John Colet, whose father, a prominent mercer, had twice been Lord Mayor of London. He and Colet had had a private discussion at the deanery which stood within the cathedral close just a few yards south of Lollards' Tower. Monoux, suppressing his anger, had broached the subject with diplomatic caution contrary to his robust instincts.

"Dean, holding the office I do I receive all manner of citizens' concerns and complaints about daily hardships, taxes, lack of conduits, maintenance of properties and so on. But since Hunne was taken into the bishop's prison I have had complaints without end about what many of our good freemen believe to be an unwarranted act of revenge for his praemunire. I understand, of course, that this is outside the province of my office but I am bound to draw attention to the sense of injustice that exists among the people."

The dean had been sympathetic but explained that he had no influence with the bishop. He was himself deeply troubled by the Hunne case but could only hope that the unfortunate prisoner would soon be released.

Colet had ended that meeting with a personal anecdote. He alluded to the passage in St John's Gospel with its thrice stated command *Feed my sheep*. In expounding this text he, Colet, had rejected the idea that, in the final declaration, *feed* referred to hospitality and entertainment. Such a precept he argued would not be enjoined on poor men like the apostles. For this opinion he had been threatened with heresy proceedings. "I say no more," the dean had concluded, shaking his head. "But these are the times we live in."

After leaving the deanery Monoux had reflected that if a man could fall foul of the Church for an innocent interpretation of scripture, what chance for Richard Hunne with his praemunire.

———————

When he was informed of Hunne's death on that Monday morning, Monoux recalled his abortive meeting with Colet. After conferring briefly with his officials he wasted no time in instructing the coroner, Thomas Barnwell, to empanel a coroner's jury to investigate the cause of death. Edward IV had granted the City of London the right to make its own appointment to this ancient office and Barnwell was therefore directly answerable to the Mayor.

Monoux was only too well aware how sensitive this case was going to be. Bills were already being pinned to the north door of St Paul's accusing the bishop's chancellor of murder. The Church authorities, on the other hand, were proclaiming the death as self-murder which, if proven, would mean that all of Hunne's estate would be forfeit to the Crown.

The Mayor's instructions to Barnwell could not have been more clear. "Thomas, you must first ensure that no persons intermeddle with the body or come to the prison. You and the jurymen will, of course, view the body at the earliest opportunity and then you must take statements from witnesses. Spare no one, and do not trouble yourself about causing dismay in high places if that is where the path leads. We must discover the truth because the whole city is in outcry over this death."

Thomas Barnwell, a solidly built man with greying hair and a florid complexion, sat at his desk in the coroner's office at the Guildhall. He was well used to being called in to investigate unexplained deaths but this case was different: there was great public clamour, the mayor was taking a close personal interest in the outcome and the Church was showing extraordinary sensitivity over the proceedings.

He had appointed a jury panel of 24 citizens from local wards and now these worthy burgers were gathered before him awaiting their instructions. After each man had been sworn in, he addressed them:

"Gentlemen, the body of Richard Hunne was discovered on the morning of Monday last. A day having already elapsed, we must view the same without delay. According to the vows you have just given you are bound by the strictest confidence in all proceedings before me as I am sure you are aware."

Barnwell led the jurors down Milk Lane into Cheapside and from there into the cathedral precinct where an angry crowd was still gathered around the north door. Passing in front of the bishop's palace and the deanery, they approached the entrance to Lollards' Tower, where one of the mayor's serjeants was standing guard. When Barnwell presented his authority the serjeant looked concerned.

"Crowner Barnwell … gentlemen … the room in which the corpse hangs is small – too small, I think, for so many."

The coroner was in agreement. "What I propose is that a company of six persons views the room at any one time. Then, after we have all looked at the scene, I shall go up with William Marler and James Page here – both of whom have knowledge of physic – and we three shall make a full examination of the body."

When Barnwell's turn came he climbed the stairs and entered the cell which in the dark days of winter had little natural light. In the dimness he noted the pitiful simplicity of the room: a makeshift bed and bolster on which was perched a wooden stool, a small chest containing Hunne's Bible, prayer book and other devotional works, and, in one corner, a bucket. There were also stocks set against one of the walls on which a snuffed out candle had been stuck with its guttering wax.

The corpse was hanging face to the wall by a black silken girdle that had been hooked onto an iron staple attached to a wall timber. The head was lolling to one side, the neck apparently broken, but the ashen and expressionless face of the victim was not in any way contorted and the mouth and eyes were closed. On closer examination, William Marler observed: "There are some few drops of blood from each nostril but otherwise there are no bodily effusions from mouth or bowel. That is unusual in a hanging."

After taking some measurements, which showed that the extinguished candle was some eight feet from the body, Barnwell began to supervise the delicate task of taking Hunne down and laying out the corpse. But before they could unhook the girdle Barnwell made a surprising discovery: "This iron chain hung from the same staple as Hunne's belt, has been laid over the top of the belt. This must have been done after he was hanged."

The silk girdle was removed and the doublet, shirt and linen undergarments stripped off. The three men then stood silently for a minute before the naked body. Barnwell made a sign of the cross and they bowed their heads. After this brief act of homage, James Page resumed the examination. He exclaimed suddenly. "How curious! There is severe chafing around the neck which most probably was caused by a metal object and not by a silken sash." This remark prompted them to look up at the iron chain hanging from the wall. "I fear that this very chain was the instrument of death," Page said solemnly. "Another thing … there are marks around the victim's wrists as if his hands had been bound. And a man with bound hands cannot make a noose to hang himself."

The three of them agreed that it was beginning to look like a murder scene. The other jurors had already reported finding considerable quantities of blood on the floor of the cell and now Marler made a further discovery. He was bending down to examine Hunne's jacket which was lying discarded in a corner. "Here is another puzzle," he said. "On the left side of Hunne's coat from the breast downward, there are two great streams of blood and under the left flap there is another mass of blood. Some person has tried to conceal this by the manner in which the jacket has been folded."

"What makes it all the more extraordinary," responded Barnwell, "is that there is no blood on the body, nor on the doublet, collar or shirt or any other item he was wearing. Everything here is inconsistent."

The three men, having completed their inspection, descended the stairs and rejoined their colleagues to whom they reported their findings.

The following day, seated at his desk in the Guildhall, Barnwell finished dictating a full account of what had been discovered in Lollards' Tower. Acting as his scribe was his trusted assistant, Matthew, a sensitive looking young man of slight build. The coroner had learned from bitter experience not to place confidence in the pool of scribes provided by the sheriff's office and, in a delicate case such as this, he wished to prevent information getting to those who might seek to influence the verdict.

Barnwell was perplexed. "Matthew, I cannot make sense of Hunne's death. The body was not injured yet a great deal of blood was spilt. And why was the corpse's linen unstained? Maybe the blood on the floor and jacket belonged to someone else. Certainly, neither I nor the jury members believe he could have hanged himself, but why would someone intent on murder leave such an incriminating scene?"

Matthew looked equally bewildered. "Yes, Master. It is a puzzle. If the cause of Hunne's death was, as we believe, the breaking of his neck by a metallic implement, possibly the chain hanging from the staple – why the blood? And who but a dunderhead would seek to hide the blood found on the victim's jacket by merely folding it over? Is it possible that he hanged himself and afterwards some rogue tried to give it the appearance of murder?"

The coroner paced up and down the room for a minute. "We must summon all witnesses who may shed light on this mystery to attend us here. I propose that each witness is sworn in the presence of at least four of our jurymen. You, Matthew, will set down what they say and after I have read this out they will subscribe their testimony. We do, however, have a difficulty. The most important witness may be Dr Horsey, but I understand he is being held incommunicado under the Archbishop's protection. We are therefore unable to question him. Spalding, the bell-ringer, is a simpleton and his testimony is of little value. The other chief witness is Charles Joseph. But they say he is not to be found at his house and may have absconded. That leaves us with the lesser fry and we shall have to do the best we can with them. Christmas is fast approaching and I would like to review all witness statements by Friday next."

"Then we shall have a lot to keep us busy," Matthew said. "I have prepared placards requesting any citizen with information to come forward. We can affix these to the Guildhall as well as to Paul's great door and we can request that one of the undersheriffs makes a declaration from Paul's Cross."

Barnwell gave a deep sigh. He did not try to disguise his anxiety: "The whole of London is in turmoil over this death and I am the one charged with determining the cause and finding the culprits. Yet at this time I am unable to make sense of it. Let us hope fervently that the witnesses can help us."

There was another worry for the coroner: he had been told that the Bishop of London, even now, was planning to try Hunne as a heretic. Such a move, he had no doubt, was designed to drown out his own inquiry and to encourage a belief among the people that Hunne surely deserved to die, whether he killed himself or not. Never before had Barnwell been assailed by so many dark forces: the suspicions of the citizenry, the fearfulness of reformers, the vengefulness of the Church and the evidence of foul deeds in Lollards' Tower that defied any rational explanation.

10

CONFESSION

BARNWELL HAD SELDOM KNOWN SUCH A BITTERLY cold winter – or perhaps he was just feeling the chill more as he grew older. He moved his desk closer to the fire and looked into its embers. Time was running out for his inquest into Hunne and he might soon be forced to reach an inconclusive verdict: *murder by persons unknown.* That would be an unsatisfactory outcome to a case that caused such consternation among the burgesses of London.

It was while he was entertaining such thoughts that Matthew burst in: "Master, there is a royal messenger here from the Tower come to see you on urgent business."

A swarthy man, wearing a tunic emblazoned with the Tudor rose, presented himself and explained his mission. "Sir, I am commanded by the Constable of the Tower to inform you that one Charles Joseph has been taken and will this very afternoon be questioned by the King's counsel concerning the death of Richard Hunne. Knowing your interest in this matter, the constable inquires whether you would wish to have some of your jurymen present."

Barnwell's response was immediate. "Please thank the constable and inform him that I shall ask several men to be in attendance." He turned to Matthew. "Send messengers to see which members of the jury may be available to go to the Tower. Those who do can report back to us here."

Errand boys were duly despatched while Barnwell paced his office, anxiously awaiting further news. He imagined that this could be the breakthrough he was looking for. If Joseph confessed to his role in the slaying of Hunne, fear of his vengeance would be lifted from others and tongues would be loosened. All might then be revealed.

As darkness was falling in late afternoon Barnwell greeted four jurymen returning from the Tower. He gestured towards the fire. "Welcome gentlemen. Warm yourselves and then let us hear what the blackguard, Joseph, has to say. Master Crofton, you may act as spokesman."

Christopher Crofton glanced at his fellow jurymen before proceeding. "Very well. Joseph has given himself up after taking sanctuary. He has tried to thwart his accusers by claiming that on the night Hunne was killed he was lying with a harlot at Neck Hill, Essex, in the house of a man whose wife is a bawd. He proposes to bring before the King's counsel both the wife and the aforesaid harlot for his purgation. It is expected they will appear at the Tower on the morrow."

For a moment Barnwell was dismayed. Then he recovered himself. "Gentlemen, we already have four good witnesses to set against the bawd and the harlot. The tailor, Thomas Chicheley, the stationer, Thomas Symondes and Symondes's wife have all sworn that they saw Joseph coming out of the cathedral at around seven o'clock on that Monday morning. And Robert Johnson of the Bell Tavern has said that Joseph's horse was left with him all Sunday night, ready saddled, and was mounted and ridden away by Joseph at eight o'clock the next morning."

Crofton looked reassured. "Their evidence will weigh in the balance much more heavily I wager."

"Indeed," said the coroner. "We have copies of the depositions here and I will have them despatched to the Tower so they may be read by the King's counsel and shown also to Joseph and his fellow connivers. Then we may hope to get at the truth."

The following day the coroner met briefly with the four jurymen at his office. They were due to return to the Tower to observe Joseph's reaction to the witness statements that disproved his alibi. "Gentlemen," Barnwell said, "we may today learn of matters that are of great moment. I suggest we meet next morning at my house in Fenchurch Street rather than at my chamber here in the Guildhall where there are too many curious eyes and ears. I will await your arrival together with as many of the remaining jurors as I can assemble."

After the men had gone, the coroner sat back pensively. He could not erase from his mind the image of Hunne hanging in Lollards' Tower. He recalled that the body had swung gently in the draught from the open window and when they had turned it round he had noticed the face, though white and bloodless, suggested a person at peace. It had struck him as particularly odd, too, that the hair was newly combed beneath the cloth cap set neatly on his head. It was as if the last thought of this doomed man was to compose himself for the moment of death.

It was very unlike the other hanging case he had recently encountered – an insolvent wine merchant found suspended from one of the wharf-side cranes in the Vintry. Some had suspected foul play but all the evidence pointed to suicide. He recollected that the condition of the corpse was in contrast to that of Hunne's: the face was convulsed and contorted, the tongue protruding, the eyes staring out and bulging. Barnwell wondered whether a man's state of mind is stamped on his countenance at the very last.

In late afternoon, Barnwell walked over to his house in Fenchurch Street and there he welcomed the jurors as they arrived from the Tower and neighbouring wards. They all crowded into his parlour where he addressed them.

"Gentlemen, Master Crofton here has brought important news from the Tower where our emissaries witnessed Charles Joseph's testimony. Please say your piece Master Crofton."

The jury's spokesman, evidently shaken by the news he had to impart, glanced nervously around the room seeking reassurance from his fellows before beginning hesitantly. "Yesterday we returned to the Tower to be present when Joseph was confronted with the depositions gainsaying his own testimony and that of his compurgators. When the King's counsel examined him closely on his whereabouts on the night of Hunne's death he fell silent and then began to swear profusely. Finally, on being brought to order, he confessed his role in Hunne's death, a copy of which signed confession I am holding."

At this point Crofton read slowly from a small sheet of parchment, his hand shaking visibly. "*Charles Joseph sayeth that when Richard Hunne was slain, John Bellringer bear up the stairs into the Lollards' Tower a wax candle, having the keys of the doors hanging on his arm. And I, Charles, went next to him and Master Chancellor came up last. And when all of us came up we found Hunne lying on his bed. And then Master Chancellor said 'Lay hands on the thief!' So all we three murdered Hunne. And then I, Charles, put the girdle about Hunne's neck. And then John Bellringer and I, Charles, did heave up Hunne, and Master Chancellor pulled the girdle over the staple. And so Hunne was hanged.*"

Everybody in the room was silent. Then one juror spoke up. "So we have compelling evidence that the bishop's chancellor was the chief villain in the wilful murder of Hunne and also in feigning the cause of his death." Another added: "But it does not stop there. We all know that the chancellor is a most faithful and loyal deputy of his bishop and has been such over many years. It is hardly imaginable that he would have done such a thing without his bishop's endorsement. This could be the greatest scandal to afflict the Church in our lifetime."

Barnwell sensed the tension in the room. However, he forestalled any further discussion by announcing his proposals for completing his investigation. "We may already have enough evidence to bring charges against those whom Joseph has incriminated. But I intend to interrogate again two important witnesses … Peter Turner, Joseph's son-in-law, and Julian Little, Joseph's servant – now that the threat of retribution overhanging them has been lifted. The bishop's summoner has sealed his own fate without assistance from them."

The jurors departed that evening surely knowing that they were on the threshold of bringing an indictment that could cause turmoil within the Church. They would also know that the ensuing trial could dramatically widen an already dangerous rift between the Church and London's citizenry.

But as he reflected on the latest twist in the Hunne affair, Barnwell's attention was focussed in another direction. He was aware that the King himself was taking an increasing interest in the case: Joseph had, after all, been incarcerated in the Tower under a royal warrant and it was said that Henry was prepared to support a bill in Parliament for the restitution of Hunne's property to his family. No doubt there was royal sympathy for Hunne's dependants but the coroner was convinced that it was the clamour of the people that was obliging their sovereign to make a public display of his concern over Hunne's fate.

———————

As Barnwell had anticipated, Joseph's confession prompted his servant, Julian Little, and the junior gaoler, William Turner, to make further revelations. Joseph had evidently confided to Little that he had killed Hunne shortly after midnight, and Turner confirmed that his father-in-law was in London that night and had kept a horse saddled up at the Bell in Shoreditch.

The coroner put the latest witness statements together with the other case documents in a leather folder. He placed the case file in an iron box behind his desk, locked it, and gave a sigh of satisfaction as he turned to his assistant. "The indictments we have prepared against Horsey, Joseph and Spalding are well supported by the evidence that has been gathered. We can say that our job is done – or will be as soon as the jury have agreed our verdict. So, on that happier note, what do you say to a visit to the bear garden on Sunday to occupy our minds with lighter fare?"

Although he showed little appetite for blood sports, Matthew was clearly flattered to receive such an invitation from his superior.

"That's settled then," said Barnwell. "St Paul's Wharf on Sunday morning where we shall take a wherry to Bankside. I shall procure it ahead of time because there will be many souls on the river that day."

Despite his outward air of confidence the coroner remained troubled by the evidence he had collected on Hunne. What possible motive could the bishop's chancellor have for killing a man who was already under lock and key and liable to conviction for heresy? And what was Joseph doing all those hours in Lollards' Tower between Hunne's death at around midnight and daybreak when he was seen emerging from the cathedral close? And why all the blood? And whose blood? Privately, he had to concede that he could make no sense of it at all, but he would reveal none of his misgivings to Matthew or to the jurors. After all, given Joseph's confession, the case against the three culprits was clear enough – sufficient to bring his enquiry to a conclusion and allow him to end his involvement in this intractable and worrisome case.

The bear garden on Bankside was a high, circular, wooden structure with galleries projecting inwards round the upper levels for spectators. Below the raised seating was the bear pit while outside the arena there were numerous sheds and kennels in which bears, bulls and dogs were kept. The shouting of revellers mingled with the barking and roaring of caged animals to produce a cacophony of sound.

Barnwell and Matthew sat in the upper gallery and looked down into the pit where a bear was tethered by its neck to a stake at the edge of the arena. Dog owners stood around the circle, holding their mastiffs at bay, waiting for their turn to loose them against the quarry. The first attack dog was released and tore into the bear which retaliated with its claws and teeth. The crowd, many of whom had made wagers on which dog would last the longest, roared as flesh was ripped and the blood flowed. Although the mastiff was severely mauled it was prepared to fight to the death but its owner forcibly pulled it back with the aid of a stick inserted into its muzzle.

The next dog was released and others followed. Two were killed, one was dragged off half-dead and the rest were judiciously withdrawn before fatal damage could be inflicted. Amid the din, Barnwell explained to Matthew. "The bear's teeth have been filed down, otherwise more dogs would be killed. You have to understand that the bear owner does not wish to lose the bear because it is a costly creature. And neither do the dog owners want to have their dogs killed. Therefore it is the owners who decide how long the combat should last."

Sure enough when the first bear showed signs of exhaustion from its exertions and wounds, it was replaced by another. So the spectacle continued with fresh mastiffs and several bears. For the last encounter, a bull was brought into the ring and the tethering stake removed to the centre of the arena. Hounds were loosed all at once against the animal until, after a prolonged fight and the death of two more dogs, the bull was itself mortally wounded and torn apart in a melee of blood spattered flesh.

Violence of a different kind had erupted in the upper gallery. Trying to make their way out, Barnwell and Matthew first had to clamber over a drunken spectator but were then obstructed by a brawl. In the general mayhem a man was dropped over the wooden rail and lay still in the bear pit below them. As they pushed their way past someone said, "He should have paid out on my wager!"

They eventually descended the scaffolding and made towards the exit. Barnwell turned to Matthew. "It happens too often. I am afraid the lower sort get over-excited at these spectacles." Passing a bull pen on the way out he added, "Bulls are different from bears. They are much less costly and so, to please the crowd, they allow one to be killed. It is because of the cost that in our smaller towns bull baiting is seen more than bear baiting."

Matthew appeared impressed by the coroner's knowledge of the sport but he also looked pale and shaken.

Barnwell felt that his assistant needed some reassurance. "Violence between men is for a purpose," he said "but these animals that are born and bred for savagery need no such justification. They fight because they exist to fight. They are but beasts and have no feelings."

Matthew appeared less than convinced but said nothing.

———

At St Paul's Wharf the two men parted. Dusk was gathering but it was a clear night and Barnwell began to walk home having turned down the link boy who offered to guide him back to Fenchurch Street. It was not long before he heard a footfall behind him and he began to suspect that he was being followed although, looking back, he could see nothing through the gloom. He quickened his pace along Thames Street and was about to turn into Gracechurch Street when he felt a blow from behind and then a sharp sensation in his back. The coroner was a powerful man and, twisting around, he swung his right arm against his assailant and brought his knee up into his groin. The attacker, evidently severely winded, groaned, dropped his knife and disappeared into a side alley.

Barnwell could feel the blood trickling down his back but he was able to stagger the short distance to his house. There his wife, Barbara, with the help of their maidservant, dressed his wound. There was relief on her face when she had done:

"It is fortunate, Thomas, that you must have begun to turn round as the blow was struck because the knife has not made a deep incision."

But Barnwell was troubled. In normal times he would have made nothing of the incident. Such assaults were common as daylight faded from London's unlit streets and there was surely no need to attribute to the assailant any motive other than avarice. However, these were not normal times and it was odd that the would-be robber, if such he was, had directed his knife at his person and not at the pouch worn on his belt – as any cutpurse might have been expected to do.

Could someone be targeting him? He was about to deliver an explosive verdict on the cause of Richard Hunne's death that implicated the Church at the highest level. And if the Church was capable of murdering a respected London liveryman, why might it not also seek to eliminate the man charged with identifying the perpetrators of the crime?

Then another possibility occurred to him. The indictment for murder of senior church officials would place the Crown in a very difficult position. Given the public outcry that would ensue, how could the King avoid a prosecution in the royal courts of those indicted in the coroner's verdict? Yet such a course of action would create a great rift between Church and State, thereby upsetting that delicate balance between the spiritual and temporal powers on which the governance of the country depended. Henry would, he surmised, do anything to avert such a dangerous confrontation. Perhaps someone in the service of the Crown was out to disrupt the inquest into Hunne's death.

That night Barnwell mentioned his fears to his wife but she chided him gently as she brought him a drink of hot ginger. "My dearest, I think this inquest has weighed too much on your mind for too long and that you are becoming fanciful in imagining all manner of evil doings. We will both be thankful when it is all behind us."

On this last point, Barnwell was fully in agreement: "Yes, I have decided that the best course is to bring things forward. I will assemble the jury this coming week to swear the verdict and indictment which I will present to the mayor without further delay."

THE TRIAL

BENJAMIN SLATHER WAS SITTING AT A TABLE IN A small cubicle adjoining Bishop Fitzjames's library, surrounded by scrolls, writing materials and books. He had just been visited by a lowly clergyman requesting an audience with the bishop. This man was but one of the countless applicants from the swelling ranks of the priesthood that crowded the corridors of the palace seeking appointments, preferments and other favours. None of these suitors could gain access to Fitzjames without the say-so of his secretary. And for this modest service Slather demanded some small consideration from each petitioner – or rather more if he was expected to put in a good word with His Lordship.

But while the perks of office were welcome, the workload now being placed on him was not. At this time, in the second week of December, bishops and clergy from all over England were gathering for Convocation which was to meet ahead of the parliamentary session called for February. Although the bishops were able to stay at their London palaces there were always accommodation problems among the abbots, deans, archdeacons and lesser clergy who poured into London to attend the Lower House of the Church's legislature. During these great assemblages Fitzjames liked to entertain his fellow bishops and this also placed administrative demands on his aide.

Slather bemoaned the fact that there was no benefit for him in all these duties – although he recalled that he had on occasion been given generous commissions by visiting churchmen to provide handsome wenches for their wellbeing and comfort.

This year his work was being greatly augmented by this Hunne business. He was already heavily involved in arrangements for the trial and had just sent out invitations to the spiritual and temporal elite of London – the Lord Mayor, the aldermen and sheriffs of the City, twenty-five doctors, several abbots and priors and numerous other dignitaries. He would have to arrange their seating in the cathedral in order of precedence – a delicate task – and there were all manner of other duties: the provision of scribes, the employment of ushers and even the positioning of Hunne's open coffin as well as the incense burners to cause least offence.

On top of everything else, his leg was causing him great discomfort and all this activity was only making things worse. He sometimes wondered whether there might not be an easier task master than the present bishop.

To Slather the trial proceedings seemed unnecessary and tiresome. He understood that Church revenues had to be protected and that those who spoke against tithes must be punished. But on the finer points of doctrine – and especially on the question of whether the Eucharist was a miracle or a symbol and remembrance – he had no opinion and cared not at all. As for prisons, public penance, executions and burnings, surely better by far to exact fines against transgressors – most of all rich merchants like Hunne – and thereby swell the Church's coffers.

There was another consideration. The bishop believed, or so Slather surmised, that the example of Hunne would instil fear into the people and bend them to his will. But suppose it went the other way? Suppose the people, already disaffected, were to be further incited by the trial and burning of the corpse of a fellow citizen deemed innocent. Then there might be consequences no one could foresee.

———————

While Parliament and Convocation were sitting, the bishop resided at his London mansion in the north east corner of the cathedral close. The palace, noted for its magnificent Great Hall, was sumptuous enough to have provided lodging for kings, but today the bishop had no thoughts of entertaining royalty for other pressing matters were on his mind. He was only too aware that this great gathering was occurring at a time of growing antagonism towards the clergy among Londoners, fuelled by leaked reports of foul play in Lollards' Tower. Conscious of the urgent need to strike a blow for the Church he was making his preparations for a counter-attack.

Fitzjames summoned his commissary, Dr. Thomas Head, to a private meeting in his library.

"Thomas, we must give very careful attention to the procedures we follow in the trial of Richard Hunne, not only to ensure compliance with canon law, but also to persuade the people of our cause. There are several particulars of the case that we need to attend to. First, there is the gathering of evidence. I understand that Wycliffe's Bible was discovered locked away in Hunne's house. Have you considered how we can use this in the proceedings?"

Dr Head had done his homework. He was, after all, standing in for the chancellor and appeared anxious to show that he could step into his superior's shoes. His reply was emphatic.

"The Bible is in English, so that the possession and reading of it is, of course, a grave spiritual offence. But the version we found contained Wycliffe's infamous prologue with its many heresies. Among other calumnies, it casts doubt on the miracle of the Eucharist, and condemns the idolatry of saints, the falsity of the pope's indulgencies and proclaims that poor men and idiots have the truth of the Holy Scriptures more than a thousand prelates and religious men. This is enough to damn Hunne in the eyes of all – the more so because marks of approval have been made in his hand against the offending passages."

Fitzjames felt reassured. Here was rich material, understandable by the most simple of minds, that would not only condemn Hunne as a heretic but show to a sceptical world the wickedness of his beliefs.

"Thomas, this is excellent work. But we will also need to call witnesses to show that this Bible was indeed in the possession and ownership of Hunne. What progress here?"

The commissary took some papers from a pouch he wore on his girdle. "My Lord, we have broken the silence of Hunne's manservant, Thomas Brooke, who has betrayed his master for fear of punishment by the spiritual court. He will testify that the Wycliffe Bible was kept in Hunne's house, together with other forbidden texts. John Cawood, parish priest of St Margaret's, will testify that Hunne showed him his great Wycliffe Bible which he used to read out loud from the doorway of his own house. Some others may also come forward to confirm these things."

The bishop was reassured that his commissary was clearly on top of his work. He nodded his approval. "Very good. I propose that ahead of the trial we bring the witnesses here to testify on oath in front of those of us who will be presiding. Slather can make the necessary arrangements with yourself. Bishop Young is in London for Convocation and he will give evidence that Hunne once argued with him that the Bible should be translated into the English tongue. The open advocacy of such a thing is unfitting for a Christian and further proof of his wickedness."

Dr Head nodded an acknowledgement of the gravity of this latest revelation of Hunne's depravity.

"Now Thomas," the bishop continued, "I am satisfied that we have sufficient evidence against Hunne but we have to consider also the opinion of suspicious people. I propose that we set out the Wycliffe Bible and its offending text in the Lady Chapel and proclaim from Paul's Cross that if anyone desires to see it they may freely do so with our goodwill.

"Also we should issue a grave warning to the people. I have instructed my preacher this next Sunday to promulgate from Paul's Cross the charges against Hunne, including the damnable points and opinions of heresy contained within his Bible. He will then deliver a denunciation of Hunne's supporters, and a caution to them if they persist in their false ways.

"Now, as for the trial, I must rely on your knowledge of the law to ensure we follow the correct procedures. I must ask you to set this out and I will send it to the chancellor in Lambeth so that he may confirm that all is in order."

If Dr Head felt any resentment that the bishop should still think it necessary to pass every point of law though his trusted deputy, there was no hint of this in his response. "My lord, this will be done without delay for we have little time. The trial has been set for December 16th and will, as we agreed, be presided over by yourself, the Bishops of Durham and Lincoln and your own suffragen, Bishop Young. It will take place in the Lady Chapel with a full attendance of both spiritual and temporal dignitaries. I believe Slather has arranged with the sexton that Hunne's corpse will be displayed in an open coffin. It will be necessary to have incense burners to sweeten the air."

Fitzjames approved the arrangements and made an appointment with his commissary for the following day when they would go over the trial procedures in greater detail.

On the morning of the trial, Fitzjames prepared himself for the biggest day of his episcopacy. All his critics would be cowed and he himself vindicated by a judicial process that would put an end to all malicious speculation about Hunne. Watched by the civic and spiritual elite of the diocese, he would stamp his authority on this troublesome city and instil fear into the souls of those who might be tempted to oppose him.

He called his manservant to help him dress in his full regalia: a gold-embroidered cope, a bejewelled mitre and across his shoulders a vermillion stole decorated with black crosses – fitting symbols for the occasion. Taking up his gilded crozier he descended to the Great Hall of his palace where his fellow bishop judges were gathered.

"My lords," he said with pride, "everything is arranged. Dean Colet has excused himself on grounds of ill health so we will be censed by the sub-dean." He motioned to a white-robed elderly man standing beside him. "We shall process into the Lady Chapel and take our positions at the far end beneath the great rose window."

The Bishop of Lincoln, tall and nervous-looking, seemed to need reassurance. "My Lord, we are all no doubt aware that the heretic John Wycliffe faced his accusers in the very same Lady Chapel nearly one hundred and fifty years ago. On that occasion, there was an unseemly disturbance which led to the abandonment of the hearing. What safeguards are in place to prevent such a debacle?"

Fitzjames was confident that he had this in hand. "I can put your mind at rest. We have engaged a number of stalwart hirelings who will eject any troublemakers. And summoners will be standing by to arrest any person giving overt support to the accused."

"Another thing ..." the Bishop of Lincoln added, "I believe that the Lady Chapel may not accommodate all those wishing to be present. Those that are forced to gather outside may become agitated if they cannot witness the proceedings."

"My dear Lord Bishop," Fitzjames replied patiently, "all this is taken care of. The choir door will be kept open and from there a priest will repeat to the crowd outside everything that is said within. All will be informed of our proceedings."

"And the burning of the body. When will that take place?"

"Ah yes. Once the sentence has been pronounced, we shall request the secular arm to make arrangements. The sheriff should undertake this task within a day or two."

Without further discussion, Fitzjames led the way down a flight of stairs to a small door that gave access to the cathedral. Once inside, the sub-dean took up his position at the head of the solemn group which then processed down the nave into the Lady Chapel intoning Latin prayers and trailing clouds of incense.

Once the bishop judges had settled themselves at the eastern end of the chapel, Fitzjames looked around at the assembled company he had called together. Senior clergy in their white cassocks and surplices were seated on one side, together with gowned and capped doctors of divinity and canon law. On the other side sat the Lord Mayor and the city aldermen in their red fur trimmed gowns, together with numerous officials. Prominent among them were the sheriff and under sheriffs. Standing spectators crowded behind the benches of invited dignitaries and, as he had anticipated, so great was the press of people that those for whom there was no space gathered expectantly outside the choir door.

Fitzjames noted with satisfaction that at the west end of the Chapel a lectern had been placed on which rested Hunne's Wycliffe Bible. In the centre stood a simple open coffin containing the accused's corpse. He could not help noticing that although the air was filled with the aroma of incense, this could not altogether disguise the distinctive smell of putrefying flesh.

Fitzjames began the proceedings by standing up and reciting the articles of heresy charged against Hunne. He read from a text held close to his eyes, his voice thin and wavering. But then his manner changed. He paused, looked up at this audience, and, with greater force and animation, announced, "There is a new charge arising out of the prologue in the accused's Wycliffe Bible. This says that the very body of the Lord is not contained in the sacrament of the altar, but merely that men receiving it shall thereby keep in mind that Christ's flesh was wounded and crucified for us."

There was an audible gasp from the clerical benches at this flagrant denial of transubstantiation. The murmurings of disapproval having at last subsided, Doctor Head rose from his seat and read out the various witness statements. This was a lengthy process and Fitzjames observed with displeasure that some of those seated on the lay benches had apparently fallen asleep.

Towards the end of the recitation the commissary read the evidence of one of Hunne's neighbours that the accused was seen standing outside his door reading his English Bible. The disclosure again occasioned muttering and consternation on the clerical benches. Suddenly someone in the standing crowd shouted. "Every man's right!" The dissent was quickly suppressed as two burly men moved in and bundled the offender outside, the bishop's summoner following a short distance behind.

As the hearing drew to its conclusion, Fitzjames issued a warning that, by prior arrangement, was read out simultaneously by a priest at the choir door for the benefit of the throng outside. "We counsel and admonish that if there be any persons that of their simpleness have been familiar and acquainted with the said Richard Hunne and his heresies, or have heard him read from his Bible or have any similar books themselves, let them come to me now and acknowledge their fault. And if they do not come of their own volition, then at their own peril be it, for the rigour of the law shall be executed against them." There was a pause to allow the warning to sink in. "And if there are any that would defend the opinions and books of Richard Hunne they should immediately come forward and be heard, according to the requirements of the law."

The people had been stunned into silence; no one was prepared to risk their own life by coming to the defence of a man who had already lost his. When there appeared not a single witness in support of Hunne, Fitzjames conferred briefly with his fellow judges before pronouncing the verdict.

"We find the said Richard Hunne guilty of the crime of heresy. And therefore the same Richard Hunne we have condemned and excommunicated and his body we have pronounced and declared to be deprived of Christian burial. And by our sentence him and his body we have relinquished to the secular arm and power."

———

On a grey, misty and damp morning five days before Christmas, a horse-drawn cart rumbled slowly along Newgate Street. The sheriff walked in front and the Bishop of London, leaning on his sub-dean, and accompanied by fellow dignitaries, followed behind. At a respectful distance further back, a multitude of onlookers splashed their way through the mire towards the elevated killing ground of Smithfield.

The sheriff's men had already prepared a stake surrounded by reeds but fresh tinder was now needed because of the damp.

The corpse, its head lolling to one side, was dragged from the cart and attached to the stake with iron chains.

As the reeds were being torched, Fitzjames, delivered a final damnation.

"You, Richard Hunne, have strayed from the path ordained by God. You have transgressed the laws of his Church and the self-same laws have been executed against you. After the fire of Smithfield, hell will receive you where you will burn forever. And let all the people gathered here reflect on the fate of this man, that they may remain on the path of righteousness and eschew that evil course that leads to everlasting hellfire."

As the flames encircled the slumped figure, Fitzjames looked at the faces of the crowd that had gathered around. The people were silent and for the most part expressionless. Were they supporters of Hunne or the Church or perhaps merely curious? He could not tell but, looking into their eyes, he observed with grim satisfaction that they were filled with fear.

The body shrank as it burned, the executioner eventually striking out the staple holding the chains, so that the remains fell into the bottom of the fire. He made sure that the bones and skull were burned to ash by breaking them into small pieces with a mattock. When the fire had died down, the grey pile of ash and embers was scraped into a barrow and taken away for secret disposal. There were to be no remains, no relics and no shrine to Richard Hunne.

PART III

❧ *1515 – 1517* ❦

GOD WILL PROVIDE

DETERMINED TO AVOID ST PAUL'S AND ITS THRONGS of gossipers Anne Hunne could not help hearing all about Richard's trial and burning. This was, after all, the chief talking point of London's populace. The thought of his poor broken body laid out for all to gloat over and demean was more than she could bear. As for the burning, how could she have stood by while Richard's wretched corpse was consumed by fire amid the incantations of his persecutors? These churchmen were no more than practitioners of sorcery and she consoled herself with the thought that their cruel actions were driven by a great fear of the man they affected to despise.

After making her solemn vow at St Paul's Anne had returned to New Fish Street to find that her house had been ransacked while her two servants were nowhere to be seen. Everything had been turned upside down. In the shop that fronted onto the street her late husband's handiwork was in disarray: flowing gowns, quilted doublets, cotehardie tunics and long houplands lay in a confused heap on the floor. The rolls of uncut cloth piled high in the warehouse at the back of the building had also been thrown around. Upstairs the living quarters had clearly been searched and on closer inspection she found to her alarm that a wooden box hidden behind their bed had been broken open: the prized Wycliffe Bible that was normally kept there under lock and key had been removed.

Anne lay on her bed and wept silently. She understood that God worked in mysterious ways and that life – all life – was accompanied by terrible afflictions. She had seen her mother die in the agonies of childbirth and the infant cut hurriedly from her womb so that a christening could be improvised before it, too, passed away. She had witnessed the lingering mortal sickness of her own baby son. And while still a child she had seen one of her close friends succumb to the sweating sickness which had swept like a biblical scourge through the country.

All these things could be born because they were part of the natural order ordained by God. What she found impossible to accept were the afflictions imposed by man on man – and, most of all, the cruelties exacted by the Church itself in the name of a just religion. The obscene burnings of supposed heretics had driven her family from Amersham and now the campaign of persecution had spread to London and ensnared both her father and her husband.

As Anne struggled with these thoughts she conceded that there was some modicum of consolation to be had. Yes, the misfortunes inflicted by God in His unfathomable wisdom were to be suffered without rancour – for there was nothing to be done in such cases but pray. But the cruel misconduct of churchmen could be defied and the pillars of their profane temple undermined. She well understood that having all these years walked in the shadow of her husband it had fallen to her, a mere woman in a world governed by men, to do justice to the memory of Richard Hunne. She would choose her weapons and do battle with the enemies of true religion.

Going through the contents of the shop, Anne had picked up a hooded cloak and slipped it on. Looking at her image in the polished metal disc that hung on the wall she reflected momentarily that, with her tall figure, sharp features and dark complexion, she could easily pass for a man. She removed the cloak and, after clearing up the living space on the first floor, left the house to collect her daughter.

Little Margaret was being looked after by her aunt Rebecca, and it would be a relief to Anne to be able to unburden herself to her beloved kinswoman. Rebecca welcomed Anne at the door and gave her a big hug. "Come in and sit down. Margaret is still pining for her father and I find it difficult to explain to her what has happened to him. But I have been able to distract her with games and she has passed a pleasant enough morning with Sarah".

Anne sat down opposite her cousin and took her hand. "Rebecca, I cannot take Margaret back to New Fish Street. It will be too upsetting both for her and for me. Could she possibly stay here for the next few days, at least until I have a more settled view of our future? I fear our house, together with all Richard's worldly wealth, will be forfeit because it is claimed he was guilty of *felo de se*. The Church authorities are also determined to find my poor dead husband guilty of heresy and have, I believe, taken our servants for questioning. Even if the coroner determines another cause of death a charge of heresy would also mean forfeiture of his estate. It seems that I will have nothing to live on."

"Of course Margaret must stay here," Rebecca said. "And should you find yourself without a roof, our home is open to you both. As to the future you are still young, and I know you have male admirers within our community. The outlook need not be so bleak."

But Anne would not be comforted. "The penniless widow of a supposed heretic is not the stuff for matchmaking. I do not think that any among our acquaintance will be leading me up the aisle. Besides, Richard was always my true love, and I would find it displeasing to be married to another. I will find some better way of keeping body and soul together because I believe that, for those who are prepared to do His work, God will provide."

So it was that Margaret stayed in Carter Lane while Anne tried to put her affairs in order. She needed to sort out her personal belongings and safeguard what meagre assets she possessed from the jointure that had been settled on her at the time of her marriage. But most afternoons she returned to Carter Lane both to see her daughter and to confide her latest thoughts to her cousin.

Shortly after the trial, Rebecca, wishing to distract Anne from her sorrows, arranged to meet her in fashionable Cheapside where her husband had opened a new haberdashery. Anne thought it paradoxical that her cousin's fortunes were on the rise at a time when her own troubles were multiplying, but as she walked up Gracechurch Street, well wrapped against the winter cold, there was anger but no envy in her heart. Indeed, the terrible events of the past few weeks had given her life a new and vengeful purpose, a spur that had strengthened her resolve and would surely enable her to confront whatever challenges she might now have to face.

She turned into Cheapside and proceeded past the Church of St Mary le Bow, whose resounding bells she heard every evening as they proclaimed the closure of the City gates and the shutting of all shops. Beyond, stood Cheapside Cross, one of the monuments erected along the funeral route of Edward I's Queen Eleanor. Anne had always thought it very fitting that a great king should exalt the memory of his adored wife with such a majestic token of his love. In much more humble manner she was sworn to honour her late husband, not in stone but in her life's work.

Continuing down Cheapside, Anne gazed at the stores and shop fronts that lined both sides of the busy street. There was a profusion of goods for sale – linen cloths, fustions, satins, jewels, oil, wine and much else. Then she saw Rebecca standing in front of her haberdashery, attired fetchingly in a green woollen dress trimmed with cream-coloured fur and matching bonnet.

Rebecca embraced her cousin and led her into the little shop. "Anne, I am so glad you came. What do you think of our new enterprise?"

Anne looked at the rich display of leather laces, brightly coloured ribbons, gloves, purses, and caps of all hues and sizes. "What a splendid assortment of finery you have here." She picked up and examined some of the items. "I am full of wonderment."

"I am glad you approve. Now I want you to choose something for yourself. Also something for little Margaret. And please do not stint in your choices."

After a few minutes of indecision, Anne selected a pair of fine leather gloves for herself and for Margaret an ingenious toy – a hollow figure with a rod within that made its tongue go in and out. She hugged her cousin in gratitude but then revealed the latest blow to befall her. "Rebecca, it is not enough that the bishops have found my poor Richard guilty of heresy at St Paul's and that his body has been taken for burning. To add to my miseries I have now received a warrant from the Lord Chancellor's office. It says I must quit our house within two weeks since it is forfeit to the Crown. They have also taken an inventory of every item which is to be surrendered and this includes our bed and all the linen. I am left with just a few dishes."

Rebecca looked shocked. "This is little more than thieving. How do they expect you to live? Please let me persuade you to come and stay with us."

"Yes, cousin. If after two weeks I have no place to live I will accept your kind offer. But I still hope to help myself".

Anne said her fond goodbyes and departed. What she had not confided to her dear friend was that a mysterious visitor had come to her house just two days before. He appeared to be a clerk but his face was partly hidden behind a cowl. The man had been ill at ease as he stood in the hallway and delivered his message in a low voice. "Mistress Anne, I have been given instructions by a nameless benefactor who wishes to ease your plight. There is a lease of a small house in Eastcheap which has fallen vacant where you and your daughter may reside without charge or rent."

Anne was astonished. "But if this be true, how am I to repay such an act of charity? And how can I discover the author of my bounty?"

"The only obligation is that you should not disclose our meeting or seek to know the source of your good fortune. The property is ready now and may be occupied by yourself for a term of five years after which time there will be a review. On this piece of parchment there is the name of a woman in Eastcheap who, when you see her next Tuesday, will show you the house. I have said all that I need to say and I have no further business with you."

The clerk then left abruptly, leaving Anne bewildered but also uplifted by the thought of a possible dramatic change in her fortune.

On the appointed day, Anne walked over to Eastcheap as directed. Here there were numerous butchers shops displaying dressed meat – pork, mutton and beef – as well as cookshops selling pies and other ready-to-eat hot foods. The street was bustling with carriers, shoppers and traders and she reflected that her own comings and goings would hardly be noticed amid such animation.

A hunched old woman was waiting outside a narrow, three-storeyed timber-framed house. Anne gave her name but the woman remained silent and proceeded without further ado to unlock the door and lead the way in. The house was hardly spacious and sparsely furnished but, with its two small bedrooms on the top floor, it would be sufficient for the needs of herself and her daughter.

She took the keys and thanked the old woman who left without a word. Was she mute or was the transaction too delicate to be the subject of open conversation? In any event, now that she was accommodated she would not after all need to impose on her cousin.

On returning to New Fish Street, she was surprised to find her local parish priest, John Cawood, waiting outside her house. He was the very last person she expected to offer comfort to her in her troubles. Cawood asked to see her privately so she took him upstairs to the parlour where they could talk.

The priest was a smooth-faced balding man in his middle years. He was portly as if well fed and well wined and he adopted an avuncular tone towards her. "My dear Mistress Anne, we have missed you at St Margaret's these past two weeks so I finally came to see you. I have been concerned about your situation and I wished to offer you my sympathy and support."

Anne felt little warmth towards a man whom she held partly responsible for bringing down her husband. "Sir," she replied, "it was considerate of you to think of my pitiful circumstances. I have been unable to come to church with all the troubles I must attend to, my servants gone, a daughter to care for and a husband to mourn."

"Quite so. And that is why I want to give you succour. You are alone without means of support and prey to great danger." At this point Cawood drew closer and took Anne's hand which had not been proffered. She noticed that he was breathing heavily and that there were beads of sweat on his ample brow. "My dearest Mistress Anne, I can give you my protection and financial help too, if only you will allow me." He suddenly pressed himself against her and she could feel his firmness against her body. She pushed him away forcefully and stood back. "John Cawood, you have already brought misery to me and my family. You now insult me and defile the memory of my noble husband with your unwanted attentions. Please go."

But with his blood now up Cawood was not yet ready to give up on his quarry. "Mistress Anne, you must be aware of your situation. You are the widow of a proven heretic. Heretical works have been found in your house and now you have abandoned weekly mass, contrary to your duty as a resident of this parish. As you well know, this is considered by the Church to be a mark of heresy. The bishop would be displeased to hear of such dereliction and if he were to be informed there could be grave consequences. For your own security you should reconsider my offer of care for yourself and your child."

Anne had heard enough. "Go from this house now! You have brought shame on the priesthood and the Christian cause you claim to serve. For myself, I with my daughter am removing myself to another parish where I shall have no need of your priestly comfort."

With no more to be said, Cawood departed, leaving Anne to contemplate how easily widows became prey to ravenous vicars.

It was the very next day as Anne was packing up her last belongings to take them to Eastcheap that a buxom woman bearing a large basket of loaves came to her door. She said that she had an urgent message that she could only communicate in the privacy of the house. Anne was by now wary of visitors but she allowed the woman in and asked her what she had to say. Her visitor put down her basket and spoke quickly without introducing herself.

"Madam, I have to inform you that there are admirers of Richard Hunne in this City who wish to relieve your pitiful state. I am required to tell you in confidence that a sum of three pounds will be paid to you each quarter. To collect the first payment you must go at noon tomorrow to the convent church of St Helen's. Sister Agnes, the almoner there, will be waiting for you in that part of the church which is reserved for the use of the nuns. She will give you the money and tell you when next to come to her. All this is of the utmost secrecy and the payments will cease if any person – any person whatsoever – other than yourself is made aware of the arrangement."

Anne was once more overwhelmed by news that suggested that her husband had had powerful friends of whom she had no knowledge. "And must I do something in return for this great favour?"

The woman shook her head. "No – this money is not charity. It is owed to you for the sacrifice that Richard Hunne suffered in performing good service for his fellow citizens. No more is to be said. But I would like you to step outside and there pay for a loaf of bread so that we may appear to be engaged in simple trade."

Anne duly obliged and that was the last she ever saw of the bread vendor.

The following morning, Anne walked through frozen streets to the church of St Helen's convent in Bishopsgate. The building was divided into two by a partition running from east to west, the northern half being for the exclusive use of the sisters. She entered this reserved area through a small door and was met by a nun wearing a wimple and the black habit of the Benedictine order. Anne gave her name and said she had been sent by a bread vendor.

"I am Sister Agnes," the nun said, "and you have been sent to me to receive alms. You may return at the same time on the Feast Day of St Anselm in three months' time." She then pressed a small leather pouch into Anne's hand and opened the partition door for her to leave.

———

Mother and daughter took up residence in the modest little house in Eastcheap. Anne calculated that on twelve pounds per annum and with no rent to pay and no servant to keep she could afford food, clothes, fuel and other necessaries and still have money left over. She was unable to explain to Rebecca how she had come by her good fortune, saying only that her jointure had yielded more than expected and that friends had been kind. However, she could not help speculating on the identity of her benefactors. Could they be one and the same? Could it be that the Guild of Merchant Taylors had made provision for her? Or was there some powerful figure in the background who had stood behind Richard Hunne? She could find no answer but determined that, since she was now a free woman, she would fulfil her vow and devote her life to serving the cause for which her husband had died.

13

JOHN COLET

CONSPICUOUS BY HIS ABSENCE FROM BOTH HUNNE'S trial and his burning was John Colet, Dean of St Paul's. Colet was not the easiest of men. His close friends observed that, though introspective and solitary by nature, he became animated when engaged in debate on his favourite topics – classical scholarship, reform of the Church and the education of young men. The resident canons who came under his care found him to be a hard task master. He had set the tone for his administration from the outset. Having gathered them together he cast his eyes over their sullen faces and stressed the need for change:

"The resident canons have thrown aside their care for the Church. They pursue their own private gain. They convert common property to their own private use. In these unhappy and disordered times, residence in the cathedral is nothing else than seeking one's own advantage and, to speak more plainly, robbing the Church and enriching oneself."

He had in mind the diversion of funds from the cathedral's three great money-making shrines: the image of the blessed Virgin, the tomb of St Erkenwald and the crucifix at the north door. But his words had caused mutterings and resentment and some said it was all very well for him for he was a rich man.

Dean Colet accepted that he would never be popular with his canons. Far more serious for him personally, however, was the bitter feud that existed between himself and his own bishop. On this Sunday, the day after Hunne's burning, he sat in his library which overlooked the cathedral close. He gazed at the bishop's palace and reflected on a relationship that was poisoning his own ministry.

His young sovereign, Henry, had taken a liking to him and his appointment to the deanery was due to royal patronage, not to the choice of his bishop. But he recognised that the supposedly scandalous sermon he had delivered to Convocation some three years before had stirred up animosity among the Church establishment. He cast his mind back to that day when he had been emboldened to speak openly of the Church's shortcomings. He had decried the covetousness of priests and the worldliness of bishops who entertained lavishly in their fine residences, mixed politics with religion and absented themselves from their dioceses. He had shocked his audience, too, by claiming that the supposed heresy of those who disputed Church doctrine was not so pestilential to the Church or the people as the depraved lives of the clergy for, as St Bernard had pointed out, there were two kinds of heretical depravity: one of perverse doctrine, and the other of perverse living – of which the last was the greater and more pernicious.

Bishop Fitzjames had not liked that sermon and took it very personally – as well he might, living at Fulham Palace in fine style and busying himself with the pursuit of heretics. He had gone so far as to cite the dean before his consistory court on a charge of heresy, the articles of complaint being that he, Colet, had attacked the worship of images, the temporal possessions of the bishops and the laziness of those who read their sermons verbatim from texts – which Fitzjames himself was accustomed to do. When Colet had refused to answer questions put to him, the angry old bishop had imposed a sentence of silence upon him.

But Colet knew that he had the protection of the King who thought highly of the scholarly sermons that he delivered at court on Good Fridays. He also enjoyed the support of Archbishop Wareham who, as Lord Chancellor, was always sensitive to his sovereign's opinions. And it was Wareham who had overruled Fitzjames and dismissed the heresy charge.

Nevertheless, Colet felt threatened by the animosity of his cantankerous overlord and knew that he had to tread carefully. He had been powerless to intervene in the Hunne case, but his sympathies lay with the victim and he now wished to make amends for his enforced silence.

He walked across the cathedral close to St Paul's School, which was his proudest achievement. The fine stone building designed to accommodate over 150 boys had replaced a ramshackle array of bookbinders' stalls that used to stand in the north east corner of the precinct. To the great annoyance of Fitzjames he had chosen the Guild of Mercers as lay trustees of the new foundation whom he considered more trustworthy than the priests of his own chapter. He had appointed as the first High Master a distinguished Greek scholar, William Lily, and it was Lily whom he now wished to see on urgent business.

Colet was taken into the High Master's library and there the two men discussed various matters concerning the school curriculum as well as a recent incident of unruly behaviour. The boys from St Paul's and St Anthony's School in Threadneedle Street had exchanged insults in public. This had led to satchels being thrown around and books spilled onto the street to the great inconvenience of passers-by. The dean gave full support to the High Master's decision to have the culprits birched in front of their fellow pupils. He then asked about the boys' prospects.

"As we intended, St Paul's now provides a classical as well as a religious education – much to the annoyance of some of our church brethren. But, tell me, do you think our best pupils will take holy orders?"

Lily, trim and scholarly, spoke with precision as might be expected of the foremost classical grammarian of his generation. "Many of the boys come from poor families and the education they have here provides an avenue to the universities and to the priesthood. I believe it very likely, therefore, that the Church will receive a great number of our pupils."

Colet gave a sigh of resignation: "I have no doubt you are right. But the sorry state of the clergy must be a concern to anyone contemplating such a life. The Church has become but another trade whereby men can obtain profit, promotion and the goods of this world. The bishops aspire to great wealth, high office in the service of the state, and leisure pursuits that compete with noblemen – feasting, hunting, hawking and other, grosser, activities I dare not mention. 'Physician, heal thyself' is what I would advise my fellow churchmen. Therefore I hope that in the course of their learning the boys are given proper instruction and guidance on Christian piety and the simplicity of life that befits a man who is called to Christ's service. There lies our hope for the future."

Lily was familiar with his patron's views on Church matters and had indeed discussed them with their common friend, the young Thomas More, an increasingly familiar figure in the deanery. Although More was less critical of the admitted failings of the Church they had all agreed that those taking holy orders should be better educated.

The dean took up another theme. "The depraved way of life of our clergy gives temptation to those good men who look for a better example. They then incline to Lollardy and other heresies that reject the priesthood in favour of Bible reading in the mother tongue. I sometimes think that supposed heretics have something to teach our spiritual leaders in the way of modest living. That brings me to the chief matter on my mind and the reason for my visit.

"I have been very troubled by this Hunne affair. I was unable to forestall the imprisonment of Hunne or his prosecution, but the case was a bad one. I now feel obliged to his widow who, under the law, has been left without support. I have entered into an agreement to take a lease on a small property to enable the widow and her daughter to begin a new and modest way of life. I need your help in arranging this, which I cannot undertake in my own name because I am already under suspicion as a supporter of heretics."

The High Master, more used to dealing with scholarly matters than engaging in Church politics, asked uneasily if he could help. "Dean, I will always be of whatever assistance I can, though I am not sure how the school can give support to Mistress Anne."

"I would, of course, do this myself but I am under threat from the bishop. Having failed to secure charges of heresy against me, he has stirred up difficulties at court. My enemies claim that my sermon at the Chapel Royal this last year was intended to denounce the war with France. It is fortunate for me that His Highness took the matter in good heart but I know that my Lord Bishop is waiting to entrap me. I cannot therefore be seen giving succour to Hunne's family. However, I can increase my provision of funds to the school so that it can purchase the lease from me for the use of one of the masters – in reality Mistress Anne."

Colet suspected that the High Master, a man of scrupulous propriety, would not be entirely at ease with such an arrangement. However, Colet was not only the school's great benefactor but also his own patron. "Dean, I will do whatever you think is necessary to ease the widow's plight. Of course, there is such an outcry over Hunne that I understand Parliament may itself seek to restore the man's fortune to his family."

Colet shook his head. "The spirituality holds sway in the House of Lords and would very likely prevent a move that would be seen as a slight on my Lord Bishop of London. But we may pray that it will come to pass. Of course, I do not wish Hunne's widow to know the source of her bounty. Although she may perhaps suppose that it comes from the Company of Mercers. I shall advise on the details of the property transfer later."

The two men parted and Colet returned to the deanery. As he sat in his library he was reminded by recent events that these were dangerous times indeed for reformers such as himself. He took some comfort from the fact that the King favoured his criticisms of the Church, especially the cult of relics and the excessive wealth of prelates. He was also pious and revered scholarship as he and Thomas More could testify. But Henry was temperamental and his actions unpredictable. Neither the Church as it stood nor the cause of religious reform were safe in such a man's hands. Today war against France, tomorrow war against the bishops? There was no telling.

Colet knew very well that if the King's favour towards himself was withdrawn, Wareham would follow and he would then be under threat from his own bishop. The advocacy of Church reform that endeared him to his sovereign was the very thing that infuriated Fitzjames. He gave a sigh. If it all became too much for him he might consider retiring from active life to the house he had built in the precincts of the Charterhouse at Sheen. There he could remove himself from worldly affairs, set up his library and indulge his passion for classical learning.

But as he gazed out across the cathedral close, he could not help but think of the terrible fate of Richard Hunne. The deanery, standing as it did at the south west corner, looked straight onto Lollards' Tower some fifty yards away. One of

Colet's servants had reported to him that on the fateful night there was a gleam of candlelight through the window of the tower between midnight and around seven in the morning. And not long after the cathedral clock had struck twelve, there had been the sound of someone crying out – not once, but several times. The dean winced as he pondered the events of that night. There was little doubt in his mind as to what had occurred, but he did not intend to disclose his thoughts on the matter to anyone.

14

OF BISHOPS, JUDGES, KNIGHTS AND KINGS

BISHOP FITZJAMES SAT IN THE PANELLED LIBRARY OF his episcopal palace adjoining St Paul's. He was in a highly agitated state and, unable to focus his thoughts, he got up and paced around. He had hoped that the conviction and burning of Hunne's corpse would settle matters once and for all, but that was not to be. In January, Charles Joseph had made his sensational confession in the Tower of London; and that, no doubt, would decide the coroner's verdict on the cause of Hunne's death. The bishop's own chancellor, Horsey, and the two junior church officers, Joseph and Spalding, could be expected to face criminal proceedings on a charge of murder.

Fitzjames was uncomfortably aware that he, too, was the subject of suspicion. Worse still, burgesses and knights were gathering for the new Parliament which was about to meet and the Hunne affair was on their agenda. Fitzjames knew that he had to try and head off the pressure that was building up for removal of the Church's ancient privileges – and especially the immunity of those in holy orders from prosecution in the royal courts. He had asked to see his trusted friend, Dr. Richard Kidderminster, Abbot of Winchcombe, who was in London to attend both Parliament and Convocation – the two legislatures being called to meet in the same month. The Abbot, a man of swarthy and robust appearance, was admitted by a servant and greeted by the bishop.

"Doctor, plagued as I am with disloyal colleagues and a fractious populace I am relieved that you are here. This coming Sunday it would be helpful to our cause if you would deliver a sermon from Paul's Cross defending the liberties of the Church and condemning those who would remove them. Because on this issue we are under assault from all sides."

The Abbot nodded and adopted a grave expression. "My Lord, it is a subject close to my heart and I shall, of course, oblige".

Fitzjames looked at his friend appreciatively. "May I suggest, subject of course to your own view of the matter, that you take as your text the biblical admonition, recently proclaimed by the Pope himself: *Touch not my annointed*. Your message to the assembled faithful can be uncompromising. You may wish to say that any bill to make clerks answerable before secular courts is against the law of God and the liberties of the Holy Church. And, by papal decree, all clerks who have received holy orders are exempt from temporal punishment for criminal causes. Those who profess otherwise will incur the censure of the Holy Church."

The Abbot nodded to his superior: "These are my very thoughts on the question and the words you have chosen are those I myself would have used – and indeed shall use."

Fitzjames moved on to the battle in Parliament that was bound to ensue. "Doctor, the wretched Hunne business has stirred up our enemies in the Commons. They are, I understand, preparing to introduce bills against Church privileges so as to allow Christ's own anointed to be treated as common criminals. We must ensure that in this Parliament we hold a majority over the temporal lords in the Upper Chamber who will certainly support the Commons. I have calculated that we have forty-nine bishops, abbots and priors to be set against forty-two dukes, earls and barons. Of course, neither all the temporality nor all the spirituality will attend but we have the advantage of letters of attorney from some of our friends who cannot be in London."

Richard Kidderminster looked triumphant. "My lord, I hold letters of attorney for six other abbots and the Abbot of Westminster holds another four. I believe that with these votes added to those actually present we have enough numbers to throw out any unwanted bills from the Commons."

Fitzjames was reassured. "Very good. I believe we have the measure of our adversaries."

The meeting concluded with pleasantries about the bishop's plans for his Fulham garden, after which the Abbot was shown out.

Having, he hoped, headed off the parliamentary threat, the bishop's next move was to try to discredit the coroner's inquest on Hunne. He decided to write a letter to Thomas Wolsey, Archbishop of York, whom he knew to be the rising power in the land and a man commanding the King's ear. He called in his secretary and dictated a letter which he then asked to be read back. Slather duly obliged:

I beseech your good lordship to shield my poor chancellor now indicted by an untrue inquest for the death of Richard Hunne, upon the sole accusation of Charles Joseph exacted by coercion. That by your intercession it may please the King's Grace to have the matter duly examined by disinterested persons of his counsel in the presence of the parties before any more harm is done in the cause. And that upon the innocence of my chancellor being declared, it may further please the King's Grace to instruct his attorney to declare the indictment void.

The bishop, not being entirely satisfied with the tone of his appeal spoke curtly to his amanuensis. "Slather, we must leave no doubt about the dangers we all face. To this end, add a final sentence as follows ... *For assured am I, if my chancellor be tried by any twelve men in London, they be so maliciously inclined to heresy that they will condemn my clerk though he were as innocent as Abel."*

The letter to Wolsey bore fruit. The bishop was invited to attend a conference of judges, lawyers and senior clergy at Blackfriars to discuss the question of clerical privilege arising out of the Hunne case. He had high hopes that the legal immunity of the clergy would be upheld and that his chancellor would be excused from prosecution in the secular courts.

The Bishop of London returned from Blackfriars in a state of undisguised fury. Dr Standish, the King's spiritual counsel, had dismissed the much vaunted words *Touch not my anointed* as having been spoken not by Christ but by King David more than a thousand years before the Saviour. According to Standish, the words spoken had nothing whatsoever to do with the priesthood. The old bishop had been stung by this rebuff to his own biblical scholarship delivered by a mere friar. But more serious by far was the wider threat to the Church posed by the explosive proceedings at Blackfriars. In an attempt to meet the danger head on, Fitzjames called a crisis meeting of his spiritual colleagues at his London palace.

Amid the storm clouds gathering round them, robed clerics congregated in the Great Hall, talking among themselves in anxious voices that echoed within the stone-walled interior. Fitzjames called everyone to order.

"Where is my Lord Bishop of Winchester?" he asked tetchily.

"He is sulking alone in his great palace in Southwark," another prelate answered. "He does not take it kindly that he has been displaced in affairs of state by Wolsey. Apart from which he is too proud and mighty to cross the water to attend here at the bidding of his fellows. He takes to the Thames only at the King's command."

Fitzjames made a dismissive gesture before addressing those assembled before him.

"My lords, the King saw fit to put forward as his delegate at Blackfriars a mean, upstart friar, Dr Standish. The friar asserts that the convening of clergy before a secular judge has long been the customary law of the land, stands well with the law of God and does not infringe the liberties of the Church. This must be taken to be the King's own view – which puts us all in grave danger.

"The lawyers have also taken against us. When we called Dr Standish before us and interrogated him on pain of heresy, the judges held that because he was of the King's counsel all those present at that hearing could be charged with praemunire. What can we do against this?"

"The King's judges have done worse than that," the Bishop of Lincoln despaired. "They have declared that the King could, if he so chose, hold a Parliament without summoning the bishops. The reason given is that the bishops are there only because of the appointments they hold from the Crown. This, surely, is a warning that we use our votes in Parliament to oppose Church reforms at our peril."

Fitzjames had difficulty controlling his anger as he summed up. "The King and his advisers have placed matters on a war footing. We are faced with a direct threat to our ancient privileges and powers. If we yield any ground, who knows what further curbs may be imposed on us."

"We could appeal to the Pope", suggested one of the prelates.

"That could stir things further," another said. "Also imagine how long it would take. But it is something to consider nevertheless."

Fitzjames explained to those present that he would make one last attempt to retrieve the situation. "I will request a private audience with Archbishop Wareham – since he is a chief counsellor who understands the mind of the King and has long experience handling matters of great delicacy."

There was general support for this move and, after messengers had been sent back and forth across the river, it was arranged that Fitzjames and the Archbishop would talk matters over at Lambeth Palace.

As he was rowed across the Thames from the wharf below St Paul's, Fitzjames was uncomfortably aware that he would have to show uncharacteristic humility. Wareham's status gave him direct access to the Pope and, as Chancellor, he was England's leading statesman. His personal retinue far exceeded that of the bishop and his palaces were considerably grander.

On reaching Lambeth Stairs, Fitzjames was met by liveried servants who escorted him through the great gatehouse into the palace. He was taken up a staircase to a richly panelled room where Wareham was consulting papers spread out on his desk.

Now in his mid-sixties, William Wareham was heavy jowled and watery eyed. He had risen from humble origins to become not only the most important cleric in England but also, as Lord Chancellor, head of the judiciary and the King's most senior political adviser. He was a wily politician whose instinct was always to look for compromise and the middle ground but he was also a man of contradictions. He had persecuted and burned Lollard heretics in Kent yet he patronised and protected liberal reformers such as Erasmus and Colet. Conscious of the importance of grandeur he was building a vast palace at Otford rivalling Wolsey's Hampton Court where he could indulge his taste for lavish entertainment. Yet he himself ate and drank sparingly and professed to admire the asceticism of his illustrious predecessor, Beckett. As for his personal life, he shrugged off all gossip about his "nephew", William, whom he promoted shamelessly to numerous profitable posts including the archdeaconry of Canterbury.

Fitzjames went straight to the point. "My Lord Archbishop, after the proceedings at Blackfriars, I and my fellow bishops believe that the Church is in grave danger. We are concerned that His Highness's judges have decided to espouse the cause of those who would harm us. How can we find a way out of this confrontation without yielding up the Church's ancient liberties? And how can I prevent my chancellor, now under your protection, from being arraigned before the secular courts?"

Wareham sighed as he moved some papers on his desk. At last he looked up. "Bishop, we are indeed in difficulties. His Highness has been angered by the Hunne affair and this has disposed him to attack the clergy's privileges. But we can perhaps detach the wider issue from that of your chancellor. His Highness is to convene a further conference at Baynard's Castle to discuss all these matters. He is unlikely to yield on what he sees as a challenge to his prerogative. But if Horsey will submit himself to the jurisdiction of the King's Court and if the threat of heresy proceedings against Dr Standish is removed, then the King may through his Attorney General gracefully declare the charge against Horsey dismissed. This will finally dispose of the Hunne case. I will propose that the question of clerical privilege be referred to the Holy Father for his adjudication – which could, conveniently, take years to determine. That way we avoid a clash of arms that could split the realm asunder."

Fitzjames was not in the habit of compromising but here was a possible way out. Knowing the sensitivities of his chancellor, he did have one reservation. "What assurance is there that my chancellor will be released if he submits himself to the court? He will be putting himself in jeopardy."

The Archbishop leaned forwards and Fitzjames observed the world-weariness written on his face. "My dear Bishop, you have my own personal assurance. And if that does not suffice you may have the assurance also of Wolsey who is privy to these proposals. It may be opportune, now that you are here, to see your chancellor who is accommodated in the guesthouse. It is best for us all if we have an agreement on the Hunne case before the conference. That way we may emerge with less damage to our cause."

It was late November and by the time Fitzjames returned to his barge at Lambeth Stairs it was getting dark. He was relieved to have seen his chancellor and to have obtained his agreement although in truth the man had little choice.

The bishop was helped on to his barge by servants carrying oil lamps, and as the boatmen dipped their oars he looked across the water at the dim outline of what was left of the Palace of Westminster. The royal apartments had been destroyed by fire just three years before and were now a burnt out ruin. The King would be residing instead at Greenwich. Within the gracious walls of this, his favourite waterside palace, Henry, too, would be giving much thought to the forthcoming trial of strength between Church and Crown at Baynard's Castle.

15

BAYNARD'S CASTLE

IN THE LAST WEEK OF NOVEMBER, ANNE WAS WALKING through Blackfriars after visiting Rebecca in Carter Lane. Down here on the river front stood Baynard's Castle, the imposing royal palace that had been rebuilt in spectacular style by Henry VII with five new towers projecting onto the river. Anne and Richard had in former times marvelled at the grandiose water frontage from a wherry boat. But now she found herself in a lane just below Upper Thames Street that ran behind the rear entrance to the castle. Suddenly she heard a familiar voice.

"Mistress Anne. What a surprise to see you here! I hope you have forgiven me for my sudden departure ... I was fearful of the bishop's men."

Anne smiled at her runaway maidservant. "Martha, of course I understand only too well why you felt obliged to leave. It was all very frightening. But tell me, how are you occupied at present?"

Martha pointed to the imposing structure behind her. "I am a maidservant to the steward at Baynard's Castle. I do errands for him and attend on the royal guests who stay here at the King's invitation." She lowered her voice. "You may know that there is to be a great conference here owing to the clamour that has arisen over my late master's death. We have many visitors arriving with their servants and all is confusion and bustle within the castle walls. The King himself will be coming here and all preparations are being made. I myself am running hither and thither."

Knowing that her former maidservant was inclined to be indiscreet, Anne seized the opportunity to find out more. "Yes, Martha, I have had word of this great event. It is strange to me that the leaders of our realm should be gathering over matters connected with my poor Richard and that I, his widow, am excluded from the proceedings or any knowledge of them. Do you know who will be present?"

Martha seemed ready to confide in her former mistress. "There will be judges, bishops and nobles. I am not permitted to enter the Great Hall but I have been able to see from the squint in my lord steward's chamber all that is taking place below … labourers bringing in benches, joiners building a platform for His Highness and food stuffs and wine casks taken through to the kitchens for those who will be residing at the castle."

Anne thought for a moment before bending her head to Martha's ear. "Martha, this squint in the steward's chamber – is it directly overlooking the hall and can you hear what is said below?"

"Oh yes, Mistress Anne. My lord steward's chamber is on the second floor and the aperture in the wall allows the onlooker to hear as well as see all that passes within."

"And will either you or the steward be watching the proceedings from this chamber during the conference?"

"No mistress. The steward will be taken up with duties in the hall and most especially attending on His Highness, and I shall be making ready some of the guest rooms. Why do you ask?"

Anne paused and held Martha's arm. "Maybe I myself could take a look at the proceedings from this vantage point. Of course you would have no part in it – what do you say?"

Martha seemed at first taken aback, but her reply was both cautious and very deliberate. "The steward's chamber can be accessed by the rear entrance over there." Martha pointed to a gateway set in the great stone edifice facing Anne. "There are stairs up to a corridor on the second floor that skirts the castle wall. You follow the corridor to the end and the steward's chamber is on the left, overlooking the river. It is unlocked during the day. But there is a serjeant at arms posted at the castle entrance as you can see."

"Thank you Martha," Anne said quickly. "I am interested to hear about your new situation. But you need know nothing else from me." She tried to press some coins into Martha's hand but the offer was resolutely refused and the two women parted with nothing more said.

The morning of the conference was crisp and cold and grey clouds overhung the city. Anne dressed herself in a long brown dress with a white apron and white mop cap. She wrapped herself in a surcoat and hurried over to Conduit Street where she found a flower seller. She bought a large bouquet of mixed fragrances – lavender, rosemary, roses and pinks – at a cost that would be beyond the reach of ordinary householders. She then joined the throng of those making their way along Thames Street towards Baynard's Castle. The King and his council would be coming upriver from Greenwich, courtiers were travelling downriver by wherry, tilt boat or barge and visiting bishops were being rowed the short distance from their London palaces to the castle stairs.

The more important travellers in Thames Street were on horseback but there were also numerous servants and attendants on foot. Anne noticed that the street had been cleared of beggars and that the dung heaps that were usually to be seen along the route had also been removed. She saw ahead of her a litter, supported by poles slung between two palfreys and caught a glimpse of the mitred occupant whom she took to be the Bishop of London – now too old to mount a horse.

Anne followed the stream of people towards the rear entrance of the castle. There were two serjeants at arms checking the identity of those entering the building and Anne wondered how she could possibly bluff her way through. As she stood in a queue behind several others she overheard a young girl in front announcing herself.

"Maidservant to Sir John Morley." The girl was motioned through without further questioning and when it came to Anne's turn she said with as much confidence as she could muster, "Flowers ordered for Sir John Morley to freshen his chamber." There was a momentary pause and a fleeting look of suspicion on the serjeant's face before he nodded her through.

Anne found herself in a vestibule with stairs leading off to the right. She pushed her way through the jostling crowd and climbed up two flights to the second floor where a long corridor, flanking the outer wall, stretched out before her. As instructed she proceeded along this corridor pausing only to observe through an aperture to the inner courtyard the hectic toing and froing of officials, counsellors and attendants preparing for the imminent opening of the conference. The corridor ended in an outer wall pierced by a small window through which she could see the river traffic below converging on the castle stairs and surrounding wharves. To her left was a door that she guessed must open into the steward's chamber. Still clutching her flowers she opened it and stepped inside.

The room was of modest size but furnished comfortably with a double bed, chest, cushioned chairs and wall hangings. Light entered through a large window looking over the river. On the inner wall adjoining the main castle frontage she saw a squint set in the stonework at chest height. She bent down and peered through the narrow opening. Below her was the great hall which rose to a considerable height somewhere above her. Rows of benches were placed along the whole length and the floor was covered with newly laid rushes. The lower walls were adorned with richly carved oak panelling and above were hung tapestries depicting biblical scenes. At the far end there was a gallery where several heralds had assembled and directly below her was a raised platform on which a gilded throne had been placed. Logs were blazing in a huge fireplace and the whole scene was framed in flickering light from oil lamps affixed to the walls.

Anne was surprised to see that those now gathering below her were segregated. The benches were divided by an aisle in the middle: on one side sat men in black gowns and caps whom she took to be lawyers; and on the other side sat clergy in their white robes. Occupying the front benches nearest the platform was a group of more colourfully attired dignitaries: courtiers with bright doublets and sleeves, judges in red tunics and bishops with their shimmering mitres.

There was a great murmur from below as everyone talked among themselves, awaiting the arrival of the King. Anne could hardly believe the spectacle before her. If the reports were true, this great assembly of the might of England had been convened with the express purpose of debating the fate of those indicted for her husband's death. She had come in the hope of learning more about that terrible event but she could not understand why the King felt it necessary to bring all these men of authority together to discuss the case. Maybe there were consequences she did not fully comprehend. If so, she would soon find out.

Suddenly there was a hush. Then everyone stood up as the heralds in the gallery trumpeted the arrival of the King who appeared from the river entrance having disembarked from his barge. Several attendants accompanied him and he was followed by the Archbishop of Canterbury and Cardinal Wolsey with their retinues. The King, tall, broad shouldered and youthful, seated himself on the throne and Anne noted the splendour of his attire: a doublet of purple and gold, puffed honey-coloured sleeves slashed with white satin, a short gold mantle trimmed with fur; and a flat broad-brimmed hat covered in feathers.

The Archbishop and the Cardinal were seated on the platform to the right of the King. Wolsey's ample form was covered in crimson damask with a round, flat-topped hat to match and a tippet of fine sable over his shoulders. He now rose and knelt before the King to commence the proceedings with carefully chosen words which Anne, placed directly above him, could hear clearly.

"Your Grace, to my knowledge the clergy have never meant to do anything in derogation of the King's prerogative. For my own part, I owe my whole advancement solely to my lord the King, wherefore I would assent to nothing for all the world that would derogate from Your Grace's royal authority. Nevertheless, to all the clergy this matter of summoning clerks before the temporal judge seems contrary to the laws of God and the Liberties of the Holy Church to which I myself and all the prelates of the Holy Church are bound by their oath to maintain according to their power."

After Wolsey's opening address there were statements from lawyers arguing in favour of the royal prerogative and contradictory declarations from senior clergy in defence of what they described as their ancient rights. Anne found this pattern of assertion and counter-assertion tedious and inconclusive but the atmosphere became suddenly charged when the King himself at last intervened. Turning his face towards the bishops sitting on the front benches he spoke loud enough for Anne to hear every word.

"It seems to us that all these points advanced on behalf of the clergy have been sufficiently answered by our own spiritual counsel, Dr Standish."

One of the bishops was so provoked by this that he stood up and exclaimed in a shrill voice. "I warrant your Grace that Dr Standish, if he persists in the views he has stated, will do so at his peril."

Anne was amazed at this admonition to the bishop's own sovereign. It also prompted a response from Dr Standish himself who rose and, appealing directly to the King, said meekly, "My Lord of Winchester threatens me. But what should one poor friar do alone against all the bishops and the clergy of England?"

At this juncture it was evidently felt necessary to cool tempers. A break in the proceedings was called and refreshments brought in by butlers and laid out on trestle tables along the wall. Anne noted that no maidservants were allowed into the hall: in this place not only were women excluded from office and their voices unheard, they were deemed too low even to serve their masters at table.

Groups of men were now huddling together in private conversation. The King, directly below her, was consulting with members of his council – and although they spoke in low voices she distinctly heard the name Richard Hunne mentioned more than once.

When the formal proceedings were resumed the atmosphere remained tense. The Archbishop of Canterbury, William Wareham, rose from his seat beside the King and reasserted the clergy's immunity from the courts. He was rebuffed by a lawyer whom, from his glittering insignia, Anne identified as the Lord Chief Justice. He pointed out that canon law offered no means to deal with a felon or murderer and that if the secular arm committed such a man to the spiritual authority for trial and sentence the culprit would escape all punishment.

At length the King, showing growing signs of impatience, decided to bring matters to a conclusion. Remaining seated he leaned forwards and spoke with great force. His words reverberated through the hall.

"By the ordinance and sufferance of God, we are King of England. And the Kings of England in times past have never had any superior but God only. Wherefore know you well that we will maintain the right of our Crown and of our temporal jurisdiction in as ample a way as any of our progenitors have done before us. And to consent to your desire more than our progenitors have done in times past we will not."

Anne stood up and was conscious of some discomfort in her back brought on by the awkward angle of the squint. The formal proceedings were now over but she bent down again and had a last look through the peephole to see men once more talking furtively in small groups.

Her thoughts were suddenly interrupted by the sound of advancing footsteps along the corridor. She was trapped within the four walls and from the heavy footfall she guessed that this was the steward himself returning to his chamber. She dared not think what the consequences might be if she were found eavesdropping in a royal residence.

She quickly picked up the flowers she had laid on the windowsill. She placed them in an earthenware jar that stood on a large chest and began with careful deliberation to arrange them, just as the door swung open to reveal a large man in a green doublet with slashed sleeves.

"What the devil is going on?" the steward exclaimed. Anne replied calmly but with subservience in her voice:

"Sir, I must apologise for my intrusion. I was commanded by my master, Sir John Morley, to bring these fragrances to your chamber as a token of his appreciation for the hospitality you have shown him. Your maidservant being engaged elsewhere, I took the liberty of placing the blooms to the best advantage. I am sorry to have alarmed you."

The steward looked confused for a moment. Then he admonished her gently. "This is most irregular. But you may tell Sir John that his gift is gratefully received. You should leave now because I have much business."

Anne bowed and left. She retreated down the long corridor and joined the throng of people leaving by the rear entrance.

Walking back slowly along Thames Street towards East Cheap she thought about what she had witnessed. From the set piece speeches it was clear to her that Church and Crown were at loggerheads over the right of royal courts to hear charges against the clergy. No agreement had been reached and the spiritual and temporal powers were surely sizing each other up for a more decisive clash of arms that was yet to come.

But beneath the carefully chosen words of the open debate something else had surely been going on. During the interlude, the King had been in private conference with his counsellors; Richard Hunne had been spoken of and it seemed to Anne that her husband was the subject of behind-the-scenes contention. She had learned nothing new about the terrible events of that night but it was some small comfort to her that Richard's death had achieved what his praemunire writ had not – an assault on the Church's powers and privileges by the highest in the land.

As Anne reached her house it was getting dark. The mist was rolling in from the river, muffling the sound of St Mary le Bow ringing out the curfew hour.

———————

The bishop was tired after the lengthy conference at Baynard's Castle. But he was partly reassured on the matter of most concern to him. He understood that behind the carefully choreographed public posturing a deal had been struck, as he later explained to Dr Head when they were alone together. "All is decided. My chancellor will surrender himself to the Court of Kings Bench and on being falsely charged with the murder of Hunne will plead his innocence. The attorney general, Sir John Ernley, will then allow the plea and dismiss the case. William Horsey and his alleged accomplices will be set free but I will lose my faithful chancellor because he will be obliged to leave London for Exeter. He will be a canon at the cathedral there and I will ensure that he has preferments enough to allow him to live as he has been accustomed."

Dr Head appeared dismayed. "It is, of course, only just that these wicked charges should be dismissed. Yet it is very harsh that a man who has given such service to your lordship should be banished."

Did the lawyer wonder silently whether his superior's misfortune might open the way for his own elevation? The bishop had his suspicions but he carried on. "The threat of heresy proceedings against Standish are to be lifted. That is, perhaps, to be expected in this settlement of our great dispute, but what is an outrage …" The bishop stabbed the air with a bony forefinger. "… What is an outrage is that this execrable low born friar is, I understand, to be rewarded for his loyalty to the King's cause with a bishopric."

The next day Fitzjames learned that Wareham had resigned the Lord Chancellorship, which was no surprise to those who had observed his state of exhaustion, and was to give way to the thrusting Wolsey. The bishop was unsure what this shift of power might portend and fretted that Wolsey was not as assiduous in the pursuit of heretics as he would wish. And while he took some comfort from Dr Horsey's release he lamented the loss of his right hand man, especially as there was further work to be done before the Hunne affair could be safely put aside.

16

A SCRIBE IS BORN

ANNE WAS NOW A FREE WOMAN. SHE SETTLED INTO her modest house in Eastcheap with Margaret and, after the horrors of the previous weeks, she was at last able to consider her future. She asked Rebecca over for a confidential talk. The two friends sat at the table, sipped small beer and spoke in hushed tones while Margaret and Sarah played.

Anne broached the subject that was close to her heart. "Rebecca, I would like to continue Richard's pious work for true believers. A member of our Bible reading group tells me that there is a scriptorium in Coleman Street where scribes copy the scriptures in English. Since I am able to write, I intend to offer my services. But I have to ask a favour … would you be able to care for Margaret in daytime hours so that I may do this work?"

Rebecca gave Anne's hand a squeeze. "My dearest Anne, I would be happy to do this for you, especially as Margaret and Sarah have become such friends. But please think it over carefully. You will be taking a great risk if you work on prohibited books. Should you be discovered you may be treated in the same pitiless way as your late husband. Is this wise?"

Anne had already made up her mind and dismissed her friend's alarm: "Have no fear. Mere women are not thought to be skilled scribes and I shall take precautions. I will go to

Coleman Street on the morrow and speak with the good people there."

Rebecca sighed. "So be it. But take care. They say the bishop's summoners are watching the streets for suspicious behaviour."

The conversation moved on to other things and Anne described Cawood's clumsy attempt to seduce her.

Rebecca expressed no surprise. "I have heard many such stories from my friends. You were fortunate that he did not persist forcefully. Only this past week a friend's neighbour, an upright woman who lives on her own, was violated by the parish priest of St Stephen, Walbrook. And some two months ago, the small daughter of another friend was molested in the vestry of St Andrew Undershaft."

Anne's anger flared. "These men do not have to answer for their lewd behaviour. Those in holy orders cannot be brought before the King's courts and the bishop's courts are blind to the wicked doings of their own clergy. And yet the supposed misdemeanours of ordinary folk, however petty, are pried into and raked over in the bishop's consistory court by men supposedly sworn to celibacy."

"The clergy are a lascivious breed," Rebecca said. "Sadly what they say is true. The only good priest is an old priest."

The next morning Anne left Margaret at Carter Lane and made her way along the muddied roads to Coleman Street. The houses were spacious and imposing here, but in the alleys leading off the main street the buildings were much more humble. Anne knocked twice on the door of a small dwelling next to a bakery. A face appeared in a front window and stared at her. After a brief wait she was admitted. Anne gave her name and the elderly stooped man who opened the door said he was expecting her. He led her upstairs to the main room on the first floor where three other men were sitting at sloping desks surrounded by books, rolls of parchment and writing materials. The older man said his name was Geoffrey and the others, in their twenties or thirties, were introduced as Jonathan, Peter and Walter.

Geoffrey spoke in a low voice: "All of us here are delighted to be working with someone so highly recommended by our brethren. Make yourself comfortable and I will explain how we undertake our secret work."

Anne sat down and listened intently.

"There are four of us who act as scribes and I myself also do book-binding when the occasion demands. We take commissions to produce Latin Bibles and other permissible works. This business provides protection for our secret work which is to make copies of the scriptures in English. You see here that at this moment Jonathan and Peter are copying from the Vulgate but Walter is copying Wycliffe's Bible for our brethren."

"So what do you do if a priest or one of the bishop's officers comes to the house?" asked Anne.

"In almost no time we can place the forbidden material under the floor" – here he lifted specially cut floorboards located under the hearth rug – "we then take the Latin Bible down from the shelves. It takes about half a minute to make this transformation so we hold suspicious enquirers at the door for this time."

Anne got up and looked carefully at the work of the scribes. "Why are there two different scripts? Jonathan and Peter are copying in one hand and Walter in another?"

"You are right. Jonathan and Peter are copying the Vulgate in secretary hand and Walter is copying the Wycliffe Bible in italic. There are two reasons for this. First, italic is easier and quicker and for our own works we want speed rather than formality. For the Vulgate formality is necessary. It is also important that the prohibited work, if later discovered after despatch from here, should not be traced to our scriptorium. If our regular copying is in secretary hand investigators are less likely to make a connection."

"And how long does it take to copy an entire Bible?" Anne enquired.

Geoffrey gave a sigh of resignation. "Regrettably, it is a long labour. A Bible is over twelve months work for one man, so our production is only two or three Bibles each year. But you must remember – and you will know this from your own Bible readings – that books are passed from hand to hand and the use thereby multiplied." He then pointed to the bundles of parchment on each desk from which the scribes were copying. "In order to speed up our production we break each Bible into four separate folios. This way the scribes can all at the same time copy from a particular book or exemplar. This is necessary because it is very costly – ten pounds or more – to purchase a Bible for copying."

Anne was amazed at the complexity of what she had always imagined to be a straightforward process. "And how is the binding done after the copying is complete?"

"If it is an English Bible I undertake the binding myself. I am not highly skilled but for our own books the binding must be merely serviceable. If, on the other hand, it is a Vulgate that has been commissioned from outside we send the folds of parchment to a skilled stationer in Paternoster Row who stitches and binds them between wooden boards."

Having briefed his new trainee on the operation of the scriptorium, Geoffrey suggested that she should try her hand at copying. "I understand your accustomed hand is italic. Perhaps we could begin with that. Of course you will become more accomplished and quicker over time and at some point it will be necessary to learn to write in secretary hand."

Geoffrey then explained how the scribe prepared for copying. "First, we have scrolls of parchment which we buy from Paternoster Row. The scribe must then cut the large parchment sheets into smaller uniform lengths. Each piece of parchment must be rubbed smooth with a pumice stone before writing on it. The scribe measures out the spacing of lines on the sheet, pricks the edge of the parchment to mark the spaces and rules lines. Now all is ready and the scribe takes a goose-feather quill, always kept sharp with a penknife such as we have here, and dips the quill in the inkpot."

Finally, Geoffrey showed her how to lay the exemplar and copy side by side on the sloping desk and to put weights on the manuscript to hold it in place. These were to be moved as she worked her way down the parchment.

Anne was set to work copying from a folio but was soon frustrated at her very slow progress. She was only too aware that her experience of writing was limited to a few verses of psalms for her Bible reading group and occasional business correspondence for her late husband. The steady concentration required over long hours was something entirely new and she had to make frequent corrections by scraping off ink with a penknife before it soaked into the parchment.

Before Anne left Coleman Street at the end of the day to collect Margaret, Geoffrey had a private word with her. "Mistress Anne, in this little workshop we only know as much about each other as is needed. Where we live, what we may do elsewhere and what we have been in the past – none of these things do we demand to know of each other. This is for reasons of security in case one of us should be taken and questioned under duress. It is safer to work this way."

Over the next week Anne came each day to Coleman Street and to her great relief and Geoffrey's satisfaction, found her competence steadily improving. On one particular morning when she arrived she was surprised to see the baker's wife from next door talking to the scribes and placing a Bible in her bread basket. On seeing her puzzlement, Geoffrey hastily explained. "You see Anne, we have to distribute our Bibles when they are finished and bound. Our neighbours in the bakery are of our persuasion and we send out our New Testament Bibles hidden under loaves of bread to friends in the neighbouring parishes."

Anne also learned that there was an internal connecting door to the bakery in the passageway, which avoided the need for suspicious toings and froings in the street. "But surely," Anne asked Geoffrey, "you do not need such precautions when you deliver only two or three Bibles each year?"

"Ah, you might think so," he said, with a twinkle in his eye, "but we lend out Bibles and other texts to people we know – just as some stationers in St Paul's lend out their permitted books. There is therefore an irregular flow of books going out of the scriptorium and coming back in – all under the disguise of bread."

Anne marvelled at the ingenuity of her friends but also reflected on the pitiless intolerance of a Church that made such measures necessary.

The weeks went by and Anne became proficient enough in both secretary and italic hand to be entrusted with copying the Vulgate as well as the Wycliffe Bible. But some time after she had settled into her new routine, news came that brought forcefully to mind her solemn vow: not just to honour the memory of her husband by continuing his work, but also to avenge his death.

17

BARTHOLOMEW FAIR

THE ANNIVERSARY OF HUNNE'S DEATH PASSED, WINTER gave way to spring and spring to summer. One warm evening, Anne was returning from the scriptorium to collect Margaret when she met in the street the wife of an old friend of her husband, a fellow merchant taylor. Mary greeted Anne warmly. "Anne, I have not seen you these past few months but I want to talk to you on a matter of urgency. Are you going to Bartholomew Fair on the morrow? Because, if so, we can meet there. I am looking after a clothing stall for my husband and I must hurry home now to help prepare our wares."

Anne had already arranged with Rebecca to take Margaret and Sarah to the Fair. The next day, being August 23rd, was the first of three days of festivities held within the monastery of St Bartholomew to celebrate the feast day of their saint.

"I shall be there, Mary, and we can certainly talk. What time and where shall I meet you?"

"Our stall is set against the north wall of the church. Could you be there at three o'clock because we will be very busy before then?"

Having agreed time and place, Anne went on to Carter Lane where she was welcomed by Rebecca. "Anne, the children are getting very excited at the prospect of the Fair. But I have said they must stay close by us because the crowds will be daunting. They say half London will be there and many more from outside."

Anne, too, was concerned for the children's safety. The Fair had earned an unfortunate reputation for drunken revelry, brawls and petty criminality. But that would not stop them enjoying themselves. "I suggest we meet here and then walk up together to Newgate and Smithfield. If we go early we will see the Lord Mayor's Procession."

So they met the next morning and joined the crowds surging towards Smithfield. Anne, however, was pensive: she could not help reflecting that Smithfield was where her husband's corpse had been burned less than two years before. And she wistfully recalled her earlier visits to the Fair when Richard had set up his own stall in what was, as he proudly proclaimed, the biggest cloth fair in all England.

No sooner had they arrived than there was a great roar as the Lord Mayor rode into Smithfield followed by twelve aldermen, all dressed in their scarlet gowns. A proclamation was read and the gates into Cloth Fair opened. In time honoured tradition, rabbits were let loose among the crowds for boys to chase and capture, several people being knocked over in the ensuing scramble.

Within the bounds of the monastery walls, every conceivable entertainment was on display: rope dancers, magicians, puppeteers, fortune tellers, performing hobby horses, jugglers and jesters; there were booths selling toys, dolls, whirligigs and magical medicines; cook shops offering gingerbread, hot cakes, pastries, meat pies and roast pork; tents advertising outlandish beasts and freak shows. All this amid the sound of drums, rattles, shouting and whooping. The Lord Mayor and his sheriffs tried to keep some semblance of law and order in this tumult through their Serjeants-at-the-Mace

– officers with powers of arrest who patrolled the monastic grounds to identify troublemakers.

The drapers and merchant taylors had set up their clothiers' stalls against the north side of St Bartholomew's church and along the churchyard wall. Here they had on display caps, rugs, shawls and rolls of cloth. Mingling in the throng of would-be buyers were "searchers" – inspectors commissioned by the great guilds to ensure that the measurement, quality and weight of cloth sold conformed to the regulated standards.

Sarah and Margaret demanded to see the puppets and then they paid a penny each to see a caged tiger – which Sarah found so frightening that they had to leave the tent hurriedly. Rebecca went to a fortune teller who told her she would live to be seventy, which pleased them all. They ate slices of pork from a whole roast pig followed by pancakes and they drank quantities of cherry and raspberry waters as well as barley tea.

Anne surveyed the extraordinary scene and calculated that the monastery must do very well from renting out space for all the booths and standings. Her merchant friends said the annual taking was eighty-five pounds or more, which would certainly help to provide a good living for a few canons.

After they had eaten, Anne noticed that Margaret was wriggling uncomfortably. "Dearest, if you need relief, you may pluck a rose against the wall here. Look others are doing the same."

Margaret obliged, but then Sarah said she needed a privy. Rebecca looked around the Fair ground. "I am told they have dug only one place of easement for all these crowds so it will not be pleasant. But let us go if you must."

When they came back, Rebecca looked disconcerted. "There is going to be much work here for the dung carriers at the end of the day. They will have to bring carts during the night to remove the waste and I can imagine that the heap at Dung Wharf in Blackfriars will be greatly added to by the morning."

Anne judged by the sun that it must be approaching three o'clock and they began to stroll towards the clothing stalls by the church. Suddenly two serjeants forced their way through the crowds towards the Smithfield entrance. Someone said there was a brawl outside the Hand and Shears Ale House, which Anne could well believe since they had trouble there every year.

It was time for her to meet Mary at her stall, so Rebecca took charge of the two children. Anne greeted her friend who was looking harassed. Mary quickly explained the reason for her agitation. "Robert has had to attend the Court of Pie-Powder now being held at the monastery guest house. The court has jurisdiction over everything that goes on at the Fair and all cases must be disposed of within a day. Robert is there as a witness because they have arrested some draper for using an unlawful yard to measure his cloth. But he should be back shortly."

Mary then asked a friend to keep an eye on the stall while she and Anne spoke privately in a quieter corner of the graveyard. Mary came quickly to the point: "Anne, Robert had some dealing two days ago at the Guildhall and was spoken to by a scribe of the sheriff's court. Knowing Robert to be a supporter of your late husband, the scribe asked if he would be interested in obtaining the coroner's secret verdict on Richard Hunne's death. He said that he could lend out the coroner's verdict together with the testimony of witnesses for one day only when his master would be abroad at the Fair. That day is tomorrow, the Feast Day of St Bartholomew."

Anne hardly knew what to think. She had only heard the common rumours about that night in the Lollards' Tower and was aware that the coroner's report would be a confidential and closely guarded document. It was painful to be reminded of those terrible events, but if there was any possibility of gaining information about those responsible for her husband's death she would do anything to obtain it. Here was an opportunity not to be missed.

"Mary, this is most important. On what terms did the scribe say he would lend the document?"

"He said he would lend it out only to Robert, whom he would charge with the responsibility of returning the documents by seven o'clock in the evening. He would demand a fee of three pounds for his services but he would require a further seven pounds to vouchsafe the return of the parchments. He said these are the original manuscripts and that the only copy of them is with the Bishop of London."

Anne thought quickly: "I will raise the money – though perhaps your dear Robert will be charitable enough to contribute two pounds to the deposit. I will come back with the money tonight before the fair closes and the monastery gates are shut. Have the scribe deliver the documents to your husband tomorrow morning and he may then put them in a roll of cloth and bring them here to your stall. I will collect them and return them to you by six o'clock in the evening. What time in the morning can Robert be here?"

"The scribe said he could have the parchments at eight o'clock, so shall we say half an hour after that time? But be sure to bring the money tonight."

Anne promised her she would and lost no time in rejoining Rebecca and the children who were again being mesmerised by the puppets. "I am afraid I must return home at once Rebecca. Do you wish to stay here or will you join me?"

Rebecca seemed aware that something unusual had occurred and insisted in accompanying Anne. Margaret and Sarah had to be dragged away with the promise that they would have one more day at the Fair and the little group retraced their steps through Smithfield and Newgate, passing many latecomers on their way to the festivities.

On the way back, Anne told Rebecca what Mary had revealed to her and she said she would have to raise the money that very evening. She had only recently collected her quarterly payment from St Helen's and had enough money for the three pound rental charge. Rebecca said she was sure her husband would be willing to put up two pounds of the security required, which, if Robert came up with two pounds also, would leave three pounds still to be raised.

Anne also needed to see Geoffrey at Coleman Street, if he could be found at home, to arrange for the material to be transcribed. There would certainly be work for the scriptorium the next day but Anne did not know how much because she had very little idea of the length of the coroner's report. She explained to Rebecca. "I will have to copy the coroner's report. I want to have a record of how my husband died so that I can study it and show it, if need be, to others."

"Anne, you would surely be endangering yourself," Rebecca said. "First, the taking of a secret court document. Second, wrongful use of the same. And most of all the retention of a copy that may be discovered. Perhaps it would be better to look at the text and then return it."

But Anne was adamant. "No, I will have it copied by my fellow scribes and then we can read it together in our own time – if you will agree."

Rebecca seemed resigned. "So be it. You know I will always support you in this."

Anne left Margaret in Rebecca's charge and walked on alone to Coleman Street. Fortunately Geoffrey was there and she gave him a full account of her conversation with Mary. He was quite animated as he outlined a plan of action.

"First, I myself will put up the remaining three pounds which you need. Then when you come back with the scrolls we must set to work. Walter is away during the Fair and Jonathan

I am not sure about but I will try both him and Peter since they are a short walk from here. We will have to separate out the parchments, divide them between us for copying and adjust the work to suit the different speeds of the copier. We will agree beforehand on any shortening of names to save us time. Let us gather here at nine o'clock in the morning."

Anne accepted the money from Geoffrey gratefully. She returned to Eastcheap to collect her own savings before walking briskly on to Carter Lane, where Rebecca gave her the contribution she had promised. Anne was now carrying coinage amounting to eight pounds and making her way back to the Fair on her own. She realised that she was vulnerable to the pickpockets and bag snatchers that infested London during the Fair.

She knew that the gates to the monastery were locked at night to safeguard the wares of the stallholders and she feared that she might be too late. She was getting tired, and, as she approached Smithfield, her progress was slowed by crowds of revellers returning home, many of whom had been drinking strong ale all day. At Cloth Fair there was a noisy rabble outside the Hand and Shears but she pressed her way through and was thankful when, breathless and exhausted, she reached St Bartholomew's Church.

Mary was now with her husband closing up their stall for the night. Anne gave the money to Robert who said he would make up the difference and deliver the manuscript the next morning. The couple insisted on accompanying Anne back to Eastcheap because, as Robert reminded her, the streets of London were not safe for a woman after the closure of the Fair.

At half past eight the next morning, Anne collected the roll of cloth from Robert's stall and hurried back to Coleman Street. Geoffrey had already prepared the writing desks with parchment, ink and quills and Peter had come to help. Anne unfurled the roll of cloth on a small table and examined the sheets of manuscript pages that had been hidden inside.

There were a dozen sheets consisting of the findings of the jury's inquest into Hunne's death, the various depositions from witnesses and the final verdict of the coroner, Thomas Barnwell. The parchment pages had been bound loosely together and Anne carefully removed the stitching while retaining the twine for rebinding. The individual sheets were divided among the three scribes but, before they began to copy, Geoffrey gave his final instructions.

"We will use the italic hand to speed up the task and do not be too particular about the formation of your letters. It is sufficient if the words can be read. But be sure not to get ink on the original manuscript."

The work proceeded intensely and in silence for they had only a few hours to complete the copy. As it turned out the amount of material was not too onerous and Geoffrey was confident that they would be able to finish their task in time.

Then disaster struck. Refilling his ink pot, Peter, in his hurry, spilt ink onto the manuscript he was copying. A large black stain spread across the parchment which there was no way of removing. Geoffrey immediately took charge: "We will have to copy the exemplar which by good fortune can still be read, using carefully formed secretary hand to conform to the original. This will take time and it is not without risk to the scribe but at least the ink is a good match."

They all knew what this meant. The writing of individual scribes varied in small details so that whoever did the copying of the replacement page would be identifiable. Yet Geoffrey unhesitatingly exposed himself to danger by insisting that he would work on the page to be substituted.

The ink spill also meant a serious delay that they could ill afford. It was now a race against time and when at last the copying was done and the manuscript papers restitched it was nearly six o'clock. After inserting the original manuscript in the roll of cloth and leaving the copy with Geoffrey for the time being, Anne headed straight back to Smithfield. Entering the monastery grounds she observed that today, on the feast day of the great saint, there were more people of fashion celebrating the occasion.

As Anne arrived at Robert's stall and handed back the precious roll of cloth the church clock rang out the half-hour which meant that Robert had barely thirty minutes to return the papers to the scribe at the Guildhall. Before setting off he warned Anne: "Take care on your way back. Attach yourself if possible to a party because there are villains around." But Anne was too preoccupied to heed this advice.

Relieved at having completed her transaction, she began to retrace her steps. By now many revellers, after drinking all day, were distinctly the worse for wear. As she passed the Hand and Shears she was greeted with shouts of "Let's 'ave you m'doxie". Ignoring the insults and jeers, she pushed her way through. After leaving the noisy rabble behind she became aware that a large bearded man had detached himself from his fellow drinkers and was following her. Suddenly he came up behind her and bundled her into a side alley, where they were alone. He wrestled her to the ground and began to force open her legs. The assailant – reeking of drink and much else – lay heavily on her making it difficult to move. But she managed to free one hand and extract a small penknife from its leather sheath attached to her cincture. The heaving man on top of her had now exposed himself and, as he arched his back to thrust himself into her, she grasped her blade and with all her strength forced it upwards into his scrotum. He bellowed like a bull as he rolled away clutching his privy parts. Anne got up and ran off – thankful that the implement she used to sharpen quills in the scriptorium had rescued her from a dreadful fate.

She hurried back to Eastcheap where, badly shaken and breathless, she slumped on her bed. She lay there for some time until, feeling calmer, she rose and began to cleanse herself. She poured out a basin of water suffused with fresh herbs, washed her body with a sponge and rinsed herself with warm rose water. Now revived and determined to put her shocking experience behind her she was able to focus her mind on what she must do the following day. She would have first to retrieve the copy of the coroner's report from Geoffrey. She had invited Rebecca over later in the morning when they planned to examine together the secret documents. She would tell her cousin at a more suitable time later about her ordeal because all their attention must be focussed now on the new evidence that was to be revealed.

Though still shaky, Anne was in a state of heightened anticipation, knowing that at long last she was about to learn the true fate of her dear husband.

SUSPICIONS

BISHOP FITZJAMES DELIBERATELY ABSENTED HIMSELF from his London diocese during the Bartholomew Fair when he found the stench, noise and ribaldry around St Paul's too much for him. He was thankful, instead, to be surveying the improvements he was making to the palace gardens in Fulham. Under his own careful instruction, his gardeners had created elaborate pleached alleys where fruit trees, privet and hawthorn had been wrought into arches and walkways, providing shade from the sun and shelter from the rain. He looked forward to strolling with his guests in this little arboreal paradise.

Within the palace itself he had commissioned a great screen of carved oak panels for his hall. He intended to celebrate the marriage of Henry and Catherine of Aragon at which he had been present and to commemorate the event by interlacing the many royal emblems with his own coat of arms – crossed swords with dolphins and an eagle.

Yet amid these pleasant distractions he was troubled. The King had shown himself to be no great friend of the Church and he questioned whether Henry's powerful new Chancellor, Thomas Wolsey, stood with the Crown or for the protection of Church privileges. He recalled the celebration of Wolsey's appointment as Cardinal only a few months ago when the cherished cardinal's hat, brought from Rome by a high official of the papal court, was carried over London Bridge through the city in great splendour and placed on the high altar of Westminster Abbey – an event that had prompted several taverns and at least one stew house to rename themselves The Cardinal's Hat.

Nor could Fitzjames forget the ceremony of installation at Westminster Abbey from which he had absented himself. What had caused him great offence was the choice of his own dean, John Colet, to deliver the sermon. Could this be a sign that the Cardinal and the King were to follow the teachings of reformists whom he had been battling all these years?

And something else was troubling him. He had never believed that Richard Hunne had acted on his own. It is true that the merchant taylor had been a wealthy man: they said his tenements and other property may have amounted to £600 excluding his plate. But what man, especially a man of business, would sink his wealth into costly – and dangerous – legal actions against the Church? Not one action, he reminded himself, but several, of which the praemunire suit had been adjourned again and again at great cost to the plaintiff. Fitzjames calculated that the expense of attorneys, pleadings, writs and other legal fees over several years must have been a heavy burden even for someone in his position. It was simply not credible that a man with a young family and the ambition to expand his business would pour his money away in such a manner.

And there was another thing: it was hazardous to bring legal suits against the Church, especially if the suitor had Lollard leanings. The Church knew how to fight back as it had done in this case, and Hunne would have been aware of the risk to which he was exposing himself. Therefore he must surely have felt – albeit in error as it turned out – that he had powerful protection from some quarter. The old bishop stroked his sallow cheek with a bony hand. There must be some person or persons behind Hunne. It was surely a conspiracy and he needed to get to the bottom of it.

That evening he was supping with Thomas Head who, now that Horsey was banished to Exeter, was acting as the bishop's chief legal adviser and right hand man. When the serving maid and butler had withdrawn Fitzjames raised the subject that had been on his mind all day. "Thomas, I wish to find out who gave support to Richard Hunne. I have been thinking how to do this. His servant told us all he could and I do not wish to pursue his widow. Being merely a woman she would not understand her husband's financial affairs and, besides, with the uproar over Hunne I must not be accused of going after his family. But perhaps Hunne's attorney, Richard Hawkes, could tell us something since he was very likely paid by the heretic's patron. Could you take it upon yourself to discover more about this man and whether there is anything we could use against him?"

Head seemed only too pleased to be asked to assist in such a sensitive matter. "My Lord, I will certainly find out all I can. Our new summoner, Robert David, has low born friends who may help us to gather such information. I will put Hawkes under our scrutiny."

The bishop expressed his gratitude and the conversation moved on to the recent decline in the business of the ecclesiastical courts which was putting pressure on diocesan finances. It was some consolation to them both that the takings of the great shrines at St Paul's were particularly buoyant that year. At the end of the evening, Head took a wherry back to St Paul's Wharf, leaving the bishop to browse among the theological works that were proudly on display in his library.

Two weeks later, Head revisited Fulham to report his findings to the bishop. It was a glorious early autumn morning and the two men strolled along the newly created walkways in the garden. Head spoke with some satisfaction about his discoveries. "My Lord, we have tracked down Richard Hawkes. He lodges in the Middle Temple where he is a bencher and he meets his clients in Westminster Hall, the Temple Church or the Antelope in Holborn. He has been observed to frequent Cock Lane, Smithfield for immoral purposes but we can do nothing about that. The Temple is, of course, a liberty and neither we nor the mayor have jurisdiction there. A summoner dare not be seen within its bounds."

The bishop sighed. "Yes, these nests of secular lawyers are like petty kingdoms. They say they have become a refuge for bankrupts, debtors, foreigners and any other scoundrels escaping arrest. What then can we do to obtain further information about this man's dealings?"

Head already had the answer. "My Lord, Hawkes has a clerk who has for some years been a student at the Middle Temple. He lodges at the Black Spread Eagle in Fleet Street. Knowing that such people are always short of money, our summoner arranged for one of his lowly friends to meet with the clerk at the tavern. For a few pints of ale and a shilling this clerk's tongue was loosened. He provided important information. He said that at the time of Hunne's praemunire his master's fees were paid not by Hunne himself but by one John Rymer, a scrivener. Your suspicions are therefore well founded."

The bishop took his trusted adviser by the arm. "Thomas, this is excellent work. Of course, the scrivener could have been acting for Hunne but why would Hunne pay his fees through someone else? Our investigation must be carried to another stage. Who is Rymer and was he under instructions from some great man?"

Head undertook to enquire into the mysterious scrivener. Several weeks passed before he was able to gather together sufficient information on his new target and by the time he presented his findings to the bishop colder weather had set in. A fire was crackling in the hall of Fulham Palace where Fitzjames was pacing up and down. He was by now impatient to identify his ultimate quarry. "So, Thomas, what do we have now? Where has this chase finally led us?"

Head gave a cautious reply. "My Lord it is not yet clear for whom Rymer was acting in Hunne's praemunire case. He is a married man living in Bread Street and is agent for a number of men of property – managing their rents, conveying houses, drawing up leases on tenements and so on. However, one matter may be of interest. He was observed several times going from Blackfriars Stairs over to Southwark. On one such occasion we had a waterman follow him and he was seen entering a stew house called the Cross Keys, at Bankside."

The bishop stopped his pacing. "Ah, then we have something against Rymer. The way to proceed is to instruct our summoner, Robert David, to visit the scrivener at his house and to demand that he appear before the consistory court for the grave moral offence of adultery and fornication. After putting him in peril of infamy, penitence and a heavy fine, David will then know how to obtain the information we require by offering lenience."

The bishop's confidante, being familiar with the Church's information gathering methods, was at one with his superior. "Quite so, my Lord, and I shall ensure that the citation by the summoner is supported by sworn statements from women with whom Rymer has had connection. This may of course take some days, but it should lead us to our prey. I must also mention the question of funds. These enquiries involve large outlays and we have exhausted the money set aside for summoners' costs."

The bishop began to pace again but then stopped. "St Erkenwald has received large oblations from the faithful this year – indeed considerably more than last – so I propose that we take what we need from the shrine receipts. I will discuss this with the treasurer."

The two men parted with a common understanding of what had to be done. They were determined to reel in the big fish that they were convinced was lurking in the deep waters of London's religious underworld.

With Advent approaching, the bishop felt obliged to return to St Paul's to attend to diocesan matters and cathedral duties. He and his retinue were rowed down river in a barge on which was painted his coat of arms. When he alighted at St Paul's Wharf he was met by a number of church dignitaries though noticeably absent was his own dean.

Fitzjames took up his lodgings in the palace and busied himself with administrative tasks. But he was even more sharp tongued and cantankerous in his dealings with others than usual. He was concerned that his London house was suffering dilapidations especially in the Great Hall. He was painfully conscious that his income of little more than a thousand pounds was much less than that enjoyed by those such as the Bishops of Winchester, Durham and Lincoln and indeed was barely sufficient for his needs. His relations with the dean remained strained to breaking point and the chapter were complaining bitterly about the austerity being imposed on them. Add to this the continuing spread of iniquitous Lollard teaching and the ever-increasing power of the unfathomable Wolsey and the overall picture was not a happy one. Even now, as he peered out of his study window, his sense of propriety and orderliness was affronted by the disrespectful behaviour of apprentice boys frolicking in the cathedral precinct.

———

It was in early December that the breakthrough came. The scrivener, Rymer, had for some time proved resistant to the summoner's threat of court proceedings but had at last given way. He evidently calculated that the humiliation and loss of business that would result from a conviction in the consistory court outweighed considerations of confidentiality. And so it was that Thomas Head, barely able to conceal his excitement, came to report to the bishop at his London palace.

The bishop was seated in his library and invited Head to take a chair.

"So, Thomas, we have come to the conclusion of our quest. What is the outcome?"

"My Lord, the scrivener would make no sworn statement, but he did at length inform us that the man who instructed him to pay for Hunne's praemunire was the former Lord Mayor himself, George Monoux."

The bishop registered his shock by standing up and walking to the window. "This is most extraordinary. Monoux is one of the foremost men in the City and this very year made Master of the Drapers Company. It seems that heresy has reached almost the highest level of the realm. Thomas, let me think about this news. We cannot leave matters as they stand but we will have to proceed with great care."

The meeting was concluded, but the bishop stood for some minutes by the window. Looking out across the cathedral close, he knew that a confrontation between London's spiritual head and one of its wealthiest and most powerful citizens could hardly be avoided.

The Spectre of Richard Hunne

19

Anne and Rebecca had arranged to meet at Anne's house in Eastcheap while the two little girls were cared for by a neighbour. Anne did not want to examine the coroner's report on her own because the memories and bitterness its findings would provoke might be too much for her. So the two friends sat together at the table behind a bolted door while Anne unfurled the scrolls of parchment and laid them out with weights placed on top to prevent them rolling up. After she had glanced through the dozen sheets of manuscript, Anne said, "There are three groups of papers here. We have the coroner's examination of poor Richard's body when it was found together with a preliminary verdict. Then the testimony of several witnesses taken at different times. Then comes the coroner's final verdict signed off by the twenty four jurymen."

They agreed to study closely each of these sections in turn, reading the script over again and making marks against those parts of the text that they believed to be of special importance. Rebecca, though able with some difficulty to read, was much slower than Anne and they worked separately on different sheets of manuscript.

They had started their work at nine in the morning but it was a good two hours before they were ready to discuss what they had found. After fortifying themselves with fruit juices and pastries, Anne suggested that they begin by examining the description of the corpse – painful though this would be.

Rebecca was surprised by the speed with which the coroner's jury had been empanelled. "Richard's body was found on the Monday morning and the jury sworn in on the Tuesday and Wednesday. It seems that they all viewed the body in Lollards' Tower on that same Wednesday, so the Lord Mayor must have acted speedily to instruct the coroner."

Anne nodded in approval. "Yes, he did his duty well, especially as the bishop and his friends were already proclaiming from the pulpit that Richard was guilty of self murder. But look what is said here … it is as if these churchmen had never seen a hanged man … *His eyes and mouth were fair closed, without any staring, gaping or frowning* and also *without any drivelling or splurging of the body.* It is stated here, too, that he had *a fair countenance, his head fair combed, and his bonnet right sitting upon his head.* If Richard had hung himself he would have kicked and struggled, his face would have been contorted and his body soiled. I have seen it myself on Tower Hill."

Rebecca was equally incredulous. "They say, too, that the silken girdle round his neck was too small to put his head in and too slight to make the marks they observed. Listen to this … *we find that the skin both of his neck and throat beneath the girdle of silk was fret and phased away with that thing which the murderers had broken his neck withal.*"

Anne was now becoming upset and angry. "How dare they insist he killed himself! Look what the twenty four honest men of the jury state*! Also, an end of a wax candle which, as John Bellringer says, he left in the prison burning with Hunne that same Sunday night that Hunne was murdered, which wax candle we* *found sticking upon the stocks fair put out about seven or eight foot from the place where Hunne was hanged. Which candle, after our opinion was never put out by him."*

Rebecca comforted Anne while citing another passage from the jury's report. *"Moreover we find that within the said prison was no means whereby any man might hang himself but only a stool, which stool stood upon a bolster of a bed so tickle that any man or beast might not touch it so little but it was ready to fall. Whereby we perceived that it was not possible that Hunne might hang himself, the stool so standing."*

"Anne you have at least one consolation. Not only did your dear husband not hang himself but it could be proved to the world, could it but see the evidence, that it was impossible for him to have done so."

Anne tried to overcome her growing anguish. "And all this blood they speak of. What terrible things did they do to kill him? They say there was a great patch of blood in the corner of the prison and yet only four drops of blood from his nose and no blood whatsoever on his doublet, collar or shirt. Listen to this … *Also, we find that upon the left side of Hunne's jacket, from the breast downwards, to be two great streams of blood. Also, within the flap of the left side of his jacket, we find a great cluster of blood and the jacket folden down thereupon, which thing the said Hunne could never fold nor do after he was hanged. Whereby, it appears plainly to us all that the neck of Hunne was broken, and the great plenty of blood was shed before he was hanged. Wherefore, all we find, by God and all our consciences, that Richard Hunne was murdered. Also we acquit the said Richard Hunne of his own death."*

Anne sat silently while the tears coursed down her cheeks. After a while she was able to gather her thoughts. "This then is the coroner's preliminary verdict. But already there are questions in my mind. Why would these despicable men choose to kill by spilling blood, which cannot easily be masked as self murder and certainly not self murder by hanging? Also why was the pretence of hanging so clumsily executed? And why did they need three men to kill a man whose arms were bound and who was already severely weakened by mistreatment?"

Rebecca agreed that these circumstances were very puzzling. "Let us examine the witness statements to see if they answer these questions. But first we need a respite and some refreshment." As they sipped raspberry juice and divided up a heavily spiced meat pie, Rebecca tried to lighten the mood by recalling the recent spectacle she had observed on London's streets: "I took Sarah to see the arrival of Wolsey's scarlet hat from Rome. The Lord Mayor and aldermen were at Cheapside on horseback to greet it and the City guilds and their liverymen were turned out on foot to line the streets and do reverence to the hat as it was born in a grand procession to Westminster. It was an occasion to remember."

Anne replied bitterly that the idolatry of a hat showed only that there was no limit to the vanity of churchmen.

There was another long silence as the two women re-read the depositions of church officials, gaolers and servants. This time it was Anne who broke the silence. "There is only a short statement here from the murderer, Charles Joseph. I suppose this is because he was examined not by the coroner but by the King's counsel in the Tower of London. A copy of his full testimony was not made and so what we have is a mere summary.

Charles Joseph sayeth that, when Richard Hunne was slain John Bellringer bear up the stairs into the Lollards' Tower a wax candle, having the keys of the doors hanging on his arms. And I, Charles, went next to him and Master Chancellor came up last. And when all of us came up we found Hunne lying on his bed. And then Master Chancellor said, "Lay hands on the thief!" And so all we three murdered Hunne. And then I, Charles, put the girdle about

Hunne's neck. And then John Bellringer and I, Charles, did heave up Hunne, and Master Chancellor pulled the girdle over the staple. And so Hunne was hanged.

"Rebecca, there are more puzzles here. Why did the chancellor describe my dear husband, who everybody knew to be honest, as a thief? And why does Joseph not say here how he was killed? Also, it is curious that he says *we three murdered Hunne.* Look now at the deposition of Julian Little, the summoner's servant. According to Little, Joseph told him: *I have destroyed Richard Hunne,* and then said ..." At this point Anne, overcome by her grief, was unable to continue and Rebecca added the missing words. *"I put a wire in his nose."*

The idea of three churchmen, one the bishop's deputy, setting out to murder a defenceless man by pushing a wire up his nose into his head was too shocking for the two friends to contemplate. But it would explain all the blood and yet the absence of visible wounds. They sat for some time in stunned silence.

Rebecca put her arms around Anne. "At least certain points are clear beyond doubt. First, Richard did not hang himself but was murdered. Second, the man who did the killing, according to his own confession, was Joseph. Third, Richard was killed with a wire, then had his neck broken with some metal object and finally was put in a girdle and hung to give the semblance of self-murder."

Anne agreed with these conclusions but was troubled by another unexplained circumstance. "According to two witness statements, Joseph left St Paul's at just after seven o'clock on the Monday morning. Yet he told Little that he had killed Richard at around midnight on Sunday. What occurred in those missing hours? And what caused Joseph to be detained so long that he had to make his escape from the cathedral at daybreak when he could be – and was – observed by witnesses?

"Now, we agree that Joseph killed Richard, abetted in some way by John Bellringer who was a junior confederate. But what about Horsey? What was his role and what is the proof against him?"

It seemed Rebecca had been considering this very question. "Well, we have first of all the testimony of Joseph who portrays the chancellor as the puppet master if not the murderer. Then we have an interesting statement. An unnamed witness, who I take it declines to provide a sworn deposition for fear of retribution from a powerful man, says something to the coroner's jury which they believe to be true. According to the inquest: *It is well proven that before Hunne's death, the said Chancellor came up into the said Lollards' Tower and knelt down before Hunne, holding up his hands to him, praying him for forgiveness for all that he had done to him and must do to him.* This surely is proof that Horsey intended great harm to Richard. The poor prisoner would therefore have been made aware that a terrible fate awaited him.

"There is another even more mysterious passage. The inquest says: *Also at the going up of the Master Chancellor into Lollards' Tower to view the body, we have good proof that there lay on the stocks a gown, either of murrey or crimson igrain with furred shanks. Whose gown it was, we could never prove neither who bear it away.*"

Anne interjected. "Is it not very odd that the chancellor should take off his fur trimmed gown on a cold winter's night in an unheated prison?"

"You are right," Rebecca said. "The inquest says the observation of the gown is proven but again there is no sworn testimony, meaning that whoever reported it was too fearful to reveal himself except to the jury. It seems that there was great trepidation of the chancellor and what he could do to those who caused him offence. The same goes for the clergy. There would surely be many who would have known the gown belonged to

Horsey and several went with him to Lollards'Tower who would have seen him carry it away. But all were overcome by fear."

Anne was increasingly uneasy. "All this shows the power of these great churchmen and the terror they could implant into those beneath them. And there is something else about the chancellor. It seems that on the Sunday of the murder he kept Richard more securely. On that evening, the gaoler, Peter Turner, was shut in with him while he had his dinner and after dinner his hands were bound. John Bellringer, who held the keys, testifies that the chancellor gave him special instructions as follows ... *I charge you to keep Hunne more strictly than he has been kept ... let nobody come to him without my licence. Neither bring shirt, cap, kerchief, or any other thing, but that I see it before it comes to him.*

"Do you see, Rebecca? Horsey, after kneeling before Richard praying for forgiveness for what he was about to do to him, was fearful that his prisoner, now knowing his fate, might harm himself. It is as if the chancellor wanted poor Richard to live and not to die. I find this very extraordinary."

"There are many puzzles here," Rebecca said, "but the final verdict of the coroner on the last manuscript page states with certainty who the murderous confederates were. It says Richard Hunne was feloniously strangled and smothered, his neck broken and after he was dead, his body hanged. The twenty four jurymen solemnly swear that *William Horsey, clerk, Charles Joseph and John Spalding, of their set malice, then and there feloniously killed and murdered the said Richard Hunne in manner and form above said, against the peace of our sovereign Lord, the King, his Crown and Dignity.*"

Anne could no longer contain herself and burst out angrily, "What kind of justice is this? Twenty four honest men have reached this conclusion yet there has been no trial! The three villains have been set free as I have been told, because to pursue charges against a high official of the Church would bring infamy to his office and cast doubt on his bishop."

"Calm yourself dearest Anne, we now know as much as we will ever know about this terrible affair. There is, I believe, nothing more to be done. Terrible injustice though it is, a mere woman is powerless against the might of the Church and its leaders. And I think it best that you burn this copy of the coroner's verdict in case it should incriminate you." She gave Anne a final hug before leaving to collect the children whom she was to look after for the rest of the day.

Anne was left alone to contemplate the events surrounding her husband's agonising death in Lollards' Tower. She would not tell Rebecca that she intended to keep the copy of the coroner's inquest. She put the manuscript scroll back in the roll of cloth and hid the little bundle under her bed. In the years to come when Margaret was old enough to comprehend these things she would show the child how her dear father had suffered and died.

And Anne entertained darker thoughts that she would also keep to herself. It was beyond doubt that Charles Joseph had set out to murder Richard Hunne and had done so in the most cruel manner. She had made a solemn vow to avenge her husband and she was not going to let this pitiless villain escape the sentence of death that a just court would have imposed on him had the matter been brought to trial. She well knew that the law of Moses said *Thou shalt not kill*. But did not Genesis also state *Whoever sheds man's blood, by man his blood shall be shed, for in the image of God has God made man?*

God, she was convinced, had appointed her the instrument of His just retribution and she would answer His call to arms.

20

EVIL MAY DAY

GEORGE MONOUX, THOUGH NO LONGER MAYOR, FELT
that as Master of the Drapers Company and Alderman it was
his duty to keep his finger on the pulse of the metropolis. And
in the opening months of 1517 he was becoming increasingly
concerned about growing popular antagonism towards the large
number of aliens who worked in the City. Foreigners had never
been popular in London. Some, like the Italian bankers who
frequented Lombard Street, flaunted their wealth; others, such
as the Hansa, in the German steelyard on the Thames, enjoyed
special privileges; those from France and the Netherlands –
shoemakers, tanners and brewers – competed for jobs with the
local artisans and journeymen; and all these groups lived and
worshipped in their own separate enclaves. Although the uneasy
coexistence between immigrants and English born Londoners
occasionally erupted into violence, the different communities
generally rubbed along well enough.

However, in the early spring of 1517 Monoux was aware of
tension in the air. Posters were affixed to church doors attacking
foreigners. There were isolated assaults on foreign merchants.
He himself had been present on Easter Tuesday when Dr Bell,
a canon of St Mary Spital, had delivered an inflammatory
sermon from Paul's Cross. This respected man of God had

denounced aliens and strangers *"who eat the bread from the poor and take the living from artificers and merchants."* He had concluded his sermon by issuing a call to arms. *"This land was given to Englishmen, and as birds would defend their nests so ought Englishmen to cherish and defend themselves, and to hurt and grieve aliens for the common good."*

Monoux was appalled by this incitement to violence. As he feared, the message from the pulpit struck a chord among the people and there were more sporadic attacks on foreigners in London's streets. But much more disturbing was the rumour that began to circulate of a general uprising planned for the May Day holiday. When the Lord Chancellor, Thomas Wolsey, got wind of this he instructed the Lord Mayor to take preventive action. The Mayor called Monoux and his fellow aldermen into session at the Guildhall on the evening of April 30th to decide on their response. The twenty-five aldermen, dressed in their fur trimmed scarlet gowns, met in the decorative splendour of the Aldermen's Court Room, presided over by the Lord Mayor, John Rest. The Mayor seemed agitated as he addressed those present:

"Fellow Aldermen, I brought you all here because of the reports, of which I am sure you are aware, that some of the more unruly elements in this City are preparing for an uprising tonight. However, matters have now been taken out of our hands because word has been brought from His Highness's Council, now sitting at Greenwich. It is the Council's command that a strict curfew be imposed, requiring everyone to be indoors and off the streets from nine o'clock this evening until seven in the morning."

Many of the assembled company looked uneasy and it fell to Monoux to voice their concerns. "My Lord Mayor, that is all very well, but young persons from all over town are already gathering to enjoy a night of celebrations ahead of the May

Day holy day. If we should attempt to clear the streets now – in midstream as it were – the revellers will be provoked and there will be trouble."

The Lord Mayor looked resigned. "I share your anxieties. But we are left with no choice. And since it is not long before the evening curfew hour I must ask you to despatch without further ado and bring word of the curfew to your wards."

Monoux hurried off on foot while some of his fellows remounted their horses and dispersed. Returning to his house in St Laurence Pounteney, he took two of his manservants and began to patrol the streets within his own Bridge ward, issuing the curfew proclamation and entering taverns to inform the landlords. In Gracechurch Street he was approaching a small crowd of merrymakers drinking outside the Bell Inn when suddenly he heard the cry of "Prentices and Clubs!" This, he knew well, was the labourers' traditional call to arms and, sure enough, clubs and weapons came out as apprentice boys, watermen and other labourers streamed in from the side streets and surged towards Cheapside.

Monoux gathered his thoughts for a moment and turned to his youngest servant, a boy of seventeen years. "Tom, since you are fleet of foot I want you to follow the mob and report back to me here outside the Bell. I must remain and discharge my duties within the ward. Take care to avoid trouble. I will see you within the half-hour."

Monoux retraced his steps along Fish Street Hill but soon realised that all the troublemakers were heading north, leaving him little to do but watch them pass by.

When Tom returned to the inn he was shaken and breathless. "The prentices have broken into Newgate and freed the prisoners. The foreigners living in St Martins Le Grand threw bricks, stones and boiling water over them, causing further rage. The mob's blood is up and they are coming back this way. Foreigners are being attacked and they say, Master, that eminent persons will now be their targets."

Monoux looked apprehensively up the street. He could hear the yelling of the mob getting closer and the sound of shops being smashed and broken into. Realising that he was powerless in the face of a general uprising and knowing full well what the rioters were capable of, he overcame his inclination to confront the troublemakers.

"Very well Tom, I will return to my house for the present. But I would ask you to again follow the path of the demented rabble and let me know what they do."

Back at his nearby mansion, Monoux bolted all the doors for his own safety and took comfort from the fact that his wife and children were staying in the country. His servants were instructed to look out for Tom and let the boy in on his return. He himself would retire to bed and receive reports of the evening's events next morning.

He slept badly that night, disturbed by what sounded like several thunder claps. He rose late and, to his great alarm, found that Tom had not come back. But before he could organise a search party, there was a loud rapping at the door. The caller was a messenger from the Guildhall who quickly explained his unexpected presence:

"I have been instructed to inform all Aldermen how things stand after last night's uprising. The rioters broke shop fronts along Cheapside and Cornhill before moving on to Leadenhall. Here they broke into the shops of foreign shoemakers, carrying away stock and hurling the rest into the street."

"So has the mob now been quelled?" Monoux asked.

"Yes," was the reply. "The streets are now quiet but this is because the forces of the Crown have taken charge. In the early hours the Lieutenant of the Tower of London was ordered to fire ordinance into the heart of the City to signal the intervention that was to come. Before daylight the Duke of Norfolk's men rode in to arrest the chief culprits and the entire city is now under direct military control. Royal troops are patrolling the streets and scolding any citizen who dares to show their face. The mayor has called a special meeting of Aldermen on the morrow but, for today, everyone is advised to keep off the streets and stay indoors."

Monoux thanked the messenger and pressed some coins into his hands as he left. Pacing up and down his library he turned matters over in his mind. He had a special responsibility for young Tom whom he had sent into harm's way. As former Lord Mayor he would hold sway over the soldiery that had been positioned around the town and he could surely ask for – and expect to receive – their assistance in helping to find his servant.

He made up his mind. He would venture out wearing his Alderman's gown and accompanied by one attendant.

He had never known London so empty and quiet. But walking up Wallbrook towards Cheapside he observed men at arms stationed outside broken shop fronts. One of them shouted out "Go home!" and another yelled "Coxcomb!" as he passed. When he turned into Cheapside he was greeted with the sound of hammering and sawing. Carpenters and labourers were at work and he asked one of them what was going on:

"Sir, by the King's command we are setting up gallows all along the route that the rioters followed last night. They will be hanged on the very streets they desecrated. See, the miserable culprits are coming now!"

Monoux looked up and saw at the far end of the street a great crowd of prisoners being driven like cattle. As they approached he saw that the entire company of a hundred or more were bound by ropes and flanked by men-at-arms. He stood back while they shuffled past, heads down. Suddenly he caught a glimpse of Tom, looking bewildered among the throng of captives. Assuming his customary air of authority Monoux accosted the guard nearest to him:

"My good man, you have there my servant who is innocent of any wrongdoing and was on the streets last evening at my request. As the former mayor of this great city I will be obliged if you would release this boy to me as justice requires."

The guard gave Monoux a disdainful look as he replied: "Sir, the King's men are in charge here now. It is not your justices, aldermen or serjeants who command but rather the King and his Council. So make way and let us fulfil His Highness's pleasure which is to bring these wretched people to summary trial and thereafter to execution."

Monoux was reduced to silent impotence. The reality of the situation dawned on him: the City authorities, having lost control over London's streets, had ceded power to the Crown and its agents. A once unchallenged leader of this town he had become a mere bystander, unable to protect a boy who had courted danger out of loyalty to his master.

Events were moving fast. Returning home, he found there was a message from the Guildhall. All those charged with upholding law and order in the City – mayor, aldermen and sheriffs – were summoned to appear at Westminster Hall where the King was to preside over a great assembly, with his Chancellor, Wolsey, in attendance.

The next day Monoux stepped off the Lord Mayor's barge at Westminster Stairs and, together with his fellow aldermen, processed into Westminster Hall which was especially appointed for the occasion. He sat next to the Lord Mayor on scaffolding erected along one side of the Hall, the lords of the realm sitting above them. The King was enthroned under his canopy of state on a raised platform at the end, attended by Queen Catherine, Cardinal Wolsey and councillors. A large crowd of onlookers packed the body of the Hall and spilled out into the street. Monoux, to his utmost distaste, was conscious of the contamination of the air caused by the press of bodies, an odour which became even more perceptible when the crowd inside made way for scores of ragged prisoners bound with ropes and wearing halters around their necks in preparation for hanging.

Monoux turned to the Mayor. "There is my poor servant boy I spoke of," and he pointed to a trembling youth with a terrified expression at the front of the group of captives. "Let us hope His Highness is merciful," the Mayor replied. "You may have heard that a dozen of the chief culprits have already suffered a traitor's death. These are the more fortunate ones."

Wolsey gave an opening address, first admonishing the rioters and then reproaching the Mayor and Aldermen for their negligence for allowing the rioting to occur. Monoux observed that the Cardinal was clasping an orange in one hand which he held to his nose from time to time, no doubt a confection to shield him against the pestilential air. At the end of his homily Wolsey turned to the King and beseeched him to grant a royal pardon to the prisoners. Queen Catherine, kneeling before the throne, made a further plea for leniency but Henry merely stared ahead. After conferring briefly with the King, Wolsey turned to the assembly. "It is His Highness's decision that the offenders be hanged." At this a cry went up from the captives. "Mercy! Mercy!" and Monoux, looking down, could see that young Tom was in tears.

In a final gesture Wolsey knelt before the King and said he would pledge himself for the good behaviour of the prisoners. Henry looked impassively on as the Cardinal stood up and proclaimed that the King had seen fit to give a pardon. Pandemonium followed as the hall erupted into cheers, the prisoners threw off their halters and friends surged around them.

Monoux wiped a tear from his eye. The most important thing for him was that Tom was safe. But he also wondered at the masterly display of royal power he had witnessed – the King first instilling great fear and then exhibiting graciousness. The whole proceeding had been carefully crafted to curb rebellious spirits and stamp the King's authority on the capricious citizenry of London.

Returning down river on the Lord Mayor's barge Monoux noticed that over London Bridge kites and carrion crows were circling in large numbers. They were no doubt attracted by the freshly decapitated heads of the riot leaders now impaled on pikes above Southwark Gatehouse.

―――――――――

On the day of the riot Bishop Fitzjames was resident at his palace in St Paul's. He had tiresome duties to perform over the Easter period that kept him in London but he was also carefully planning his forthcoming showdown with George Monoux. He had decided to take his opponent unawares by inviting him down to Fulham to see his newly planted gardens in all their spring glory. Late May would be ideal and an invitation would shortly be despatched. He would have to make careful preparations for what he expected to be a very difficult encounter with the former Lord Mayor, a man renowned for having a high opinion of himself. In order to underline the wealth and status of his office he would borrow servants from the residentiary canons and his own London palace; he would order a sumptuous lunch and the very best Gascony wines; and he intended to place a placard emblazoned with his own coat of arms, depicting crossed swords, against the fireplace in the dining hall. He would also choose a suitable moment to remind his guest that Queen Catherine had stayed at the palace after Prince Arthur's tragic death. Once caught in his web, the bishop would entice his guest with warm hospitality and ingratiating conversation. Then, when he had drawn him out and exposed his iniquity, he would strike.

It was while entertaining such thoughts in his study on May Day eve that the bishop was suddenly made aware of tumultuous events outside. Several hundred apprentices had gathered in St Paul's churchyard shouting and brandishing clubs and sticks. The rabble surged towards Cheapside and it was not long before the sounds of breaking shop fronts a few streets away could be heard within the cathedral close. The bishop slept fitfully that night and was woken first by the sound of cannon fire from the direction of the Tower and later by the sound of horses' hooves on the roads around St Paul's.

When Fitzjames learned about the events of the preceding night from one of his servants, he was resigned. He had for some time taken the view that the decline of true religion would lead to decay of the social order and the uprising had proved him right. What was particularly worrying to him as Bishop of London was that a few clerks in holy orders were reported to have been among the rioters, meaning that the pernicious teaching of reformers was undermining the Church from within. He would have to investigate the priesthood in his diocese to ensure that corrupted clergy were removed from their office. In the meantime he intended to pursue his campaign against Lollards whose attacks on the Church leadership had undoubtedly contributed to the breakdown of law and order. After all, if civic authority were so weakened that a Lord Mayor could lend his support to a proven heretic, it was no surprise that humbler men had lost their bearings

———————

Across the close, John Colet had also witnessed the previous night's extraordinary events from his deanery. He had been sitting in his study looking onto the cathedral, reflecting on the direction the Church was taking now that Cardinal Wolsey was at the helm. He recalled the sermon he had preached at the Cardinal's installation in the Abbey. His subject was humility and he had reminded his audience that cardinals came not to be ministered unto but to minister and he had cited the biblical text *Whosoever shall exalt himself shall be abased, and he that shall humble himself shall be exalted.*

But Wolsey had not humbled himself. As Lord Chancellor he had introduced new laws regulating the nation's apparel and diet in accordance with a person's station in life. Burgesses had to wear homespun, but the clergy were encouraged to appear publicly in silk and velvet. Three dishes a meal was the dietary limit imposed on ordinary gentlemen, six on lords of Parliament, Lord Mayors or knights of the garter but nine was the statutory number of dishes he allowed himself – a benefit he enjoyed wherever he went since the dietary rule was determined by the rank of the most distinguished guest.

It was reported that Wolsey was spending 200,000 gold crowns building Hampton Court Palace to show that he could live as graciously as any cardinal in Rome and it was common knowledge that he was extending and refurbishing York Place in Westminster to rival Lambeth Palace's claim to be the greatest house in London. Colet was appalled at the scale of this clerical ostentation and when he learned about that night's rioting he blamed the behaviour of the lower orders on the gross excesses of their supposed superiors. It was the flaunting of wealth, he was convinced, that had created the resentment and rebellious mood among the poor.

A few days after the riots, his old friend, Sir Thomas More, had found time within his busy official schedule to visit the deanery. The two men discussed the disturbances and had some difference of view. More adopted a robust approach to the rioters. "The poor must be cherished but when they become unruly they must be put down."

When Colet questioned whether charges of treason should have been brought against the riot leaders, More had his answer ready. "Under our statutes, anyone who attacks persons such as aliens who enjoy the King's safe conduct, are traitors. It is therefore proper that, when convicted, they, in common with heretics, suffer the most extreme penalty."

More and Colet parted on amicable terms, but Colet noted that his good friend's views had become a little harsher since becoming a royal counsellor.

———

Anne was in her house in Eastcheap with her daughter on the evening of the riots. She was turning over in her mind how justice could be delivered to Charles Joseph. First she would have to discover his whereabouts – no easy matter if he was lying low. Besides that she would need an accomplice and the question was whom could she rely on. It was while wrestling with this problem that she was alerted to the distant noise of shouting and banging towards Cornhill. She opened her door and as she did so a crouched figure came stumbling towards her. Her immediate reaction was one of fear but then she saw that the contorted shape was that of a man, his head covered in blood. When he looked up and saw Anne, he called out to her in a thick foreign accent. "Madam, I beseech you give me help and the protection of your house. I have been attacked by a mob because I am a foreigner."

In the gathering gloom Anne could see shadowy figures lurking under the overhang of houses further up the street and without further thought for her own safety pulled the injured man into her front room. She told Margaret to bring water from the tub and began to examine the man's injuries. Removing his bloodied flat cap she found he had several cuts to the head and appeared to have lost a considerable amount of blood. He was also passing in and out of consciousness and groaning. Anne bathed the wounds by candlelight, applied yarrow and then forced some ale between the man's lips and placed him on a mattress.

Before leading Margaret upstairs to their bedroom Anne took a closer look at the man she had so boldly let into her house. He was possibly in his mid-thirties, tall, clean-shaven and flaxen haired. His clothing suggested considerable wealth: he wore a dark tunic and a black surcoat, under which could be seen scarlet sleeves of silk; his hose and shoes were of the best quality and he wore a richly bejewelled ring – a lustrous ruby encircled by diamonds.

Anne was expecting Rebecca to call early the next morning and there would be some explaining to be done.

21

A German visitor

When Anne came down at daybreak the next morning her overnight visitor was already stirring. Clearly much recovered, he hastened to introduce himself: "Madam, I am Hermann Wedig, a Hanseatic trader from the Rhineland. Much of my work is here in London at the Steelyard on the river front. I am deeply grateful to you for giving me the protection of your house." Anne noted his German accent but the English could not be faulted.

"It was a small thing to do. But tell me, how did you come to be so viciously assaulted?"

"Last evening I was visiting a banker in Lombard Street when, coming out of his house, I saw a crowd of young men coming towards me. One of them shouted out, 'Kill the foreigner!' When they came after me I ran down Gracechurch Street but some caught up with me and assailed me with clubs. I managed to escape their clutches and turned into Eastcheap which is how I find myself here."

At this moment there was a knock on the door and Rebecca appeared in an agitated state. After Anne had explained as best she could how she came to be harbouring a handsome German merchant, Rebecca was impatient to tell her story. "Anne, you cannot imagine! Many more than a thousand were gathered just two streets north of Carter Lane! They say the shop fronts are broken into along Cheapside, Cornhill and Leadenhall and the stock either taken or destroyed. Thankfully our haberdashery is spared! These people are no more than thieves though they claim all manner of grievances. You must have heard the guns firing from the Tower in the night and now the streets are full of soldiers. To avoid them I had to come here by a back way, through Old Fish Street and St Swithin's Lane."

Hermann offered his own opinion on the outbreak of lawlessness. "The danger has been building for some weeks. There were some isolated attacks on foreigners before last night and I hear from my English friends that a few influential men, among them priests, were telling the poor that we traders were taking bread from their mouths. Also, of course, these young men were full of drink as I well know from having their breath in my face."

Anne kept her thoughts to herself. She believed that the poorer classes would only behave in this way if they felt that no one listened to them. Rebecca had said that women were among the rioters and this did not surprise her. After all, women as mothers and housekeepers suffered most from poverty and yet had no voice at all.

Wedig said he thought he should be getting back to the Steelyard where he would be missed but Anne and Rebecca insisted that he stay and have something to eat with them before he returned. Anne called out to Margaret who was dressing up a little figurine to show to Sarah: "Dearest, bring some ale to the table and also the bread and whatever cheese is there."

When they were sitting round the table, Rebecca showed her curiosity about the visitor. "So, tell me, Herr Wedig, what happens behind those great walls of the Steelyard that I see when I walk down Thames Street?"

"Ah, we are like a separate realm governed by our own rules. We have within the enclosure our own guildhall where we meet to discuss matters of common concern. We elect an alderman each year to represent us in the City. We have our own kitchen for banquets, our own garden with vines and fruit trees and a treasury where we keep our valuables. You might say that we are a city within a city."

Rebecca's husband had told her that the Hansa had secured special trading privileges but she had not realised how entirely separate this community of merchants had become. "You make it sound like a place to spend holy days but what about the work that goes on there?"

"Madam, you are right to correct me. The Steelyard is above all a place of work. From the river you may have seen that we have cranes mounted along the quay where our ships unload."

Anne broke the bread. "And what goods are taken off there?"

"We import not only merchandise from the Rhineland – wines, furs, metals, smoked fish, grain and hemp – but also items from more distant countries, especially dates and spices. I myself import for the most part Rhenish wine but also other articles as the occasion suits. I should also add that we have built great warehouses along the quay which are rented to all the German merchants in London."

Anne poured the ale into pewter tankards. "And where do the Hansa worship? Is there a church within the enclosure?"

"Madam, we have only a chapel within the Steelyard. This is not big enough for the needs of our community and so many of us worship at All-Hallows-the-Great in Upper Thames Street – a fine church with pleasant cloisters."

Anne was conscious that she and Rebecca were unfairly interrogating their visitor who had, after all, been severely bludgeoned the night before. But seldom did they have the opportunity to speak to foreigners, least of all men of distinction such as Hermann Wedig. "And perhaps you do not mind me asking what Bible worshippers use in your country. Would this be the same Latin Vulgate that our own priests read from?"

Up to this point the German merchant had been merely courteous in answering the two women's questions. But he now showed a keener interest in the subject. "Certainly our churches employ the same Latin Vulgate as that used by the priest at All-Hallows-The-Great. But for some fifty years we have had a German Bible – that is a translation from the Vulgate into German – which is printed in Strasbourg. This Bible has been reprinted many times and is read quite commonly by the faithful."

"But surely," Anne said, "the Church authorities in Germany prohibit the German Bible just as here they prohibit the English Bible."

"No, it is different for us. The Church does try to discourage the use of the Bible translated into German. But its leaders turn a blind eye. They fear that any attempt to do otherwise would cause great discontent among their flock. The result is that people who can afford it are generally able to buy and read the Bible in their own tongue."

Anne did not disguise her astonishment at this information. But she was not yet willing to confide in a man she had only just met. So nothing was said about the scriptorium in Coleman Street that laboured to produce two or three Bibles each year and where the scribes were daily risking their lives. Nor did she voice what was on her mind: that access to the printing press would transform the English market in prohibited religious books.

Hermann Wedig got up from the table. "Ladies, I have taken up too much of your time. I am sure you have work to do and so have I. However, I have a proposal. I shall be departing shortly for Bishop's Lynn in Norfolk where the Hansa do business and after that I shall be sailing for Antwerp. Before I leave London

I would like to entertain you both at the Steelyard Tavern by Cosin Lane where we can dine in some comfort. What do you say?"

Anne and Rebecca looked at one another. Anne was about to speak when Rebecca interjected quickly, "That is a most generous offer Herr Wedig. But I have family commitments that would make it impossible for me. Anne, on the other hand, is free of such duties and perhaps would welcome a visit to the Steelyard."

"I quite understand," said Wedig, "but I would be honoured if you Mistress Anne would dine with me two days hence. I can come here first to accompany you."

Anne was embarrassed at her cousin's impetuous response on her behalf. "I may not have many family commitments but my daughter Margaret is not to be discounted lightly and I am also engaged in regular work. Besides, we must be sure that the streets are safe once more. But of course your offer is most appreciated. If I may I will let you know how matters stand tomorrow by leaving a note addressed to you at the Steelyard. It is no distance for me."

When the door closed Rebecca gave Anne an artful look, but Anne took no notice. She was thoughtful for a minute. "Rebecca, I think I may take up Herr Wedig's offer. I would like to learn about the Hansa merchants and, of course, the form of worship among Rhinelanders. I will tell them at the scriptorium not to expect me and perhaps you would be kind enough to have Margaret as usual."

The next morning Anne walked down towards the Steelyard. The streets were quieter than usual and there were soldiers posted at crossroads. She had heard rumours that suspects were being rounded up and that savage retribution would follow. At the main gateway into the Steelyard, which during the riots had been protected by a great portcullis, there was an official door keeper. Anne asked if he could take a note to Herr Wedig and, after looking her up and down curiously, he readily agreed.

Once back at Eastcheap, Anne mused that she need not make a special effort to present herself to her best advantage. It would be absurd for her, an avowed widow, to dress up for a passing stranger. But then she did not want to be the cause of embarrassment at this man's tavern so she decided after all to take some pains to appear at her best. She would look out her finest kirtle and overgown and wear a simple linen coif on her head.

The Steelyard Tavern was a cut above the run of London's ale houses. Set beside gardens and provisioned with the best Rhenish wine and imported luxury foods it attracted not only well-to-do merchants but also diplomats and even courtiers. Anne and her companion were seated in a quiet corner by a window looking on to the garden. When the wine arrived in an earthenware jug Hermann poured it into two goblets and asked Anne how she liked it. "I am not accustomed to drinking wine but I find the sweetness and fruitiness pleasing."

Hermann gave a grin of satisfaction. "It is just as well. I myself import this wine which is stored in casks here at the Steelyard. Of course, we do not compare with the biggest wine importers from Gascony. They unload and store their wares at the Vintry wharf just up river from here."

Plates of food appeared: smoked fish, sturgeon and a selection of meats, all garnished with exotic spices. Anne asked about the curious sign she had observed hanging outside the tavern, which looked to her like a gallows surmounted by a bunch of golden grapes.

"Ah yes, many are puzzled by this motif. The steelyard is a specially designed balance hung from a beam which is used to weigh heavy merchandise. The balance has given its name to our trading settlements in Hansa towns and is depicted on inn signs not only here but in those places too." Anne was struck by the pride of these German merchants and the careful ordering of their business. Hermann was looking at Anne with a warm smile. "I have answered some of your points but without wishing to cause offence tell me, how does a woman of your standing and intelligence come to be living on her own in a small house in Eastcheap?"

Part of Anne was affronted by the directness of this question but the wine was having an effect and the questioner sounded sincere rather than merely inquisitive. She began defensively. "I am happy in my house which is more than sufficient for the needs of myself and my daughter. However, it is true that I lived in much greater comfort near London Bridge when my dear departed husband was alive."

Having touched on her widowhood it seemed impossible not to go on. Aided by the wine and occasional prompting from her companion, Anne revealed the story of Richard Hunne and his supposed heresy. When she had told her story Hermann looked grave and placed his hand on her arm. "My dear Anne, we live in difficult times. In my part of the world there is less persecution of religious dissent but I have to say that things are stirring. There are those who seek to reform the Church from within but there are many others – among whom I count myself – who believe that the Church leadership has become so distanced from the faithful that nothing less than a new start is required."

Anne felt that she had already revealed too much about herself and decided to say nothing about her work in the scriptorium – especially as it might risk the lives of others. She was, however, curious to know more about her friend's personal circumstances.

"So when you have been to Antwerp, do you return home to your family in the Rhineland?" she asked.

"I will visit the Rhineland certainly, but my wife died in childbirth three years ago and my two daughters live with my sister. I have a house in Cologne where I do a lot of my business but I would not call it a home."

"I am sorry to hear that," Anne replied. But she could not help thinking that a Hansa merchant's life would go on much as before when his wife died, considering his travels and long spells in foreign steelyards. She wondered whether a man could truly love someone whom he saw only on short visits between voyages. But then she looked at her dining companion and imagined that a woman might well love such a man even if he was seldom at home.

As the tables were being cleared Anne said it was time for her to go because she had to collect Margaret from Carter Lane. She thanked her host and said how much she had enjoyed their talk. Hermann insisted on accompanying her and, as they walked up Thames Street he said he would like to keep in touch. "I shall be returning to London after my travels towards the end of this year. I will write to you at the Steelyard and they will have instructions to bring the letter to you. In the meantime, take care of yourself and please invite no more strangers into your house at night. It is a dangerous practice."

They laughed, and when they reached Rebecca's house he left her. Before entering she watched his tall figure disappearing down the street. After he was out of sight she stood there thoughtfully for a minute before turning her back and closing the door.

22

CROSSED SWORDS

GEORGE MONOUX WAS SURPRISED TO RECEIVE AN invitation to dine with Bishop Fitzjames at Fulham Palace. As a leading spokesman for the City, the former Lord Mayor was known to be an active supporter of the anti-clerical movement during the last Parliament. It was he who had ordered an immediate investigation of Hunne's death in Lollards' Tower – a dreadful affair that had poisoned his relations with the prelate. He surmised that the old war horse was anxious to mend fences but he was a little suspicious. The bishop was an uncompromising man whose recent public pronouncements suggested little desire for an improved understanding between mitre and mayoralty. Also, dining in Fulham and awaiting the tides would mean taking a whole day out of his busy schedule.

Despite his reservations, Monoux graciously accepted the invitation. After all, the bishop wanted to show him his garden and, as the owner of a grand estate in Walthamstow, he himself had an interest in things horticultural. Besides, he might want some favours from the Church: his wife had expressed a desire to have the sacrament administered to her in the oratory at their country house. And for this he would need to obtain a special licence.

When Monoux alighted from his wherry at Fulham Palace stairs, he was mildly surprised to be met not only by the bishop but also a large retinue of his staff. Fitzjames greeted his guest warmly and after some brief formalities the two men took a walk in the grounds. They were accompanied by the bishop's head gardener who pointed out recent plantings of roses and marigolds laid out around a central fountain. They moved on to the herb garden, then the vegetable garden and ended their tour by strolling along the bishop's overarched walkways. It was while they were returning to the house that the bishop commented on Fulham Palace's royal connections. "You may know that the present Queen stayed some time at the palace after the death of Prince Arthur. I believe she is very attached to these gardens although there have, of course, been great improvements since she was here."

Monoux acknowledged that a garden laid out beside a flowing river was a delight. "I myself have constructed a moat around my house, Moones, in Essex and the River Lea runs close by. However, too much water can be a problem. The roadway is impassable when the meadows are flooded. I am therefore building a causeway over Walthamstow Marsh for the benefit not only of myself but other travellers."

Conversation between the property owning magnates continued along pleasant and inconsequential lines before dinner. The two men then sat down at a great oak table, big enough to accommodate twenty guests. After their goblets had been filled by the butler, Monoux, himself a wine importer, noted with approval the quality of the Bordeaux. "My Lord Bishop, I must congratulate you on your cellar. The wine complements the meat as well as any I have tasted in Drapers Hall."

The bishop responded that good wine was essential to ease the burdens of high office. He then motioned to his servants to leave the room and turned to more serious matters. "Now tell me, what do you think of the riot and the punishment administered to the culprits? I was there in St Paul's when they were gathering and a fearful spectacle it was."

Monoux put down his goblet and wiped his mouth. "The mob is an ever present danger to the City's prosperity. When the passions of the humblest sort are unleashed there is no limit to the havoc they may wreak. We aldermen had a council meeting on that fateful evening and I was of the view that to deal with the threat the soldiery should be brought in without delay. Our serjeants cannot contain a riot as was painfully proven. When the people's blood is up the troops must be used to strike down the chief troublemakers so as to leave the monster headless."

The bishop nodded in approval as he picked at the platter of choice meats before him. "I believe those who commit such felonies are like heretics. They break the rules of the civic order just as heretics break the rules of the spiritual order. Felons should be hung and unrepentant heretics burned. That is the way to uphold temporal and spiritual regularity in these troubled times."

Up to this point the two men had found common ground in their conversation but at the mentioned of heretics Monoux froze. The bishop surely knew that he disapproved in the strongest terms of the relentless persecution of men and women whom he considered harmless. "My Lord Bishop, on this point I must disagree. Many good citizens live in fear of heresy proceedings which are not conducted in accordance with the strict requirements of secular law. It seems that any man or women may be traduced by ill-disposed neighbours or a false summoner. And when the Church pronounces judgement on the putrefying corpse of a respected freeman of this City it brings ignominy on itself and its officers."

The bishop appeared to have braced himself for this moment. Monoux suspected that he wanted to draw him out so that he might condemn himself from his own mouth.

Fitzjames leaned forwards and wagged a knobbly finger at his guest. "Sir, what you have said is a great insult to our noble Church. And since you object so strongly to the condemnation of Hunne's heresy what is your opinion of the man's possession and reading of the Wycliffe Bible?"

Monoux now realised that he was getting into a fight and he was not going to yield any ground. "What a man does in his own house or among a few friends by way of Bible reading is not, in my opinion, a matter for ecclesiastical courts and summoners' investigations – still less for the cruel sentence of death."

The bishop seemed to be emboldened by this rejoinder which Monoux himself was aware came very close to expressing support for heretical practices. "Your refusal to denounce Richard Hunne is of some interest to us. Because we have information from your agent in a statement made before two witnesses, that it was you yourself who provided support to Hunne. We understand you went so far as to transfer money to his attorney in the praemunire suit against our church officers who were justly fulfilling their judicial duties. What do you have to say to this?"

Monoux felt like picking the bishop up and rattling his bony frame. "So you have terrified my agent into revealing confidences. Well let me give you a solemn warning that you are here stepping into waters much deeper than you suppose. I advise you to leave all this alone or you will heap troubles on yourself and your office."

The bishop evidently felt that he had scored heavily against his opponent and Monoux could see he was now going for the kill. He dismissed the threats with a wave of his hand. "I have to tell you, sir, that your actions in abetting a proven heretic and also this heretic's treacherous suit against the authority of the Church, makes you an inciter and promoter of heresy. For that you may be charged with the very same offence."

George Monoux leaned forwards and placed his elbows on the table. He allowed some moments to elapse in order to collect himself and then proceeded in more measured language. "My Lord Bishop, you have placed me in a position where I shall have to tell you more than I should and more than you need to know. But let me say first that my interest in Richard Hunne arises from several considerations. He was a near neighbour of mine in Bridge Ward, he was a fellow cloth merchant known for honest dealing and he upheld the highest principles of the Guild of Merchant Taylors of which he was a liveryman. In short, he was a valued citizen of this great city which I was privileged to serve as Mayor. Therefore the circumstances of his death were of direct concern to me ..."

The bishop intervened with an impatient gesture. "None of this has to do with the charge of heresy! A man may be liked but if he espouses heretical views he must suffer the consequences. Those who have his interests at heart should prevent him from straying. But once he has strayed his friends must stand aside."

Monoux dismissed his adversary's point with a sweep of his arm. "Hunne's religious views are not of the smallest interest to me. I personally adhere to the Catholic faith in all its particulars. I believe in the miracle of the Eucharist, the communion of saints, the use of the Latin Bible, the importance of confession and the redemptive power of good works. It may interest you to know that I have been restoring at my own expense St Mary's Church in Walthamstow where I am also building alms houses and planning to endow a school after the manner of St Paul's. A charge of heresy against me would make the bishop a fool and the Church a laughing stock. More strictly, if you try to lay hands on me, the riots we have witnessed would be as nothing compared to the fury that would be unleashed against the Church."

"Then why", demanded the bishop in a clipped voice, "did you incite Hunne's praemunire?"

"From my own standpoint, Hunne was pursuing a just cause. He had made a very fine Christening gown for his deceased boy – a gown valued I think at the considerable sum of nearly seven shillings. The priest was demanding this item for a burial service. Now I am a man of business and I ask myself whether it is just or proper for a man of God to demand for an hour or two's work a sum which many honest men would be pleased to earn over many weeks. But these are merely my personal views and they are of no account."

Monoux looked the bishop in the eye before making the devastating revelation he had been building up to. "The reason I supported Hunne's praemunire is that I was requested to do so by the Attorney General, Sir John Ernley, who, as you are aware, is one of his Highness's most intimate counsellors. You can surmise as well as I where this instruction came from and you may also easily guess the reasons behind it. After all, the over-weaning power of the ecclesiastical courts is a cause of disquiet at the highest level of the realm."

Bishop Fitzjames was reduced to an uncharacteristic silence. But Monoux had not finished with him. In the absence of the butler he helped himself to more wine: "I must congratulate your Lordship on the size of your retinue, the magnificence of your palace and the beauty of your gardens. But I would remind you that the wealth of the Church is obtained at the expense of our citizenry who are daily subject to spiritual dues, tithes, probate fees and other exactions which are not easily born by poor honest craftsmen and labourers."

Monoux took a final swig of wine and got up to leave. As he reached the door he turned round. "My Lord Bishop, I have been admiring your coat of arms on the placard by the fireplace but the thought presented itself to me that perhaps a dove would be more fitting as an emblem than crossed swords for one of Christ's representatives on earth."

As he was being rowed down river Monoux began to calm down. He would much rather have kept to himself the circumstances of his support for Hunne but he had been left with no choice. The malignant old bishop would in any event not dare to take matters further with the King or his council. Such an intervention could only result in an open breach between Church and State. Furthermore the bishop was already in a weak position with the King due to his shrill advocacy of clerical privileges in the last Parliament. But it was just as well that Fitzjames did not know that he was supporting Hunne's widow from his own pocket by means of his niece, an almoner, at the convent of St Helen's.

———————

Back at Fulham Palace, Bishop Fitzjames was left in a state of impotent fury. For some minutes after Monoux's departure he sat frozen at his table, contemplating the gravity of what he had just heard. Was it really conceivable that his own sovereign had moved covertly to undermine the Church's judicial powers?

But then he recalled the experience of his old friend, Bishop Nykke of Norwich, who in the previous reign had been plagued by praemunire suits against his chancellor and other officers of his consistory court. The man Nykke held responsible for promoting these proceedings was none other than James Hobart, Attorney General under Henry VII. Could the King be secretly harassing Church courts through praemunire writs as his father had done before him? He shuddered to think what might happen if Henry himself should decide to wield such a terrible weapon in open warfare against his bishops.

A WINCHESTER GOOSE

ONCE THE HANSA MERCHANT HAD DEPARTED, ANNE determined to fulfil her vow to avenge her husband. There was no doubt in her mind that God had countenanced this as a just act: *Whosoever sheds man's blood, by man his blood shall be shed, for in the image of God has God made man.*

Her mission was to track down Charles Joseph and ensure that he paid with his life for the crime he had committed in Lollards' Tower. She must find out where he was hiding and she would need an accomplice to do the deed. The question was: who could be relied upon to assist in such a project without danger of betrayal?

The thought struck her that Peter, the scribe at her scriptorium, could be the man. He was young and robust and a true Lollard for whom Hunne was a revered martyr. To deliver justice to Hunne's killer would surely be considered an honour, especially as he had read the gory details in the coroner's verdict.

Anne thought it best to talk matters over away from the scriptorium, so she persuaded Peter to walk across to the parish church of St Stephen's just off Coleman Street. There, in the privacy of a side chapel, she revealed her intentions to him and asked for his help in the task she had set herself. Peter was thoughtful for some time before giving her his answer: "Anne,

I am willing to do this – not as a favour to yourself, worthy though that would be, but because your husband's death should not go unpunished. Our cause is simply that of administering the justice that was demanded by the coroner's jury but denied by the King's court. Besides, I have no family to fear for and my work as a supposed heretic scribe already invites each day the summoner's knock on the door."

Anne clasped his hand. "We must first discover where the rogue is living. Perhaps it will be easier for you than for me to make enquiries at the Bell in Shoreditch where he used to drink."

The initial plan of action was agreed. And it was only a few days later that Peter brought news. He spoke in hushed tones in the sepulchral gloom of St Stephen's church. "Joseph has taken flight to Southwark. He told his friends that he intended to set himself up as a fulltime pimp and brothel keeper. He is using an assumed name, but what that name is and where precisely he is conducting his new business no one could say."

Anne envisioned that nether world just across the river. "Then we will have to explore the Southwark stew houses around Bankside and talk to the whores in the hope of identifying Joseph."

"I agree," Peter said. "But we must take care not to alert him when making our enquiries."

On a warm summer's evening, Anne and Peter took a wherry across the river from Blackfriars Stairs to Bankside. The waterman warned that he could not bring them back after dark when all boats were required to be moored on the London side of the river. When Anne enquired the reason, he explained that the regulation was designed to stop undesirables entering

London by night when the gates of London Bridge were closed. This way the City was protected from Southwark's criminal underworld during the dark hours.

As they approached the south side of the river Anne could see more clearly the row of stew houses along Bankside. Their Thames frontages were whitewashed and painted on the walls were the names and motifs of the various establishments: The Boars Head, The Cross Keys, The Castle, The Crane, The Bell – the total numbering over a dozen. The colourful display was obviously intended to catch the eye of potential customers crossing from the City for, as the waterman pointed out, the stews were not permitted to interfere with river traffic by affixing projecting tavern signs.

Stepping off the boat at Bankside Anne and Peter arranged with the waterman to be returned to Blackfriars shortly before nine o'clock when the river curfew would come into force. They walked up from the little pier and along the Bankside road, flanked by a low wall beside the river and a row of stew houses on the landward side. Women were standing by doorways while men of all ages and descriptions strolled leisurely along the street eyeing the young – and not so young – flesh that was on offer. Anne suggested that they go to a neighbouring tavern to find out about the pimps and bawds who ran the brothels. It was a matter for wry amusement to them both that the tavern they found themselves in was The Cardinals Hat. "In these parts, south of the river," Peter remarked, "the Cardinal's Hat signifies the extremity of the male organ. The painted sign shows the resemblance." But Anne pretended not to hear.

Among the throng of drinkers there was an older woman on her own. Ordering ale for himself and Anne, Peter offered to buy the woman a drink which she gratefully accepted. They engaged her in conversation and it turned out that she was an old hand in these parts. She had had some education in a convent but then served her time in local brothels before becoming a "trot" or procuress.

"It's a drear life," she said, "but once you are in there is no way out – except by the common burial pit, for the likes of us cannot be placed in consecrated ground. Those who are diseased or are with child are put out of the stews and reduced to working the streets or begging. After a few years of this life girls become ill and die before their time."

Anne asked about the ownership of the stew houses. The woman prattled on: "In times past the Bishop of Winchester, besides having his great palace, owned most of the property here. But the ownership is now in the hands of men living in fine houses on Long Southwark who have grown rich from the work of us poor women. Indeed, it was not so many years ago that the Mayor of London himself owned stews, which he farmed out to a Dutchman."

Anne was curious to know why the women in the stews were called Winchester Geese. "As I say, in times past the bishop let out the houses to bawds. Even now the stews fall within his rule. Truly, therefore, we are all his geese. And if we transgress we are taken to his Court Leet and the fines exacted from us go directly into the bishop's coffer. For that reason his steward would rather impose fines than have us put in the Clink."

They ordered more ale before Anne asked the question that had been on her mind all along. "And who are the stew-holders at the present? Have most of these men been in place for some time or have there been new leaseholders?"

The woman gave a hoarse laugh. "You ask about men. But the bawds who have taken the leases here as stew-holders are in nearly every case women. I believe there are only two men who live as bawds in Bankside – and one of them has taken his lease only these past few months."

This was proving a most productive chance encounter. Anne shrugged. "Well, I suppose, as with all kinds of business, people come and people go. Yet I imagine that a woman is better able to look after both the girls and their rakes than a man. Tell me, which stew house has this last adventurer taken his chance on?"

"It is The Castle, just by Maiden Lane. I do not know the gentleman concerned – my business is with The Boars Head and The Crane – but I understand he is looking for women to rent his rooms."

Anne and Peter, having obtained the information they needed, thanked the woman, gave her money for another drink and left. Once outside Peter looked encouragingly at Anne. "We have our man. Let us take a close look at The Castle from the river side."

They walked once more beside the stew houses along Bankside until they came to The Castle – a detached building abutting the road with gardens at the back. A girl lolled against the door eyeing the passing men. Peter turned suddenly to Anne. "I have a proposal. I shall approach the drab and go inside with her so that we may discover more about Joseph and in which part of the house he resides. You stay here and I will return within the half-hour."

Anne had strong misgivings. For one thing they were due to be picked up by the waterman in half an hour. She wondered too what Peter might get up to in a stew house with a comely girl. But most of all she worried that a woman on her own in Bankside invited approaches from the prowling rakes. "Very well, Peter," she said at last. "But do not overstay your time."

Peter had a few words with the girl and disappeared into the house. Anne walked away and strolled beside the river wall gazing out at the north bank. She thought it strange that the river frontages of the great episcopal palaces along the Strand stood a little upriver from the stews of Bankside. Two very different worlds beholding each other uneasily across the water.

Absorbed in her own thoughts Anne recollected that some years before, when she was betrothed, Richard had at great expense hired a tilt boat for the day and taken her with her father and a maid servant on a river outing. They had been rowed upriver with the tide to Westminster where they watched the horse ferry going back and forth between Lambeth and Westminster Stairs. They had returned with the ebb tide after being served with delicacies and cold meats, stepping off at St Paul's Wharf in high spirits.

During the trip they had observed the extent of the Church's lands and wealth along the Thames. On the north bank the great episcopal palaces – Worcester, Exeter, Bath and Durham among others – extended all along the Strand and beyond to York Place. There were also the monastic lands of Blackfriars and the riverside property of the Templars, now let out to lawyers. On the south side stood the Augustine Priory of Southwark, the Bishop of Winchester's palace and his surrounding swathe of property and the grandiose edifice of Lambeth. "In London at least," Richard had said, "the Church's wealth rivals that of the Crown – what a temptation that might be for a covetous prince!"

Anne walked downriver towards the Bishop of Winchester's palace and London Bridge and heard the clock of St Mary's Overie striking the half-hour. She turned back, realising that the waterman would soon be at the pier. When she reached The Castle, Peter emerged alone with an enigmatic look on his face. Without further discussion the two of them walked down to Bankside pier where the wherry was waiting.

During the river crossing to Blackfriars Peter asked the waterman about tides. Then Anne wanted to know whether any of the clergy took wherries across to Bankside but the good boatman would not be drawn on that sensitive subject.

It was still light when they arrived at Blackfriars Stairs. After paying off the waterman they walked up to Thames Street in time to hear the nine o'clock curfew bell ringing out from St Mary-le-Bow in Cheapside. Peter now began to tell Anne what had happened when he entered The Castle.

"I went upstairs to this little room with the girl – Miranda was her name. After some brief conversation I told her that I was desirous but unable to engage with her because I had consumed too much strong ale. However I said I would pay her and she was grateful enough to tell me something about the stew house."

Relieved that he had not succumbed to Miranda's dubious charms, Anne asked what he had learned about Joseph.

"He has assumed the name of William Godfrey and lives in two upper rooms of the house, which are served by a separate staircase that is reserved to him alone. This gives him the privacy he requires to entertain his own women friends."

"That sounds like the man we have learned about from the coroner's inquest," Anne commented. "But how might a stranger come to him in his room?"

"I understand that he takes his ale and nourishment in The Kings Arms tavern. Miranda described one other interesting circumstance. Godfrey – as we may now call him – always takes new initiates to his room, shares a drink with them and takes pains to inform them of all the laws and regulations concerning their profession. I believe this is done to comply with the duties imposed on stew-holders."

By the time they reached Eastcheap and Peter had gone his separate way, a plan had begun to form in Anne's mind. There were risks, of course. But she was only too willing to incur danger if this was the price to be paid for redeeming her pledge and ridding the world of Charles Joseph. She would confide her thoughts to Peter next day in the privacy of St Stephen's.

RETRIBUTION

THE FOLLOWING MORNING, ANNE AND PETER TOOK A short break away from the scriptorium to plan their next moves. In the side chapel of St Stephen's Anne disclosed her thoughts in hushed tones. "We know Joseph alias Godrey is to be found at The Kings Arms. I can go there, ask the taverner to point him out and approach him, posing as a whore wishing to rent a chamber. If Miranda is correct in what she says, he will take me up to his own room at The Castle and explain what is expected of me while we are sharing a drink. I will administer a strong potion and put it in his ale so that after some short lapse of time he falls into a deep sleep. We can then together take him down his backstairs, carry him outside and push him over the river wall into the water."

Peter looked doubtful. "It is no easy matter to find such a potion and if Godfrey detects it you will be in his power. Also, his removal from the house would have to be undertaken after dark – so we could not get back across the river that evening. Another point, too, is that the tide would have to be at its height to ensure that the body is carried downstream without fetching up on mud banks. And beyond all this, Godfrey's hands would have to be tied to stop him struggling either when he is carried or when floating in the river."

Anne assured Peter that she knew of apothecaries in Bucklersbury who would be able to produce the necessary herbal compound. As for getting back to the City they could stay overnight at one of the great hostelries in Southwark that served travellers coming up to London from Dover and Canterbury.

It was agreed that Anne would go that very afternoon to purchase the potion, while Peter would buy some cord and then go down to St Paul's Wharf to check the time of high and low tides from the watermen.

Bucklersbury, by Wallbrook, had long been London's market for grocers and apothecaries. Anne found herself among the stall holders talking to one of the oldest vendors of herbal medicines. Anne explained that her husband was in great pain, found it impossible to sleep and needed a very strong opiate to allow him respite. The apothecary assured her he had the very thing: "I can make up a compound of ground poppy seed heads, hemlock and black henbane that will induce deep sleep within half an hour. Your husband will thank you for this."

He made up the potion with a pestle and mortar and poured the mixture into a small glass phial. "It was the Augustinian monks who found this remedy for their infirmary. Take care with it because more than a thimbleful at any one time could cause a seizure."

Thanking the apothecary for his good advice, Anne took the phial and returned to the scriptorium where Peter was already back at work. Later, as they left together at around six o'clock in the evening, Peter whispered to Anne that the tides were right that very night. The high watermark would be reached at half past ten, which was just after dark. "Then we will do it tonight," replied Anne.

Deciding that a boat would be too public, they began to walk across London Bridge towards the inns on the other side of the river. Some of the buildings along the Bridge were seven stories high and overhung the narrow road in between to form a dark tunnel. One of the few gaps among the buildings was at the central drawbridge, and here they paused and looked over the parapet walls. Anne gazed down at the waters sluicing through the arches below and the flotsam caught up around the projecting starlings that protected the piers.

While Peter walked slowly on Anne looked into a chapel on the bridge dedicated to St Thomas a Becket which had been built to attract Canterbury pilgrims coming out of London. She knelt down for a moment and prayed that God would guide her actions and that she was doing her husband right.

Moving on beyond the bridge to Long Southwark, they passed The Tabard Inn on their left, an imposing hostelry that Peter said was overpriced because of the fame it had gained from Chaucer's *Canterbury Tales*. Next to it was The St George Inn, and it was here that they decided to take one of the rooms facing the courtyard. There would be so many late night travellers with their horses and baggage arriving from Kent and the southern counties that their own comings and goings would not be noticed.

It was now half past seven and time for Anne to go to The Kings Arms in search of her prey. Leaving Peter outside to shadow her movements, she entered the tavern and looked around. There were large numbers of drinkers in the bar area as well as groups sitting at tables taking late supper. She went straight up to the tapster who was drawing beer and asked whether William Godfrey was to be found in the tavern that night. He pointed to a corner where a man was eating alone. He was gaunt, even cadaverous, with a scabby face and long dark hair that highlighted the pallor of his complexion. To Anne he looked like the devil himself and she approached with some trepidation.

"Sir, please excuse me for imposing on you but my name is Elizabeth Grey and I am looking for a room to rent. I believe you are William Godfrey and I have been told you might be able to assist me."

He waved her to sit down and spoke slowly in a hoarse voice. "That could be. But you look to me both older and more gracious than the women who have their business here. How is it that you are selling your favours?"

"Sir, I have no occupation, no husband and two children to provide for. I must have money to live."

He nodded, looked her up and down and then said they should talk privately. He finished his meal quickly and the two of them left the tavern and walked down to Bankside. When they reached The Castle, Godfrey opened the door and led Anne down a short passage ending in a back staircase. She followed him up creaking wooden stairs onto a small landing with two doors leading off. He opened one of the doors and led her into a sparsely furnished attic room. The windows looked onto the Thames and in the late evening light the great spire of St Paul's towered over the City and its shimmering waterway.

Godfrey invited Anne to sit down and filled two goblets of ale from a flask on the side table. He then sat opposite her. At this point she had to make a quick decision. Since there was no means of administering her potion unnoticed she contrived to knock her drink over accidentally. She apologised profusely and as he got up and turned his back to refill her goblet she took the opportunity to pour some of the contents of the phial secreted in her cloak into his ale.

"There is no need for nervousness," he reassured her, "but as the leaseholder of this business I am bound to inform you of the rules laid down by the judicial powers here in Southwark. The Bishop's Court exacts heavy fines if these are breached and I have to protect my pocket."

She said she understood very well and she would of course abide by the requirements. Godfrey continued: "First I must know that you are not married, with child, or a member of a religious order."

"I can assure you of that." She watched him take another sip of his ale.

"You must dress according to the status of your profession. You must not wear clothes trimmed with fur or coloured hoods and, for the protection of honest housewives, you must not wear an apron."

"I understand and will observe these rules," she said.

Godfrey went through the other regulations, some of which imposed duties on her and some on him as stew-holder: rooms to be vacated during holy days, men not to be drawn or enticed into the stew house, the room rental to be fixed at fourteen pence per week, no victuals, ale or coal to be sold on the premises and, to observe the river curfew she must lie the whole night with any man staying after dark. He then sat back in his chair and looked at her, his sunken eyes staring out of a ravaged face. "I now come to a bothersome requirement. The bishop's officers carry out a search each month and if it is found that I am harbouring a single woman who is with disease I shall be subject to a fine of twenty shillings. I must therefore examine you now to be sure that you are in good health."

Anne had not bargained for this. The idea that this ogre, her husband's murderer, should touch her intimately was utterly repugnant. But if she was to carry through with her plan there was no way out. So she stood up and allowed him to lift her dress and examine her.

When he had done he said that all was well, but she noticed that he was beginning to slur his words. As he lit a candle to lighten the gloom, he appeared unsteady on his feet. After they had both taken another drink he addressed her again. "We now have an agreement between us. You may not be aware but all stew-holders must be married to obtain their licence and the woman who passes for my wife will be coming here tonight. She will show you the room, answer any questions you may have and later introduce you to the other tenants."

Godfrey had struggled to get out these last words and now he sank back in his chair, holding his head in his hands. After a few moments his arms dropped and his head fell back, lolling to one side with his eyes closed. He had lost consciousness. Anne waited to be sure of this before quickly descending the stairs, proceeding along the passage and opening the door onto the Bankside road. Here Peter was waiting for her in the fading light. She beckoned to him to come inside and together they went up to the room where Godfrey was slumped, dead to the world. Peter laid him on his stomach and tied his hands with cord while Anne looked anxiously out of the window.

"He took me by surprise when he said that a woman would be visiting here tonight. It would be safer to be out of the house but we cannot take him down until it is properly dark."

They waited in the eerie silence until Anne distinctly heard the tread of feet on the staircase. She dishevelled her hair hurriedly and adjusted her clothes to expose her bosom. There was a knock on the door and she opened it ajar in a state of breathless agitation. Before the visitor could announce herself, Anne spoke urgently and in a low voice. "William Godfrey is occupied this evening and it is not possible for him to see anyone until the morning. I trust you understand and he sends his apologies."

With that she shut the door and the woman on the other side stood cursing the perfidious Godfrey before eventually retreating down the stairs.

It was now dark outside and, after waiting a few minutes, Peter left the room to see if all was clear below. When he returned they dragged Godfrey down the staircase as quietly as they could, pulled him outside and hauled him across the Bankside road to the river wall. With only the moon to guide him they manhandled him onto the wall and pushed him over. The high water mark being only three or four feet below the top of the wall the body fell into the river below without a great splash – though Peter and Anne imagined that it was sufficient to attract the attention of the entire neighbourhood.

Their mission accomplished, they made their way furtively towards Long Southwark. They had to skirt round the extensive complex of the Bishop of Winchester's palace and then the priory church of St Mary Overie – "over the river", as Peter had explained to Anne. They eventually emerged by London Bridge and as they did so Anne froze. She pointed in the direction of one of the near arches where debris had collected around the pier. There, caught up among branches and other detritus – starkly visible in the moonlight – was the unmistakable form of a body.

"He is stuck there and he is alive – I think I saw his head move," Anne said with panic in her voice.

Peter could see only too well. "Dead men don't float," he said, trying to keep calm. "We cannot leave him there. After curfew a serjeant is posted at this end of the bridge. He may be spotted at any time. If taken alive from the water he will, of course, be a witness against you. And if dead there will be an inquest."

"Then what are we to do?"

"There is only one thing we can do," said Peter, "and that is to dislodge the body."

"But at this time of night there are no boats. They are all moored up on the other side of the river as the law requires."

"Not quite true," said Peter. "The Bishop of Winchester may be able to help us out. I noticed that his palace has its own wharf where a wherry is tied up."

There was no time to lose. Hurriedly retracing their steps, they climbed over the palace wall. Down by the river they found the wherry tied to a post as well as a boat hook and two oars stored conveniently in an adjoining boathouse.

Before embarking Peter paused. "Anne," he said, gravely, "this is risky. The water gushes through the arches as you have seen. Shooting London Bridge is dangerous at the best of times. But here there is only moonlight to relieve the darkness. And one of us will have to use the boathook to catch the body as the current propels us under the bridge."

Anne was undaunted. Stepping into the boat she said, "I take it neither of us can swim. So we will have to get it right."

Peter slipped the mooring and climbed in, taking the oars and handing the boathook to Anne. "We are making for the third arch. The body is protruding from the left pier. The water will be turbulent but you will have to try to hook the ropes tied round his arms to get a purchase as we go past."

Anne could feel the current pushing them towards the bridge, Peter all the while doing his best to steady the boat. She peered into the semi-darkness and could just make out the shape of a human form wedged against the pier. Suddenly the boat surged and the bridge was rushing towards them. Peter shouted something but his voice was lost in the roar of the river. Anne, desperately trying to maintain her balance, raised the boathook and lunged at the man's clothing as they shot by. The hook failed to take hold, and succeeded only in dislodging a long branch. The boat had been thrown around and was now awash with the filth of the Thames. But Peter managed to manoeuvre towards the bank and in the calmer water they looked back.

He was still there. But the trailing branch had broken free, thereby loosening other debris around the pier. Slowly – agonisingly slowly – the jammed body was released into the stream, gathering speed as it was carried down river. Watching it sweep silently past Anne had the impression that its eyes were staring at her accusingly. But then it was gone into the night.

Peter rowed towards a jetty belonging to an imposing house east of the bridge. There they tied up, got out and made their way through narrow lanes back towards Long Southwark. At the St George Inn, the courtyard was still bustling with activity as ostlers dealt with the last travellers from Dover. Their room off the courtyard was noisy, and after wringing out their wet clothes they had to share a bed with a bolster between them. Before turning in for the night, Peter tried to reassure Anne. "William Godfrey should be at Rotherhithe by now and by first light he will be carried past Blackwall." But her sleep was disturbed by images that kept surfacing in her mind of a half-submerged body with staring eyes, twisting and turning in the tides and currents of the Thames as it was born downstream to an unknown destination.

The following morning, Peter and Anne crossed London Bridge and made their way to Coleman Street. But something was wrong. There was a serjeant standing outside the scriptorium. Documents, books and writing materials were being carried out of the building by men who looked like court officials. The baker's wife hurried over to them from the shop next door.

"Quick! Stop! Get out of here before they arrest you. The scriptorium has been raided and Geoffrey and his collaborators have been taken. You must not be seen here."

Needing no further prompting they disappeared into a side street without looking back.

25

NEWGATE PRISON

ONCE THEY HAD DISTANCED THEMSELVES FROM Coleman Street, they stopped and Peter turned to Anne. "We are both now in grave danger. I will take to the road and settle in Essex for some time. I have friends and family there. But your situation is more difficult."

Anne considered the implications for herself. "Walter and Jonathan knew nothing of me or my connection with Richard Hunne. Therefore they cannot inform against me. Geoffrey knows much more though I hope he will not betray me even under duress. But you should go and go quickly."

After a brief but tearful farewell, they went their separate ways knowing that they would never see each other again.

Anne returned to Eastcheap where she was surprised to find her friend Mary waiting for her in a highly agitated state. Once inside the house Mary explained breathlessly why the scriptorium had been raided. "Robert has been to the Guildhall where there is a great scandal. A scribe has confessed to lending out manuscripts for money. When they learned that the Crowner's Inquest on Hunne had been lent out they examined it and found that it had been tampered with. They were able to match one sheet of manuscript with the scriptorium in Coleman Street."

"Then I am to blame for all this!" cried Anne.

Mary comforted her. "No, not at all, my dear. It was Robert's idea, which he then brought to you. But my great fear is that the scribe will tell the sheriff that it was Robert who borrowed the documents."

"And what about our scribes from Coleman Street? Does Robert know where they are being held?"

"I am told that they are in Newgate awaiting criminal charges for taking the property of His Highness. I must get back to poor Robert. I need hardly add that you please say nothing that could incriminate him."

After Mary had left in haste Anne wondered whether she should destroy her copy of the Coroner's Inquest but she decided to take no action. In the afternoon she walked over to Carter Lane where Rebecca was looking after Margaret. Rebecca had already heard the news, which was spreading rapidly within their little community. She hugged her friend and spoke through tears. "Anne, I fear for your safety. They say that the sheriff's men have found the Wycliffe Bible and other prohibited writings at Coleman Street. The bishop has been informed and there is bound to be a big stir within the Church over this."

Anne realised that the copying of the Wycliffe Bible would be sufficient grounds for heresy charges against all of them. Poor Geoffrey and his two assistants would face the full force both of the King's criminal law and the Church's spiritual proceedings. Surely it was only a matter of time before the trail led to her and how then could she escape the bishop's clutches?

———

Bishop Fitzjames was still residing at Fulham Palace some weeks after his bruising encounter with George Monoux. He had been deeply disturbed by the revelation that those in high places were seeking to undermine the authority of the Church. But his determination to pursue heretics had been reinforced, and when he heard that a Lollard scriptorium had been uncovered by the sheriff he called in his legal adviser, Dr Thomas Head.

"Thomas, the villainous scribes of the iniquitous Wycliffe Bible are being held in a secular prison awaiting trial in the Court of Kings Bench. However, the charge of heresy that we can bring in the spiritual courts is a graver offence than the theft of manuscripts. Tell me, how does this stand in law? Can we request the sheriff to entrust these men to our care in Lollards' Tower?"

Dr Head answered without hesitation. "By law, the sheriffs must assist bishops and their officers in arresting Lollards. When an arrest is made by the secular arm, the sheriff is obliged to deliver the supposed heretic to the spiritual authorities within ten days. Therefore I believe we may require the sheriff to release these men into our custody."

The bishop expressed another concern: "Thomas, the Church has long experience of rigorously questioning suspects and holding them securely in our prisons. By contrast, I understand Newgate to be a place of common intercourse where uninvited visitors may freely come and go and the prisoners are not sufficiently constrained. Therefore it is important that these Newgate prisoners are committed to our care without delay, so that their confederates may be discovered."

Dr Head acknowledged the urgency of the situation. "My Lord, the longer these men are in Newgate the less opportunity we have of discovering their supporters and accomplices. I will at once inform the sheriff of our concerns and request their immediate removal to Lollards' Tower."

But the bishop was to be disappointed. The sheriff made it known that he had no intention at present of delivering his captives into the hands of the Church. They had been arrested not on grounds of suspected heresy but because they had stolen and then tampered with documents belonging to the Crown. This was a matter touching on the rights and honour of His Highness and the alleged perpetrators had to be charged, tried and, if convicted, sentenced before they could be handed over to the bishop. Furthermore, the bishop's officers were not at liberty to question the suspect felons while they were being held at Newgate.

This unwelcome response was conveyed to Fulham by Dr Head, just as the bishop's craftsmen were putting the finishing touches to the great oak screen he had erected in commemoration of his episcopacy. "My Lord, sadly we will now have to await the conclusion of the criminal proceedings against these men. But I have made a discovery that will be of interest to you. The leader of these so-called scribes is one Geoffrey. This is the self-same Geoffrey Chandler who was brought before you some years ago on a charge of heresy. At that time he abjured and did penance for his grave transgression. However, there is nothing at present against his two confederates."

The downcast bishop was revived by this news. "Thomas, when we obtain custody of these villains we will make an example of them. We will use every means at our command to wring confessions from them so that they yield up their fellow conspirators and supporters. And when all this has been done we will have another burning at Smithfield."

While Fitzjames waited impatiently for his new batch of Lollard prisoners, Anne determined to visit Geoffrey in Newgate. But when she told Rebecca of her intention to visit the gaol her friend warned of the conditions she would find. "The poor husband of one of my close acquaintances was there for a short while on account of his debts. The office of keeper of the gaol has for some time been sold by the sheriff to the highest bidder. The winner of the commission must then charge the prisoners to redeem his outlay. He does this by requiring payment for all kinds of services.

"What sort of services?" asked Anne.

"Everything. Even putting on and removing shackles or providing as bedding a plank and filthy blanket instead of slabs of stone."

Anne was shocked. "And what about food and drink?"

"That is the worst of it," replied Rebecca. "The keeper is supposed to charge no more than a penny for a loaf of bread and twopence for a gallon of ale…"

"But what if they cannot pay?"

"Then friends or kinsmen may bring food, or else the prisoner must starve. And another thing," Rebecca added. "They say there are informers within the prison walls to report on suspicious visitors who may be accomplices of the inmates. Take care you do not give yourself away."

Anne took heed of her cousin's warning. To avoid detection she felt it would be prudent to go in disguise. So she bound her scarf tightly around her chest to flatten her bosom, tied her hair up and slipped on a hooded cloak which was the one article of her husband's clothing that she had managed to retain in remembrance of him. She then practised speaking slowly in a low voice that would not betray her femininity.

Standing at the northwest entrance to London's ancient wall, Newgate Prison was located within the original gatehouse that guarded the entrance to the City. Approaching the prison from Newgate Street, Anne could see a strange assortment of people milling around outside the prison walls. Arriving at the gatehouse, she asked a large buxom woman with two small children why there was such a gathering of people.

"You must be new here, Sir," she replied. "You have creditors seeking repayment, well-wishers, friends and wives, such as myself, and also …" She glanced in the direction of a pitiful looking waif of a girl who could scarcely have been more than twelve. "There are those who may be selling their bodies."

Anne noticed an emaciated man in shackles slumped against the prison wall. "And what of him?"

The woman's response was matter of fact. "They have some inmates who have no money for their board. The keeper allows them to beg in shackles outside the walls so they can pay him for their food. That way he makes more money than if they were to starve. But this man here will soon be beyond begging and the carcass carriers will then take him away."

Anne thanked the woman and spoke to a prison official standing outside the gatehouse whom she took to be the turnkey. She told him that she wished to visit Geoffrey, the scribe, who had been taken in during the past few days. The turnkey led her without further question to a room on the ground floor.

Here she was assailed by an over-powering stench as she searched for Geoffrey among the crowd of faces. When she did find him he was barely recognisable – hunched, unshaven and wasted he seemed to have aged by a good ten years in less than a week. And he was wearing leg irons. He did not at first recognise her so she helped him to a quieter corner and there revealed her identity and her great distress at his situation.

"Geoffrey, I am to blame for all this," she whispered. "It was because I pressed you to grant me a favour that you are here."

But he would have none of that. "Anne, I took my chance in this business and it was always likely that they would catch me one day. But take care." He glanced around to make sure no one was listening. "This is a dangerous place for you."

"I, too, am willing to take my chance," she said. "I have brought you money so that you may buy food and bedding."

He thanked her. "What of Walter and Jonathan?" she asked, anxiously. "Are they here?"

"They are in another chamber. I have seen them and I understand they have friends who have given them food. The keeper has told me that the three of us will be removed to Lollards' Tower to face charges of heresy once our present case has been heard in the King's court. This they expect in two or three weeks."

The turnkey announced that it was time for visitors to leave, so Anne pressed some coins quickly into Geoffrey's hand. She squeezed his arm and said, "I shall be back next week when we can talk more fully."

On the way out she observed that there was a little makeshift chapel in the corner consisting of a simple wooden cross and a table altar. A prisoner was sitting there on a bench with a priest officiating before him and what looked like a coffin lying open by his side. Responding to her puzzled look, the turnkey explained. "This is the condemned pew where prisoners who are to be executed next day are given a benediction. Young Tom here will be taken to Tyburn in the morning."

Anne returned to Eastcheap and removed her disguise before walking on to Carter Lane to collect Margaret. It was early autumn and there was already a slight chill in the air. When she arrived, Rebecca had more upsetting news for her.

"Anne, it is known within our community that your friend Geoffrey has already done penance. He was convicted some years ago for supposed heresy. As a relapsed penitent he must be considered dead in the hands of the bishop."

Anne thought of poor Richard's treatment. "Rebecca, if he and his two assistants are put in Lollards' Tower and subject to duress there is no saying what they may disclose – though not of their free will. I am concerned for the baker and his wife next to the scriptorium and all those members of our community who have borrowed forbidden books from Coleman Street. The bishop may find he has a big catch in his net."

Rebecca chided her friend. "You always understate the danger to yourself, Anne. The biggest threat is that your name is made known, and where would you and little Margaret be then?"

Anne sighed: "Perhaps we must trust to the fortitude of these men. After all, my dear Richard betrayed no one when he was captive."

"Yes, indeed," Rebecca said. "But then look what befell him."

A week after this conversation, Anne returned in her disguise to Newgate to see Geoffrey, but visitors and bystanders were being kept well away from the prison walls by sheriff's men and no one was allowed entry. Anne asked someone what had occurred and the reply came in two words.

"Sweating sickness."

She knew about sweating sickness. There had been an outbreak ten years before and at that time she had witnessed the death of one of her friends. First cold and shivering then, after only a few hours, fever and sweating. Unlike the plague, there were no sores on the body, but the distemper raged within, leading eventually to delirium and in most cases death. The end came very quickly, within hours of the onset of illness, but it was said that if the victim lasted for a day and a night they would live. She also knew that an overcrowded prison was where the disease could spread fastest and that Geoffrey and his fellow scribes would be in grave danger.

Anne and Rebecca thought it best to keep their girls indoors when the pestilence was at its height and it was Rebecca, through her wider acquaintance, who brought the latest news to her cousin.

"They say Oxford and Cambridge have lost half their citizens through this scourge. It is much more severe than the last time it brought terror to our people. Several at court have died. They were taken ill while feasting and did not last the night. They say the King himself has fled and gone into the country."

Anne was desperate to know how Geoffrey and his friends had fared in Newgate, but she herself had no means of finding out. Rebecca was again the source of information. "You will not wish to hear this, Anne, but Geoffrey and both his friends have succumbed to the terrible disease. According to my acquaintance who heard it from the turnkey, they were, after the outbreak, put in the same chamber from which there were few who survived. The criminal charges against them are dismissed."

Anne was stunned into silence and Rebecca embraced her. "Cousin, I know this is deeply upsetting to you but it may be for the best. Better that the bishop should be denied and that poor Geoffrey should be spared the horrors of burning. The pestilence has cheated the Church of its prey and we may all breathe a little more freely knowing that Lollards' Tower will have no scribes as prisoners."

Anne would not be consoled even though she knew that Rebecca was right.

———————

Then the sickness came to Eastcheap. Looking through her window, Anne saw a carcass carrier pass by with two corpses slung across his cart. Later that day another victim was hauled past her door. The poisonous vapour must now be swirling around her house.

It was in the evening that Anne noticed Margaret was unwell. She was whimpering and shivering and her forehead was cold. Within the hour Anne herself began to feel an icy chill and started to shake. It dawned on her that they had succumbed at the very same time to the dreaded sickness.

There was little time to act while she still had strength. She quickly put straw outside her door by way of warning as the ordinances required. She then took her treasured beeswax candle that she kept for special celebrations and lit the wick from embers in the fire on which she had been cooking. She took the candle up to her room and placed it on a sill above her bed, calculating that the wax would burn down after a day and a night. By that time the danger would be past or else death would have intervened. She brought up a pitcher of fresh water which the water carrier had fetched from the conduit and took from the shelf Richard's book of Aesop's Fables. She then put Margaret in her own bed, lay down herself and cuddled her close.

Anne knew that above all else neither she nor Margaret must be allowed to fall asleep. That would be the end. So she read story after story aloud while also nudging Margaret from time to time. For the first few hours she managed well enough, even though she felt exhausted and had severe aches in her neck, shoulders and limbs. When the sweating phase was reached, however, Anne felt she might die and little Margaret, too, became feverish. Every few minutes she put water to their lips to quench the intense thirst they both felt. During the next few hours the sense of tiredness and the desire for sleep became overwhelming and Anne, in desperation, put her forefinger into the candle flame. The searing pain sharpened her senses and kept her awake, and at one point she shook Margaret gently to arouse her from the slumber of death.

As the hours went by, Anne sensed that she was slipping away. She again put her fingers to the flame until the smell of charred flesh caused her to withdraw. The pain made her wakeful for two or three hours more during which time she continued to talk into Margaret's ear. The fever was reaching its climactic phase and the sweat poured from her brow. The candle had burned far down its stem but now she began to lose all sense of time and space. She was no longer able to resist the lure of oblivion. In her half sleep she had visions of Richard and her father, their faces appearing, dissolving and reassembling themselves. Another face came in to view, this time much closer to her own. She could hear a voice as if some spirit from another world had spoken. But the voice became more urgent and she felt small fingers touching her cheek. Margaret's familiar features came into focus and her cry was insistent.

"Mama, wake up! I am thirsty!"

Anne slowly stirred herself. She looked up and saw that the candle above her bed had been reduced to a pool of guttered wax. A full day and night had elapsed and they were still alive. The sweating sickness had let slip its kill.

During the remaining days of autumn, Anne had time on her hands. She was able to spend more of each day with Margaret teaching her to read and, when the sweating sickness died down as quickly as it had come, taking her to the open fields beyond Moorgate.

It was in the early days of November when the first household fires of winter had been lit that Anne received a letter from the Steelyard.

> *Dear Anne,*
>
> *I trust you are in good health. I shall be returning to London early in December and I hope that we may renew our acquaintance at that time. I shall write to you again when I have more exact knowledge of my arrival.*
>
> *Yours,*
>
> *Hermann Wedig.*

Anne had convinced herself that she would not hear again from her unexpected German visitor but when she did she was unwilling to admit to herself how much she looked forward to meeting him again.

PART IV

❦ *1517 – 1522* ❧

26

MARTIN LUTHER

IN THE SECOND WEEK OF DECEMBER ANNE FOUND
herself dining once more at a secluded table in the Steelyard
Tavern in the company of Hermann Wedig. There was a roaring
fire in the grate, a platter of venison placed in front of them and
a flask of warming red wine from Burgundy to fill their goblets.
The Hansa merchant was in genial mood as he surveyed his
fellow diners. "Well Anne, not much sign of fasting for Advent
here."

Anne looked around at the portly shapes and florid
countenances of the assembled company. She could detect in the
general hubbub of conversation the guttural accents of German
and Dutch as well as the softer intonations of French and
Italian. This world of merchants, it seemed, brought all nations
together in a spirit of comradeship. And yet, she reflected, it was
only a few months ago that foreign traders had been attacked
by the London mob.

"Yes, there is a festive atmosphere today," Hermann
remarked. "These past months the people have been afraid to go
to taverns or to meet together. Now that the sweating sickness
has left us they are celebrating their new freedom. We, too,
can rejoice in your own and little Margaret's escape from its
clutches."

"Have you come across this frightening malady on your travels?" Anne asked.

"Indeed, I have," replied Hermann. "There have been outbreaks all over Europe from Hamburg to Calais. There is no protection. It kills the young as much as the old, the rich as much as the poor and the country dweller as much as the townsman. The only point in its favour is that death is very quick. But let us not dwell on this mournful subject – I have interesting news to report."

He poured wine into their goblets and leaned forwards speaking softly. "Anne, you must be patient with me for it is a long story. But the conclusion of it is no less than this … that the roof of our universal Church, both in my country and, I believe, in yours, is shortly to be blown off by a religious tempest such as has not been witnessed these past thousand years."

Anne wondered for a moment whether she was being mocked but the sincere and animated expression on her companion's face persuaded her otherwise.

"Let me begin with one of our German princes – Albert of Brandenburg. It has been his great ambition to be appointed Archbishop of Mainz which would make him also the primate of all Germany. He has no special claim to this high office and he already holds two other sees. So he knew he would have to pay the Pope a good sum to secure his prize. The price eventually agreed was 10,000 ducats which Albert had to borrow from the great banking house of Fugger. Pope Leo X – a self-indulgent spendthrift who seldom takes off his hunting boots – gave Albert a special concession to enable him to repay his loan from the bankers. This was the privilege of selling indulgences in his territories for eight years."

Anne was perplexed "But surely a prince cannot dispense indulgences? Only the Pope or his bishops can do that."

"Ah, you may think so. But if the money is right, the Pope may claim to devolve his power to an earthly Prince who, as you must remember, is now made Archbishop."

Hermann helped himself to a haunch of venison. "This year, Albert announced that a plenary indulgence had been issued by His Holiness the Pope to defray the expenses of rebuilding St Peter's in Rome. Subscribers would enjoy a complete remission of their sins and be restored to the same state of innocence as if newly baptised. Everyone was expected to contribute according to their means ... Kings and Queens, Archbishops and Bishops were to give twenty-five gold florins ... Abbots, Counts, Barons and other great nobles, twenty florins ... the lower nobility, six florins ... burgers and merchants, three florins and the humblest orders one florin."

Anne was horrified: "If I understand you correctly the Pope has sold the Archbishopric to Albert, the purchase price being advanced by a banking house. The Pope, knowing this, grants Albert the right to sell indulgences so that he may repay his loans. What iniquity is this?"

Hermann smiled in approval. "You have understood the entire transaction."

"Albert also pretended that the money from selling indulgences was to be used for rebuilding St Peter's and not to meet his own debts. Is that right?"

"Yes, the whole business was a fraud. I know this because we Hansa have close dealings with the Fugger bankers.

"But it does not end there. Albert has entrusted the selling of indulgences to a Dominican, John Tetzel, who has long experience of cozening the faithful. It so happens that a few weeks ago I was doing business in Berlin-Cölln, a trading centre in Brandenburg. The word went round that John Tetzel was coming to town. Being curious I, along with everyone else, from the wealthiest burger to the humblest menial, gathered in the market square to hear him. He was met by local dignitaries who joined in a solemn procession, a cross bearing the papal arms preceding them and the Pope's Bull of Indulgence carried aloft on a gold embroidered velvet cushion. I watched as the gilded cross was planted in the middle of the square and then, with the crowd hushed, Tetzel began to deliver his message which he no doubt repeats in towns throughout the principality."

Anne drew her chair closer. "And what was his message?"

Wedig would not be hurried and refilled their goblets from a flask on the table. "I remember very well what he said. Let me give you his words as best I can."

Keeping his voice low, Wedig nevertheless contrived to assume a menacing tone.

"Listen to the voices of your dear dead relatives beseeching you and saying: 'Pity us, pity us. We are in dire torment from which you can redeem us for a pittance.' Hear the father saying to his son, the mother to her daughter 'We bore you, nourished you, brought you up, left you our fortunes and you are so cruel and hard that now you are not willing for so little to set us free. Will you let us lie here in flames?'"

Wedig dropped his impersonation. "Of course, Tetzel also terrorises people into paying money to save their own souls but the effect is the same. The florins pour in and are delivered not to the needy but to the vaults of bankers. It is a nice little business."

Anne knew about the indulgences granted at St Paul's but Hermann's account raised a question to which she had never been able to find an answer. "How can the people believe this nonsense? Purgatory is not to be found in the Bible, indulgences are not to be found in the Bible. As for the idea that God would remit sins for the payment of money on the instructions of a decadent Pope, this is an affront to all good Christians."

"Part of the answer to your question, dear Anne, is that

people are inclined to follow the crowd. To my great shame when Tetzel's gilded offering box came round I felt compelled, in the full view of others, to put in my florins. It is also true that the humblest sort of people do not think for themselves and are happy to be led – and fleeced – by their supposed superiors. But there are many middling people among the merchants and artisans in Germany who know very well that the sale of indulgences is an abuse. Such disbelievers have been waiting for a powerful voice to rouse the people against all the exactions, deceits and knavery practised by the Church."

There was a lull in the conversation as plates of almond leech were brought to the table and the last of the wine was poured. Hermann leant towards Anne and looked into her eyes: "The whole point of my story is that such a voice is now being heard; and the people all over Germany are being stirred up against religious oppression."

"And whose voice is this?"

"His name is Martin Luther. Six weeks ago, on the eve of All Saints Day, he pinned a placard to the door of the castle church in Wittenberg, setting out his objections to the Church's teachings – and especially the sale of indulgences. He cited and ridiculed a little rhyme used by Tetzel to persuade his listeners to give money:

As soon as the coin in the coffer rings
The soul from purgatory springs'

Luther listed ninety-five criticisms against the Church and sent a copy to Albert of Mainz."

Anne was puzzled. "But why should this man's opinions carry such weight beyond the good citizens of Wittenberg? Where lies his power to incite others?"

"Martin Luther is one of the Church's own. He was a monk before he was appointed to the University of Wittenberg. He is a biblical scholar, writes his criticisms of the Church in best Latin and cites the scriptures in making his arguments. The Church authorities cannot ignore him because he speaks in their tongue. Also he is fearless in stating his opinions."

Anne was wide-eyed in disbelief: "But surely he will very soon be arrested and charged with heresy? That is what would occur here in England."

Hermann shook his head. "Luther has for the moment the protection of his Prince, Frederick of Saxony. There the Church cannot touch him. He has a following that is growing by the day. His arguments have been translated into German and are even now being printed. His opinions are becoming widely known in my country and it cannot be long before his works are read here."

Anne was amazed. No one in England would have the audacity to publicly attack the Church in this way, and if they did they would be in the bishop's prison in no time. And how could prohibited teaching be disseminated throughout the land by the printing press? In England the printer would be arrested, his business shut down and he and his books burned.

She wanted to know more. "Besides denouncing indulgences, what else does Luther say against the Church?"

Hermann paused while he finished his wine and the maidservant cleared the table. "Luther says that the Bible is the only source of religious truth. The scriptures must have primacy over the teachings of the Church and the pronouncements of the Pope and his bishops. As you can imagine this doctrine is very unwelcome to the highest dignitaries of the Catholic Church."

"Our own John Wycliffe, now long dead, and his followers would fully support Luther on this."

Hermann nodded. "He also states that Christians cannot reach salvation by their own acts but only through their faith and God's grace. Good works such as bequests to the Church and offerings at shrines cannot of themselves secure salvation. This again is objectionable to church leaders because it strikes at their revenues.

"Luther also objects to the idea – propagated by the Church over many centuries – that Christ and the saints through their holiness, have built up a surplus treasury of spiritual merit that can be distributed to the faithful to remit their sins. This doctrine is used by the Church to justify the sale of indulgences. Luther's assault on the doctrine is seen both as an attack on the cult of saints and as a threat to the Church's wealth."

"Those of Wycliffe's persuasion are dead against the idolatrous worship of saints and their relics," Anne said. "But Luther appears to be challenging also the accepted theology."

"Exactly so," said Hermann. "Finally, Luther has caused great offence to the Pope himself by asserting that, since he is richer than Croesus, Leo X should build the basilica of St Peter with his own money rather than seeking the donations of poor believers."

Anne nodded. "I find myself in agreement with this Martin Luther. His beliefs have much in common with Lollards although he goes further in his objections to Church doctrine. So what is next?"

Hermann gave a shrug: "I cannot say – except that when this man speaks the people take note, the printers spread his message and the Church trembles. Certainly, there is here the makings of a great religious upheaval. In fact, I believe that it has already begun."

The Hansa merchant moved his chair closer to Anne. "Come now. I have said too much already about these lofty issues, important though they are. I did not bring you here to discourse on Church doctrine: I am much more interested in Anne Hunne than in Martin Luther. What of yourself? And little Margaret? Will you celebrate Christmas together at Eastcheap?"

And so, as the tables around them emptied and their fellow diners departed the conversation turned to more personal matters. Hermann reported on his travels and complained that he spent too much time alone. Anne described her recent happy outings with Margaret but said she wished she had something more to fill her life. While they lingered at the table in fading light he placed his hand gently on hers – and they looked into each other's eyes and laughed.

27

To have and to hold

It was only three days later that Anne received a note from Hermann suggesting that they meet for a Sunday stroll in the fields beyond the City, weather permitting.

The winter sun shone brightly that day though the air was crisp and cold. Plumes of smoke rose from innumerable chimneys as the pair walked towards Moorgate and then out into Moor Field. Here washerwomen were at work scrubbing London's dirty linen in great tubs and hanging the clothes and sheets on tenterhooks.

In Finsbury Field archers were testing their bowmanship on ranges that had been specially marked out for target practice. The spectacle of men bracing the string to the bow and drawing the yew against their bodies brought back memories for Anne. When the new King had required every able-bodied man to acquire a bow and train with it, Richard had welcomed the chance to develop his archery skills. She would look on proudly as her husband exhibited his prowess with England's deadliest weapon and she remembered especially the occasion on which he had won the prize in a target shoot against his fellow merchant taylors.

But now she and Hermann were getting a little too close to the action. "We must keep clear of the butts," Anne cautioned.

"They have many archery ranges here as you can see from the target posts. Accidents to passers-by are commonplace."

"I am impressed by all this preparation for war," Hermann replied. "In Europe we favour the crossbow, although I have to concede that the English longbow has fared better in battle."

As he spoke a strapping bowman who had been standing nearby adjusting the fletching on his arrows, shouted out:

"Foreign scab! Spy! The Devil take you!"

The incensed man turned on Hermann and threatened him with a dagger which he drew from a sheath hanging on his belt. For a moment Anne thought her companion would be knifed. But in a quick movement Hermann forced the bowman's arm back to his shoulder and held it there. "I have no great interest in your archery practice," he said coldly. "Bows and arrows have been used since ancient times. There is nothing new here. I could if I were so minded kill you on the pretext of self-defence. Besides which I am a privileged alien living under the King's protection. So mind your manners churl."

The bowman glared at his rival for some moments and then slowly dropped his arm before spitting on the ground and shuffling off to the sound of foul mouthed cursing.

Anne took Hermann's arm and they walked on. They turned eastwards towards Shoreditch, passing several windmills whose sails hung motionless in the windless air. They reached Bishopsgate Street Without, where a great upright cross stood guard at the intersection, and headed south again.

"There are some fine houses with extensive gardens spreading beyond the City limits," Hermann commented. "This would be the place for me. Fresh air, space, tranquillity and ease of travel to the City markets."

They were now approaching Bishopsgate and Anne pointed to a single storey building centred around a courtyard with a chapel in the middle. "You would not find peace and quiet within the walls of Bedlam Hospital here. All the inmates have lost their minds and one can often hear their ravings from the street. What misery there must be inside!"

They were both silent as they walked through the arch of Bishopsgate back into London's busy thoroughfares. Hermann drew Anne towards him.

"I enjoyed our walk, despite the threat to my life! But I now have a surprise for you. I have reserved a private room for the two of us tonight at the Pope's Head tavern in Cornhill. What do you say to a quiet evening together?"

Anne hesitated only because of Margaret but she knew that Rebecca would not mind keeping her overnight. "I would like that," she replied, as he took her hand.

A link boy accompanied Anne and Hermann to the Pope's Head – an imposing stone building bearing the royal coat of arms that was reputed to have belonged to King John. They were led upstairs to a private room where a table was laid out for two in front of a fire. The air was sweetened by an exotic aroma and Anne noticed that late blooming flowers with small white petals had been placed in vases on the side board.

"Jasmine", Hermann said seeing her enquiring look. "The symbol of divine love and heavenly happiness. It is I think fitting for this occasion."

They sat side by side at the candlelit table looking into the fire while food and drink was placed before them. Anne was amazed that all this had been arranged for her benefit but her surprise was even greater when a lute player entered, bowed and began to pluck a soft melody.

When their goblets had been refilled with wine Hermann held Anne's hand and lent forwards to kiss her brow. She responded by stroking his cheek affectionately. He sighed. "Anne, I realise we have known each other only a short time. But it is time enough for me to know that I love you. We should surely be together. Will you agree to us living as man and wife?"

Anne had a great longing to be with this man who had so recently and unexpectedly come into her life. She had, of course, to protect the memory of her husband and respect the laws that scripture had proclaimed for men and women. But there had been little joy for her since Richard's passing. She herself had just escaped the jaws of death and she could not bear to forego the chance of renewed happiness, however fleeting. She looked up at him. After some moments of reflection she gave her answer. "My dearest Hermann, yes. Let us live as man and wife –so long as we are made man and wife."

"Then we shall marry", he replied. "We can do this without any delay or ceremony. After all, consent and witnesses are all that is required in the eyes of the law and God."

"It could be a secret marriage," said Anne.

"It would have to be secret because the Hansa do not approve marriages to foreigners. Our union would be unusual in other ways. I would continue to live mostly outside England. Such estate as I have is in Germany. And, even here in London, I would have to steal myself away from the Steelyard where I am supposed to reside. But let us put all that aside and seize this very moment."

He took her in his arms and Anne felt at peace as all the sadnesses of the past few years melted away.

They were to be married at the Church of St Sepulchre without Newgate. Anne and Richard had some years earlier admired this gracious building where one of Richard's ancestors, a crusader knight who had returned from Jerusalem, was buried. They had gazed up at the beautifully wrought porch ceiling with its richly carved groining and bosses representing angels' heads, shields and roses. They had joked that the image of the church's founder sculpted on the porch bore an uncanny resemblance to Richard himself. "I would consider it a great honour to have my face chiselled into the stonework of a fine church," he had said with a smile. "But the diocesan authorities would never allow the effigy of a Wyckliffite to upset their dignity. The world will therefore be spared such a spectacle."

Anne believed that her departed husband would have approved this setting for her union with Hermann and she wished, above all else, to be true to his memory.

On a cold and damp December morning there was a small gathering in front of St Sepulchre just beyond the City wall. A bystander might have thought that Rebecca, in her high waisted pink damask gown and elaborate conical hat was the bride-to-be, whereas Anne wore a simple blue dress and wimple.

The two gentlemen were introduced to each other by Rebecca. "Hermann Wedig, this is my uncle, Jack Honiker – a seafaring man who has had dealings with Hansa merchants. My husband cannot be here because he is attending a trade fair in Kent. We two are to be witnesses, sworn to secrecy."

"Let us stand in the porch for our vows," said Anne. "Hermann and I have agreed to seek the protection of the Church but we do not want the blessing of a priest."

They moved into the porch just as it began to rain lightly. Hermann, holding a piece of parchment, stood opposite Anne and made his vow in the time honoured manner. "I take thee, Anne Hunne, to my wedded wife, to have and to hold, from this day forward, for better for worse, for richer for poorer, in sickness and in health and thereto I plight thee my troth."

Anne responded in similar vein after which Hermann placed a simple gold ring on his bride's finger.

After the brief exchange, Jack said quietly, "You are now man and wife and we are witnesses to this."

28

1518
HAPPY NEW YEAR

BISHOP FITZJAMES HAD A DEEP DREAD OF THE
Christmas season. His official duties required him to be present
at St Paul's and there to witness the carousing and merrymaking
of the London populace. He particularly objected to the ancient
custom of the Boy Bishop. On December 6th, the Feast of St
Nicholas, the choristers would choose one of their own to
take on the role of bishop for the two days December 27th and
December 28th . The Boy Bishop would lead the community
in all things apart from taking the mass and his tenure would
end with a procession through London to bless its citizenry.
To Fitzjames these proceedings were a heathen practice that
undermined respect for the Church, his personal authority and
the dignity of his office.

Fitzjames also believed that the twelve days of Christmas were
several days too many. All work on the land stopped until Plough
Monday (the first Monday after twelfth night) while women
ceased spinning altogether. As for the pagan practice of appointing
a Lord of Misrule to preside over Christmas revelries this, in his
view, inevitably led to excesses and improper behaviour. One such
case brought to his attention was at the Inner Temple where by

long tradition a fox and cat were let loose in the hall on St Stephen's Day and hunted with a pack of hounds. The masks, feasting and wassailing that took place on Epiphany were, in the bishop's eyes, a further manifestation of religious decadence on a holy day that should celebrate with dignity the coming of the Magi.

This year Fitzjames found the whole business of Christmas especially burdensome. He had not been feeling well and was only too conscious that his days were numbered. He was now contemplating both his earthly legacy and his prospects in the world to come. He had designated a prime position in the nave of St Paul's for his final resting place. He would be interred beneath the central northwest pillar within a raised grey marble tomb surmounted by a small chapel. Meanwhile his coat of arms had been sculpted on the cathedral ceiling, while here and at Fulham Palace, his name would be commemorated in the memorials he had mounted on gateways and walls. He would leave his library of theological works to Merton, his old Oxford College, and he planned to endow a school at Bruton in Somerset where his family had their roots.

But the bishop hoped to be remembered above all, for his unrelenting fight against the enemies of the Church. His campaign against Lollard heretics had been maintained over the past twelve months with thirty-six convictions yielding thirty-four recantations and two burnings – his biggest catch in recent years. He was confident that his record of upholding traditional religious doctrines would be given due recognition after his death, although he was also aware that there was much work still to be done to stamp out the virulent pestilence spread by Wycliffe's followers. His main regret was that he had been unable to deal as he would have wished with his own dean who, as a dangerous reformer, had been a constant thorn in his side.

On the other side of the cathedral close, John Colet, too, was looking back on his life. Having only recently turned fifty he was some thirty years younger than his bishop but he had been severely affected by an attack of the sweating sickness and sensed that he had not long to live. That year he had delivered his last Good Friday sermon before the King and he was soon to be forced to absent himself from cathedral duties.

Since he had declined to publish his own scholarly works and sermons Colet was aware that his greatest legacy would be St Paul's School whose future was assured thanks to ample endowments. In the will he was preparing he made no requests for obits, commemorative masses or chantry priests to pray for his soul, and from his considerable private fortune he intended to bequeath no money to religious houses. Having a strong aversion to all pomp and ceremony he had arranged to be buried on the south side of the cathedral choir in a modest sepulchre bearing the simple inscription: "IOAN.COL".

Sitting back in his chair, Colet looked up at the shelves of books lining his library. His eye lighted on the copy of *Utopia* recently given to him by Thomas More. The dean affectionately referred to his great friend as *Britanniae Unicum Ingenium*, the ablest man in Britain, but now he felt a twinge of envy. More was ten years his junior and in the prime of life. As a rising man and newly appointed adviser to the King he would, of course, be looking ahead, not back. He was making money, he had the ear of both Henry and Wolsey, and took pride in his growing family. He could hope for high office, a great estate and honours to match. All this, on top of his writings which had already made his name familiar both at home and abroad. More would be enjoying the warmth of a family Christmas while he, Colet, faced illness and death with no one close to comfort him – apart, that is, from his dear servant boy, William Bowerman, who would provide some solace.

As he contemplated his end and began to put his affairs in order, Colet was reminded of some unfinished business. He wanted to ensure that the widow of Richard Hunne was provided for in a more permanent way than that offered by the tenancy he had managed to arrange for her. But as Dean of St Paul's he could hardly make an explicit provision in favour of a heretic's family in his will. Therefore he would have to meet with Mistress Anne herself and explain to her what he had in mind.

For Anne the Christmas season was darkened by the thought that December marked the third anniversary of Richard's death and burning. However, she was determined to create a festive atmosphere in her house, partly for Margaret's sake but also because she now had a close companion and husband who would be staying with her over Christmas.

Hermann Wedig, having absented himself from the Steelyard for a few days, was only too pleased to show his new wife and her daughter how Christmas was celebrated in Germany while they in turn explained to him the way things were done in England. Anne bought a large Yule log which she laid upon the coals in the hearth saying that it would be kept burning for the twelve days of Christmas. She made a hoop from willow, placed a small effigy of the Christ child in the middle and hung the Holy Bough inside the threshold of the house with mistletoe suspended beneath it. She explained to Hermann what was meant by this ancient tradition:

"Anyone who calls at the house during this season must show the good will they have brought with them by embracing under the Holy Bough. And for each stolen kiss beneath the mistletoe a berry is removed until there are no more kisses to be had." Hermann was quick to respond to this invitation. He took Anne is his arms and kissed her so many times that all the berries except one had to be removed. The last he kept for little Margaret from whom he stole a final kiss. Anne then had to replace the mistletoe which, as she said with feigned irritation, was not strictly within the rules.

On Christmas Eve, Hermann said that Anne and Margaret must leave their boots by the chimney and fill them with straw. "In Germany, long before we celebrated the feast days of the saints, we acknowledged a hunting god called Odin. Odin led a hunting party through the sky on an eight legged horse called Sleipnir, which could leap great distances across the heavens. Children were asked to leave straw by the chimney to feed Sleipnir on his heavenly journey and this tradition continues to this day – although it is now St Nicholas whom we are pleased to welcome into our homes."

After the straw had been laid out, Anne took some mince pies round to her neighbours – a butcher and his family – and when these had been consumed they all went off to Midnight Mass at the little parish Church of St Clement, Eastcheap. "My neighbours are discrete," Anne whispered to Hermann, "but it is better that we are in a large group when appearing before the priest."

On Christmas morning it was clear that Odin had paid a visit to Eastcheap. The straw was gone but the boots were full of presents: leather gloves, a pomander and various scented items for Anne and all manner of sweets, marzipan and other delicacies for Margaret – but most prized of all a beautifully carved figurine of Sleipnir, the eight legged horse.

Later that day the three of them walked over to Carter Lane to enjoy a Christmas feast at Rebecca's. After they had gorged themselves on the roast goose, Hermann surprised them all by producing a traditional German desert – a pastry concoction of cardaman, coriander, cloves, cinnamon and sugar which he had obtained from the Steelyard kitchen.

On Holy Innocents Day, December 28th, Anne, Hermann and Margaret went to see a masque put on by the students of Grays Inn. The staging and costumes were lavish, but Anne noted that the portrayal of the seven virtues was marred by the appearance of Temperance in a distinctly intoxicated state. When it was the turn of the seven deadly sins Avarice and Pride, both looking suspiciously like Wolsey, were loudly booed by the audience but Lust was given a hearty cheer by some of the students present. The evening ended with Justice rounding up the Vices and leading them off the stage to the accompaniment of raucous jeers and hissing.

On New Year's Day, presents were exchanged. Anne gave Hermann some embroidered handkerchiefs and Hermann gave her a jewelled brooch in the form of a miniature steelyard balance. The seasonal festivities came to a conclusion on Twelfth Night, when Rebecca and her family came round to Eastcheap and a steaming brew of cider, ginger, nutmeg and cinnamon was passed round in a wooden bowl.

Anne had taken great joy in sharing the Christmas and New Year celebrations with her new husband. Yet she was also troubled by the thought that the work of those who had suffered and died for the cause of religious liberation – first Richard and now Geoffrey and his friends – had still to be fulfilled. Her own contribution to the cause had been suddenly closed down and as the winter days went by she wondered how she could discharge the solemn vows she had entered into three years before.

It was at this point, only a few weeks into the new year, that Hermann came up with an idea that would renew her commitment while taking her life in an entirely unexpected direction. But before that could happen another surprise awaited her.

THOMAS MORE AT HOME

EARLY IN THE NEW YEAR A NOTE WAS DELIVERED TO
Anne's house in Eastcheap. The bearer did not wait for a reply
and the brief message was unsigned. It requested Anne to
come to the deanery of St Paul's at eleven o'clock the next
morning and to enter by the back door. Anne could not make
sense of this cryptic and anonymous communication but she
had no fear of the dean whom she knew by repute to be a man
of generous temperament and reformist sympathies. So she
appeared at the deanery at the appointed time where she was
met at the back entrance by a manservant and ushered into the
great man's study.

Anne was immediately struck by Colet's sickly appearance.
He sat by a window looking onto the close and a shaft of
sunlight accentuated the pallor of his still handsome face. He
rose from his chair and greeted his guest in a weak voice that
bore little resemblance to the stentorian tones in which he had
sermonised from St Paul's Cross on the two occasions Anne had
come to hear him.

"Mistress Anne Hunne, I must apologise for the obscurity
of my rather undignified communication but I am pleased you
have come. You, above all people, will appreciate that we live in
difficult times and that even deans have to watch their backs."

Anne stood awkwardly. "Reverend Dean, I fully understand the need for caution and I am honoured to be received in your house. But I confess I am puzzled as to the purpose of our meeting."

Colet motioned Anne to sit down as he resumed his seat. "Let me try to put you at your ease, although I shall be brief. I was and still am deeply saddened by the circumstances of your late husband's tragic death. I was especially concerned that his family was deprived of his estate and left without means of support. Therefore I made arrangements for you to have the tenancy of your present house in Eastcheap."

Anne was stunned, but as she tried, with tears in her eyes, to express her overwhelming gratitude Colet interrupted. "There is no need for you to feel indebted to me. Thanks to the enterprise of my late father I am a man of considerable means and it was a small matter to help to remedy a gross injustice visited on yourself and your daughter. However, I am now a sick man and my life is drawing to a close. Before I am called to account for my actions before God I wish to ensure that your own enjoyment of the house in Eastcheap is made permanent." He indicated a bundle of papers lying on the table beside him. "I have prepared deeds and documents that will transfer the freehold to yourself. I could, of course, have made such a provision in my will but you will understand that there is a certain delicacy about the matter, so I prefer to make an *inter vivos* gift."

For a moment Anne was left speechless. One of her benefactors had at long last revealed himself to her and now he was proposing to do more. Tears coursed down her cheeks as she rose to kiss his hand and it was some minutes before she could collect her thoughts. "I cannot say how much this means to me. I hope only that the good Lord restores you to health so that you may continue your work in His service for many years to come. The Church is sorely in need of you."

Colet smiled and said he was resigned to whatever fate awaited him. He was satisfied that his school was in good hands and that his chapter was in better order than when he was first appointed. As for the wider Church, he acknowledged that there were grave problems. He had made known his views on the need for reform but it now fell to others to bring that about.

Before they parted Anne plucked up courage to ask the question that weighed so heavily on her mind. "Tell me, Reverend Dean, I know little of what befell my poor Richard in Lollards' Tower ..." She turned to the window and looked at the very building standing only a few yards away. "Can you enlighten me on the events of that night?"

Colet looked grave. "Mistress Anne, I have my own views on what may have transpired, but I am not privy to the facts of the case. The man who knows as much as anyone, because he was closely involved in all the enquiries into the matter, is my good friend, Thomas More, now counsellor to His Highness. He may be able to enlighten you. If you are so minded, I am happy to write a note to him to propose that he should see you."

Anne said she would be very grateful if he would do that but wondered whether such an eminent and busy man would be prepared to find time to talk to her.

Colet chided her gently. "Well, I am sure I am neither as eminent nor as busy as my friend More but I dare say he will deign to see you just as I have done if I request him to do so."

Anne blushed and regretted her clumsiness, but Colet was clearly amused rather than insulted by her indiscretion. He said the documents he had prepared for the transfer of the freehold at Eastcheap would be sent round to her within the next few days. He also reminded her that the whole transaction was, of course, highly confidential.

As Anne got up to leave, he gave her a word of warning. "My friend Thomas is a man of great intellect and learning and

I also consider him to be fair-minded. But at the end he will always defend the Church and you should have that in mind when you see him."

Anne thanked the dean for this final piece of advice before departing discreetly through the back door of the building.

It was about a month later that Anne received a communication from Thomas More. This time the messenger waited at the door for a reply and the note itself was signed. Anne conjectured that the dean had to take precautions because he was answerable before a vindictive bishop whereas More, being close to the King, had no such need. It was arranged that Anne would be received at More's own house, the Old Barge, off Wallbrook, where she duly presented herself at the appointed time.

The Old Barge was a very large ramshackle building of stone and timber set on the south side of Bucklersbury. Anne was taken by a servant into a lobby area where she was asked to wait. An enormous bird cage hung from a beam presumably for the amusement of guests and she watched fascinated as a variety of colourful small birds twittered, pecked, hopped, and preened. While she waited she went through in her mind the best way of conducting herself during the interview. She would, of course, give no hint that she was familiar with the coroner's report but rather present herself as a simple innocent widow enquiring into her late husband's death, the reasons for the charges against those who had custody of him and the reasons also why those charges had been dismissed. The rest she would leave to Thomas More.

After some minutes, Anne was summoned into a large chamber furnished comfortably with rugs and wall hangings and warmed by a blazing fire. More was sitting at his desk in the centre of the room and she stood there, rather awkwardly, in front of him as a suspect might appear before a judge.

More was a dark, full-faced and smooth skinned man in his late thirties. Anne felt a little intimidated by the severity of his expression and she thought she detected a hint of cruelty in his penetrating eyes and the firm set of his mouth. When he spoke he did so with a commanding and silky eloquence that befitted England's most brilliant lawyer.

"I am pleased to welcome you to my house, Mistress Anne, although I must apologise for the rather disordered state of our domestic arrangements. The Old Barge is too big for our needs and we have tenants in part of the building. You may be interested to know that the name is owing to the fact that before the Wallbrook was paved over in the last century barges were towed up to Bucklersbury and moored hereabouts."

After thanking her host for seeing her, Anne explained that her only desire was to know everything that could be known about her late husband's death so that she could settle her mind on the subject.

More nodded in sympathy. "I understand your wish to satisfy yourself as to your late husband's fate. My friend Colet was right to direct you to my door because as undersheriff I was engaged closely with the case. I was present at your husband's post-mortem trial at St Paul's; also at a conference convened at Baynard's Castle to examine the merits of charges brought against certain church officers; and I have personally spoken with almost all those connected with the events that concern us – excepting the deceased himself. You might say that I know the case from top to toe."

Anne was surprised that More made no reference whatever to the most important evidence of all, namely the report of the coroner's inquest, to which she imagined he must, as undersheriff, have had ready access. He would of course assume that she was unaware of the document because it remained confidential.

More leaned back in his chair. "Let me say first that I understand your husband to have been an honest man in his dealings, and of good substance and repute. As for the heresy proceedings against him I believe it is best for us both if we do not go into that painful subject – except for me to say that I did myself witness his Wycliffe Bible with its markings."

Anne could not help asking a question at this point, knowing full well that she was treading on dangerous ground. "Being but a simple woman of poor understanding, may I be so bold as to ask whether it is seemly and proper for a man or woman to read the scripture in their own tongue?"

More gave her an inquisitorial look. "That depends on the Bible and also on the reader. Not all translations are of equal merit and some have wicked prologues or glosses. Similarly those who wish to read the Bible in their own tongue include both heretics and good Catholic folk. But surely if the bishop gives his approval both to the English Bible in question and to he or she who would read it for their use only, he may allow it for their devotion. Be that as it may, the Church must at all times direct the means by which the word of God is received by the people."

Anne thanked him for enlightening her on this point, but confided to herself the thought that More must surely know that the priesthood's power over the faithful would be forfeit if they were to read and interpret the scriptures for themselves.

More now addressed directly the question that had prompted Anne's visit.

"Mistress Anne, the purpose of your presence here, as you have said, is to discover how your late husband died. You will be aware of the Church's view that he hanged himself and that charges later brought against the bishop's chancellor and his subordinates were dismissed in the secular court. Let me now tell you what I know and what I think.

"You must forgive me for saying so, but your late husband, in bringing his praemunire suit, was, I believe, set on the glory of a great victory, which he trusted would be spoken of long after his days as 'Hunne's case'. When he perceived that the suit was about to fail in the temporal court and when also he was faced with a well-founded charge of heresy in the spiritual court, he must have feared the public shame which would shortly be brought upon him. Therefore I believe it more likely than not that, for weariness of life, he killed himself."

Anne marvelled that this lofty man could presume to know the inner thoughts of her late husband whose burning faith, she knew, would never allow him to despair. "But what of the charges brought against the bishop's chancellor and his two officers?" she asked.

"The coroner's jury were no doubt right honest men who found their verdict according to their consciences. But in this charge against the bishop's chancellor they were mistaken. The chancellor had no good reason to kill your late husband because he had already gathered sufficient evidence against him to bring shame upon him and perhaps even shameful death. Furthermore, after the whole matter was examined exhaustively before the King at Baynard's Castle, His Highness, in his wisdom, perceived that Dr Horsey was innocent and commanded his attorney to accept the plea of not guilty – which he would not have done unless he was satisfied that the chancellor, as well as the two others indicted with him, were truly innocent. As for myself, having heard all the arguments on both sides, I cannot believe that the chancellor murdered your husband."

Anne called to mind again that More made no mention of the overwhelming evidence of foul play presented by the coroner's jury. She therefore tried to draw him out. "But were there not reasons given by the jury for their verdict of murder?"

More addressed Anne as a patient schoolmaster might speak to a slow-learning pupil.

"Some suspicious circumstances were laid out but when later examined they were fully answered. Let me suggest to you something by way of a parable, if I may. Consider a man called to give evidence before the Lords at the Baynard's Castle conference.

"A layman reports words said to have been spoken by the chancellor, a most pious man. 'My Lords all,' says the layman, 'So help me God, Master Doctor here said unto me from his own mouth that if Hunne had not sued the praemunire, he should never have been accused of heresy.' And so the Lords inquire of the chancellor. 'How say you, Master Doctor? Is that true? Or, if not, then what did you say?'

'Surely, my Lords', says the chancellor, 'What I said was that if Hunne had not been accused of heresy he would never have sued the praemunire.'

'There my Lords!' says the layman, 'I am glad you find I have spoken the truth. Do you command any further service from me?'

'No, not at all,' replies one of the Lords. 'You are free to go. For it seems that as long as the words are the same it matters not to you in which order they are placed; a horsemill or a millhorse, drink before you go or go before you drink.'

'I will not drink God bless you,' says the plain old honest man, leaving the Lords laughing at his simplicity."

Anne considered herself insulted by More's childish play on words, as if it cast any light on a matter so critical to her own peace of mind. However, she gave no indication of the offence she felt and, since the interview was clearly over, merely declared her gratitude for the opportunity to talk to someone of his eminence who was so familiar with the case.

More gave her a condescending smile and expressed the hope that she would take some comfort from what he had told her. A servant was called to accompany her out and as she passed through the lobby with its aviary it occurred to her that in the mind of this masterly lawyer she was no more than one of his little caged creatures, a twittering bird whom he could easily appease by casting a few seeds in her direction.

As Anne reflected on the interview there was no doubt in her mind that More was deliberately holding back on the true story of Richard Hunne. She knew that lawyers were accustomed to tell lies on behalf of their clients, and that this lawyer's greatest client was the Church which, as Colet had warned, he was prepared to defend to the last.

Certainly her host had set out to deceive her. But there was one curious inconsistency in his account which she found surprising in a lawyer. He was entirely convinced that the bishop's chancellor was innocent of her late husband's murder but he was prepared to say only that it was more likely than not that Richard had killed himself. Yet if More allowed even the possibility that her husband had been killed by others how could he be so sure that the chancellor was not implicated? Anne understood that lawyers, and especially very clever lawyers, are careful about the words they use. So here was a puzzle to be added to many others surrounding the events in Lollards' Tower.

A New Career

IT WAS LATE MARCH AND THE FIRST INTIMATIONS OF
spring were to be seen in the crocuses, primroses and fresh grass
blanketing the fields and river banks around London. Hermann,
unable to escape from work, wanted to talk to Anne privately and
suggested that they take a stroll in the cloisters of All-Hallows-
the-Great near the Steelyard. The sun's rays warmed the old
stones of the vaulted arcade which echoed to the sound of their
footsteps. Seeing they were alone, Hermann took Anne's arm.
"I find the monastic regime imposed on me at the Steelyard an
increasing burden. I must stay so many nights there, sleep in my
monkish cell, eat at the common refectory and have only men as
visitors. I cannot admit to having a female companion still less
a foreign wife and when I stay with you I am like a schoolboy
playing truant."

Anne kissed his cheek. "The rules of the Hansa are like those
imposed on our own priests. They will always be disobeyed by
ordinary men of flesh and blood."

"It is an ideal that goes back to the Teutonic Knights,"
Hermann explained. "But enough of that, I have not come here
to complain about a course of life that I have chosen freely. I have
something of much greater interest to tell you. I have received
letters from Germany informing me that Martin Luther

continues his campaign against the Church. He has questioned the primacy of the Bishop of Rome, asserted that the Pope may err, that church councils may err and that only scripture is the final authority. He has even questioned those sacraments which cannot be justified by Holy Scripture. The German people are listening to him and there is a great thirst for his sermons and tracts which printers in Cologne, Wittenberg and many other centres are unable to satisfy."

"Is the Pope unable to lay charges against this man?" Anne asked.

"It is only a matter of time before the Pontiff orders his arrest," replied Hermann. "But there is a difficulty. Luther's attacks are founded on scholarship and even his enemies are impressed by his knowledge of scripture. The Church wants to outwit him by confronting him with known scholars in public debate. That way, they hope to discredit him before they bring charges. There is another problem … the German princes would prefer that he be tried, if tried he must be, in Germany rather than Rome, while Frederick of Saxony is loath to have him tried at all."

Anne tried to imagine how the Bishop of London would deal with such a man as Luther. There would be no public debates or scriptural refutations. Without further recourse, two swarthy summoners would no doubt appear unannounced at his lodging, put him in shackles and drag him off to Lollards' Tower where the world would hear no more of him. After many weeks of hardship he would be declared a heretic at a hearing of bishops and given the choice of public recantation and penance or the fire at Smithfield.

Hermann now lowered his voice as he led Anne along the passageway to a point furthest from the church entrance and furthest also from prying eyes and evesdroppers.

"Now, Anne, I am a simple merchant and everything I undertake is for profit. But I am also, like you, a strong believer in allowing the faithful to read the Gospels in their own tongue. Also in the need to break the hold of the Pope, his bishops and the priesthood over the lives of ordinary men and women. It so happens that there is an opportunity here. The people want to read the words of Luther and other reformers; and the printing press makes that possible. Printing is in a far greater state of advancement in Germany than here in England and there is money to be made by shipping Lutheran books and tracts from river ports such as Cologne and Antwerp to London. The English Church itself commissions Latin Bibles, brevaries and prayer books from printers outside England. Now I propose to use these same foreign printing presses to attack the English Church."

"But surely these works are presently printed in Latin or, perhaps, in German. Why would English readers wish to buy such books?"

"A good question Anne. There is already a strong demand for the Latin writings of Luther among scholars, universities, lawyers and the like. But I foresee that very shortly – within a year or two and maybe sooner – these and other works will be translated into English for interested persons here in England. I wish to begin now in a small way to bring in reformist religious books and then take my opportunity when the tide comes in – as certainly it will."

Anne well understood the power of print. After labouring in the scriptorium she was astounded at what Hermann had already told her about the speed of the press, the scale of production and the ease with which new editions of the same book could be issued.

Hermann continued. "A good sized book can be produced by a small printing house in, say, Cologne, for less than one shilling a copy. The price for merchants when landed in England would be around three shillings and for retail the price would be perhaps four shillings. This allows a good profit for the importer after allowing for the cost of shipping. Even so, the price to an English buyer would be far below the cost of the same book in manuscript which would run into several pounds. You see, Anne, the press has the power to change the world. Even now, the printed word is allowing a humble monk in Wittenberg to shake St Peter's throne in Rome."

Anne was sceptical: "But what about the risk of detection and the danger that forbidden books will be seized and destroyed by those in authority – as well as the threat that the importer and his associates might be imprisoned or worse?"

"True, there is some peril in all of this. But precautions can be taken. I am an importer of wine from Germany and northern France and books can be hidden in casks of wine. Furthermore, the Steelyard, as a fortified wharf with its own trading privileges, denies access to customs house officials. There is however the problem of finding some sound man to distribute the books stored in the Steelyard. He would need to understand the risks of the business and have connections with those of our religious persuasion. Do you by chance know of such a man?"

Anne thought for a moment: "Yes, I think I know the very person you need. If you come to Eastcheap on the morrow at around noon I can arrange for him to be there to meet you."

Hermann readily agreed to Anne's suggestion. They left the cloisters and walked slowly back along Thames Street, still arm in arm.

The next day Hermann appeared at Eastcheap as promised. Anne embraced him and then took him into the parlour and asked him to wait. "Our friend whom I want you to meet is upstairs. He is a retiring and rather mistrustful person and I must encourage him to come down."

Hermann expressed puzzlement at the timidity of a man who was supposed to be robust enough to carry out undercover work but he nevertheless agreed to wait patiently. There were sounds of movement above and after a few minutes a figure emerged in a dark cloak and a Tudor bonnet. The stranger took Hermann's hand, bowed and said simply, "Thomas Hendrick at your service, Sir."

Anne could see the astonishment in Hermann's eyes and guessed he was all but convinced that the person before him was a gentleman. Such was the effect of her simple disguise: tying her hair up under a round hat, flattening her chest, donning a cloak and lowering her voice.

Hermann recovered himself and joined in the charade: "I am honoured to make your acquaintance Sir," he replied. "I believe you have been advised of my business and the vacancy that I have for someone to distribute foreign printed books hereabouts."

They burst out laughing simultaneously but it was not long before Hermann adopted a more serious tone. "Anne, if you are truly putting yourself forward as a contender for the post I have in mind, I must be honest with you. Selling books is more dangerous than importing them. After all, if suspicions arise I can hope to escape from my fortified enclave and take ship to Germany but if you were discovered you would have your daughter here and nowhere to go. Believe me, too, it is not women's work. Even in the Steelyard where Hansa rules apply, the language of the merchants is often coarse and unsuitable for a woman's ears."

Anne dismissed Hermann's concerns: Rebecca would look after Margaret if anything happened to her; she had already exposed herself to grave danger by working at the scriptorium; she had gained experience of undercover work and she had direct access to London's Lollard communities who would provide a market for the imported books. As for bad language, did he really believe she could not handle that?

Hermann admitted reluctantly that she was perfectly suited to helping in his new line of business. "Well, perhaps there is a role for Thomas Hendrick, but first I would like to extend an invitation to this gentleman to dine as my guest at the Steelyard to see how he finds the company of Hansa merchants – and to discover also how they find him."

Anne was happy to accept this test of her new persona and it was agreed that she, as Thomas Hendrick, would sup with the Hansa. To prepare for this she was given a brief lesson on how to conduct herself at a merchants' table while she for her own part practised her assumed voice and manner.

Two days later, Anne found herself seated next to Hermann in the panelled refectory of the Steelyard. They were served with beer and bratwurst – a mixture of pork, veal and spices stuffed in a casing and smoked.

"This is our common fare," explained Hermann, "but on feast days we have venison, best Rhenish wine and all manner of delicacies. Let me now acquaint you with my fellow Hansa, Georg Gisze, sitting beside you, who prides himself on his good English."

Gisze made known that he was an importer of beeswax, which he shipped all the way from Russia, Livonia and his homeland, Prussia. Anne was introduced as Thomas Hendrick, a London merchant who had previous connections with the cloth trade but who was now hoping to assist Hermann with his business.

"I had thought that those English merchants who are members of The Worshipful Company of Wax Chandlers had command of the wax trade in these parts," Anne ventured.

"Ah, by no means", replied Gisze. "The need for beeswax, above all for the Church, is so pressing that English chandlers cannot satisfy all. Consider that the cathedrals and churches require wax tapers for masses, the high altar, their chantries, funerals, marriages, baptisms, processions and also to light up their shrines. Why, the great rood at the north door at St Paul's alone consumes many tapers each day. Let me tell you that Hansa imports of beeswax into England can be measured in several thousand hundredweight each year to help meet all these needs."

Anne knew that the price of beeswax far exceeded that of the humble tallow used in households and could imagine the huge cost of feeding the Church's insatiable appetite for wax tapers.

"Of course", added Gisze with a chuckle, "there are other uses for wax. I have heard, for instance, that young damsels, fearful of being with child, use hot wax to stop up their wombs."

Anne thought it best to laugh coarsely at this point.

"My fear is that the present good times could come to an end. If these cursed Lollards, reformers and Lutherans were to have their way, the use of tapers for devotion and Church ceremony would be greatly curtailed and my trade would suffer."

Anne gave him a sympathetic look. "Let us indeed hope that wax tapers continue to illuminate the worship of us Christian souls. After all, the Church teaches us that pure beeswax is symbolic of Christ's flesh, the wick his soul and the flame his divinity. It is very fitting, therefore, that tapers should light our path to his heavenly kingdom." What she omitted to say was that tapers, in her mind, were used not only to beautify the sacraments but also to bewitch the simple minded.

Gisze beamed. "I am very glad you see things the same way. Unfortunately, many of my fellow Hansa merchants here are of a different persuasion. It is a privilege to make the acquaintance of someone with such well-formed opinions."

The evening's proceedings ended after platters of hazelnuts, figs and dates had been consumed. And it was clear from the reassuring expression on Hermann's face that Anne had acquitted herself well in her new identity.

GET LUTHER

IT HAD BEEN ANNE'S IDEA TO TRAVEL TO GERMANY
with her new husband. After all, she was his London agent and
it would help to know more about the printing of the books
she imported and distributed. Also, she was curious to see
the country that Hermann described lovingly and the city of
Cologne where he spent much of his time.

Hermann himself had been enthusiastic about the suggestion
but he insisted that Anne should travel not as his wife but as
Thomas Hendrick. He said that in Germany, as in England,
women were excluded from business and the Hansa would in
any case expel him if they found out that he had married an
Englishwoman. So, while they could be man and wife behind
closed doors, they must be business partners in the eyes of the
world. The voyage was planned for April to coincide with the
spring Frankfurt Book Fair which they hoped to attend. They
had boarded the Danzig, a large three masted Hansa vessel, in
London and now here they were standing on the foredeck as the
ship sailed into the port of Cologne. The sea crossing had been
rough and the ship had pitched and rolled but as soon as they
reached Rotterdam things had calmed down, the wool-laden
vessel sliding peacefully down the Rhine past castles, towers and
walled towns.

Amid much shouting in English and German, warps were flung onto the quayside and wound around mooring posts. Once the bow and stern lines had been secured a treadwheel harbour crane was made ready to hoist the ship's cargo out of the hold.

"They will land some of the cloth here," Hermann said to Anne, "but the bulk will be taken further downstream to the River Main and then to Frankfurt and Nuremburg. As for ourselves, we must gather our baggage. I will hire a cart to take us to my house in the centre of town."

As they trundled through the city, Anne was struck by the prosperity of the place. Many of the buildings were in stone, there were numerous fine churches and the people were well clothed, with women in kirtles of rich fabric and men in leather tunics and loose hoods. The carrier halted outside a stone house which, in common with neighbouring properties, featured a steeply pitched and stepped gable.

The housekeeper was a portly and self-important woman. When Anne was introduced to her as Hermann's English agent, she looked at her with suspicion – the more so when Hermann insisted that they would occupy only one room on the second floor. Climbing the stairs Hermann whispered to Anne, "Helga is rather severe. But she guards my interests like a tigress. It is better that she is not in on the secret, for the sake of the business we have here."

Once in their room, Hermann took Anne in his arms. She sighed. "It is difficult to go on playing this part for so long. When I want to take your arm or slip my hand into yours I must stop myself."

Hermann gave her a squeeze. "Dearest Anne, behind this door we are still man and wife. We can manage the pretence for a week or two." She nodded and he wiped a tear from her eye. "At least we can talk freely since Helga does not understand a word of English."

The next morning Helga served them a leisurely breakfast. Hermann smiled at Anne. "Thomas, I must go to the Hansa office here to see what news they have and also to arrange a ship for our return. Perhaps you would like to see our cathedral which is only a few minutes from here?"

"An excellent idea," Anne replied. "I have heard all about the relics of the three Magi. I will join the pilgrims at the shrine, though not as a fellow idolater."

"There will be many innocent souls seeking solace from this icon. You can put in a prayer for me," he said with a mischievous smile. "Later on today we can visit the printer who will tell us about the production of books."

Anne made her way through narrow passageways overhung with trade signs to the cathedral precinct. Hermann had warned her that she might be disappointed and she could see why. The eastern façade of the basilica was complete and imposing but the western frontage was only half-built, a crane surmounting one of the unfinished twin towers. Such was the scale of the structure that this city, with all its wealth, had run out of money.

She entered the eastern end of the building and was confronted by a dense crowd of pilgrims, jostling and pushing to get as close as possible to the shrine of the three wise men. This was displayed immediately behind the high altar in the form of an enormous basilica, gilded and ornamented with enamels and gemstones.

Some people were crossing themselves while others were on their knees in a show of unrestrained devotion. The press of people, the wailing of tormented souls and the foul air were too much for Anne. She left hurriedly and felt greatly relieved once outside and able to breathe freely. She walked back to her new lodging and waited for Hermann in the parlour – a warmly furnished room on the first floor overlooking the bustling street.

When he returned from the Hansa office he had an excited air about him but he was giving nothing away. "The printer I spoke to you about is expecting us. So we can see him now and you will be able to learn all about his trade."

"That is hardly likely," Anne replied tartly, "seeing that I have no knowledge of your language. But I may at least watch the printing press perform."

Hermann said little as they made their way through winding alleys to a modest building with a painted sign depicting the tree of knowledge. The door was opened to them by a youth in an ink-spattered apron. Entering the print shop, Anne was immediately aware of a strong aroma – a curious blend of oiled wood, damp paper and soot.

There were four operatives in the print shop, supervised by a dark haired and gaunt young man who greeted Hermann as an old friend. Hermann, speaking in English, introduced Anne as Thomas Hendrick, his London agent and then turned to Anne. "Thomas, Peter Quintel here came over to Germany from England to learn his craft and now has his own business here in Cologne." The master printer, responding to the surprised look on Anne's face, added: "I did my apprenticeship in Mainz. There are many foreigners working in print shops in Germany because everything is more advanced here."

Looking closely at a contraption that resembled a wine press, Anne asked, "And how do you go about printing your books?"

Peter pointed to a long wooden box of metal letters adjoining one wall. "It is very simple really. We take these letters and arrange them in a tray – as Johann here is doing – to form a page of text. The compositor who does this must be well versed in German and Latin because we produce books in both languages."

"What is that boy doing with those pads?" Anne asked.

"That is the next stage. The pads are infused with ink which is then transmitted to the typeface."

"The ink smells of soot. Why is that?" Anne asked.

"Because it is soot." Peter replied. "It is a mixture of lamp soot and oils that give it adhesion."

"And the apprentice over there?" Anne pointed to a youth with a sponge.

"He is preparing the paper, which must be damped to absorb the print. The sheet is then held between two frames and placed on the flat surface beneath the press. The windlass is used to turn the press screw, the base bearing down on the paper which is imprinted with the typeface beneath. This is a hard labour for Helmut who repeats the process many hundreds of times each day."

Anne was astonished by the inventiveness and careful organisation that had gone into all she was seeing. When compared to the scriptorium it seemed that a new age had dawned for the reproduction of the written word. And what power lay in this modest print shop!

"Tell me, how many pages can you print in one day?" she asked.

"Maybe five hundred pages, printed on both sides – that is one thousand imprints in all. Perhaps more if the apprentices are working at their best."

Hermann looked triumphantly at Anne. "You can see now how a man can reach out to the world. Ideas can be spread in no time through the printing press. And bear in mind that this is just one of hundreds of print shops scattered in towns all over Germany."

Anne noticed that there were printed pamphlets and texts laid out on a table set against the wall. There were anti-Lutheran tracts with covers depicting the monk as an ass, a devil or a wild boar and there were others that she took to be Lutheran works, some in Latin and others in German.

Peter must have noticed what had caught her attention. "I take commissions for all manner of works. Although in this town I have to be careful because the people do not favour Luther – perhaps because of the money that pilgrimage brings in. For instance, take Luther's latest work, *The Babylonian Captivity of the Church* ..." He held up a slender volume. "There is great demand from outside Cologne and I am happy to print it but I leave no printer's mark."

Anne was doubtful: "I can see that in print shops there is great opportunity to instruct the world and increase understanding among people. But there is surely an equal possibility of spreading harm and falsehoods throughout Christendom."

"That may well be true. But who is to say what is false and what is true? As a humble printer I make no such judgement: I simply print whatever is put into my hands."

"Well my friend, I have some business to put into yours hands today," Hermann said. "I wish to commission one hundred copies of the *Babylonian Captivity* in Latin for despatch to England. Leave them at the quayside with my agents who have special instructions for loading."

When they were departing, Peter gave Anne as a memento an anti-Lutheran pamphlet whose cover depicted a pipe-playing devil wrapped around the monk's head. "Master Thomas, this may not be to your liking but it is an example of our art and you will be safe with it in England."

———————

Anne and Hermann dined at home that evening on fish from the Rhine served by Helga. Pouring Rhenish wine into their goblets, Hermann divulged the news he had heard from the Hansa office that morning. "Thomas, Charles V's Imperial Diet is meeting at Worms right now. This is the most important assembly in Europe and what I have learned today is that Martin Luther himself has been summoned by the Emperor to appear before him at the Diet. I think we should go to see this great spectacle."

Anne pushed away her platter and stared at Hermann. "This is something momentous. When is he making his appearance? And how long would it take us to get to Worms?"

"The town is about two days sailing up river from here. Luther is required to defend his opinions before the Emperor within the next few days. We have to take a boat in the morning if we are to be there for the confrontation. Of course, we may not be able to witness the scene but Worms will be full of excitement and we will find out about the proceedings."

Anne's interest was now thoroughly aroused. "It is worth travelling all this way just to be in the very place and on the very day of Luther's examination. I am all for going."

"That is settled then. I checked at the Hansa office and one of our boats is heading towards Nuremburg tomorrow morning. We must be at the quayside soon after first light with whatever belongings we need."

"Where will we stay?"

"Worms will be overflowing and the inns will be full but there is a hostelry I know that will always find room for a Hansa merchant."

It was evening when they sailed into Worms. The port was heaving with human activity and full of vessels, large and small. The boatmen had to moor alongside a carrack and, helped by a porter, Anne and Hermann clambered awkwardly across to the quayside with their baggage. Once on land, Hermann led the way through jostling crowds to a quiet cul-de sac where the sign of a black boar projected from a tall timber-framed building. Soaring above them, in the neighbourhood beyond, was a great cathedral of red sandstone whose lofty towers and twin domes had caught the last rays of the setting sun. For a moment they both stood staring at the fiery edifice. "That is where Luther will be heading", Hermann said. "The hearing will be in the bishop's palace adjoining the nave. We must now try our luck here. It is a favoured hostelry for the Hansa."

The innkeeper, a giant of a man with a midriff the size of a beer cask, greeted Hermann as an old customer. There followed an earnest conversation in German during which Hermann grasped the other's arm and pointed to their baggage. Anne assumed he must be pressing their need for accommodation but the innkeeper's initial response was to furrow his brow and shake his head. Hermann leaned over to Anne. "He says everywhere is full and so great is the crush of incomers that tents have been erected outside the city and some are sleeping in cowsheds. Here at the inn, the Duke of Brunswick has demanded that his men occupy all the rooms."

But after much head scratching there appeared to be a change of mind. Following a shouted exchange with a woman somewhere at the back of the building they were led up several flights of rickety stairs to what was little more than a box room containing a single bed. Their host was all the time talking with animation, the only word recognised by Anne being *Luther*.

When they were alone, Hermann explained the excitement. "Our host, Wilhelm, says Luther came into town around midday in an ox waggon. Cheering crowds went out to meet him and followed him to his lodging at the house of the Knights of St John."

"So in this town the people are in favour of Luther?" Anne asked.

"It seems so. But as Wilhelm pointed out the monk is up against the full might of the Empire and all its emissaries. Small chance for him I fear."

Lying in bed that night, Anne felt overwhelmed by the strangeness of everything. Moving from Amersham to London had been disorientating. But here she was surrounded by a harshly spoken foreign language, steep roofed buildings of alien appearance and men and women in novel attire. And now she found herself thrust into the middle of an extraordinary drama affecting a far wider world than she had known – an all embracing empire of many nations of which she had little concept. All this was far removed from the comfort of her own home, the narrow confines of Eastcheap and the familiar voices of family and friends.

She turned over restlessly and reached out to feel the warmth and reassuring presence of the man beside her.

The sun rose next day on a city full of expectation. The historic encounter between the priest from Wittenberg and Emperor Charles V, scion of the house of Hapsburg and ruler of domains larger than any since Charlemagne, was due to take place that afternoon in the bishop's palace.

Hermann and Anne joined the crowds assembling around the cathedral. Anne was struck by the magnificence of the eastern apse which cascaded downwards in tiers of Romanesque arcades like folds of molten lava. After speaking with officials posted outside the adjoining palace, Hermann reported to Anne that there was no chance of gaining entry to the building. So they, along with several thousand others, waited impatiently for news of the proceedings.

After scarcely half an hour figures began to emerge from inside. Rumours swept through the crowd and Hermann said,

"I think it is all over. They say Luther has declined to uphold his writings and that all proceedings against him are to be dismissed."

Anne felt betrayed. "What a dismal ending! His faith has failed him. I wish we had never come."

Hermann held her arm. "It is one thing to take on the world through the printed word. It is another to stand face to face with the Emperor and the leaders of Christendom who have power over life and death."

With the subdued crowd beginning to disperse they made their way back to the Black Boar. "We can take a boat back to Cologne in the morning," Hermann said, gloomily. "But I shall drink a beer with Wilhelm tonight."

Anne said she was tired and retired early to bed. Lying there disconsolate she wished she were back at home. She was an outsider in this country and never more than a passive onlooker, separated from all around her by language and nationality. The thought that Luther had thrown in his hand added to her distress. The cause of Church reform would be set back, perhaps indefinitely, not only here but in England. And the demand for imported Lutheran books would collapse once it was known that their author had publicly recanted.

She was dozing off when Hermann came bounding up the stairs and burst into the room. "It is not what we thought! We were drinking with Wilhelm. A junker aide to the Duke of Brunswick was there. He attended the hearing and told us everything."

Anne sat up. "I cannot believe there is any more to be said."

"Let me tell you what happened. Luther was asked only two questions … first, whether he was the author of the books they set out before him and, second, if so, whether he would renounce the views expressed in those works."

"Well he could hardly deny his authorship," Anne said curtly.

"Of course not," Hermann replied. "But on the second question he would give no immediate answer and asked for more time. The Emperor's response was to give him just twenty four hours. He will be recalled to the assembly at the same time on the morrow."

Anne was not in the mood to take much encouragement from the news. "It comes to the same thing. He is prevaricating because he fears the consequences of standing firm. He has already shown his weakness and betrayed his cause."

Hermann shook his head. "You are being too harsh on him, Anne. I believe he wishes to prepare a full answer. In any case we have a chance to witness the scene because the Burgundian junker says he can get us into the bishop's palace."

Anne was sceptical. "Yes we should go. But I will not raise my expectations too high. We could be about to witness the dissolution of the reformist movement and a final victory for the old Church."

"Or perhaps the martyrdom of a great theologian and reformist leader," Hermann said. "They have him in a corner … if he recants, his credibility is destroyed and all his works become empty words. But if he reaffirms his views they will kill him as a heretic and outlaw, cutting short his mission and leaving his followers leaderless. They have worked it out. Either way, they get Luther.

32

THE WARTBURG

THE NEXT DAY AT FOUR O'CLOCK IN THE AFTERNOON, the dignitaries of the Holy Roman Empire – Electors, princes, bishops, nobles and courtiers – were assembled in the audience hall of the bishop's palace. Presiding over them was the Emperor Charles V, seated at one end on a raised throne over which hung a canopy. Anne and Hermann were among a group of privileged onlookers, able to witness the scene from an anteroom whose doors onto the hall were held open.

Anne surveyed the scene noting that there was not a single woman to be seen either in the hall or indeed among the onlookers around her. What caught her eye were the colourful berretas of bishops, papal nuncios and priests, the rich fur trimmed gowns of ambassadors and the nobility of Europe and the Emperor, holding his sceptre, draped in gold and scarlet damask. In stark contrast, standing in the centre of the hall, facing all these notables of Empire and Christendom, was a tonsured monk in the humble habit of his Augustinian order, before him a table on which were displayed his printed works.

After everyone was called to order, a high official, whom Anne took to be a spokesman for the Emperor, turned to Luther and addressed him first in Latin then in German. The monk, undaunted by the forces arraigned against him, responded in

Latin in measured and respectful tones. The high official then asked him to repeat what he had said in German, which he did. But towards the end of his statement he raised his voice and looked up at his accusers with an air of defiance. It was clear, even to Anne, that he was flatly refusing to renounce his views and this became even more apparent when he finally raised his arm in a victory salute as might a triumphant knight after winning a jousting bout.

For a few moments the assembly descended into uproar and hissing before order was restored by the Emperor's official. "He's done for," Hermann whispered to Anne. "We should leave right now because there could be trouble when the crowds outside get to know."

Hurrying back to the inn, Anne asked. "What happens next? Should we not wait until we see what they decide to do with him?"

"There is no point in staying. They say he has a safe conduct to allow him to travel back to Wittenberg. Certainly, he will be allowed to leave Worms but thereafter who can say. It is quite likely that he will be attacked en route given the stir he has created."

On entering the Black Boar, Wilhelm greeted them and handed a letter to Hermann which he took upstairs to their room. Sitting on the bed with Anne he read the contents twice over before looking up at her. "The Hansa in Cologne are worried about Luther's safety if he refuses to recant. Knowing I was here, they have asked us to follow the monk as he departs the town. They fear an assassin. But of course, we cannot oblige them."

"Why not?" Anne demanded.

"Because it would be too dangerous. Your safety dearest Anne is more important to me than Luther's. I cannot possibly expose you to the risk and in any case –"

"You must not refuse this request on my account," Anne cut in. "I can ride a horse and am well able to look after myself."

Hermann made a dismissive gesture. "This is not an assignment for a woman – and certainly not for my beloved wife whose wellbeing I prize above everything."

Anne stood up, glaring in defiance. "That I am a woman has no bearing on it! The real point is this … Since coming to Germany I have observed this and I have witnessed that but I have not been part of what is going on around me. Now I can have a role in these events! Following this man out of Worms would be an honour. So please let us not argue over the matter."

Hermann got up and walked over to the window. After some moments of reflection he turned to Anne. "Very well. I can see that there is no point in opposing you. We will have to hire horses, we must carry arms and we will follow Luther and his group of companions at a distance which gives no cause for suspicion. We will lodge here at the inn until they depart."

Anne's spirits lifted and she gave him a hug.

But he cautioned her. "This is not an adventure. Religious passions in this country are running high and anything can happen out there beyond the city walls of Worms."

From his travelling bag he extracted a sheathed short-sword. "This is my trusty seax, wielded in battle by my Saxon warrior forebears. We will have to buy a similar weapon for yourself in the market." He held up the single edged blade. "You must leave me to tackle any assailant. Your sword will be for your self-defence only." To which Anne made no response.

———————

Luther remained in Worms long enough for Anne and Hermann to learn that the Emperor had personally pronounced against him. It would only be a few days more before the Diet followed up with an edict outlawing the heretic monk, making him a legitimate target for any would-be assailant.

Mounted on their hired horses, Anne and Wedig watched the saxon ox-cart that had brought Luther to Worms carry him out of the city. A large crowd of well-wishers cheered him as he and his companions passed through the city gates. Hermann turned to Anne. "Little do they know. The louder their acclaim the more the Church will want him dead." They stood by for some time to allow the excitement to subside before riding out on the trail of the humble equipe.

For several days they travelled through small German towns – Oppenheim, Grunburg and Hersfeld – staying at cheap hostelries when their quarry halted for the night. On the open road they kept well behind in the hope that their pursuit would not be noticed among all the other travellers.

Shortly after entering the forested area of Thuringia they passed through Eisenach where Luther was feted by the residents. Here, Anne and Hermann halted their horses on the outskirts of the town.

"I think we have done our duty," Hermann said. "Luther is entering his home territory and should be safe. We will see him through the woods and then we can return to Worms.

"A long and uneventful journey. But we were right to do it – also I have seen so much more of your wonderful country. And to follow in the tracks of such a man!"

They followed Luther's entourage through dense woodland. Then, in a clearing ahead of them, there was a sudden commotion. Masked knights had emerged from the trees and, with loud shouts, surrounded the waggon. Anne saw a cowled figure forcibly removed from the cart, placed on a horse and led away into the forest.

All this had happened in an instant. They were too far behind to offer any assistance and in any case they would have been no match for the heavily armed knights. When they reached the scene of the abduction the driver of the waggon, though unhurt, was in a state of shock. "They pointed a crossbow at his head," Hermann told Anne. "The poor man could do nothing."

"We should follow them, surely," Anne said in a state of agitation. "We must see where they take him."

Hermann needed no such prompt. He spurred his horse and motioned to Anne to follow. They abandoned all caution as they rode along a winding forest path where fresh hoof prints and broken brushwood betrayed the flight of the abductors. They continued uphill until they saw towering above them a mighty fortress straddling an escarpment, the sheer stone cliff on which it sat rising over a thousand feet above the surrounding woodland. But before they could take in this awesome spectacle there was a violent movement from behind. Powerful arms pulled Anne from her horse and Hermann was unsaddled and pinned to the ground. Their ambushers were two armed knights who must have held back from the party ahead after spotting them on the forest path. The two men said not a word but bound their victims' hands after taking their weapons and led them on horseback up a steeply winding track towards the forbidding castle perched above them.

It was nightfall when they arrived eventually at a back entrance to the fortress. A torch bearer led the group across a wide courtyard to a bastion flanking the main gateway. Here Anne and Hermann were dismounted and pushed into a dank and foul smelling dungeon. After their hands had been unbound and their baggage taken away they were left in total darkness for the night by their captors, one of whom shouted something before he clanged the door shut.

"The commander of the castle is going to see us in the morning," Hermann said in a strained voice. "Things are not as they seem. This castle is the Wartburg, which is under the control of Frederick of Saxony. And Frederick is a strong supporter of Luther."

Anne was bewildered. "Why, then, would they abduct Luther and incarcerate him here against his will?"

"That was not a convincing abduction. There was no violence, no resistance by the victims and it all went a little too smoothly. I suspect Luther was forewarned and that the purpose is to keep him in isolation and out of harm's way."

"In that case, we can justify ourselves. We can explain that we, too, are here to protect the monk."

Hermann seemed more doubtful but, exhausted from the day's exertions, they said no more on the subject but lay down on filthy mattresses to drown their uneasy thoughts in sleep.

They awoke next morning as shafts of light radiated from the cell's barred window. They were brought bread and water by an orderly and, not long after, the commander made his appearance with an armed guard. He was a tall angular man with blond hair who walked with a stick, possibly as the result of a wound. He introduced himself as Hans von Berlep and began to interrogate Hermann who, pointing to Anne, explained that his companion was English. Von Berlep nodded towards Anne. "I speak a few words. When I fought as a Landsknecht there were some English with us."

He spoke quickly in German to Hermann whom Anne could tell was trying to convince the commander of their innocent intentions. But von Berlep kept making dismissive gestures. Suddenly he produced from his surcoat the anti-Lutheran tract with its devilish cover which Anne had been given in Cologne and had stowed in her travelling bag. He held up the abusive image and, looking directly at Anne, shouted "English spy!" He then gestured to them to look out of the cell window. Anne peered through the small aperture and scanned the sheer drop plunging hundreds of feet onto a rocky outcrop far below. She drew back and Hermann took his turn. That was the end of the interview because von Berlep motioned to the guard and the two men left.

Hermann, looking dazed, took Anne's hand. "We are in deep trouble."

"But this is absurd. We are on the same side."

"He is convinced that because we tracked Luther and possessed both arms and a pamphlet attacking him, we must be implicated in a plot to get rid of him. The fact that you are English makes it worse because it is known that England has anti-Lutheran agents operating in Europe." Hermann looked up at the window. "He says the easiest course for him is to drop us over the castle wall which would avoid the need for a judicial hearing and official reports. The wolves would finish the job for him. He is coming back later today and if we don't then confess all and give names of our backers the sentence will be carried out. We had better come up with something or else our journey ends here."

Anne stood by the cell window and stared out. "Surely the only thing we can do is tell him about our business of importing Lutheran and reformist texts into England. You can tell him about the German printers we deal with."

"I will certainly do that," Hermann said. "The only problem is that our familiarity with the illicit book business could equally be viewed as suspicious. Spies would be well informed on such matters and why would book traders want to chase Luther up here?"

"What about the letter from the Hansa in Cologne?" Anne asked.

"I put it on the fire at the inn. We have no proof of our innocence."

After the orderly had brought them more food and water they awaited the commander's return. Anne prayed and cried silently when she realised she might never again see Margaret and Rebecca or experience the sights, sounds and smells of Eastcheap.

Von Berlep and the guard appeared in late afternoon when light in the cell was already fading. Anne could do little more than look on anxiously as Hermann and his interrogator, seated on wooden stools, engaged in an intensive and, at times, angry discourse. This went on for perhaps half an hour before the commander stood up and, with what seemed to Anne an almost sorrowful look, gave a little bow, turned and left.

Hermann put his head in his hands and Anne knew that their fate had been sealed.

"The commander admitted that he could not know one way or the other whether our story was true or whether we were possible assassins." Wedig explained. "But he insisted he had been given a very heavy responsibility – I take it he means the custody of Luther – and that he could take no chance on us."

"So he is still open to a change of mind?"

"It is too late for that. We are to be taken up to the ramparts as first light and dropped into the valley below."

There was little more to be said. The moon cast a pallid light on the cell walls and from far off the unanswered call of a lone wolf was carried on the wind. After praying for deliverance, Anne sought comfort in her husband's arms.

———

The sun had risen and the upper stonework of the Wartburg was bathed in gold. Anne and Hermann, arms bound, were led up steps to the top of the castle tower where a wooden platform was raised against the parapet. Armed guards stood on either side of them and immediately opposite stood the commander. Anne looked over the edge and glimpsed the seemingly bottomless void below. As she prepared herself for death the commander shouted out something:

"He is asking whether we wish to say anything," Hermann said.

"I shall say a short prayer," Anne replied. "Please translate so the commander can hear."

Looking into the eyes of von Berlep, Anne raised her voice:
Lord, give me grace to hold righteousness in all things,
That I may lead a clean and blessed life and prudently
Flee evil and that I may withstand the treacherous and
deceitful falseness of the devil.
Make me mild, peaceable, courteous and temperate
And, when I am called, make me steadfast and strong.

Then she added slowly, her eyes fixed on von Berlep: "These are the words of John Wycliffe, which are written in my own hand on the blank page of the pamphlet that was taken from my travelling bag. I am a follower of Wycliffe, our English Luther, and because of that I die a loyal follower of your own German Luther."

Hermann again translated and it was clear that the words had struck home. After some hesitation, von Berlep raised his hand to stay the proceedings and ordered the two prisoners to be brought down.

Standing in the courtyard below the commander spoke to Hermann. "Thomas, he is asking you whether you can give further proof of your adherence to this man Wycliffe."

Anne again looked directly at her captor. "I believe you have Martin Luther in custody here. He will know about Wycliffe and I can prove to him that I am a follower by citing passages from Wycliffe's English Bible that I have learned."

Hermann translated. The commander's brow furrowed and he shouted angrily. "He insists Luther is not held in the castle," Hermann said.

Von Berlep was evidently weighing up whether or not to carry through with the summary execution. But a thought seemed suddenly to strike him and he motioned to the guards to take the prisoners back to their cell. Some minutes later he himself appeared and addressed them. Hermann explained to Anne. "He says there is a knight residing as a guest in the castle who is steeped in knowledge of the Bible. Von Berlep has challenged you to make your case to this man who is ready to see you now."

Still bound and guarded they followed von Berlep outside and across the forecourt to what appeared to be a timber framed guest house. Hermann whispered to Anne. "I believe you are about to be examined by none other than Martin Luther, though the pretence that he is not here must be kept up."

Anne felt overwhelmed. The idea of being questioned by the most contentious figure in the whole of Christendom was daunting, but she knew she had to hold her nerve.

They entered a panelled room where a man dressed in a tunic and cap sat at his desk. Anne had not been able to study him closely at the Diet of Worms but now she was a few feet away. He was heavily built and broad faced, and he looked unslept and unkempt. They said his searching eyes were like those of a hawk and she could see why. There was something predatory about him – a giant bird of prey full of stored energy, poised to launch against whatever moved.

The man was introduced as Junker George and Anne and Hermann were invited to sit on chairs facing him. Hermann again acted as translator for Anne as Junker George turned his gaze to Anne.

"While I have studied classical languages – Greek, Latin, Hebrew and Aramaic – I have had no cause to learn English. But I understand that you are familiar with the English Bible of John Wycliffe, which I know to be a great work of translation from the Latin."

Anne was aware that her moment had come: "I have always followed the words and teaching of John Wycliffe, who has guided me since childhood. My family have suffered at the hands of the English Church for their devotion to his beliefs but I continue to study his bible as the truest source of scripture."

Junker George nodded. He leaned forwards and Anne for a moment saw him as a projecting gargoyle. Hermann translated. "I now want you to cite for me the first verses of the fourth chapter of the Gospel according to St Mark."

Anne's mind went back to her Bible reading group and her recollection of the words came gradually into focus.

"And after Jesus began to teach at the sea; and much people was gathered to him; so that he went into a boat, and sat in the sea, and all the people was about the sea on the land.

And he taught them in parables many things. And he said to them in his teaching:

Hear ye, Lo! A man goeth out to sew and while he seweth some seed fell about the way, and birds of heaven came and ate it. Other fell down on stony places where it had not much earth; and anon it sprang up for it had not deepness of earth. And when the sun rose up, it wilted for heat, and it dried up, for it had no root –"

Hermann had translated Anne's recitation this far when their interlocutor interrupted. His words were passed on by Hermann to Anne. "That is enough. You have convinced me. Wycliffe was a great figure in the history of our Church who upheld the supremacy of scripture. We all owe him a great debt. I am honoured to have met one of his followers."

The commander indicated to Anne and Hermann that it was time to depart. They stood up, bowed and left the mysterious scholar-knight at his desk surrounded by books and papers.

Outside von Berlep addressed Hermann who communicated his instructions to Anne. "He says we are free to leave on our horses though he will keep our weapons as a precaution. For the first day we will be escorted out of the area and we must not return. Also, spreading false rumours about the supposed whereabouts of Luther would endanger both our lives and his, so we should take care."

———

As they negotiated the steep path leading down to the valley floor Anne looked back for the last time at the imposing stronghold above. She wondered what great project might be undertaken by the commander's scholarly charge during his forced residence in this isolated place. And she wondered, too, whether she would live to see the product of his endeavours.

A BOOK BURNING

WOLSEY SAT ALONE IN THE MAJESTIC AUDIENCE chamber of York Place after a long day of meetings with foreign emissaries, government officials and senior churchmen. Now that he had a brief respite from the press of business he could focus his mind on his future prospects.

True, he had good reason to be pleased with himself. The son of an Ipswich innkeeper and butcher, he had risen in little more than ten years from being a humble chaplain in the household of the Governor of Calais to become Archbishop of York, Cardinal, Lord Chancellor of England and Henry VIII's leading counsellor. But Wolsey saw himself not as a prelate but as a great renaissance prince with an entitlement to all the perquisites that went with such worldly eminence: he had a concubine, Mistress Lark, by whom he had a son and daughter; he had built palaces at Hampton Court and York Place fit for a King; he boasted a retinue of over four hundred servants and an income of £9,500 per annum; he held sway over the kingdom's entire domestic and foreign policy as well as all ecclesiastical matters. As others had noted, his form of address had gradually changed from "His Highness will do so and so" to "We shall do so and so" and, finally, "I shall do so and so".

Yet as he contemplated his achievements from the comfort of York Place – where visitors had to traverse eight rooms before arriving at the audience chamber – Wolsey felt that England was too small for his ambitions. He had in mind nothing less than the Papal See, should a vacancy arise, where, as a Roman potentate, he would be able to act on a European stage surrounded by the glittering splendour of his own palatine court.

But first he had to deal with the problem of Martin Luther. He had already concluded that something had to be seen to be done about this man whose teaching was the cause of much handwringing within the House of Hapsburg and the Curia in Rome. What was needed from him was a grandiose spectacle that would not only daunt the populace but also convince the papal and imperial courts that the Church's ancient practices and privileges were secure in his hands.

After much thought he decided that a ceremonial burning of Lutheran texts at Paul's Cross before the people and foreign dignitaries, himself presiding, would send out the right message to the wider Christian world.

The winter of 1521 had been severe and the bitter cold had eaten into the bones of the aged Bishop of London. He had been called to York Place to discuss an unnamed matter of urgency with the Cardinal but nowadays he disliked even short journeys and resented the summons. He took with him his secretary and, disembarking from his barge at York Stairs, noted the far reaching river frontage of the newly extended palace. He was led by liveried attendants through successive richly adorned chambers into an anteroom hung with tapestries, gilded chandeliers and a large arras.

Sitting uncomfortably on an unpadded carved oak chair, Fitzjames waited impatiently. Messengers were scurrying back and forth and he wondered at the volume of business that Wolsey must conduct through the day. He felt demeaned by the delay and eventually turned to his secretary. "I have no doubt that we are meeting here to serve the political scheming of the Cardinal." He was about to carry on but Slather pointed to the twitching arras. The bishop fell silent again, judging that a man such as this must have spies everywhere.

Eventually a gentleman usher appeared and conducted them into the imposing audience chamber where Wolsey, florid and corpulent, sat behind his desk, his Lord Chancellor's chain of office glittering before them.

He spoke briskly. "My Lord Bishop, I am much obliged for your presence here and I regret that I have kept you waiting on account of the press of important business."

The bishop was about to say something but Wolsey ignored him.

"Now the issue I wish to bring before you is this ... Martin Luther, that impious German priest, is, as I am sure you are aware, the cause of great disquiet within the chancelleries of Europe. It cannot be doubted that the Emperor and His Holiness the Pope would take it kindly if we were to make a grand gesture to suppress the infamous works of the renegade monk. That way our credit – that is the credit of His Highness – would rise abroad. Therefore I have decided that a special service and ceremonial burning of Lutheran texts should take place at Paul's Cross. What do you say?"

Fitzjames was gratified that Wolsey, whatever his true motives, was at long last doing something to stamp out pernicious doctrines. "Your Grace, I believe the burning of forbidden texts is to be applauded. We ourselves have seized many such works and my secretary here, Master Slather, can make all necessary arrangements for the burning. Our new dean, Richard Pace, can of course attend to the cathedral service. However, I fear that due to my infirmity I cannot myself be very active in this matter."

"That is understood, my good Bishop," Wolsey replied warmly. "My assistants will handle this with your secretary and you need not be troubled."

On his return to St Paul's Wharf Fitzjames was helped back to his palace where he took to his bed after instructing Slather to prepare for the book burning.

For his part, Slather, realising that his master was not long for this world, had begun to contemplate his own future under a successor – rumoured to be the austere and scholarly Cuthbert Tunstall. Conscious, too, that it was important to seize every opportunity for private gain while his bishop was alive but enfeebled, he sent a note to his friend the sacristan requesting a meeting in the cathedral vestry. In the privacy of this small vaulted chamber he explained what was in his mind:

"Brother Roger, we have been presented with a great opportunity. I am to gather in forbidden texts from searches and raids on booksellers. All these, together with those we have already seized and which are now in the crypt, we are to burn in front of the people. I myself have been entrusted with this task."

Brother Roger, a long faced man whose expression betrayed a tendency to melancholia, seemed puzzled. "I do not see how this can benefit us. Indeed, it would entail much labour."

"Think of it this way," replied Slather. "These heretical works and Lutheran texts are much sought after. Purchasers will pay several shillings for them as any bookseller in this neighbourhood will tell you. Now if we fill our baskets with approved but worthless books which are damaged beyond repair – I have in mind those many Bibles deposited in the undercroft which suffered in last winter's flooding – then we can retain the forbidden books and sell them at a good price. What do you say?"

The sacristan's air of gloom lifted. "You mean we could place a few forbidden works on top of each pile in the baskets and conceal the other texts beneath."

"Exactly so!" Slather exclaimed triumphantly. "So long as we two – and we alone – are in charge of the books and their burning no one can know."

When the sacristan began to look doubtful, Slather was quick to reassure him. "We would be performing a useful service and I will tell you why. The burning of forbidden books reduces the stock of such books and, the demand being constant, has the effect of expanding the orders to printers and increasing their sales. By preserving the books intended for burning and selling them to booksellers we are fulfilling a demand that would otherwise be met by the iniquitous printers in Antwerp, Cologne and elsewhere. So, have no fear. We would be striking at our spiritual enemies."

Roger could not dispute his friend's logic and an agreement was made there and then to share the profits of their joint enterprise.

April had been a bitterly cold month but now the spring sunshine had brought people onto the streets. Doors and shutters had been left open to let out the smell of tallow and the accumulated foul odours of a prolonged winter.

Slather, too preoccupied to appreciate the fine weather, accompanied the Lord Chancellor's men to the book shops clustered around Paternoster Row and St Paul's Churchyard. The booksellers were busy at work, stacking their wares, displaying the most popular items on their counters and engaging in trade with passing customers as well as each other.

The market activity was brought to an abrupt halt when the Lord Chancellor's men rode in. After dismounting they targeted a number of booths directed by the limping Slather. The chosen bookstalls were ransacked, their stock tipped into the street and prohibited works removed. The bishop's secretary held a blacklist of Lutheran texts whose Latin titles he shouted out to two clerks acting as searchers: "*The Ninety-five theses, The Sacrament of Penance, The Treatise on Good Works, The Babylonian Captivity of the Church, The Freedom of a Christian* – seize all these together with any other works published in Germany."

Where prohibited material was discovered, the fragile timber framing of the offending shop was smashed and the bookseller taken away for questioning. But not every suspicious shop was investigated. As Slather had explained to the sacristan, "We will need vendors to sell the books we impound from their fellows."

As the confiscated books were being thrown into a horse-drawn cart, Slather spoke to the carrier. "You can take your cart through the north door into the cathedral and unload the contents at the entrance to the crypt. I will follow you. We will carry the books down and store them in the undercroft until needed."

They were joined in the cathedral by the sacristan and the three of them stacked the sequestered volumes in a far corner of the crypt where other books were stored. After the carrier had left Slather addressed his friend. "We will fill our baskets with these flood damaged texts." He pointed to a large heap of dilapidated books. "And top them up with German works."

The sacristan picked up a dog-eared and mud-stained volume from the pile and inspected it. "The pages are still damp. I hope these books burn because if not we will be found out."

Slather sought to reassure him. "Of course they will burn. We will have to use more rushes and brushwood, that is all."

On the appointed day for the book burning, Fitzjames was too ill to attend but his secretary took his place in the cathedral. The spring sun streamed in coloured shafts of light through the rose window as Slather watched the procession of bishops progressing slowly up the great nave headed by the Cardinal, and censed by the new Dean. When he reached the high altar, Wolsey stood beneath a canopy of gold held aloft by four doctors of divinity. Looking at the majestic scene, Slather could not but admire Wolsey's style and brazen magnificence. He reflected that here was a low born man, unencumbered by too many religious convictions, pursuing a career in the Church directed only to the accumulation of wealth and power and to personal aggrandisement. Nor could he help thinking that the ecclesiastical order would be better served if more of its senior churchmen followed the Cardinal's example by avoiding contentious issues of dogma and promoting instead the resplendence of their office. Sadly he was only too aware that he could never aspire to any high preferment. His lameness and deformity, which they said was a mark of the devil, condemned him to a position of servility in the Church.

After Wolsey had made his obeisances, the procession retraced its steps down the nave, leaving by the north door, the congregation following behind. Slather filed out with the rest and took up his position with the sacristan by Paul's Cross where a pyre had been prepared. A tiered platform had been constructed for the dignitaries and the scarlet-robed Wolsey seated himself under his canopy at the summit, a gold cross set on either side. The Pope's Ambassador, the Imperial Ambassador and the Archbishop of Canterbury were seated directly below him, with the rest of the bishops spread out to left and right.

Bishop John Fisher of Rochester, as the foremost preacher of his day, had been designated to address an audience now numbered in thousands. As the bishop climbed the steps to the canopied pulpit of Paul's Cross, Slather spoke urgently to his collaborator. "The bishop is renowned for his long sermons but when he has accursed all the works of Luther he will at the end denounce anyone who has kept his writings. This is the signal for us to torch the rushes and let the book burning begin."

"What would these eminent men think if they knew it was Vulgate Bibles and not Lutheran texts that were going up in smoke?" the sacristan replied, nervously.

"You don't have to worry about that. And in any case I am sure the Cardinal doesn't care what we burn. He is interested only in the show."

To Slather the bishop's prolonged diatribe against the reformist doctrines of the German monk seemed like an eternity. At last Fisher began to castigate all those who possessed Lutheran books. Taking his cue, Slather put a torch to the rushes and kindling wood that formed the base of the fire. He and the sacristan then busied themselves throwing the contents of the baskets onto the blaze. The flames leapt high into the air while the assembled dignitaries looked on solemnly from their perches above.

But as more and more books were added they began to sizzle and hiss, emitting large billows of thick smoke that spiralled upwards. The suffocating fumes reached the upper tiers of the viewing platform, causing the Imperial Ambassador and his fellow notables to cough, rub their eyes and turn their faces away.

"Quick, more rushes," Slather said, hobbling away from the fire's noxious emissions. They hurriedly gathered more reeds from the bundles stashed nearby and fed the flames. They had to go on working hard to keep the blaze going and they were greatly relieved when the contents of the last basket were safely burned. At this point Wolsey and his distinguished guests led the way out of the close towards St Paul's Wharf where barges were waiting to take them to York Place for a sumptuous banquet – to which Slather, to his great chagrin, had not been invited.

CONVENTICLE

THE WHERRYMAN DIPPED HIS OARS INTO THE MURKY waters of the Thames and the boat created a small bow wave as it glided over the smooth surface towards Westminster. It was a bright summer's day and Anne was taking Margaret on her first river trip. "Here on the left is Lambeth Palace, dwelling of the Archbishop of Canterbury and over there ..." She pointed to Wolsey's newly extended palace on the opposite bank. "Over there is York Place where the Archbishop of York lives."

"Are bishops the richest men in all England?" Margaret asked.

Anne smiled: "You might think so. They live like kings."

Margaret looked puzzled. "But do they have queens?"

"No, dearest. They live on their own in their great houses surrounded by servants."

"And what do they do?"

Anne pondered before replying. "They tell everybody how they should think and what they should do."

"Just like Mama," Margaret said, and Anne laughed.

Disembarking at Paul's Wharf Anne decided that they should walk back through the book market in Paternoster Row and St Paul's Churchyard. She had heard all about the book burning that had occurred a few weeks before while she was in

Germany. Now she was encouraged to see that the traders were recovering from the raids that had preceeded the burning, with businesses reopening and shattered shop fronts being repaired. She pointed out to Margaret the array of painted signs hanging above the book stalls – The Bible, The Bishops Head, The Mitre, The Rising Sun and many more. They stopped opposite one deserted shop whose timber frontage had been smashed and splintered.

"Who broke everything?" asked Margaret.

"Some wicked men," replied Anne.

"Will they be punished?"

"Certainly. God will punish them."

"But will He punish them now?"

"No, not now. Later."

Anne cast her mind back to happier times. Before Margaret was born it was a favourite diversion of hers and Richard to wander curiously among the bookstalls in Paternoster Row, examining with eager eyes everything on offer. They had bought some printed devotional works but they also scoured the shelves for history and poetry. Their favourite acquisition without question was an early printed edition of Chaucer's *Canterbury Tales* complete with woodcut illustrations. They delighted in Chaucer's irreverence and would read to each other some of his more scathing portraits of the clergy, especially those contained in the Summoner's and Pardoner's Tales. Amid such light hearted amusement little did they think that Richard's life and her own happiness would be brought to a sudden end with a summoner's knock on the door.

Saddened by these thoughts, Anne led Margaret into the cathedral close where boys were using catapults to target the crows that sat on the nave roof. An angry verger emerged from the building and remonstrated with the culprits, pointing to a broken clerestory window. They turned and walked back to Eastcheap.

The next day, after dropping Margaret off in Carter Lane, Anne walked over to a shoemaker's house in Cordwainer Street where her Bible reading group was meeting. She had rejoined the conventicle after the scriptorium had been shut down and now its proceedings were dominated by the controversy surrounding Luther. Hermann, attending to his business in Germany, had kept her informed of the religious turmoil in his home country through correspondence addressed to her at the Steelyard. And while giving a full account of Luther's battles as reported to him by his fellow Hansa, he was always careful to avow his disapproval of the man. After all, the interception of letters coming into England from Germany was now commonplace.

When it became known that she was recounting the unfolding story of Luther's revolt based on information from Germany, her little reading group was overwhelmed by those wanting to attend. Many were excluded and all those present had to be scrutinised to ensure that there was no informer in their midst. But those who did attend passed on what they heard to their friends, thereby enabling an ever-widening circle of Lutheran sympathisers to follow the course of this man's trial of strength with the temporal and spiritual powers of Europe.

Earlier in the year, Anne had told them about Luther's attack on the papacy and his call for religious orders to be dissolved, pilgrimage abolished and clerical celibacy abandoned. And at the last gathering, just after her return from Germany, the audience had listened spellbound as Anne described what she had witnessed at Worms – although nothing was said about her adventure in Thuringia.

Those present could only marvel at the thought of Luther confronting the might of the Holy Roman Empire but Anne drew other lessons from this man's ability to command the world's attention. Her dear late husband, Richard, had tried to challenge the Church single handed by invoking the secular law against the priesthood, but the spirituality had been too strong and his great sacrifice had gone unnoticed by the people. Yet this lowly German monk, using only his own scholarship and the printing press, was able to attract a great following throughout Christendom and cause even emperors, popes and princes to quake in their palaces.

At today's meeting in Cordwainer Street Anne was asked by a fishmonger about Luther's views on the sacraments.

"My correspondent in Germany tells me that Luther accepts only two sacraments … the Lord's Supper and Baptism. He says confirmation, marriage, ordination, penance and extreme unction are without foundation as sacraments because they are not instituted by Christ. Of course, the Church is aghast at these pronouncements, especially because the repudiation of ordination places the priesthood on the same footing as those they serve."

The fishmonger had wanted to know more. "So what does this mean for our priests and their power over the faithful?"

Anne's correspondent had provided the answer. "Luther says that, according to scripture, all those who are baptised are priests without distinction, and those we call priests are merely those chosen from among the faithful to minister to us."

The assembled company murmured support for Luther's daring declaration but many present were puzzled why, after the events at Worms, he had not already been burned.

Anne tried to explain. "It is said that he has the protection of Prince Frederick of Saxony and that he will continue his fight while removed from the eyes of the world."

As the proceedings were being brought to an end, a bookbinder had the last word. "I believe His Highness Himself is to issue a riposte to Luther. I have heard this from a printer who has been commissioned to prepare the text."

They all agreed, as they dispersed, that the King's intervention in the debate could signify a harder line against Luther's supporters. They would have to be on their guard against informers.

―――――――

It was less than a month after this meeting that Rebecca visited Anne in an agitated state. As they sipped rosewater and the girls played upstairs she unburdened herself. "My dear husband, Samuel, is fearful about our familiarity and frequent visiting."

Anne was entirely taken aback: "Why is that? He knows we have been the closest of friends these past twelve years. What has changed?"

"He says everything has changed. You must know that the King has published an attack on Luther in his own name."

"Yes I am well aware," said Anne, "His *Assertion of the Seven Sacraments* is a direct rebuttal of Luther's *Babylonian Captivity of the Church*. But how does this affect us?"

Rebecca looked pained. "Samuel says that those who sympathise with Luther have become a danger to themselves and to others." She paused awkwardly and added, "He forbids me to see you."

Anne took her time before replying with tears in her eyes: "Rebecca, if your husband forbids you to see me and you feel you must obey him then we must say our goodbyes."

Rebecca raised her voice: "No! I would never accept that!" and she embraced Anne. "Of course we will go on seeing each other. Margaret is old enough to come to Carter Lane to be with Sarah and I will visit you here – just as often as before."

They wept together for a time before Anne spoke. "Rebecca, in some ways he is right. The King coming out strongly against

Luther is one thing. That Sir Thomas More is supposed to have written this damning work is another."

"Why so?" asked Rebecca.

"Because More is a fanatical upholder of the old order and a cruel enemy."

Anne continued to receive letters from Hermann at regular intervals. He was travelling north from Cologne to visit Bremen, Hamburg, Wittenberg and Lubeck, after which he intended to return to England via Antwerp. She knew that as well as occupying himself with wine exports he was meeting with printers and book dealers in these towns but, of course, there was nothing of this in his correspondence.

Some days before Hermann's arrival in London, a Hansa ship, the *Lubeck*, was due to dock at the Steelyard wharf with a consignment of Hermann's Rhenish wine shipped from Cologne. Assuming the role and outward appearance of Thomas Hendrick, Anne turned up at the Steelyard to await the vessel.

It was her task as a registered agent to supervise the unloading and stacking of the casks of wine in the riverside warehouse. She kept in mind the painstaking instructions she had received from Wedig:

"Those casks with a chalk marker must be separated from the rest. You must arrange for their collection by a waggoner who will then deliver to the houses of selected wholesalers, carefully approved by yourself. When the casks are broken open the hidden compartments will be exposed containing closely packed printed books in the smaller, octavo, page size. These pocket sized volumes can then be sold discreetly in the retail market to known sympathisers in London and the surrounding area."

By now Anne was familiar with the procedure but she knew only too well that a single informant within the distribution chain could prove to be their undoing.

She stood gazing at the ships coming up river with the tide to see if she could identify the *Lubeck*. But as she turned around she became uncomfortably aware of a hooded figure standing on the other side of Thames Street evidently watching the entrance to the Steelyard. Could the German trading post be under surveillance? She knew that neither the sheriff nor the customs authorities, still less Church officials, would dare to set foot in this privileged enclosure. But if the Crown itself found cause to send in its officers to carry out a search, that was a different matter. Given the furore over Lutheran books and the suspicions attaching to German merchants, Anne felt it was time to make alternative arrangements for distributing their contraband literature. After she had embraced her husband on his longed for return, she would have to tell him that the Steelyard was no longer safe.

35

THE DEVIL'S TAVERN

ANNE ROUSED HERSELF FROM A DEEP SLEEP AND
touched the cheek of the man lying beside her. As he stirred she
whispered: "Dear heart, it is such a comfort to be together. But
today we must go in search of a new place to bring in our wares."

Hermann yawned. "I would much rather the soft delights of
Aphrodite than the weighty tomes of Luther. But you are right.
The Steelyard is under suspicion and we must move on."

Anne peered through the unshuttered window. "It would
be safest to go beyond the City walls to the east and further
downriver than Tower Wharf."

Hermann, now fully awake and alert, adopted a business-
like manner. "I agree. We will need a landing place hidden from
the eyes of the world. It must allow us to bring in a small boat at
high tide from our Hansa ship anchored in midstream."

"I am told," said Anne, "that small boats come into Wapping,
which I believe is a wretched community of those serving the
river trade. Perhaps we should take a look. It is not much more
than an hour's walk from here. But I will go dressed as Thomas
Hendrick since he is the one to help you in this task."

They walked along Cornhill and Leadenhall Street,
through the City gates at Aldgate and beyond the walls to East
Smithfield. From there they headed south across a marshy and

treeless wasteland towards the river. It was not long before there came into view a huddle of mean houses standing at irregular angles, the consequence of having settled into the mud on the banks of the Thames over many years.

"What a desolate and godforsaken place," Hermann muttered.

"But that is what we are looking for," Anne replied. They walked slowly along the water's edge beside a crumbling wall, which was evidently intended to keep out flooding from the river. There were yards in front of some of the dwellings where men were engaged in maritime trades: mast, oar and block making; sailmaking; victualling and boat repairs. Set apart from the houses was a larger building with a projecting inn sign depicting a weather-battered pelican. Just beyond the inn a flight of stone stairs descended to a jetty from where small boats could come and go.

Hermann drew Anne's attention to several merchantmen that were anchored opposite them in the middle of the river. "These large vessels can go no further upstream and must therefore berth in the deep water here. They bring their goods ashore in smaller boats taken upriver beyond London Bridge. A Hansa ship would not be out of place here."

Anne's spirits had been dampened by the desolation of the place but she could see that this isolated spot with its river anchorage would serve their purpose very well.

A man was sitting on the wall beside the steps and Hermann decided to engage him in conversation. "Sir, can you tell me if the Pelican is a good hostelry for the likes of us? We are strange to these parts."

The man turned towards them and Anne noticed that one side of his face was wasted away by disease. He spoke as if with effort. "Jonah is the innkeeper there. He is not too particular about the company he keeps and there are all sorts who drink his ale. There are some who call it the Devil's Tavern. Down here in Wapping men do as they please, there being not much call for serjeants or law officers or the like. Jonah and his kind may be a little suspicious of respectable gentlemen such as yourselves. But, for all that, he is a good man, right enough."

Hermann thanked him and asked whether he worked in the neighbourhood. "I used to be a true ferryman before I had my illness," the man replied gruffly. "Now I am a boatman still but only between ship and shore. I am waiting for a call from the Madonna out there. They need to purchase provisions."

Anne pointed down river. "There appears to be a wooden frame emerging from the shallows of the river beyond here. Is this set up by fishermen?"

The man gave Anne an intent look as if she had no business to ask such a question. "Sir, I cannot answer to that. You had best ask Jonah."

Anne looked at Hermann and they walked away.

"He seemed fearful," said Hermann, as they approached the entrance to the Pelican. "Anyway, let us try our luck here because the innkeeper sounds like a man we could do business with."

Entering the tavern, they found themselves in a dingy low ceilinged room, sparsely furnished with a few benches and tables. A stuffed pelican with malevolent eyes and a scabrous face peered out from a cage set on a stand in the corner. There was a pungent smell of tallow, the flaking plaster walls were stained with damp and the stone floor slabs were spattered with mud and debris.

There were no other customers but a man whom they took to be the proprietor appeared promptly. He was bearded, of middle height and bore a long sword slash of a scar that ran down the length of his cheek from the point where his missing ear should have been. He gave a cautious welcome to the visitors in a rasping voice. "Good day, sirs. It is a rare thing to see unfamiliar faces here but I am happy to serve you with such humble fare as we have to offer. Jonah is the name."

After they had ordered ale and cheese and a tankard of strong brew for the landlord Hermann looked round the room and then touched on the topic that was uppermost in his mind. "I take it there is no one behind these doors."

Jonah gave a deep laugh. "Rest assured I am a widower. My dear departed was inclined to overhear things but there is none other that would dare to do so for fear of finding themselves at the bottom of a well."

"Then let me speak my mind," said Hermann. "You are a man of business and so am I. I bring merchandise from Germany – mainly wine but also other goods that might not be so well regarded by the powers that be in the City. If there were a handsome profit in it for you, would you entertain the idea of storing these more contentious items here for distribution among the faithful? I am speaking of printed books and texts that are harmless except in the eyes of certain of our churchmen."

Hermann motioned to Anne. "This is my assistant in the project."

Jonah put down his ale and wiped his mouth. "Sir, you have not given me your names and perhaps it is best you do not. As for your proposal there are two matters of concern to me. First the risk to myself and my business. I can say that neither the bishop's nor the chancellor's writ runs here and we are a community mainly outside the law. On the landward side certainly we are secure. But the river is a different matter – there we have always to be vigilant. Second, I will need to examine closely the benefit to myself. I am unlettered and have no interest in the Church's teachings or priestly sermonising. Therefore I care not one tittle about the books you may bring in. But for the trouble and the danger I would want to be rewarded."

This was the opening Hermann had been hoping for. His manner was brisk and down to earth. "I will from time to time deliver in person shipments of books. These will be conveyed by boat from a Hansa ship berthed in mid-river and brought ashore at Wapping Stairs. You will agree to store the books in the tavern secreted in casks of ale, which I will provide. Distribution of the books to purchasers comes within the remit of my assistant here."

Anne responded to the cue. "Yes, I will appoint three or four wholesalers who will be made known to you. They will collect books from yourself for distribution to the faithful in and around London."

"And if you agree to all that," Hermann continued, "you will receive a fixed fee for each shipment of books and a percentage of all sales. What do you say?"

As Hermann anticipated everything depended on the precise financial terms. After a prolonged negotiation, agreement was reached and tankards were filled again to seal the compact.

Aided by the drink, spirits rose and Anne asked about the curious timber frame they had spotted in the river that had so upset the boatman on the waterfront. Jonah's lighter mood was immediately dissipated. His eyes blazed and he banged his tankard down on the table but then he composed himself and apologised for his anger. "This is a subject that touches my heart, and let me tell you why. The object you saw is a gallows set up by the admiralty court at the low tidemark, the admiralty having authority only on the river. Those whom the court judge to have committed felonies or piracy at sea are brought here to hang."

Having related this much the innkeeper paused and seemed to struggle to find words. But he carried on. "My own son, Tom – as a mere lad – was a boatman in Blackwall. They said he had pilfered a sack of corn from a merchantman on the river. After conviction by the admiralty court – for it was held that it happened on the high seas – he was taken from the Marshallsea prison and brought here. I saw him myself in the cart with a priest and the hangman." Here he stopped and took a swig of ale. "There was a great multitude of people from the city who had come to watch – some gathered here on Wapping Wall and others on boats hired for the occasion. I looked on as they put Tom in the noose, which was attached to the gallows by a specially shortened rope. So when he dropped his neck was not broken and he jigged and danced as he fought for breath. It was some twenty minutes before his face went blue and he ceased struggling. He was left there, lashed to a post, as is the custom, until three tides had covered his head. Only then could I claim the body."

Jonah looked intently at Anne and Hermann. "You will understand my rancour when I have to witness this execrable gibbet every day beyond my door."

Anne and Hermann felt chastened as they walked back to the City across the windswept wasteland of Wapping marshes. Approaching Aldgate, Anne held Hermann's arm tightly. "Above all else," she said, "we must beware the river and the baleful watch of the admiralty."

PART V

❧ *1524 – 1527* ☙

A New Bishop

ANNE HUGGED HERSELF AGAINST THE COLD AS SHE walked up Ironmonger Lane towards Lothbury. The conventicle was meeting there that afternoon at the house of a draper and she had news to impart to her eager audience.

The onset of winter reminded her that it was almost ten years since she had stood before Paul's Cross and learned the fate of her husband. She slowed her pace as she cast her mind back. She trusted that she had honoured Richard by carrying on his spiritual work. She had cared, too, for their daughter who was now an attractive young woman, working with her Aunt Rebecca in the family's haberdashery. As for her new companion, she believed that Richard would not have wished her to live as a nun. He would surely have approved of Hermann's business skills and, especially, his mastery of the trade in printed books that allowed so many of the faithful to read enlightened texts.

And there was something else: the carefully worded letters that Hermann wrote to her at the Steelyard provided regular intelligence on the religious upheavals gripping Germany – information that she then shared with her fraternity. They in turn passed the word on, thereby giving encouragement to the reformist communities in London and beyond.

Anne had also vowed to avenge her husband's death. And she comforted herself that she had destroyed the man most clearly implicated in his murder. Nevertheless, there were still unanswered questions and unfinished business to which she would have to return. When she had shown Hermann the coroner's report on Richard's death he had agreed that the findings left important matters unaccounted for. The praemunire action provided the killers with a motive. But why would they choose to shed blood – and such a profusion of blood – when other, easier, methods of killing could be employed? And Hermann had also repeated the question asked by Sir Thomas More: why would church officials go to such lengths to murder Richard when they already had him within their power? Anne acknowledged to herself that only the former bishop's chancellor, Dr William Horsey, now reported to be in faraway Exeter, could provide the answers.

As she walked on, Anne's thoughts were disturbed by the harsh sounds of the foundry and metal working businesses that occupied this corner of the City. Ahead of her, and set back from the street, was a large merchant's house. Here, away from the din, Anne stopped. She looked round to make sure she was not being followed and gave two taps on the door, which was quickly opened.

Expectant faces looked up as Anne entered the high ceilinged hall. The draper's wife welcomed her and after the gathering had settled down, those who could read were asked to take their turn reciting passages from the scriptures. Anne then stood up and recounted the latest news from Germany.

"As I have said before, in Wittenberg there has already been a rejection of the old religion. Priests and nuns have married, at mass wine is given to the laity, many parts of the mass are now recited in German, not Latin, and images have been removed from the churches. Now my informant tells me that the overthrow of the Church's old ways has spread to Worms and other cities. No one is able to defy the will of the people."

"And what of Luther and his writings?" asked a young man.

Anne made an expansive gesture. "His translation of the New Testament into German is distributed throughout the land. I am told it has been reprinted many times and that the production of his works are now to be numbered in hundreds of thousands. The monk, through the printing press, has caused the people to revolt."

Someone asked whether anybody was planning to print an English translation of the Bible for distribution in England.

"I cannot say for certain," said Anne, "but it is said that an English scholar, recently arrived in Worms, is working on such a project. Until we see the results of his endeavour we must content ourselves with the reformist works we have brought in from the printers across the British Sea. Master Gavin will give you the prices and you can let him have your orders. The books will be delivered directly by him."

Many of those present gathered round to give their orders and pay their money. As Anne explained, the texts would be collected from their undisclosed depot and distributed discreetly to purchasers at their door.

When Anne left the draper's house she noticed that the metal workers were closing down their foundries and furnaces for the day. She was in good spirits because the meeting had gone well and orders for books, even German books, were increasing all the time. She could just imagine the demand there would be for a printed English Bible. The new Bishop of London and his lackeys would be powerless to hold back the tide if such a text should be released into the country and circulated among the people.

Slather sat at his desk adjoining the palace library. He was transcribing notes dictated by the bishop which were to be redrafted as letters ready for final signature.

It was over two years since Cuthbert Tunstall had been elevated to his London see, and although Slather was relieved to have been reappointed to his own position as secretary and chaplain, he was not altogether at ease with the new bishop. True, Tunstall was a respected scholar – a graduate of Oxford, Cambridge and Padua, proficient in Latin and Greek and a noted mathematician. A clever and sharp-eyed man indeed. And it was for that reason that the bishop's secretary had felt compelled to curtail his extra-mural business activities.

Yet there was also something strangely unworldly about this erudite churchman who seemed to have no conception of how ordinary people made their living or how men of affairs conducted their business. Slather feared that the meeting with the Master of the Stationers' Company, which he had been asked to attend as scribe, would provide ample proof of His Lordship's simplicity in matters of commerce.

The cathedral clock chimed the quarter hour and Slather realised that the guildsman would soon be arriving. He put away his quill and went through to the library where the bishop was waiting to receive his guest. Reginald Quire, Master of the Stationers' Company, was ushered in by a liveried attendant. The Master was himself resplendently attired in the livery of his guild – a deep-blue robe and cap, all trimmed with gold. His manner conveyed the impression of a man judiciously balancing his own self-importance with the deference due to a prince of the Church.

"I am grateful for your visit," the bishop began, "the Stationers have served this city well over many years and long may they continue so to do. Indeed, my purpose in requesting your presence here today is to ensure that the Company's proud record is upheld in the difficult times in which we find ourselves."

"My Lord," Quire replied, "I can assure you we shall be of whatever assistance we can."

"As you are aware, His Highness and his spiritual advisers are concerned that heretical works are appearing with increasing frequency. Accordingly, we are taking new measures to protect our Christian community from false doctrines. In future, no new book may be printed in England without the consent of a commission whose members are myself, Archbishop Wareham, Cardinal Wolsey and Bishop Fisher of Rochester. In addition, all books coming into this country from abroad must from now be personally approved and licensed by myself. I would be obliged if you would inform all members of your fraternity and ask them to bring to my attention any suspicions regarding possible breaches of these decrees."

"My Lord," Quire responded, "in jealously guarding our own good reputation we will certainly seek to enforce these new edicts. I will instruct our wardens to undertake searches where there are grounds for disquiet."

"I am glad of that," said the bishop. "My secretary here has written out a copy of the ordinances and punishments which should be made familiar to all the booksellers, limners and printers of your guild." Here he motioned to Slather to provide Quire with the documents.

"One further point, "the bishop added. "There is great apprehension that an unauthorised English Bible may shortly be printed overseas. We should all be on our guard against that danger. In the meantime we have alerted our agents in the Low Countries so that they may buy up any such books before they can be brought clandestinely into England."

The meeting was over and the Master of the Stationers' Company bowed before being shown out.

Back at his own desk Slather felt that his earlier misgivings about the bishop were amply justified. Certainly, London printers might be raided and would not dare to risk their business and their liberty by defying the Church. But as for books brought in from Antwerp, Cologne, Basel and any number of foreign cities, these could not be kept out. There were inlets and jetties all along the Thames between Tower Wharf and Gravesend, besides Yarmouth and all the countless ports and landing places along the eastern seaboard. And he knew very well that the profits for those who imported prohibited books were so large as to ensure that there would always be those willing to bear the risk of detection. A stationer had told him that books might be bought wholesale for thirteen pence per volume in the Low Countries and sold to eager buyers in England for two shillings and fourpence or even two shillings and eightpence. That, he confided to himself, was enough to tempt even a bishop's chaplain. As for buying up prohibited books, he could hardly credit the artlessness of the bishop. Such purchases would put money straight into the hands of printers who would thank the Church for its bounteous concern for their wellbeing – and proceed to use this unexpected treasure to expand their production.

Furthermore, if it were true that an English Bible was being readied somewhere in Europe for circulation in England, it would be better by far that the Church should superintend and direct the project. He recalled that only the previous summer, a young scholar bearing the name William Tyndale had sought out the bishop with a high recommendation from a prominent courtier. Tyndale had applied to become a member of the bishop's household and to be given licence to translate the Bible into English under His Lordship's tutelage and guidance. But Tyndale had been sent away. It was said that after this rejection he was introduced to Hansa merchants at the Steelyard who gave him money as well as German connections to enable him to sail to Hamburg. So the accomplished scholar who could have laboured under the watchful eye of the bishop was now set loose in a Lutheran country, perhaps to take revenge on the Church that had cast him aside.

Mulling these thoughts, it occurred to Slather that some of these very clever churchmen, with their deep understanding of ancient languages and biblical texts, when it came to the world they lived in, had no wisdom at all.

He looked at the papers on his desk with disdain. It had never been his own plan to enter the Church. Through his family's links to the royal household he had hoped to obtain a position at court. But his father had cruelly insisted that his disfigurement would make him an object of ridicule in courtly circles. He had been induced to train for the priesthood but without any enthusiasm for the Christian beliefs he was supposed to uphold. And now that the body ecclesiastic appeared to be on the threshold of a great upheaval he worried about the future. If the reformists were to prevail and the King were to eventually endorse them he would need to have a foot in their camp. But the old order was still in command and the time was not yet ripe for making such a move.

37

A Pirate's Fate

In the guise of Thomas Hendrick, Anne trod the sodden track beyond East Smithfield towards Wapping. Swathes of mist lay low across the wetlands and a veiled sun cast a pallid light over a flat landscape. Dew-laden sedge brushed against her cloak and colourful splashes of water marigolds and violets testified to the end of a hard winter.

Anne was conscious of the importance of the message she was about to deliver. It was nearly eighteen months since she had told the gathering at Lothbury that a young English scholar was thought to be preparing an English Bible for printers in Worms. Now that Bible was in production and clandestine orders were coming in from all over the country. As she and her Hansa friend had long anticipated, the printing houses of Europe were feeding the people's hunger for texts that they could read for themselves. First Germany and now England – the uprising of the faithful against obfuscation, priestly ascendency and idolatry was spreading throughout the land.

As she approached the Pelican, she could hear the coarse voices of drinkers coming from within. She decided to go round to the back door and wait in the rear passageway. After some minutes Jonah appeared carrying an empty cask. He motioned to her to step outside where they spoke in hushed voices. Anne got straight down to business:

"Jonah, I have had directions from my master. He tells me his ship will be sailing shortly from Cologne and is likely to reach London on Thursday next. It will come in on the tide and ride at anchor in midstream here. He has two hundred English Bibles that are already reserved and to be paid for at three shillings per bound volume."

Jonah's face lit up at the mention of such handsome takings but there was caution in his response. "Sir, that is well and good, but how will such a large shipment be brought to the tavern?"

Anne tried to reassure him. "These are New Testament Bibles in a small octavo size and they will, as before, be concealed in casks. My master will himself load these onto the boat kept here which must be rowed out to him. Please make sure the boatman is standing by."

"That can be done," said Jonah, "but what warning should I display if the landing here is for any reason unsafe?"

"In that event, my master has requested that you hang a white sheet in the upper window to alert him."

The innkeeper was anxious on one other matter. "They say searchers have been sent out by royal warrant to discover heretical books. I will be loathe to store these new volumes for any length of time for fear of detection."

Anne sought to put his mind at rest. "You should be secure in this remote place. But since the books are already sold I will order their collection as soon as they are landed. You will have them for no more than a day or so."

Having satisfied the innkeeper as to the arrangements, she departed.

––––––––––

As Anne waited impatiently for Hermann's Hansa ship to sail up the Thames and to be reunited with a man who spent all too short a time on English soil, she became increasingly nervous.

For precautionary reasons, correspondence was no longer delivered to her house in Eastcheap. Instead, in her new role as Hermann's assistant, she would go down to the Steelyard to collect any letters and instructions from her employer. It was on one such errand that she had encountered Hermann's friend, Georg Gisze, at the gatehouse. He looked grave as he put his hand on her shoulder. "Thomas, there has been a great upset here at the Steelyard and you should give warning to your master. Last evening we merchants were sitting down to supper in the refectory when armed men forced their way in, led in person by Sir Thomas More. He called us to order and declared that he had reason to believe that some among us were bringing in the works of Martin Luther. Several suspects were arrested there and then while searchers examined each merchant's possessions, afterwards taking away suspect books."

The violation of the Hansa's privileged enclave by royal officials had clearly come as a great shock. But it was precisely what Anne had feared and she was thankful that she and Hermann had moved their base to Wapping.

"What will happen to those detained?" she asked.

"I understand there is a great spectacle planned for Shrove Sunday. Those Hansa convicted of possessing heretical works will be paraded before the people at Paul's Cross. No one from the Steelyard will come to witness such an affront to our fraternity."

"I am grateful for this information, Sir," said Anne, "and truly sorry that your merchants have been treated in such an insulting manner. I will pass all this on to my master who will be returning to England shortly."

Believing it to be her duty, Anne had gone to Paul's Cross to see what degradation the Hansa prisoners would be forced to endure. She watched with dismay as four merchants were led past, seated backward on donkeys and wearing pasteboard mitres to which were pinned printed extracts from offending texts.

She was standing next to a rough-looking woman carrying a baby, the mother red in the face from bellowing abuse at the men paraded in front of her. Anne wondered whether she, along with other jeering onlookers, knew anything of the teaching of Martin Luther. Much more likely, it occurred to her, that the City's meanest sort were emboldened to pour scorn on those brought lower even than themselves. Anne herself was determined to remain impassive throughout the cruel pageant, for she could see that priests were stationed within the crowd and she was anxious not to give cause for suspicion.

After the Hansa merchants were dismounted they were required to kneel with bundles of faggots tied to their backs. A fire was lit for their books to be burned and they were made to carry their faggots three times round the blazing pile before throwing them into the flames – a reminder of the fate that awaited them if they should offend again.

Anne was now worried that the raid on the Steelyard carried dangers for their enterprise. Could someone have disclosed their business at Wapping? Might her letters from Hermann have been intercepted? And could commerce on the river now be under close surveillance?

Whatever the dangers that lay ahead, she had no way of warning Hermann who even now was under sail and heading for London's river gateway.

However, it occurred to her that there was another possible consequence of recent events: the Hansa merchants were proud and would not easily submit to their debasement before the people; if the opportunity were to present itself, they would surely seek revenge.

On the appointed Thursday, Anne and Jonah stood beside Wapping Wharf scanning the river as it swelled with the incoming tide. Two ships swept up on the powerful current, sails billowing, and passed on towards Tower Wharf. A third vessel was already berthed in midstream with a barge alongside.

In the distance, a ship's prow became dimly visible and the innkeeper was quick to identify it.

"That is a Hansa merchantman. I can see the red and white pennant fluttering above its mainsail."

As the vessel came clearly into view Anne could make out the name *Lubeck* painted on its side. And then she saw a familiar figure on the foredeck waving his arms. The anchors were rattled out and the *Lubeck* berthed astern of the moored ship.

"Come Jonah!" Anne said, "Instruct the boatman to prepare to bring my master and his laiding ashore!"

The innkeeper obliged and the boatman rowed out to the new arrival. Two casks were lowered by ropes on to the boat but as Hermann was about to embark Anne noticed that armed men were boarding the barge upstream of the *Lubeck*. "Jonah!" Anne said in a growing panic, "This is a snare! Quick! Run to the tavern and hang a sheet in the window!"

But it was too late. Even as she spoke Hermann clambered into the boat and the boatman began pulling on his oars. The barge, now manned by six men, quickly closed in. There was a struggle as the bargemen forcibly overcame Hermann, bound him in ropes and brought him back to what Anne now realised must be an Admiralty ship.

She stood there incredulous and unable to think or move. Then she became aware of a scuffle on board the Admiralty ship. Hermann must have freed himself from his captors. She looked on as he jumped into the water and began to swim. There was a single shot from the ship's foredeck and the swimmer immediately began to flounder. As the fugitive was hauled on board again, she could seek him clutch his bloodied shoulder.

After a few moments' silence Jonah spoke calmly but forcefully to Anne. "You must leave now and not return. They will shortly send searchers to ransack the tavern. They will find nothing because I have no books in stock and although I will be under deep suspicion there will be no evidence against me. I shall say that the casks were to be collected by a nameless brewer directly from the jetty. And I have as many witnesses from around here as I care to call upon."

Anne tried not to give herself away by showing her anguished state of mind. "But what will happen to my master?"

"Your Hansa merchant will I believe be kept in the Marshalsea prison and then sent to trial at the Court of Admiralty. What the outcome will be I cannot say."

Anne noticed that as he spoke the innkeeper looked with apprehension at the shallows only a hundred yards away where the gallows of Execution Dock, half-submerged by the high tide, protruded above the water – a sinister reminder of the Admiralty's jurisdiction on the river.

Over the next few days, Anne was tormented by the absence of any news about her husband. She walked past the Marshalsea prison in Long Southwark several times and stood before its turreted lodge. But access to prisoners was barred. In desperation she wrote to Georg Gisze, the Hansa merchant lodged at the Steelyard whom she had met on several occasions and whose portrait by Holbein hung alongside that of Hermann in the Steelyard Hall. After an exchange of letters it was arranged that they would meet at All-Hallows-the-Great in Thames Street.

Shafts of sunlight pierced the elaborately sculpted arcading of the cloisters as Anne, for the last time disguised as Thomas Hendrick, exchanged greetings with Georg Gisze. "This is a terrible business Master Hendrick. Several among us have on occasion brought in forbidden books but for it to come to this and befall a man so highly regarded by us all ..."

"Indeed. But what can you tell me of my master's fate? What of his wounds? Do we know how he fares?" She feared her voice betrayed a degree of anxiety which was perhaps beyond that to be expected of a merchant's assistant.

Gisze shook his head. "No one has been able to visit him. But it is not the practice of gaolers in the Marshalsea to take great pains with the welfare and bodily health of their charges. The worst may therefore be feared."

"And what of the legal proceedings?" Anne asked.

Gisze looked grave. "I have to tell you that, in his struggle to escape from his captors, Hermann hit one of them with a spar with such force that the man later died. Therefore they have charged him with murder and piracy."

"But surely piracy is a crime committed only on the high seas."

"Not so. Some of us at the Steelyard spoke with an attorney who is versed in maritime law to see what could be done for our brother merchant. The attorney said that the Admiralty has jurisdiction over all crimes committed in the main stream of great rivers, below the bridges, where the tide flows unimpeded. That stretch of water is considered to be on the high seas for the purposes of piracy law."

Anne remained puzzled. "As for piracy, that surely is committed by the men of one ship against the men and property of another ship. There was no piracy here."

"Piracy is a flexible term. It may apply to any felony committed on the high seas. Here we have the alleged murder of a crewman on one of His Highness's vessels and that, certainly, can be viewed as piracy in Admiralty law."

Anne was in despair. "Then what can be done for our prisoner?"

Gisze shrugged. "The attorney said the only course was for Hermann to enter a plea of guilty and throw himself on the King's mercy."

"That mercy will not be forthcoming," Anne said. "After the raid on the Steelyard and the discovery of heretical works they will wish to make an example of a Hansa merchant."

"Exactly so," Gisze concurred. "Whatever our forebodings, we may expect to see the court's judgement posted on the walls of the Marshalsea prison before long."

Anne must have shown her distress because Gisze rested his hand on her shoulder and said something she was later to recall. "Thomas, I cannot disguise from you that the outlook for this case is anything but dark. But of one thing you may be sure ... Hansa merchants will always come to the aid of a fallen comrade."

Each morning after the meeting at All Hallows Church, Anne walked over London Bridge and up Long Southwark to the Marshalsea prison to see whether a verdict had been posted. She did not have to wait many days. The news she had dreaded was blazoned in large print on a placard affixed to the prison wall:

The Lord High Admiral hereby declares that one Hermann Wedig, a German merchant lodged at the Steelyard, has been found by the Court of Admiralty to be guilty of murder, mayhem and piracy on the high seas, the said Hermann Wedig having assaulted and killed a servant of the Crown, James Meredith, on His Highness's ship, Adventure, while seeking to evade arrest on suspicion of trading in prohibited books. And the said Hermann Wedig will suffer the penalty of death by hanging which, by command of the Admiralty Marshall, will be carried out at low tide on Friday May 14th at Wapping Stairs.

EXECUTION DOCK

ANNE WAS DISTRAUGHT AT THE THOUGHT OF Hermann's cruel fate. She wondered, too, how she would cope if he were to be taken from her. They had been together as man and wife for only a few weeks each year; their wedlock had resembled not so much a marriage as a succession of trysts between long absences. Yet their souls had touched in those first moments of intimacy in the Steelyard Tavern – and so it had been ever since. During their enforced separations they knew that each thought only of the other. And when they were reunited in those joyful homecomings their tenderness was like that of newly joined lovers. It seemed that this great solace in her life was now to be wrenched away.

As soon as she had read the poster outside the Marshalsea prison, Anne lost no time in reporting the bleak Admiralty message to her cousin in Carter Lane. But once the word was out it travelled fast and Rebecca had already heard the news through one of her many informants. Anne now broached the question over which she had been agonising: whether or not to be present at Wapping when the sentence was carried out.

"Rebecca, my mind is in turmoil. On the one hand nothing could be worse than witnessing the last terrible moments of my Hansa husband on the scaffold. And yet I believe within my heart that I should be there to lend whatever pitiful support I can offer during his lonely ordeal."

"I am not so sure it would be a good idea," said Rebecca. "And at the very least you cannot think of going down to Wapping unaccompanied. You would need to have a friend's shoulder to cry on and an arm to hold you."

"In that case, would you take a boat with me? As onlookers together we could comfort each other."

Rebecca put her arm around Anne. "We women find it especially difficult to witness such cruel events. But it would be easier to endure the ordeal if we were accompanied by a staunch gentleman. Besides, there will be many people of the rougher sort and two women on their own would be an enticement. My uncle Jack Honiker may be just the man. He is staying with us having only this month taken leave from his ship."

Anne was reassured by this suggestion.

"That is settled then," said Rebecca. "I will ask my uncle to join us in this distressing venture. I will tell him only that we believe Hermann to be innocent of all charges. If he agrees, we will take a wherry and I will bring food for us all. We must depart early that morning. The crowds will gather around Wapping to satisfy their malign curiosity and we will need to secure a place."

"Crowds are what they wish for," Anne said, bitterly. "Church and Crown are united in this. They want to tell the world that traders – especially *foreign* traders – who bring in forbidden books and defy the authorities will be made to suffer."

———

Jack Honiker was a sturdy mariner with a leathery, weather beaten face and a no nonsense manner. In twenty five years of active service at sea he had seen just about everything. Even so he made clear that he did not relish the prospect of witnessing a hanging at Execution Dock and he questioned whether Anne and Rebecca really knew what they were in for.

Anne, Jack and Rebecca met up in solemn mood at Billingsgate wharf. They embarked on a wherry just below London Bridge in order to avoid the dangerous rapids through the arches – a hazard with which Anne was only too familiar. There was a strong westerly wind blowing as the three passengers were rowed down river on an ebb tide towards Wapping. Anne was relieved to see that Rebecca had chosen a suitably sombre outfit for the occasion but she noticed that the occupants of other boats heading the same way were gaudily attired as if en route to a carnival.

They carried on beyond the Tower and the ancient hospital and monastery of St Katherine's to the mud flats that surrounded Wapping. Here they instructed the boatman to get as close as possible to the wharf so that they would have a clear view of the gallows that lay just beyond. They tied up at a post and Jack and Rebecca ate their meat pies but did not press Anne to eat hers. Little was said as they watched the crowds gather along the banks and the boats anchor in the shallows on both sides of the river. Jack pointed out a sleek-looking ship that was manoeuvring in midstream. "A Portuguese caravel. One of the fastest vessels afloat."

He looked up to where the sun appeared intermittently between scudding clouds driven by the strong wind. "It is around two o'clock. We have only another half-hour of the ebb tide. They will need to get it over within the next hour."

As he was speaking, two carts appeared on the river bank, each drawn along the muddy track by paired horses. The first contained four soldiers and an important looking official bearing a silver oar. The second cart carried three men, including the bound prisoner and a priest.

"The silver oar is the Admiralty Marshall's insignia of office," explained Jack. "The man accompanying the priest and the prisoner is the executioner."

Anne was not listening. Her eyes were fixed on the prisoner who was slumped against the side of his vehicle, his face hidden from view. She willed him to raise his head and catch her eye so that he could be reassured that there were friends among the jeering mob. But he remained motionless.

The gallows were by now almost fully exposed by the low tide and the prisoner's cart was driven against the upright to provide a platform. The horses were then re-harnessed with long ropes attached to the rear of the platform so that, from dry land, they could pull it away at the critical moment.

The Admiralty Marshall appeared to be making an official pronouncement but his voice was drowned by the wind blowing fiercely down the river and rattling the rigging of the nearby ships. Meanwhile the prisoner was made to stand, albeit it far from steadily, on the makeshift scaffold while the executioner climbed up on spikes to the cross beam to check the attachment of the rope. Once this had been done the noose was placed around the prisoner's head, at which point Anne was reminded of Jonah's comment about the drop being too short to break a man's neck.

It was only now that Anne could see Hermann clearly. His left arm was hanging limp and one side of his shirt was covered in blood. They had done nothing for his wound nor even changed his linen, she noted. And then she saw the discoloration of his face and the stupefied look in his eyes. He was obviously a very sick man.

Anne's thoughts were interrupted suddenly by a loud exclamation from Jack. "God's wounds!" he said "Something is amiss. The caravel's pinnace has come too close and is being warned off."

Anne could see the boat rowed by four men, pushing into the shallow waters just beyond the gallows. Then a shot rang out from the caravel, which had edged closer to the near shore.

The loud crack of the firearm caused the horses to take fright. Those attached to the prisoner's cart pulled away from the gallows, leaving the prisoner himself hanging in mid-air and kicking wildly as he fought for breath. But a plank was now thrown from the pinnace on to the mud, allowing two of the oarsmen to jump out. One climbed up the gallows and cut the rope, the other gathered the prisoner as he fell into the mud and dragged him into the boat. The four oarsmen, using all their strength, then rowed back through the flotilla of small craft to the caravel which was readying itself to set sail down river.

On the landward side of the gallows there was great commotion of another kind. The Admiralty Marshall's cart had been dragged by the frightened horses into the spectators gathered along the bank. The soldiers had immediately leapt out and raised their guns but they held their fire for fear of killing bystanders and those on the river. Before the Admiralty Marshall could collect himself and decide on a course of action, the pinnace had been hauled aboard the caravel which hoisted its sails. As the ship ploughed forwards Anne could see a red and white flag fluttering from the masthead.

Jack, too, had seen it. "The emblem of the Hansa!" he said. "Declaring victory no doubt."

But Anne realised that it was not yet over because the Admiralty boat, *Adventure*, was getting ready to give chase.

She looked on as the crew of the *Adventure* busied themselves on deck in preparation for a hurried departure. But it was some minutes before the anchor could be raised and even then the captain was hemmed in by all the small boats that had clustered together on this stretch of the river. By the time the *Adventure* was clear and under full sail the caravel had a precious advantage.

As they were rowed back towards St Paul's Wharf on the incoming tide, Rebecca asked her uncle whether the Hansa ship would be able to escape to the sea.

"That depends," he said. "They will shortly be facing an incoming tide. However the tide is weak at this time and they have the advantage of a very strong wind behind them. Also, the Hansa are skilled navigators and know the Thames waters well. They will try to keep out of the main stream and stay in the lesser currents. I cannot imagine that the *Adventure* will catch them, nor close the distance to allow the use of her guns."

"What about beacons?" asked Anne: "And could they not send a messenger on horseback and intercept them down river?"

"No time for that," Jack replied, "and no one to stop them at Gravesend. Once on the open sea the caravel will be away with the prevailing wind behind them."

For two whole weeks there was no news of the caravel's fate or that of the man it had plucked from the gallows. Yet Anne felt strangely calm. After hearing what Jack had to say she had little doubt that the Hansa ship had escaped. She guessed that it would head for Hamburg where Hermann might write to her through the Steelyard. However she did have other, darker, thoughts. Perhaps it was a lover's instinct but the man who had stared out from the scaffold seemed to her to have the mark of death upon him. And even if he was still alive she would surely never see him again, for he could not return to England.

At the end of the month a package was delivered to Anne's door by a messenger from the Steelyard. She took it in and on removing the wrapping found a richly bejewelled ruby ring. There was also a note written in neat script:

It is a great sadness that Hermann Wedig did not survive his wounds, but was buried at sea with full honours. It was his last wish that you, being cherished by him above all others, should receive his ring.

Rebecca seemed surprised by her cousin's outward composure in the face of the latest turn of events. Over mugs of steaming ale and ginger, Anne explained to her: "Both he and I are at peace. Every parting from him was like a death and this is but another. And better by far that he should die with honour among comrades than that he should choke to death at the end of a rope before a jeering mob and have his corpse exhibited. I would not have had this happen, but in some way it is a fitting end to everything."

Yet Anne was not being entirely truthful about her feelings. With this man's death part of her, too, had died.

PART VI

❧ *1535* ❧

REVELATION

ANNE SAT IN HER PARLOUR IN EASTCHEAP, KEEPING an eye on little Tom as he tottered about the room. Margaret would soon be back from the shops and then she would walk towards Cheapside to attend her conventicle.

Over two decades had elapsed since the death of Richard. Through all those years she had faithfully promoted the Christian beliefs he held dear and now it was time for a new generation to take over. She had no doubt that her son-in-law, Roger Whaplod, would continue to advance their common cause, although she had to acknowledge that he could be unbending and impulsive. He had only recently had a short spell in prison after being caught up in a riot and she had worried then that he might lose his employment as a joiner. That would have been a severe blow to him and Margaret but also to her, now that she depended on their rent as lodgers.

Anne had already decided that this would be her last appearance as a leading member of the conventicle. Reformists were now in the ascendant and although there was still much to be done she felt that this was a good moment to withdraw. But there was another reason. She was feeling tired these days and she wished to conserve her remaining energy for one final undertaking that would assuredly tax both her mind and body to the limit.

When Margaret returned with her basket of shopping Anne gave her a kiss. "I shall return for supper from my meeting in Poultry – and if I am late, tell your ravenous husband to leave a crust for me."

"Why," said Margaret, "I myself have just come from Scalding Alley by Poultry where I purchased this chicken, all plucked and scorched and ready to cook."

Anne gave a sigh. "Plucked and scorched is how I sometimes feel after these meetings. There is so much argument over Luther's teachings on salvation by faith, the Eucharist and absolution. I am content from now on to absent myself and leave the field to others."

The poulterer's house was modest and those assembled were obliged to stand. After the customary readings Anne, the longest serving member of the fraternity, was asked to speak. "My friends," she began, "it should be a matter of great satisfaction to us that over the past several years our reformist cause has been favoured by so many in high places. Parliament has recorded its objection to many Church practices we abhor. The most powerful man on the King's Council, Thomas Cromwell, is inclined towards our views. The new Archbishop of Canterbury, Thomas Cranmer, is a reformist formerly suspected of Lutheran beliefs. And, this very year, we have witnessed the appointment of three reformist bishops, including Hugh Latimer, who has preached openly that the Bible should be read in English. We should take comfort from all these things."

"But what of the King?" a barber surgeon asked. "Where does our sovereign stand on Church reforms?"

Another answered him. "His new Queen is most certainly a reformer. As for the King himself, we must judge him by his actions. He has imprisoned in the Tower two of our greatest enemies, Sir Thomas More and Bishop Fisher of Rochester. And the elevation of Archbishop Cranmer is surely a further mark of his wish for reform."

The barber surgeon was more cautious: "We must hope that you are right. But Fisher and More are charged with treason, not heresy. And in matters of doctrine some say the King is of the old thinking."

In bringing the meeting to a close Anne announced that it was time for her to make way for others and that she would not from now on be taking a leading part in the proceedings of their group.

What she had told no one was that some weeks before she had written to the Archbishop at Lambeth Palace. Encouraged by the progress of reformist views she calculated that the Archbishop would take a much more sympathetic view of Richard Hunne than his predecessors had done. She had humbly requested a meeting in Exeter with Canon Horsey, if he was still alive, so that she could put to him some questions that remained in her mind about her late husband's death and thereby comfort her soul before she went to the grave. And now she had received by messenger a reply which she read and re-read.

> *His Grace the Archbishop has considered your request for an audience with Dr William Horsey, formerly Chancellor to the Bishop of London and now Canon of Exeter cathedral. His Grace has seen fit to communicate with the Lord Bishop of Exeter and the reply received form the Bishop is that Dr Horsey is willing to receive you in Salisbury where he will be residing during the month of June on account of a family matter that calls for his presence there. You should present this letter to the Close Porter at the South Gate of the cathedral when you arrive in order to be admitted.*
> *Benjamin Slather,*
> *Chaplain to His Grace, the Archbishop of Canterbury.*

Anne had saved money for this expedition but she was nevertheless greatly relieved that she would not have to travel to Exeter, a journey that would take ten days or more and entail heavy costs.

When Margaret was informed of her mother's intentions she became anxious. "Surely you cannot undertake this journey on your own. It would not be safe."

Anne sought to reassure her daughter. "I have looked into this, Margaret. I will travel with a known carrier in his waggon – a man who goes back and forth each month between London and Salisbury conveying merchandise. It is a long journey of perhaps four days but I shall rest every night at a good hostelry."

Margaret continued to show concern for her mother's welfare, but knowing her obstinacy, she made no further attempt at dissuasion.

<hr />

The waggoner had insisted on an early start and the sun was low in the sky as mother and daughter walked behind Roger Whaplod, Anne's large leather travelling bag protruding from under his arm. "There," said Margaret as they entered Bishopsgate, "I take it that is our man with his waggon outside the Black Bull?"

The carrier, a short man with unkempt ginger hair and a red face, took the bag and stowed it on the covered waggon which was harnessed to four champing horses.

"We must set off without delay!" he said impatiently. "We are to be in Staines tonight and the distance is not much short of twenty miles."

Anne said her goodbyes to Margaret and Roger and was helped up onto the waggon. She was dismayed to see that she would have to share her journey with sacks, boxes, paniers, bolts of cloth, books and bags of letters. She was thankful that there were no other passengers because there was scarcely room to sit. She wondered how she would cope with long hours in such confined conditions but soon put away such thoughts as the equipage rumbled across London to Ludgate Hill. Since moving to London, she had barely travelled on land outside the city walls beyond Wapping to the east and Westminster to the west and the prospect of adventuring into unknown regions lifted her spirits.

On that first day time passed quickly, despite the discomfort, as they jolted over rutted tracks heading west. The carrier, who introduced himself as Sam, told Anne with some pride that he was the only waggoner plying his trade between Salisbury and London, the rest being mere carters, driving two wheeled vehicles. Reaching Staines well before dusk, Sam suggested that Anne put up at the Swan Inn where he had to deliver packages and letters. He said he would sleep on the waggon as was his custom.

The next stopover was the White Lion Inn at Hertford Bridge, and from here there was a short ten-mile stage to Basingstoke. In this busy town which was full of carts and travellers on horseback, some heading west towards Exeter and others south to Winchester, Sam dropped off several boxes and picked up letters from the Pen and Parchment Inn where Anne stayed overnight. The following stretch was nineteen miles to Andover, the rough road threading its way through fields of wheat and cattle grazing on pastureland hewn out of the surrounding forest. On a particularly desolate stretch, Anne wondered what it would be like in winter and how the waggoner would manage if he lost a wheel.

Sam was a man of few words, which suited Anne well enough. But on reaching Andover he became more animated. "This is a place full of manufacture – cloth, leatherwork, hats and shoes – and I shall be stowing as much as I am able for delivery to London merchants when we return. But for the present we will have a new passenger for the final stage to Salisbury, as the inn-keeper has informed me."

"And who might that be?" Anne asked.

"A friar, I believe, returning to his religious house."

Anne did not like the sound of this but said nothing. After they had driven into the yard at the back of the Angel Inn, Sam began to unharness the horses: "I have stabling here," he said. "I change horses for both the up and the down journeys. I myself will be staying elsewhere in the town tonight." Anne detected a note of anticipation in his voice and guessed that it was not only the horses that would be revitalised during the brief stay over.

The next morning Sam was in good spirits and expressed the hope that Anne had passed as good a night as he had. While she was watching him harnessing the fresh horses a shadowy figure appeared at the sunlit entrance to the yard. She could see that the indistinct form was that of a man of medium build wearing a black cowl and cloak over a white habit and carrying a bundle that appeared to consist largely of books. She could not at first make out his features behind the cowl but as he came into the yard he spoke clearly and with authority.

"Is this the carrier destined for Salisbury?"

On being so assured he climbed up onto the waggon after Anne and sat on some packaging beside her. She was aware immediately of a waft of foul air and judged that this ascetic churchman never washed. She glanced at him and saw piercing eyes set in a long dusky face – perhaps a natural hue but more probably, she thought, a discolouration due to ingrained grime.

As the waggon trundled out of Andover on the Salisbury road, the stranger introduced himself. "My name is Barnabas Cardew. I am a Dominican from the friary in Salisbury where I am returning after preaching for a few days in Andover. And you?"

Anne wished to remain as anonymous as possible. "I am Anne, visiting an elderly kinsman in Salisbury."

To her discomfort the friar seemed determined to engage her in conversation. He turned towards her and she could feel his stale breath on her face. "We blackfriars have a good foundation in Salisbury funded generously by our benefactors. But we must preach to eat, and in Andover there are many tradespeople willing to pay their farthing."

Anne felt she had no choice but to show interest. "And on what subjects do you preach?" she asked.

"Our brotherhood is sworn to stamp out heresy wherever it may arise. Our purpose is to teach not only scripture but the writings of our learned fathers and the canonical books. We uphold the supremacy of the Holy Father, the seven sacraments, especially penance, and the veneration of saints."

Anne tried not to wince or give any outward sign of her unease. "And do you find some who dissent from this teaching?"

"It is certainly true that there are Lutherans, Lollards and other heretics in every town. I make it my business to talk to the faithful who, in the true spirit of Christian fellowship, are willing to give me the names of those who are suspected of heresy. These are then brought to the attention of the bishop."

"And what should happen to such people?" Anne enquired.

"Over two centuries ago our revered father, Thomas Aquinas, whose philosophy and writings inspire all our work, made this clear. He said it is a much graver matter to corrupt the faith that quickens the soul than to forge money that supports the temporal life. Therefore, if criminals are condemned to death by the secular authority much more reason there is for convicted heretics to be put to death. Those are his words."

Anne remained silent while gazing out at the patchwork of fields and hedgerows through which they were passing.

The friar, however, carried on. "We friars have uncovered secret conventicles and nests of unbelievers in many places. I myself have discovered heretics hereabouts in Salisbury and Shaftesbury. Our brothers, the Greyfriars, have also been active in this role. And some few years ago – before my time – the friars of Aylsbury achieved our greatest triumph when they helped to track down many Lollards in Amersham of whom I believe no less than seven were burned at the stake."

Anne froze. This foul smelling man beside her was a pernicious example of the breed of churchmen who had destroyed her family. She now considered him to be dangerous but the revulsion she felt must not be detected. Instead, she tried to disguise her anguish by asking about the bundle of books.

"I preach from all these learned authors whose texts are held in our library."

"But surely you need only preach from one book, that is the Bible – the sole source of Holy Scripture and spiritual authority." As soon as the words were out she regretted her impulsiveness.

He gave her a searching look, his eyes glinting like a weasel's from beneath his cowl. "That is what our enemies might say," he replied calmly. "Tell me, Anne … in which parish do you worship?"

Anne was conscious of a slight menace in his voice so she evaded his question. "As a humble and impoverished widow, I stay with kinsfolk in different places. I have no settled parish."

He looked at her suspiciously. "And where are you staying in Salisbury?"

Again, she parried the question. "My kinsman has no room for me. But I understand that there are many inns in the town and I will procure a bed when I arrive."

After this exchange they fell silent. Anne knew that one false move on her part and he would ensnare her like a stoat catching a rabbit.

As the waggon bumped and jolted its way through the chalk downs of south Wiltshire the long-horned dairy herds gave way to sheep. Set apart from the downland grazing stood fields of barley and wheat, tilled by horses and wheel ploughs. On one stretch of road they encountered a flock of sheep numbering hundreds being driven north by two drovers. While waiting for the animals to pass, Sam turned to Anne and pointed to the wide grassy road verges. "The sheep feed as they travel. No need to find provender for these creatures. Whoever devised the drove roads with their long acres alongside knew what they were about."

When at long last they approached Salisbury, its cathedral spire soaring above the surrounding wetlands, Sam dropped off letters and packages in outlying hamlets. Anne was greatly relieved when, at one of these small settlements, the friar clambered down from the waggon with his bundle, paid his fare and, without a goodbye or a glance back, disappeared from view.

After nearly five days of travelling the waggon rolled into Salisbury where Anne, now full of anticipation, put up at the Pheasant Inn – taking care to give a false name to the good innkeeper. Sam said he had further deliveries to make but would be returning two days later to London, so her business would have to be conducted on the morrow.

Next morning, Anne presented herself with her letter at the South Gate. The Close porter asked her to wait while he sent for Canon Horsey who was staying in the bishop's guesthouse. Looking about her, she marvelled at the soaring cathedral spire but she reminded herself that she was here not as a curious visitor but on a mission that would surely settle her mind once and for all regarding the fate of her husband. She must collect her thoughts and take advantage of the opportunity now offered to her.

After she had waited an hour or so, the porter accompanied Anne across the Close. Arriving at another gateway he said, "Canon Horsey will see you here at St Anne's Gate. Follow me up and take care on the stairs to the chapel above for they are steep and narrow."

Anne realised that she was to be received as a humble supplicant and mere woman before a churchman no doubt full of self-esteem and disdain. But she had no intention of fulfilling the subservient role to which she had been assigned.

She was shown into the modest chapel where sun was streaming in through a window set in the west wall. Dr William Horsey was seated on a heavy oak chair overlaid with red velvet that had been placed on a step in front of the altar. From this elevated platform he motioned to Anne to sit on the pew below him.

She looked at the man before her. His pale complexion had a ghostly, translucent quality as if sculpted from finest wax, and his ghastly pallor suggested to her that he had lived his days indoors and seldom ventured out. She noted that his white cassock was trimmed with fine lace and that he wore a ring, which he rubbed nervously.

"Mistress Anne," he said, his soft voice almost a whisper. "As you know, my Lord Bishop of Exeter has requested that I see you. It is convenient that I am called here by the grave illness of my dear sister – God rest her soul – who has for many years been a pious nun at Shaftesbury Abbey."

"I am sorry to hear of her sickness," said Anne. "And I thank you for seeing me in such sad circumstances."

"I understand that you are seeking information about the death of your late husband, Richard Hunne. I may be of some help to you in this, but before I can say anything I must ask you to swear that nothing that passes between us will be committed to writing nor will you divulge to anyone a single word of our discourse."

Anne had not expected this but, having little choice, she took the required oath of secrecy with her hand placed on the Bible he handed her.

"Now, perhaps it is best that you put to me your questions about this unhappy affair, bearing in mind that many years have passed and not everything can be recalled."

"That is understood," said Anne. "However, the question that troubles me most is this: I am aware that Charles Joseph, the bishop's summoner, confessed to murdering my husband and in so doing implicated yourself. Also, the Coroner's Inquest delivered a verdict that indicted yourself along with Joseph and the gaoler, Spalding. It seems that at the very least you were present in Lollards' Tower when Richard died. Can you tell me what happened to cause his death?"

Horsey seemed taken aback by the directness of this question and for a minute he sat silently, rubbing his ring. Then, avoiding direct eye contact with Anne, he answered. "I think I had better tell you what occurred from the beginning. After all these years it is perhaps right that you – and you alone – know the truth. The only other person alive who is familiar with what I am going to say is Sir Thomas More, though from what I hear he may, sadly, not be alive for much longer."

Horsey put the palms of his hands together as he focussed his thoughts. "Richard Hunne had pursued the Church through the courts. He also had heretical views, as his trial demonstrated. We – that is myself and my late Lord Bishop Fitzjames – decided to take this troublesome man into custody. We knew that he must have like-minded backers but he withstood all attempts to elicit the names of these pernicious reprobates. Therefore we – the bishop and I – took the decision to use duress as canon law allows and to undertake this in scrupulous accordance with the rules laid down by the authorities in such cases."

Anne was taken aback. "When does your esteemed canon law allow torture?"

"His Holiness Pope Innocent IV issued a decree *Ad Extirpanda* nearly 300 years ago. This asserts that torture may be used to obtain confessions from heretics, for they are no more than thieves of men's souls."

Anne was suddenly reminded of Joseph's confession which, puzzlingly, had said the bishop's chancellor, on going up to Lollards' Tower, had called poor Richard a 'thief'.

"However," Horsey continued, "torture is a final resort so that the accused cannot already have confessed. Also there must be half proof or credible evidence against the accused. In the case of Hunne, we examined him in Fulham where he made a declaration of his fault though without any signed confession. Therefore the half-truth was attested and duress could be applied."

Anne was shocked. "So you contrived a preliminary examination at which he was not permitted to sign a confession in order that you might torture him according to the requirements of your law."

"Mistress Anne, you are not a legal scholar as I am and you cannot possibly understand these matters. Everything we did was in accordance with what is ordained. The procedures laid down state that I, as interrogating judge, could not myself administer the torture. This task was to be performed by one of the two other junior church officials who, according to requirements, must be present. I put it to the bishop's summoner, Charles Joseph, that he should carry out the torture – though not to shed blood or maim or kill, such being forbidden by papal decree."

At this point Anne felt confounded. The role of Joseph was not what she had been led to believe from his own confession. She asked: "Did Joseph show willingness to perform this task?"

"At first he refused absolutely to obey my command. So I said to him that if he did not agree to do what I asked I would put him out of his office. I also made mention that if he undertook the task and Hunne then disclosed his backers and confederates he, Joseph, would be rewarded with handsome fees. Joseph remained disinclined for he had formed a mistaken regard for Hunne when ministering to him as gaoler. But eventually he came round."

Anne was appalled. If what was being said was true it portrayed Charles Joseph's role in an entirely different light. But she sat tight-lipped as the rest of the story unfolded.

"At all times strict procedures had to be followed as stipulated by learned jurists. I gave Hunne warning by coming to him and seeking forgiveness for what I must do to him; I ensured that he was fasted nine hours before his ordeal; and the duress was to begin only after midnight on the Sunday because on a holy day it is forbidden.

"That night we three – Joseph, Spalding the Bellringer and myself – came up to the chamber in Lollards' Tower where Hunne was lying on his bolster with his arms bound. I invoked the papal decree *Ad Extirpanda* against him and questioned him about his confederates but he would yield nothing. So Joseph heated a wire in the candle and put it up Hunne's nose to cause him pain – but he pushed too deeply because Hunne began to bleed profusely. We could not staunch the flow of blood which poured over his apparel and onto the floor. So great was his loss of blood that Hunne went into a faint and after some lapse of time stopped breathing – whereupon the bleeding also stopped."

Anne felt sick but she was determined to hear this man to the end. He carried on, always looking askance and never directly at her.

"We were at a loss to know what to do. At last I decided that the Church must be protected so Joseph and Spalding cleaned up the blood as best they could and put fresh linen on the body. They then broke Hunne's neck with a metal chain hanging on the wall and suspended him by his own girdle to give the semblance of self-murder. All this being undertaken with the object of safeguarding the standing and spiritual authority of the Church."

There was a long silence as Horsey fidgeted with his ring and Anne collected her thoughts. Trying to suppress her emotions she asked, "Why did Joseph confess to murder jointly with yourself and Spalding?"

"Joseph was a cunning knave. He had killed Hunne without intent, but to do so when engaged in torture is, in canon law, an offence as grave as murder. To protect himself he wished to implicate me so that the bishop would be obliged to intercede to have the case dismissed. And that is what occurred."

Something else had long puzzled Anne. "And what of the body of my husband? How was it that his hat was placed neatly on his head, his hair combed and his eyes closed?"

Horsey looked surprised. "It seems to me, Mistress Anne, that you know much more of this than you should. But I can tell you that it was Joseph's doing. I left him to clean up the chamber because I was obliged to attend the canons' early morning prayers. But instead of ensuring that all spillage of blood was removed he took it upon himself to make the body seemly – I dare say out of remorse for what he had done."

"And did you not leave your fur-trimmed cloak in Lollards' Tower? Can I ask why on a cold winter's night you would wish to remove this garment?"

Horsey was clearly agitated. "Everything had to be done before daybreak. We were in a race against time. All three of us helped to cleanse away the blood – there was so much of it – and I did not wish to stain my cloak. I then had to hasten away and in so doing forgot to pick it up – which was done later."

There was a long pause, the former Chancellor evidently feeling that he had said rather too much in answer to her impertinent questions. Having composed himself he placed his palms together, raised his eyes to the vaulted ceiling above and had his final say. "In concluding let me assure you of this. At every step of this unfortunate affair I conducted myself with painstaking correctness. All my actions have been guided by the desire to uphold true Christian belief and to root out pernicious doctrines. The means chosen were those prescribed by ancient authority and established law. The disguising of Hunne's accidental death was, furthermore, amply justified by the worthy purpose of avoiding any damage to the Church and its spiritual leadership. Therefore, while I regret the manner of your husband's death, I was right to do what I did."

Anne could hold back her anger and distress no longer. "Let me ask, venerated canon lawyer that you are, where in biblical text can you find the justification for pushing a wire up a man's nose to torment him, allowing his life blood to drain away and then perverting the course of justice by breaking his neck and pretending that his agonising death was by his own hand?"

Horsey was clearly shaken by her adversarial tone. "Mistress Anne, you seem to be wilfully unfamiliar with the writings of scholars, jurists, the works of our revered church fathers and papal decretals, all of which over many centuries have enriched the teaching of the Church. These are the authorities I look to guide me."

Anne, her blood now up, came back at him: "The simplicity of scripture has been overlaid and traduced by these jurists, serpentine commentators and – yes – dusty canon lawyers who have never been out in the world or know what it is to share the love of our fellow beings."

From her cloak she produced a small volume. "This is William Tyndale's English Bible" she said, with triumph in her voice. "I have read it and you will find nothing in its pages to exonerate your behaviour, to absolve you from the heinous crime you have committed against my late husband or to justify the gross deception you have sought to practice on the world."

Horsey stood up in anger. "I may call the bishop at this very moment and have you placed in custody for reading a prohibited book, possession of which is a mark of heresy."

It was Anne's turn to stand up. "I have no fear of you. If I am imprisoned and tried I will break my vow to you in deference to a higher vow that I have made to my dear departed husband. I will tell the world of your infamous participation in the death of Richard Hunne. After all, the reason that you swore me to confidence was to save you from the ignominy and shame that would befall you should your actions be exposed."

Horsey looked dazed. There were beads of perspiration on his waxen face – or were they tears? Anne could not be sure. She prepared to leave but before doing so delivered a final salvo. "Dr Horsey, the world is moving on. The reformist views for which Richard Hunne died are now being espoused by the King's ministers, by Parliament and, yes, even by the clergy. It will be your destiny to live out your remaining years not only in deep shame at your despicable misconduct but also in the knowledge that the bigoted and despotic Church you so cherish is no more."

She turned her back on him, descended the stairs and went out through the South Gate.

TOWER HILL

ROGER WHAPLOD BROKE HIS BREAD WITH UNNECESSARY force. "The old devil is to be executed on the morrow at ten o'clock. We should go to see justice done."

Margaret, who was feeding little Dunstan, looked up. "That man has been the scourge of reformists. And think of poor Thomas Hitton whom they burned some years back. It is surely God's will that he should pay with his life for his past misdeeds. I would certainly go with you to Tower Hill if someone would take charge of Dunstan."

Anne, who had barely touched her breakfast, was quick to offer her help. "Margaret dear, I am happy to stay here with Dunstan while you and Roger go and see the execution."

"That is not what I intended," Margaret said. "I can take the boy to Aunt Rebecca and then you could come with us. After all, it is not every day that our enemies are brought low in public. We should all be there to witness the downfall and humiliation of this man."

Anne gave a sigh. "You had better leave me here. I am tired after my long journey to Salisbury and the walk would be too much."

Margaret was not so easily deterred. "Of course you must not walk. But we can hire a horse and cart from the neighbouring butcher. He is very obliging."

"Give me a little time to think about it." Anne recalled that John Fisher, Bishop of Rochester, had first been arraigned over a year ago on a charge of treason for refusing to accept the King as Supreme Head of the Church. His imprisonment in the Tower had been the subject of heated discussion within her conventicle. Some had rejoiced at his captivity and one among the fraternity, a bookseller, had reminded them all of events that occurred some years before. "Brethren, you should all be aware how the Bishop of Rochester brought about the ruin of poor Thomas Hitton. Thomas, a priest, was familiar to those of us in the book trade as a supplier of prohibited works, especially those of Tyndale. He was returning to Antwerp when intercepted at Gravesend by the Archbishop's men and brought before him. The Archbishop examined Thomas who persisted in denying purgatory, denouncing images of Christ and the saints and, in short, stating boldly all those things we here agree with. Thomas was then sent to the Bishop of Rochester who questioned him further and, when the poor man refused to abjure, was condemned to burn by the two churchmen."

A stonemason had expressed a different view. "The Archbishop, wishing that Hitton would recant his supposed heresy and thereby save his life, sought the aid of the Bishop of Rochester. This was because he, the bishop, was known to be a peaceable man, best able to dissuade Hitton from his obstinacy. It was only when Hitton had, with great boldness, refused all attempts to have him renounce his beliefs, that the bishop committed him to prison and later to burn as a heretic. Certainly, Fisher was gravely at fault, but even more so were the Church laws that guided his actions."

A master from St Paul's School had voiced his misgivings. "Here is a person most distinguished as a scholar, professor of divinity, elected lifetime Chancellor of Cambridge University, friend of Erasmus and promoter of learning in the ancient languages. We should not rush to condemn such a man to an ignominious death."

A draper had added: "The bishop is damned because he has thwarted the King at every point. He disapproved the dissolution of his marriage, he tried to block his curtailment of the Church's privileges and now he has opposed his sovereign in the matter of the supremacy. The King's anger is the greater because inwardly he esteems the man who has persistently defied him."

At the meeting, Anne had come down firmly against the Bishop of Rochester. She reminded her audience of his withering assault on the works of Luther, delivered at the book burning some ten years before, and he had led those in the Lords who obstructed all Church reforms put forward by the Commons. Above all else, Anne considered him to be dangerous because of his oratory, an eloquence that papists and other supporters of the old order were able to use as a powerful weapon against their adversaries.

She now pondered again on the fate of the aged bishop with the silver tongue. Only the previous month, the Pope had elevated him to the College of Cardinals with the purpose of saving him from the scaffold. But everyone knew that this action had further enraged the King who could not bear to see Rome meddling in his realm. It was now said that there would be no head on which to place the Cardinal's hat.

Would Fisher use his scaffold speech to broadcast his opinions? Would be denounce reformers and uphold the ancient privileges of the Church? How would be conduct himself? With these questions on her mind, and being curious too, about a man who would not bend to the will of his indomitable sovereign, Anne decided to join her daughter and son-in-law.

The butcher's horse and cart arrived on the high ground of Tower Hill, northwest of the Tower itself, after nine o'clock. A crowd was already gathered around the scaffold but the newcomers stationed themselves a short distance away.

"Standing on the cart we can see very well from here," said Roger. "And we shall avoid the crush of the onlookers."

They did not have to wait long. Looking down towards the river Anne saw an armed escort of helmeted pikemen emerging from the Tower Gate. Among the troop, two of the sheriff's men were carrying a chair occupied by the frail old bishop – though now stripped of his office. Anne noted that the burden must be light because the carriers climbed the slope without any sign of exertion. They halted at the scaffold and the bishop was offered assistance. But he refused and, to the sound of jeers and shouts of "Papist!", he slowly climbed the steps to the wooden platform unaided. He wore a white shirt, a doublet and gown, and a furred tippet round his shoulders. As he prepared to speak Anne heard the sombre peel of the passing bell – the Church's forewarning of impending death – rung from nearby All Hallows, Barking.

His voice was faint but distinct as he addressed the hushed crowd. "Christian people … I come hither to die for the faith of Christ's Holy Catholic Church. And I thank God, that hitherto my stomach has served me very well so that I have not yet feared death. Wherefore I desire you all to help and assist with your prayers that, at the very point and instant of death's stroke, I may stand steadfast. And I beseech Almighty God of his infinite goodness to save the King and this realm and that it may please him to hold His holy hand over it and send the King a good counsel."

The executioner knelt down, ready to do his office, and asked forgiveness in the customary manner. The prisoner's gown and tippet were removed, leaving him standing in his doublet and hose. Anne noticed that he was severely wasted, with scarcely any flesh clinging to his bones.

Someone standing near them said scornfully. "He is clearly dying. I do not know why they bother with all this." But Anne knew very well why. His death was not enough: the people had to be shown that the old Church had been humbled before their mighty prince.

The prisoner knelt for a few minutes in private prayer before placing his neck on the block. The onlookers gasped as the axe was raised, its menacing face glinting in the morning sun. When it fell, the head was severed in one blow. Some among the crowd groaned but most jeered.

Roger turned to his wife. "That was a task well done. He showed courage at the end but he deserved to die. I am only surprised that he did not say more."

Margaret said: "No doubt the Lieutenant of the Tower informed him that it was the King's desire he should be brief. But it is perhaps surprising that he was not permitted a priest for his comfort at the last." She looked at the sun. "We must return because I undertook to gather up little Dunstan at midday."

Anne remained silent, aware only of the measured tolling of the death knell that now filled the air. As they were leaving she looked back at the scaffold. The corpse had been stripped and was being laid out naked for the people to view. The head had been wrapped in a cloth to be taken away and impaled on London Bridge.

41

ATONEMENT

THAT NIGHT, ANNE WAS TORMENTED BY A DISTURBING dream. She saw indistinctly, as through a veil of mist, the whole of humankind from the beginning of time to the end, stretched out in an endless chain of death. All the souls who had been and all the souls who were yet to come were entangled in a great heap extending from one horizon to the other. Then she saw the torch of life passing slowly across the mound of death and as the light shone on them, so the bodies began to stir and writhe, slithering over each other as they strove to fulfil their earthly desires. And when the torch had passed on she saw the squirming shapes, their short day done, falling back and fading, motionless, into the shadows and stillness of everlasting sleep.

Anne was in an agitated state. She wondered whether the bleak images that she had witnessed signified that life – all life – is but a spasm, each generation lost to eternity as the next succeeds.

When she drifted off to sleep again the dream returned. But this time, as the torch of life passed over, some few souls remained framed in its glow, as if they had become beacons to all who came after. Anne could make out the faces of some of those who were lighting the way: there was John Colet, and her own departed husband, Richard and, yes, there too was the face of Geoffrey the scribe. But then came a shock. There could be no mistake: she could see the pale and finely chiselled features of Bishop John Fisher luminous in the surrounding darkness.

When she rose the next morning Anne felt weak and faint. She sat in the parlour for a few minutes to gather her thoughts, her mind racked with self-doubt. The dreadful images of the night troubled her deeply and she began to question the rightness of her actions and beliefs. Was that old adversary of reformists, John Fisher, to be ranked among the chosen alongside those who had died for a cause he reviled? How could this be? And then it slowly dawned on her: in matters of religious persuasion those who believe one thing may be no more right or wrong than those who believe another. Perhaps the real delusion – and sin – is to espouse a narrow view of the truth and denounce all those who cannot share it.

Anne got up slowly and went into the kitchen where Margaret was feeding little Tom. "Margaret dear, I am going out for a short time. I wish to see a bookseller in St Paul's."

Margaret looked anxiously at her mother. "You should have something to eat before you go. You have lost weight and need to feed yourself up."

"No. I have no appetite for the present – but I shall revive. I shall not be gone long."

She left the house and set out to walk the familiar route to St Paul's. The late June sun was strong but she felt strangely chilled. After a short distance she became breathless and was forced to pause. When she reached Paternoster Row she wandered thoughtfully among the book stalls examining the occasional text. She was struck by the increase in books and the decline in their cost since printed works had come in. She knew, too, that there were stalls where, if she were to ask discreetly for a Tyndale Bible, it would be found for her from the back of the shop with no trouble. Such was the power of the printed word.

But many of the tracts and devotional works that were on display were now distasteful to her. She found the language of religious zealots extreme, venomous and an incitement to hatred and violence. They were deaf men – always men – shouting at each other in apoplectic fury from their pulpits; and in all this hate-filled cacophony, reason and compassion were drowned out. She felt that true wisdom lay in perceiving that for a good Christian there are many tenable views, none of which should be upheld by heaping scorn on others. Did not Christ Himself tell us that *In my Father's house are many rooms?*

She had been deluded. Anne saw now that neither she nor any man or woman could be the rightful agent of holy retribution. It was a vain presumption to believe that the killing of another would be divinely ordained. What she had heard was not the voice of God but only a false echo going round and round within her own head. But she knew that the wisdom she had acquired at such cost to herself and others could not be passed on. Self-proclaimed devotees of some religious sect or another would go on killing with righteous intent, conducting holy war and aspiring to do God's murderous work in ignorance of his true purpose. And for all eternity the heavens would look down and weep.

It saddened her to think that this wisdom had come to her at the end of her life, too late to be of any use. It also pained her that her own child and son-in-law, if they ever gained such a precious insight, would likely do so only at the last. Each generation seemed destined to afflict one another with the shrill certainty of blind faith. And so it would go on until the day of judgement.

Anne suddenly felt more tired than she had known. She turned into the cathedral precinct and rested for some minutes on the steps of the bishop's palace. She cupped her head in her hands. She had lost the two men she loved but at least their memories could be cherished and honoured. But now she had lost her faith – and there was only shame to be felt in recalling her earlier convictions.

She rose with difficulty, crossed over to the north door of the cathedral and entered. The choir was in session, preparing for the forthcoming annual service celebrating the feast day of the saints Peter and Paul. As she moved slowly and with faltering steps down the lengthy nave, the sung *Te Deum* resonated through the great spaces of the building and swelled up into the vaulted roof voids. When she reached the entrance to the undercroft she descended the stairs, clutching at the wall for fear of falling. She was now standing in the parish church of St Faith – a gloomy, half-lit dungeon divided by three rows of massive pillars that supported the roof vaulting of the undercroft, directly beneath the choir.

Seeing that she was alone in this sombre place of worship, Anne knelt before the altar as she had done some twenty years before. Then she had been defiant, but now her tone was remorseful and her voice weak as she prayed aloud.

"Mighty God of heaven and earth, I beg forgiveness from the bottom of my heart. I have killed a man in the mistaken belief that he set out to murder my dear husband. I have harboured a great hatred for those of the old form of worship in the mistaken conviction that they were evil through and through. I have entertained the delusion that reforms would set things right whereas I see now that one kind of persecution is replaced with another ..."

Here she broke off as the tears rolled down her cheeks. In the stillness she could hear the triumphant strains of the Gloria soaring above her. The feeling of overwhelming tiredness returned and she struggled to compose herself as she ended her supplication.

"I have made a grave error in believing that there is but one path to God whereas now I see clearly that there are many avenues into his heart. I pray forgiveness for all these things. God rest my soul and those of my dear departed husband, Richard, and my beloved erstwhile husband, Hermann."

Anne tried to get up but she had not the strength.

Early next morning the body of a woman was found by a priest preparing for matins in St Faith's. He called the verger who was doing his rounds in the cathedral and the two men searched the corpse to see if there was any means of identification.

"This is a very unusual, not to say valuable, ring she is wearing." The priest remarked. "She must have connections. We should post a notice on the door of the cathedral so her kin can claim the body."

The verger looked disdainfully at the dead woman: "What was she doing down here alone? And pinned to the very flesh of her breast a scrap of parchment with a hand imprinted on it. Without doubt she was a madwoman."

EPILOGUE

RICHARD HUNNE WAS A LOLLARD. THOSE WHO thought like him desired to read the Bible in their own language, to return to the simplicity of biblical texts as the central theme of Christian worship and to do away with perceived superstition. Among the targeted practices were pilgrimages, shrines, relics, icons, obits, chantries – and, indeed, the whole indulgence industry as well as the doctrine of purgatory that underpinned it. Lollards also condemned the wealth and power of the Church and its bishops, the reach of ecclesiastical courts and the exorbitant fees charged for burials and probate of wills.

Within thirty-five years of Hunne's death the religious reforms that he and his fellow Lollards were crying out for had been enforced on an unwilling Church by Crown and Parliament. Pilgrimages were condemned, shrines and images removed and chantries abolished. The Church's powers were drastically curtailed: Convocation could no longer pass laws without the King's consent; the clergy's privileged legal status was ended so that priests became answerable before the secular courts; and mortuary and probate fees were capped by legislation that introduced a scale of charges linked to the means of the payer.

The old heresy acts were repealed, depriving bishops of their power of arrest on suspicion and requiring prosecutions for heresy to be initiated by indictment – a secular procedure. There were eighty-one executions for heresy in the reign of Henry VIII but only two under Edward VI and four under Elizabeth I. However, in the savage throw-back of Mary's intervening reign, when the heresy laws were revived, there were no less than 283 executions for heresy in little more than three years. The then Bishop of London, Edmund Bonner, was once more at the forefront of these judicial burnings. But now the state, rather than the Church, was the prime mover in prosecutions.

In the revolutionary upheaval of the Reformation one reform stands out above all others: the introduction of the first authorised English Bible. Until the late 1530s, anyone who obtained or read a Bible translated into English could be convicted of heresy while those who published an unauthorised vernacular text were risking their lives. Yet in 1539 a new translation by Coverdale which had been sponsored by Thomas Cromwell was placed in every parish church. Attached to the podium beneath the pulpit so that it could be read by all but not removed, this mighty volume became known as the 'Chained Bible' or 'Great Bible'.

During the Reformation years, the Church was stripped of much of its wealth. By threatening the entire clergy with the charge of praemunire, Henry VIII exacted a staggeringly large fine of £118,000 payable over five years. Nine hundred religious houses – monasteries, convents and friaries – were dissolved and their assets seized, while nearly 2,500 chantries suffered the same fate. Over 14,000 monks, nuns, canons, friars and chantry priests were made redundant and pensioned off with modest annuities. The bishops lost nearly 200 manors with an estimated annual value of around £6,000. And many of the great episcopal palaces lining the Thames fell into private hands or became the property of the Crown – York Place, Durham Place, Norwich Place and Bath Place among them.

Old St Paul's bore witness to the new religious order. One November night in 1548 under the cloak of darkness, the great rood outside the north door, together with the crucifixes and images in the cathedral, were pulled down and removed, while its vestments and altar cloths were taken away and sold off. With its chantries dissolved, its icons gone, its guild chapels closed down and the tapers of the faithful extinguished, post-Reformation St Paul's would have looked much more austere than in its bejewelled Catholic heyday.

After its introduction in 1539, six copies of the Great Bible were chained to pillars in different parts of St Paul's. A placard was affixed beside each volume, admonishing readers to conduct themselves reverently and "not to draw multitudes about them, nor to make exposition of what they read, nor to read aloud in time of divine service, nor enter into disputes concerning it."

The physical fabric of the cathedral was later to fall victim to several cataclysmic events. During the reign of Edward VI, Protector Somerset pulled down the chapter house and its cloister in order to utilise the stones for his pretentious new palace, Somerset House. The churchyard was dug up and five hundred tons of bones carted away to Finsbury Field where they were piled into a mound that became known as Bone Hill – now Bunhill.

Then, on June 3rd 1561, a violent thunderstorm burst over London. The steeple of St Paul's was struck by lightning, its timber framework caught fire and its lead covering melted in the heat and poured down onto the roof which was burned through. Within a few years the roof had been renewed but the steeple was never replaced. Another casualty of this fire was the monument of Richard Fitzjames, former Bishop of London: the carved timber chapel, with steps leading up, that had been built over his marble tomb, was burned by falling debris and had to be taken down.

King James I, wishing to restore the cathedral to its former glory, commissioned Inigo Jones to build an imposing but incongruous portico at the west end. However, during Cromwell's protectorate in the 1650s the portico was let out for shops and the cathedral nave was turned into a cavalry barracks. An order was issued prohibiting the soldiers from playing at ninepins from nine in the evening until six in the morning as the noise disturbed residents in the neighbourhood. During these years of iconoclasm and profanity the building fell into serious disrepair and by the time of the Restoration urgent action was required to save London's great church from collapse. Funds were raised and timber scaffolding erected around the outside in preparation for major structural repairs – but before the work could begin the Great Fire of London intervened.

The fire began in the early hours of Monday September 2nd at a bakery in Pudding Lane just off New Fish Street. Fanned by a strong easterly wind the conflagration spread rapidly through the narrow streets: southwards halfway across London Bridge before a gap in the houses stopped its progress; northwards up New Fish Street and Gracechurch Street; and eastwards along Thames Street where warehouses, full of combustible materials – oil, brandy, pitch and tar – fed the flames.

As the fire took hold, Londoners tried desperately to save their possessions. Some buried valuables in their gardens while others took their goods to churches, mistakenly believing the stone structures to be secure. The Thames was covered with barges and boats laden with household belongings; the streets were full of carts loaded with movables heading for the city gates; and in the comparative safety of the outlying fields beyond the city walls, terrified citizens encamped with their goods under makeshift tents.

Within the City the cathedral of St Paul's was thought by many to be impregnable. The massive stone structure had the advantage of standing on the high ground of Ludgate Hill, separated within its own precinct and perimeter wall from the surrounding buildings. Some took their goods to this perceived safe haven and the book sellers and stationers in the immediate neighbourhood carried their stock down to the undercroft which was quickly filled with printed works, manuscripts and texts of all kinds.

But St Paul's was far from being invulnerable: wooden scaffolding encased the exterior walls; there was timber in the roofing structure; the roof was overlaid with several acres of lead sheeting which would melt at a temperature of 327 degrees centigrade; the crypt, now crammed with books and paper, had become a major fire hazard; and while the cathedral stood in solitary splendour there was no protection from the burning debris that was carried on the wind all over the city.

On Tuesday, the second day of the fire, St Paul's succumbed. The roof timbers caught fire and the building was soon assaulted from all directions: molten lead poured like lava from above, enflamed scaffolding torched the side elevations and the flammable contents of the crypt generated intense heat from below. By the time the Great Fire had burned itself out on the Wednesday, four-fifths of the city was destroyed and St Paul's was a ruin. The combination of weakened mortar and heat-induced expansion of stones had caused walls and pillars to collapse. Anything combustible had been consumed. The rose window had been burned out and the roof had fallen into the nave and the body of the choir into St Faith's, leaving a mound of rubble where once had stood one of the finest chancels in medieval Europe. London's cathedral, within whose ancient walls so many had been condemned to burn, had itself suffered the fate of martyrs.

The work of generations of craftsmen had been demolished along with five hundred years of history. Also lost were the tombs of the great: Saxon kings, Tudor courtiers and a line of bishops going back to Edward the Confessor. However the remains of one bishop survived: a lead coffin had broken open, revealing the body of Robert Braybroke (died 1404), Bishop of London under Richard II. It is recorded that "the whole corpse was so dried up, the flesh, sinews, and skin cleaving fast to the bones, that being set upon its feet, it stood stiff as a plank."

But of Bishop Richard Fitzjames there was no trace. Some charred bones among the smouldering debris was perhaps all that remained of this once mighty pillar of the Church establishment. At the last his corpse suffered the same fate as that of Richard Hunne whose body he had committed to the flames at Smithfield a century and a half before.

As for Richard Hunne himself, no physical vestige of his life has come down to us – except that in 1999 a Wycliffe Bible, now held in a private collection in California, was identified as having belonged to him. The Bible contains the notorious prologue against which marks have been made – those very same marks that the Church seized upon to convict Hunne's corpse of heresy over 500 years ago.

HISTORICAL NOTE

NEARLY ALL THE LEADING CHARACTERS IN *MURDER IN St Paul's* are based on real historical figures. Our knowledge of Richard Hunne comes from the sixteenth century martyrologist John Foxe and Thomas More's account of the Hunne case. We know a good deal about Bishop Fitzjames, Mayor George Monoux and Dean John Colet but less about Chancellor William Horsey, Coroner Thomas Barnwell and Summoner Charles Joseph. Other characters, notably Anne herself and members of her immediate family, are mentioned briefly in the historical records while Holbein's portrait of Hermann Wedig hangs in New York's Metropolitan Museum of Art. Of the other leading characters only Chaplain Benjamin Slather and Anne's cousin Rebecca are wholly fictitious.

Most of the major incidents described are based on contemporary accounts. The following, in particular, are well documented: the burning of the Amersham martyrs, the legal proceedings between Richard Hunne and the Church, the post-mortem trial of Hunne's corpse and ensuing conference at Baynard's Castle, the riots of Evil May Day, the presence of a Lollard scriptorium in Coleman Street, Wolsey's ritual book burning, Thomas More's raid on the German Steelyard, and Luther's two day trial at Worms as well as his subsequent abduction and incarceration in the Wartburg under the pseudonym of Junker George.

The Pelican Inn at Wapping was the precursor of the still surviving pub, The Prospect of Whitby. Those unfortunates who were buried in the common pit for single women are today commemorated on the South Bank by a plaque at Cross Bones Graveyard honouring the outcast dead.

The Hunne case is analysed in great detail in Arthur Ogle's book *The Tragedy of the Lollards' Tower* (1949). Ogle, in common with most other historians, concludes that church officials deliberately murdered Hunne though others believe that Sir Thomas More was right in insisting that it was suicide. I have myself attempted to resolve this historical mystery in *The Death of an Alleged Heretic* published by the Journal, Reformation and Renaissance Review (2013) – a more accessible version appearing in History Today under the title *Murder in the Cathedral* (2014). Among the many secondary sources I have consulted in the course of my research for this book I would mention *The Later Lollards 1414-1520* by John Thomson, *Torture and the Law of Proof* by John Langbein, *London and the Reformation* by Susan Brigden, *The Detection of Heresy in Late Medieval England* by Ian Forrest, *Thomas More* by Richard Marius, *Wolsey* by Albert Pollard, *The Life of John Colet* by Joseph Lupton, *Germans in Britain since 1500* by Panikos Panayi, *The German Hansa* by Phillippe Dollinger, *Luther and the Reformation in Germany* by Charles Beard and *A History of St Paul's Cathedral* by William Dugdale.

The primary sources I have consulted include John Foxe's *Acts and Monuments* (1583 edition), Edward Hall's *Chronicle*, Robert Keilwey's *Memorandum* (on the Baynards Castle conference and the parliamentary aftermath of the Hunne case), Thomas More's *Complete Works* (especially his *Dialogue Concerning Heresies*), John Stow's *A Survey of London* and, for